LIKE CLOCKWORK

LIKE CLOCKWORK

Steampunk
Pasts, Presents, and Futures

Rachel A. Bowser and Brian Croxall
EDITORS

University of Minnesota Press
Minneapolis / London

Copyright 2016 by the Regents of the University of Minnesota

All rights reserved. No part of this publication may be reproduced, stored in a retrieval system, or transmitted, in any form or by any means, electronic, mechanical, photocopying, recording, or otherwise, without the prior written permission of the publisher.

Published by the University of Minnesota Press
111 Third Avenue South, Suite 290
Minneapolis, MN 55401-2520
http://www.upress.umn.edu

Printed in the United States of America on acid-free paper

The University of Minnesota is an equal-opportunity educator and employer.

22 21 20 19 18 17 16   10 9 8 7 6 5 4 3 2 1

Library of Congress Cataloging-in-Publication Data
Names: Bowser, Rachel A. | Croxall, Brian.
Title: Like clockwork : steampunk pasts, presents, and futures / Rachel A. Bowser and Brian Croxall [editors].
Description: Minneapolis : University of Minnesota Press, 2016. | Includes bibliographical references and index.
Identifiers: LCCN 2016003054 (print) | ISBN 978-1-5179-0062-5 (hc) | ISBN 978-1-5179-0063-2 (pb)
Subjects: LCSH: Steampunk fiction—History and criticism.
Classification: LCC PN3448.S73 L55 2016 (print) | DDC 809.3/876—dc23
LC record available at https://lccn.loc.gov/2016003054

WE DEDICATE THIS BOOK to our kids—
Chaz, Finn, Gwen, and Sadie—whom we hope
will always know the joy of playing dress-up,
the power of knowing history, and the value
of collaborating with a good friend.

CONTENTS

Acknowledgments ix

Introduction.
It's about Time: Reading Steampunk's Rise and Roots .. xi
RACHEL A. BOWSER AND BRIAN CROXALL

I. Steampunk Spaces and Things

1. Steampunk and the Victorian City: Time Machines,
Bryan Talbot, and the Center of the Multiverse 3
DAVID PIKE

2. How to Theorize with a Hammer; or, Making and Baking
Things in Steampunk and the Digital Humanities 33
ROGER WHITSON

3. The Steampunk City in Crisis 51
CATHERINE SIEMANN

II. Steampunk Bodies and Identities

4. From Steam Arms to Brass Goggles:
Steampunk, Prostheses, and Disability 73
KATHRYN CROWTHER

5. The Aesthete, the Dandy, and the Steampunk;
or, Things as They Are Now 97
STEFANIA FORLINI

6. Punking the Other: On the Performance of
Racial and National Identities in Steampunk 127
DIANA M. PHO

III. Steampunk Reading and Revising

7. Seminal Steampunk: Proper and True 153
   MIKE PERSCHON

8. The Alchemy of Aether: Steampunk as Reading Practice in Karina Cooper's *Tarnished* and *Gilded* 179
   LISA HAGER

9. Out of Control: Disrupting Technological Mastery in Michael Moorcock's *The Warlord of the Air* and K. W. Jeter's *Infernal Devices* 199
   JOSEPH WEAKLAND AND SHAUN DUKE

Contributors 219

Index 223

ACKNOWLEDGMENTS

Brian and Rachel are thankful for:

Our authors, for their excellent work and their attention to neverending e-mails, edits, and steampunk puns;

Rise-n-Dine restaurant in Emory Village, for the sausage tacos that fueled us toward these initial ideas, almost ten years ago;

Marie-Luise Kohlke, for her rigorous work with us on the steampunk special issue of *Neo-Victorian Studies,* which inspired the beginnings of this volume;

Doug Armato, for his faith in the project, and Erin Warholm-Wohlenhaus, for her invaluable help in preparing the manuscript;

Sarah Aloe Peterson, for her equal amounts of patience and eye-rolling during these many years of hearing about steampunk;

Our partners, Amber Croxall and Brian Kyle, for keeping straight faces almost always, for all this time.

INTRODUCTION

It's about Time
Reading Steampunk's Rise and Roots
RACHEL A. BOWSER AND BRIAN CROXALL

Every Labor Day weekend, more than 70,000 fans of science fiction, fantasy, comic books, and more descend on Atlanta, Georgia, for Dragon*Con. One of the highlights of the convention each year is the parade that features attendees marching down Peachtree Street, dressed in their best costumes to cheering throngs of observers—around 75,000 of them in 2015, and the numbers keep growing.[1] The cosplayers in the parade don costumes from their favorite corners of popular culture. A group of high elves from *The Lord of the Rings* will be followed by Disney princesses and villains who are in turn followed by twenty different Doctor Whos, each of them dressing as their personal favorite of the twelve different incarnations of the Doctor. Throughout the parade one sees Indiana Jones, Han Solo, Captain Jack Sparrow, and Edward Scissorhands, often walking next to one another. There are fairies, dwarves, storm troopers, and zombies—literal hordes of them. And there are steampunks. Men, women, and even some children march by in Victorian topcoats, spats, cravats, bowlers, bustles, crinolines, and lace gloves. But along with the period clothing, they carry fantastic armaments and adornments that feature exposed gears and rivets, ornate embellishments, and rich woods, materials ranging from brass to leather to copper. Most of the steampunks wear goggles of one sort or another; some pairs are pulled down over their eyes, while others are shoved up onto the brim of a hat in what could only be described as jaunty nonchalance. Alongside those marching, some ride boneshakers, some drive modified wheelchairs, and some walk their steampunk-attired pets.[2] In recent years at the Dragon*Con parade, these steampunk cosplayers have made up a sizable percentage of the fan costumes, surpassing every other form of fandom except Star Wars.

It hasn't always been this way. When we first began attending the Dragon*Con parade in 2005, there really wasn't any steampunk to speak of. By 2008, approximately twenty people joined the parade with their goggles, parasols, and waistcoats. In 2010, there were easily five times as many people marching in the parade, and the costumes had improved significantly, with one gentleman in a pith helmet carrying a blunderbuss with a gramophone-horn muzzle. By 2013, steampunk had become so familiar that when a group of five people dressed as cogged and riveted versions of the blocks from a classic puzzle game walked by, Brian's daughter immediately identified it as steampunk.

"But what," she asked, "is Tetris?"

Steampunk: Why Now?

In the second decade of this new millennium, steampunk has arrived—and in a big way. Steampunk, the mode that finds imaginative ways to combine everything from steam technology and gene splicing to Tetris and brass cogs, has advanced well beyond its Victorian and literary roots. Comic and fan conventions taking place in Atlanta and across the country regularly see large numbers of steampunk participants. Indeed, steampunk has become enough of a cultural phenomenon that

FIGURE I.1. The Steampunk Tetris cosplayers in the 2013 Dragon*Con parade in Atlanta show the popularity and adaptability of the style. Photograph by Brian Croxall.

entire conventions are devoted to it. Bellevue, Washington, hosted five annual Steamcons, beginning in October 2009.[3] Not to be shut out from activities in the Pacific Northwest, Fairhaven, Washington, held its fifth annual Steampunk Festival during July 2016.[4] Steamathon launched in Las Vegas in 2015 and continued into a bigger second year.[5] On the East Coast, the Steampunk World's Fair in Piscataway, New Jersey, competes with the Watch City Steampunk Festival in Waltham, Massachusetts, to see who can draw more participants in the spring of each year.[6] New York City got into the picture with its first Steampunk Weekend in 2013, and its participants developed it into an ongoing Steampunk Social Calendar.[7] Showing that steampunk is not limited to festivals in New York City, a recent condo development in Manhattan's Hudson Square—15 Renwick—adopted a steampunk theme for its design and marketing.[8]

Of course, steampunk is not a phenomenon that is confined to the United States. Predictably for a genre or scene that draws so heavily from tropes of nineteenth-century European culture, there is a vibrant community of steampunks across the Atlantic. Conventions have taken place in England, France, the Netherlands, Luxembourg, Germany, and more. A pan-European steampunk festival began in 2012 with the goal of "creat[ing] a steampunk event literally spanning the whole continent" and continues to run multiple events in different countries across weekends in September and October.[9] According to Ay-leen the Peacemaker, a blogger who covers steampunk culture at both *Beyond Victoriana* and at Tor.com (and who appears in this volume as Diana M. Pho), the number of steampunk conventions held each year has been steadily increasing: twenty-five in 2011, thirty-two in 2012, more than forty in 2013.[10] By 2014 there were enough steampunk events happening that Ay-leen the Peacemaker began writing a monthly blog post rather than a yearly summary; those monthly summaries continue to be filed at the time of our writing.[11]

Literary steampunk has kept pace with this growth trend. The steampunk enthusiast or novice can now delve into the genre via any number of anthologies: *Steampunk*, which appeared in 2008 (ed. VanderMeer and VanderMeer), was followed in 2010 by *Steampunk II: Steampunk Reloaded* (ed. VanderMeer and VanderMeer) and again in 2012 by *Steampunk III: Steampunk Revolution* (ed. Ann VanderMeer). Alternatively, the reader could consult *Extraordinary Engines: The Definitive Steampunk Anthology* (ed. Gevers, 2008), *The Mammoth Book of Steampunk* (ed. Wallace, 2012), *Clockwork Fairy Tales: A Collection of Steampunk Fables* (ed. Antczak and

Bassett, 2013), *Steampunk! An Anthology of Fantastically Strange Stories* (ed. Grant and Link, 2013), *The Mammoth Book of Steampunk Adventures* (ed. Wallace, 2014), or *Steampunk World* (eds. Lake and Liu, 2014). Those interested in longer fiction have had no shortage of novels to choose from. Cherie Priest's multipart Clockwork Century series, which Catherine Siemann discusses in this volume, and Gail Carriger's five-volume Parasol Protectorate novels, both of which initially appeared in 2009, have won many fans to the genre. Steampunk young adult fiction has truly taken off, including notable series like those from Philip Reeve—the Mortal Engines quartet (2001-6) and the Larklight trilogy (2006-8)— and China Miéville's *Un Lun Dun* (2007) and *Railsea* (2012). Miéville, of course, was already known to steampunk enthusiasts for his three novels set in the world of Bas-Lag: *Perdido Street Station* (2000), *The Scar* (2002), and *Iron Council* (2004). Scott Westerfeld published the immensely popular Leviathan trilogy (*Leviathan, Behemoth,* and *Goliath*) from 2009 to 2011, to which we return later in this essay. On the opposite end of the spectrum, steampunk erotica is a fully formed genre of its own, including anthologies like *Steam Powered: Lesbian Steampunk Stories* (ed. Vanderhooft, 2011), *Carnal Machines: Steampunk Erotica* (ed. King, 2011), and *Steampunk Erotica I* and *II* (ed. Le Brocq, 2010 and 2011). The proliferation of steampunk fan fiction and self-published texts in Amazon's Kindle store evidences the DIY ethos so important to its fans, while the steampunk elements of Thomas Pynchon's *Against the Day* (2006) testify to the genre's shift away from the margins to venues more likely to be considered as canonical literature.

Given such evidence of a literary shift, we should not be surprised at steampunk's making great inroads not just within its fan community but also with the general public. The potential for steampunk's broader reach is apparent in the number of steampunk how-to books now on the market. From *Steampunk Accessories: 20 Projects to Help You Nail the Style* (Tedman and Skeate, 2012) to *A Steampunk's Guide to Sex* (Professor Calamity, 2012) to *The Steampunk Adventurer's Guide: Contraptions, Creations, and Curiosities Anyone Can Make* (Willeford, 2013), any interested party can find the resources to steam up her ethos. Unsurprisingly, the visual hallmarks of steampunk are increasingly familiar—not only to our children at Dragon*Con but also to fashion designers. Prada's fall/winter 2012 collection featured four Hollywood actors, Gary Oldman, Garrett Hedlund, Jamie Bell, and Willem Dafoe, in what the company termed "a subtle parody of power and role-play" that was explicitly reminiscent of the late Victorian and Edwardian periods.[12] Instead of using these period-specific terms, however, most of the press coverage for the campaign described the clothing as steampunk.[13] Clearly it's not just our children who know steampunk when they see it.

Other mass media of the last decade have similarly drawn on elements of steampunk for their costuming, visual design, or narrative. *Warehouse 13* debuted in the United States on the Syfy channel (formerly SciFi) in 2009, the same year as Guy Ritchie's first steampunk Sherlock Holmes film. Infusing the general backstory of the X-Files franchise (1993–2016) with comedy, two secret agents must track down supernatural artifacts with the help of a computer whiz who regularly dons steampunk goggles and a mad scientist whose keyboard is an ornate nineteenth-century device (produced for the show by late steampunk artisan Richard "Datamancer" Nagy), all while carrying a ray gun created by Nikola Tesla. Less than a year before *Warehouse 13*, Syfy also debuted *Sanctuary* (2008–11). The eponymous institute provided a shelter for so-called abnormals: humans and other creatures with supernatural abilities. *Sanctuary* looked to steampunk not so much for design inspiration for characters' accouterments as it did for the architecture of the underground city Praxis, a place where humans and abnormals lived and worked together. But steampunk has more than one home on television, as evidenced by the Cartoon Network's 2012 *The Legend of Korra*, which also features steampunk technologies and cityscapes. Even the Internet has gotten involved with steampunk serials: Web series such as *Dirigible Days* (2012) or *To Kill a Princess* (2013) explicitly make use of steampunk settings. The interest in such series is evidenced by the success of *The World of Steam* on the crowdsourcing Kickstarter website during October and November 2012. Earning more than $100,000 in thirty days before production even started, *The World of Steam* promised a six-episode first season to be delivered sometime in the near future.[14] Three and a half years later, a pilot episode, "The Clockwork Heart," has appeared, and the creators of the project are in talks with television networks, suggesting that while production has proven more elusive than anticipated, steampunk continues to generate interest among audiences and content producers.[15]

Beyond film and television, video games have been another consistent place to find steampunk recently. All of the games in the *BioShock* trilogy (2007, 2010, 2013) take place in metropolitan environments that are rife with real mechanical technologies from the nineteenth century—automatons, diving suits, voxophones, and kinetoscopes—and with imagined devices that nevertheless bear the visual design of the Victorian era. The third game, *BioShock Infinite,* featured a particularly steampunk enemy: the Motorized Patriot. Originally designed as tour guides for the city of Columbia, the Motorized Patriots are automatons in the likeness of George Washington, Abraham Lincoln, and others. Reprogrammed by some of the divisive forces within the city, the Patriots hunt down the player who inevitably exposes their clockwork innards when she is forced to destroy them. Similar to the *BioShock* games, the 2012 release *Dishonored* is set in a city that is in disarray (itself a common trope in steampunk fiction, as discussed by both David Pike and Catherine Siemann in this volume), and the art direction highlights several machines made of brass and rivets and powered by steam. A prominent opponent in the landscape is the Tallboy, a member of the city watch who patrols in a heavily armored, mechanized two-legged stilt suit that is powered in part by whale oil tanks—one of the device's few weak points for the player's assassin character. But steampunk within video games is not only the domain of the dystopic and its

FIGURE I.2. A partially destroyed Motorized Patriot from *BioShock Infinite* (2013) exposes the gears that enable it to pursue the player's character. Screen shot from Irrational Games and 2K Games, used according to fair use guidelines.

accompanying brutal violence. Appearing the same year as the original *BioShock* game, the *Professor Layton* series is aimed at players aged ten and up and has become one of the best-selling games on the Nintendo DS platform. While the game play is all about solving puzzles—math, logic, and otherwise—the series has a distinct visual style that depends on its setting in a steampunk London and the characters' use of appropriately anachronistic technologies.

This essay is of course not the first place to note the increasingly mainstream appeal of steampunk. To wit: in January 2013, just six months after Prada's steampunk campaign was released, major media outlets began reporting that steampunk was poised to become a new retail trend. A largely below-the-radar movement that had begun to make inroads into boutique merchandisers or influencers like Prada, "steampunk styling" would, according to the reports, show up by 2014 "in mainstream clothing, furnishings, and accessories." What was most interesting about this forecast of fashion was that it didn't come from established fashion channels like *Vogue* or *Harper's Bazaar*. Instead, it was a prediction from IBM.[16] IBM hadn't suddenly hired a fashion consultant who saw this retrofuture on the horizon. Instead, the organization reached this conclusion through their Social Sentiment Index. Analyzing the traffic of social media networks such as Twitter, Facebook, and Pinterest, as well as thousands of blogs and online forums, IBM's software is able to sift for movements that are on the rise and about to become mainstream. According to IBM's report, online conversations about steampunk increased elevenfold from 2009 to 2012 and have leaped across several "cultural domains (such as fiction, visual arts, etc.)."[17] The demographics of the people discussing steampunk online further helped IBM to declare steampunk the major (retail) trend of tomorrow: 63 percent of people discussing steampunk online are under thirty years old; 70 percent of tweets about steampunk are written by women; and 33 percent of steampunk fashion conversations take place on sites that are primarily about video gaming.[18] IBM predicted that these individuals represent a vanguard of awareness about steampunk and that they will influence others to make purchases when steampunk-inflected objects become more readily available through mass market retailers. Indeed, when a real estate blog decided to name "the 50 most steampunk cities in America," a large part of their metrics were connected to the prevalence of retail spaces, including antique and hardware stores.[19]

So: steampunk is big and is (possibly) about to get bigger. If the list of fashion, films, games, and fiction we've provided isn't enough to convince, IBM is more than happy to provide the hard numbers to prove its point. Whether considered through a close or distant reading methodology, steampunk is clearly present. But what neither this enumeration nor IBM's big-data approach accomplishes is to answer perhaps the simplest question about steampunk: why now, and why not before? After all, when the seminal fiction in steampunk was written in the 1970s (see Mike Perschon's essay in this volume); when the term was coined in 1987 by K. W. Jeter; when the role-playing game *Space: 1889* made use of a neo-Victorian setting on Mars in 1988; when that same role-playing scenario was adapted into a video game in 1990; when William Gibson and Bruce Sterling published *The Difference Engine* in 1990; when the incredibly popular video game series *Final Fantasy* departed from its medieval setting to a steampunk world in 1994's *Final Fantasy VI*; and when Alan Moore and Kevin O'Neill published *The League of Extraordinary Gentlemen* in 1999, the same year that the Will Smith steampunk film *Wild Wild West* appeared, one must ask, halfway through the second decade of the twenty-first century, "Why is steampunk finally happening now?" Is the current momentum of steampunk somehow operating like clockwork, a sort of fantastic machine that was wound forty years ago and is only now beginning to move appreciably? Or is there something more that is motivating the rise of steampunk in the last five to ten years that mark it differently than the previous thirty? Ironic as it might be to consider the timeliness of a genre or a movement that defines itself precisely on its atemporality and anachronism, the question of steampunk at the present moment lies at the heart of this volume.

The dramatic surge in steampunk's presence within cultural consciousness, and the specificity of its timing, is of interest to scholars and enthusiasts in a variety of fields. Steampunk may in fact be a uniquely positioned cultural phenomenon, able to capture the varied interests of scholars because of its notably hybrid nature. The Victorian antecedents for so many of its stories and aesthetics are, obviously enough, evocative for Victorian studies as well as neo-Victorian studies, both fields in which the afterlife of Victorian culture is frequently examined.[20] As a literary genre, it is frequently discussed under the umbrella of science fiction and speculative fiction, raising interesting questions for critics about the relationships among technology, history, and ideology, as well as about what counts as science fiction. The speculative technologies featured in steampunk texts frequently involve steam-powered prosthetics (as in Cherie Priest's 2009 novel *Boneshaker* and the 2005 film *Steamboy*, for example) and nonnormative bodies, raising questions that disability studies scholars have been answering with increasing prominence. Steampunk's revisitation, and sometimes revision, of imperialist history and content is of interest to postcolonial studies. Similarly, the speculative history that grounds much steampunk literature provides a platform for interrogating historical and received gender identities, and the varied success of that interrogation has been of interest to feminist scholars. In addition, steampunk is as much a material culture as it is a literary one, defined by many via its carefully wrought objects and modified gear. Accordingly, theorists of material culture have been (and are in this volume) interested in the ideologies embedded and circulated via steampunk objects. Steampunk is, finally, a participatory culture, dense with the meanings embodied by its cosplayers and rich for analysis within the context of fan culture. This volume contains readings and arguments that intersect with the above fields and that converge on the question of why steampunk's ascendance seems to happen when it does.

The matter of steampunk's historicity has been discussed in a range of frequently cited pieces, such as Jess Nevins's introduction to the first VanderMeer and VanderMeer anthology, "The 19th-Century Roots of Steampunk," and is revisited in this volume by Mike Perschon, but the timing of its emergence, a phenomenon with the potential to engage the paradigmatic questions of several fields, has been less remarked on.[21] Elsewhere, in our introduction to the special issue of *Neo-Victorian Studies* on steampunk, we wrote, "Steampunk's rise in the last few decades . . . has everything to do with this punk sensibility regarding technology: a politics of taking back *control*."[22] This claim, emerging from a discussion about the tinkering impulse inherent in steampunk, evidences the relevance of steampunk's rise to scholars working in material culture and maker studies. It is also a claim we still stand by, though, as this introduction will demonstrate, we have a more expansive sense of the sorts of control steampunk seems to offer.

Each of the essays in this book, written by scholars engaged in work in the aforementioned fields and beyond, proposes a reason, in one way or another, to think about why steampunk is currently so popular and omnipresent. Some past writing about steampunk—in both the popular and scholarly press—has tended to define the genre. Indeed, we see precisely that happening in Jeph Jacques's single reference to steampunk in the Web comic *Questionable Content* (2003–present), albeit with comedic intent.

FIGURE I.3. In this 2012 Web comic strip, Marigold attempts to explain steampunk to her father, highlighting a growing cultural awareness of the mode. "Number 2198: Concise Explanation," from *Questionable Content* by Jeph Jacques, www.questionablecontent.net. Image used by permission of the artist.

But while steampunk may have some frequently recurring parts—brass, Victoriana, goggles—we are persuaded by David Pike in this volume's "Steampunk and the Victorian City," who argues that steampunk is more of a mode than a genre. There is no precise combination of features that definitively marks an object or text as steampunk; rather, a commitment to blending and combining (histories, technologies, ideologies) seems to bind the mode together. The mode's expansion has brought us to a moment when, instead of trying to define steampunk, it's simply easier to say that we know it when we see it. And, according to IBM, the "we" in that statement will soon include far more people than the contributors to this book. In this moment when it is more helpful to move from a prescriptivist to a descriptivist definition,[23] it is perhaps equally reasonable to move beyond the "what" of steampunk to its "why" and "why now." In our efforts to consider this "why now," we want to first turn backwards to consider, in part, "why then?"

Steampunk: Why Then?

In our previous work on steampunk, we considered the particular Victorian antecedent of Charles Lyell's *Principles of Geology* (1830–33), which revolutionized conceptions of time by insisting there has been no great catastrophe, no massive geological rupture in Earth's history.[24] We still find this a useful paradigm for thinking about steampunk's cultural resonance and for reminding us not to lose sight of the specifics of the genre's setting, and find ourselves interested in forging a connection to another of the nineteenth-century's titans of science as we approach this volume. Charles Darwin's 1859 *On the Origin of Species* changed the imaginative possibilities for his Victorian readers and, enabled by Lyell's insights about geological epochs, instantiated a new paradigm for thinking about time. Lyell's uniformitarianism—which we have argued can be understood as the temporal paradigm that undergirds the steampunk's imagination—catalyzed Darwin's inquiry into the explanation for biodiversity. Looking through steampunk lenses (or goggles, if you will), we can see Darwin's inquiry as resulting in a new framework for understanding the connectedness of the diverse inhabitants of the planet and can hazard a link between the steampunk mode and this argument from the century that mode so frequently invokes.

While much of the revolutionary significance of *Origin of Species* has to do with common ancestry, much of the actual text is devoted to establishing the Earth's vast biodiversity. The reason for the incredible number of species on the planet is, in fact, the question Darwin intends to answer in the book. Deliberately and carefully, he provides that answer: natural selection. In building the case for this answer, Darwin uses the framing paradigm of biodiversity to illustrate the surprising number of features that diverse populations share. He writes, "All the members of whole classes can be connected together by 'chains of affinities,'" and then methodically traces out those chains through a broad range of species and kingdoms.[25]

Homologies among different animals are the foundation of Darwin's argument for natural selection. As in this passage about similarities in skeletal systems, the ability to apprehend affinities among diverse organisms is Darwin's key imaginative insight: "The framework of bones being the same in the hand of man, wing of a bat, fin of a porpoise, and leg of a horse, the same number of vertebrae forming the neck of the giraffe and of the elephant, and innumerable other such facts, at once explain themselves on the theory of descent with slow and successive modifications."[26] The "slow and successive modifications" insight is supplied by Lyell's *Principles of Geology*, but the uniformity (and incredible length) of the geologic timeline is not enough to explain where all the Earth's variety comes from; one must also have a keen vision for shared features in order to apprehend the possibility of common descent.[27]

The significance of these homologies was not lost on Darwin's Victorian audience, and their explanatory potential was especially troubling for his critics. Bishop Samuel Wilberforce led the chorus of nineteenth-century objections to Darwin's work, drawing particular attention to the reliance of the argument on interspecies affinities, referring to homology as "the theory that really pervades the whole volume." He continues, sarcastically,

> Man, beast, creeping thing, and plant of the earth, are all lineal and direct descendants of some one individual *ens*, whose various progeny have been simply modified by the action of natural and ascertainable conditions into the multiform aspect of life which we see around us. This is undoubtedly at first sight a somewhat startling conclusion to arrive at. To find that mosses, grasses, turnips, oaks, worms, and flies, mites and elephants, infusoria and whales, tadpoles of to-day and venerable saurians, truffles and men, are all equally the lineal descendants of the same aboriginal common ancestor, perhaps of the nucleated cell of some primæval

fungus, which alone possessed the distinguished honour of being the "one primordial form into which life was first breathed by the Creator"—this, to say the least of it, is no common discovery—no very expected conclusion.... If Mr. Darwin can with the same correctness of reasoning [as is evident in Newton's work] demonstrate to us our fungal descent, we shall dismiss our pride, and avow, with characteristic humility of philosophy, our unsuspected cousinship with the mushrooms.[28]

Wilberforce's extended meditation on the stakes of homology in Darwin's argument reveals the threat of the concept. Wilberforce lines up turnips, tadpoles, and truffles as an absurd family tree before alluding to the "pride" that would be swallowed at embracing "cousinship with the mushrooms." His condescension belies the concept's threat: if the similarities among all creatures are their most explanatory features, their individuality—and, obviously, especially man's status as a special creation—pales and wavers, swallowed by epochs of geologic time. These strenuous objections evidence the central role homologies occupy with Darwin's argument. Intraspecies commonalities are the foundation on which the paradigm is built.

Like Lyell's uniformitarianism, Darwin's homologies give us a metaphor for the imaginative insight that mobilizes steampunk. The chains of affinities between centuries, technologies, and ideologies enable the mash-ups, alternate histories, and recombinations that so frequently characterize steampunk. The surprising exposure of these affinities is often what makes steampunk so compelling. As we wrote in *Neo-Victorian Studies,* steampunk may be most recognizable for blending the features and technologies of the Victorian and contemporary moments, but it also blends "the apparent incompatibilities of Victorian literature and science fiction (high literature versus popular literature; canonical fiction versus genre fiction)."[29] If the introductory paragraphs above, which enumerate the many venues of steampunk's expansion, are any indication, these surprising commonalities and compatibilities—what Wilberforce might call the improbable "cousinship" among iPads, brass cogs, Dickensian street urchins, and skaters—are more readily identifiable than ever before.

To turn to a literary example, Scott Westerfeld's Leviathan trilogy (2009-11) literalizes the Darwinian metaphor we are using to help think about steampunk's informing ethos. Westerfeld's alternative history of World War I replaces the Allies and the Central Powers with

Darwinists and Clankers, respectively. While the Clankers respond to the assassination of Archduke Franz Ferdinand by mobilizing steam-driven industrial war machines, the Darwinists rely on fabricated animals that combine the features of "naturally" occurring species. As the latter moniker might imply, these novels are set in a speculative world in which Darwin discovered the secrets of DNA (or "life threads," in the novel's terms) and gene splicing. In Westerfeld's nineteenth century, the first stage of the Industrial Revolution may have seen machines replacing humans, but the next step saw fabricated animal hybrids replacing machines. Deryn, the novel's young protagonist who has disguised herself as a boy so she can join the British Air Corps, reflects on the progression:

> She remembered how Da had said London looked in the days before old Darwin had worked his magic. A pall of coal smoke had covered the entire city, along with a fog so thick the streetlamps were lit during the day. During the worst of the steam age so much soot and ash had decorated the nearby countryside that butterflies had evolved black spots on their wings for camouflage. But before Deryn had been born the great coal-fired engines had been overtaken by fabricated beasties, muscles and sinews replacing boilers and gears. These days the only chimney smoke came from ovens, not huge factories.[30]

Although the Clanker armaments consist solely of retrofuturist improvements on nineteenth-century mechanical technologies, for the Darwinists in Westerfeld's dazzlingly imaginative universe, steampunk is ironically made by replacing London's steam engines with hybrid animals.

While the Clanker powers place an emphasis on mechanical technology, it is important to note that they have still been influenced by Darwinist experiments. In conversation with Prince Aleksander, the other protagonist of the novel and the son of the murdered Franz Ferdinand, Deryn suggests, "Clankers wouldn't have invented walking machines without our example to follow." Alek scoffs at this idea: "How else would a war machine get around? On treads, like an old-fashioned farm tractor? What a preposterous idea."[31] In this exchange, we see not only Westerfeld's playful denigration of the tanks that the Central Powers actually invented during World War I but also—and more importantly—that chains of affinities exist between the Clanker and Darwinist powers. These connections become even more clear in the second book in the trilogy, *Behemoth,* which takes place in Istanbul, where Clanker machines are designed explicitly in the shape of elephants, scorpions, and other animals. Deryn is surprised by this departure from typical Clanker behavior and inquires whether all of the walkers in Istanbul are in the shape of animals. Dr. Nora Barlow, the chief scientist on board the *Leviathan,* provides an answer: "Most of them, yes.... Our Ottoman friends may be Clankers, but they haven't forgotten the web of life around us."[32] In having Dr. Barlow point out the connections and homologies between machines and animals, Westerfeld points back to Darwin's insights in *Origin of Species,* and he does so unambiguously, as Nora Barlow is Darwin's granddaughter—in both the novel and real life.

The animalistic machines and fabricated creatures in Westerfeld's novels all have practical functions, as is the case with the "Huxley ascender," a hybrid creature "made from the life chains of medusae—jellyfish and other sea creatures" that serves as a personal zeppelin for aerial scouting.[33] In *Leviathan*'s world, Darwin's recognition of interspecies homologies supplies the explanation for the world's biodiversity while simultaneously enabling the utility of creatures built upon those homologies. It is a profoundly generative insight, one that seems to allow the Darwinists' hybrid creatures to function as metaphors for the hybrid literary and cultural genre their novel inhabits. Indeed, the eponymous Leviathan is introduced in language that the editors of this volume, at the very least, cannot help but associate with the features of the broader steampunk genre: "The Leviathan's body was made from the life threads of a whale, but a hundred other species were tangled into its design, countless creatures fitted together like the gears of a stopwatch."[34]

Indeed, Westerfeld speaks to this "fitted together[ness]" in the afterword to *Leviathan,* in which he offers some paradigmatic thoughts about steampunk:

> So *Leviathan* is as much about possible futures as alternate pasts. It looks ahead to when machines will look like living creatures, and living creatures can be fabricated like machines. And yet the setting also recalls an earlier time in which the world was divided into aristocrats and commoners, and women in most countries couldn't join the armed forces—or even vote. That's the nature of steampunk, blending future and past.[35]

The preeminence of "blending" in Westerfeld's conception of steampunk helps us think about why the Darwinian metaphor is so important for him—and us. It is precisely these chains of affinities among diverse objects, creatures, and histories that enable new insights and connections. Westerfeld here invokes the blended temporality so often associated with steampunk, but he also emphasizes the other blendings that ground the novel: the implicit homologies between the production and functionality of machines and animals, which allow Westerfeld to blend their ontological figures such that machines walk through the landscape while animals are built to utilize it.

The hybridity of the airship *Leviathan*, made possible by these chains of affinities between creatures, allows it to survive a crash landing in the Alps in the first novel. Attacked by German aeroplanes, the body of the whale is punctured, and it crashes onto a glacier in Switzerland. But because the *Leviathan* is a living creature/ecosystem, it can repair its own tissues, given time and energy. Indeed, the question of whether it will have the latter is the central problem for the book and how Deryn and Alek end up meeting. By the end of the novel, however, the ship has become even more of a hybrid. The *Leviathan* is originally powered by small electric motivator engines, which help nudge the ship forward, helped by cilia that grow along the flank of the whale's side. Small as they are, the engines are sufficient to help the *Leviathan* outstrip every German airship for speed records. But in the crash and an ensuing attack by the Clanker powers, the motivator engines are destroyed. Unable to travel quickly without the engines, the *Leviathan* appears to be a sitting duck, despite its regenerative ability. Alek provides a somewhat literal deus ex machina, supplying the large diesel engines from his damaged Stormwalker—a bipedal battle engine—to take the place of the motivator engines. The strangeness of the engines on the airbeast is made clear when Deryn contemplates their addition to the *Leviathan*: "The forward engines were partway down the airship flanks, thrusting out like a pair of ears. The tops of both pods had been removed, and a muddle of oversize Clanker machinery stuck out in all directions."[36] Neither the engines—with their parts all ajar—nor the *Leviathan*—with its new "ears"—are what they used to be; instead, things appear to be just a "muddle." Similarly, Alek finds the combination of machine and fabricated animal uncanny: "It was still strange, seeing the Stormwalker's needles and gauges out of their usual place in the pilot's cabin, and the gears and pistons that belonged in the walker's belly splayed in the open air."[37] The reader not only sees how "strange" Alek finds this combination but also observes that he thinks of his machine in biological terms, with its "belly splayed." When the *Leviathan* finally lifts off and the cilia along its flank start moving to guide the airship, he realizes he's piloting a heretofore unheard-of hybrid: "Alek swallowed, unable to take his gaze from the undulating surface of the airbeast. Working on the engines, he'd tried to think of the airship as a vast machine. Now it had become a living creature again."[38] With the help of the diesel engines, the Darwinists, as well as Alek and his men, escape from another German attack. In summarizing the escape, Deryn again places emphasis on the increased oddity of the ship: "Whatever sort of tangled crossbreed the Clankers had made her into, the *Leviathan* had survived."[39] The partnership between Alek and Deryn uncovers the fact that previously unobserved affinities exist between their cultures' respective technological paradigms. These homologies make it possible for the altered *Leviathan* to do more than was previously possible and—in true Darwinian style—survive. This airbeast, already emblematic for steampunk, becomes even more representative of the ecosystem of its world—one of fabricated animals and complex, nineteenth-century mechanical technologies.

The two books that follow *Leviathan* are at equal pains to demonstrate the advantages of both technological and cultural hybridity. *Behemoth* finds Deryn and Alek in the Ottoman Empire trying to prevent its ruler from aligning with the Clankers. The titular entity in this book is again a fabricated creature that steers much of the plot. The Behemoth is the companion creature to the warship *Osman*, which was being built by the British on behalf of the Ottomans. Despite already being paid for, the British seized the ship and the Behemoth since they were "strong enough to change the balance of power on the seas."[40] Paralleling actual World War I events in more ways than one, the Clankers see an opportunity to win the Ottomans to their side and make a gift of the S.M.S. *Breslau* and S.M.S. *Goeben* to the Empire.[41] The Germans hope to use these ships to close the Dardanelles and starve the Russian forces, which in Westerfeld's world are anchored by gigantic fighting bears whose "shoulders [stand] as tall as a house."[42] To prevent this happening, various machinations ensue, including a SEAL-like sabotage mission for Deryn and Alek's fomenting a popular rebellion against the Sultan that is carried out with spice bombs. In the end, everything lines up in time for the Behemoth to attack the Clanker vessels; it dismantles them in only moments. But the Behemoth can only do this in conjunction with the *Leviathan*, which provides not so much air support but instructions to the sea creature through spotlights. As is the case in *Leviathan*, it is a hybrid animal—a creature created from the possibilities of homologies—that is working in an ecosystem with other creatures in tandem with mechanical technology that triumphs over a machine that attempts to operate apart from its ecology.

Given the trajectory of *Leviathan* and *Behemoth*, a reader might easily expect the final book in Westerfeld's trilogy to feature another fantastic and eponymous creature. Instead, *Goliath* is titled after a machine built by Nikola Tesla, whom Deryn, Alek, and the crew of the *Leviathan* meet in Siberia, where the inventor is investigating the Tunguska event. Tesla claims he has invented a new weapon that can control massive electrical currents from thousands of miles away. Tesla hopes that this weapon will stop the war because both sides will be powerless against its power. (Although this plot seems initially like something that only a steampunk novel could dream up, Goliath is clearly based on the real Tesla's work on a "teleforce" weapon, which he claimed could destroy "10,000 enemy airplanes at a distance of 250 miles." Like the character in Westerfeld's novel, Tesla believed that his "death-beam" would be a "defensive weapon only."[43]) Alek spends much of the novel using his fame to help raise money for Tesla's work, as he hopes to end the war with another deus ex machina. Again, the previous two volumes in the trilogy suggest that Alek's hopes will be borne out by the end of the novel. Instead, a surprise attack by Clankers on the compound in New York State where Goliath is being built leads Tesla to attempt to fire the weapon at Berlin. Alek stops him, but the energy built up by the machines burns up not only the nearby walkers but also Tesla's own machinery. Goliath never gets its chance to save the world and instead ends up destroying its creator. Indeed, as the novel's conclusion makes clear, Tesla's science was faulty; as Dr. Barlow puts it to Deryn, upon discovering that the Tunguska event was caused by a meteorite rather than Goliath: "It means . . . that Tesla was a fraud. . . . Or perhaps a madman—he seemed to *think* he could destroy Berlin." So even if Tesla had fired Goliath, it wouldn't have done much beyond "chang[ing] atmospheric conditions."[44]

But perhaps it's not that surprising that a sterile machine isn't enough to produce a happy conclusion to Westerfeld's books. After all, the whole of the novels have been about steampunk which is, to use Westerfeld's own word, a "blending" of disparate parts. Yet a new hybrid is created at the series' end. In a move that surprises no one, Deryn and Alek end the novels finally able to confront their feelings for one another and embark on a new relationship. (This conclusion is so foregone that Westerfeld dedicates *Goliath* "to everyone who loves a long-secret romance, revealed at last."[45]) Deryn and Alek's relationship points to the possibilities of the bringing together the technological ideologies of their respective cultures. Indeed, throughout the series, the two have grown more hybridized. Deryn, who often sketches what she sees, ends *Leviathan* drawing the Clanker engines: "The pistons were the trickiest bits to draw. There was something about the way they fit together—the Clanker logic of them—that blistered Deryn's brain."[46] But by the middle of *Behemoth*, she is repairing walkers to help prepare for the uprising in Istanbul, and by the beginning of *Goliath*, her "German was good enough to follow most conversations."[47] Clearly Deryn's brain has adapted to some Clanker mannerisms, and her adaptability makes her all the more fit and able to survive as a soldier. Alek experiences similar hybridization, growing so comfortable on the *Leviathan* that by the beginning of the second book in the series he professes to Deryn (in a moment that puts both the reader and the still-disguised Deryn on edge), "It's almost as though . . . I'm in love with your ship. . . . It feels *right* here. . . . As if this is where I'm meant to be."[48] While Alek and Deryn aren't able to single-handedly stop the war, as Alek had hoped Goliath would be able to do, the fact that these two star-crossed—and cross-dressed, in Deryn's case, for most of the three books—lovers are able to come together at the end of the novel suggests the affinities that exist not only between technologies but also between socioeconomic status (a prince and a commoner). All of the important events in the novels are generated by these two characters and their abilities to think across the ideological, national, and gender boundaries that should separate them. Perhaps even more than the fantastic technologies and biologies that Westerfeld imagines, it is this attention to compatibility that underscores this world as steampunk.

The whole of the Leviathan trilogy provides an exemplary valorization of hybridity, with Westerfeld's fabricated creatures serving as an especially on-the-nose example. But hybrid creations are, of course, all over the steampunk universe, always showing us unexpected affinities. We might think of the spaceship/pirate vessel hybrids in Philip Reeve's *Larklight* trilogy (2006–9) or the newt/human monarch in Paul Di Filippo's story "Victoria" (1995). The brass-fitted iPods and cog-laden laptops of steampunk's material culture also come to mind, along with the surprising recognition that nineteenth-century gears and studs look well suited to Tetris blocks. Within steampunk texts and communities, these hybrids are often created by individuals who are tinkering, fiddling around with available, compatible materials to make a better ... something—or maybe just a more interesting something. Steampunks, according to *SteamPunk Magazine*, insist on "using what is available."[49] Amateur enthusiasts, whether in steampunk fiction, film, and material culture, find themselves deploying the tools and pieces at hand, a fundamental trait of the tinkerer. The specific version of tinkering at play in steampunk seems to involve not just a practical application of available pieces but also an aesthetic delight in the homologies uncovered by the ensuing combinations. This recourse to the materials at hand produces unexpected combinations and emphasizes the chains of affinities among so many of steampunk's—and steampunk enthusiasts' creations'—constitutive parts.

Steampunk's Shared Structures and Adaptations

The figure of the tinkerer is useful here not only because it is so often associated with steampunk but also because it has been instrumentally associated with Darwin and the mechanism of natural selection. In a seminal and beautiful essay published in *Science* in 1977, François Jacob argues that tinkering is the best metaphor for describing the mechanism of natural selection:

> [Natural selection] works like a tinkerer—a tinkerer who does not know exactly what he is going to produce, but uses whatever he finds around him, whether it be pieces of string, fragments of wood, or old cardboards; in short, it works like a tinkerer who uses everything at his disposal to produce some kind of workable object. . . . None of the materials at the tinkerer's disposal has a precise and definite function. Each can be used in a number of different ways. In contrast with the engineer's tools, those of the tinkerer cannot be defined by a project. What these objects have in common is "it might well be of some use." For what? That depends on the opportunities.[50]

Jacob's elegant explication of natural selection here may as easily be a description of the steampunk impulse. The "everything" at the disposal of tinkering steampunks—both those who make physical objects and those who create narratives in prose, pixels, or paint—may have initially looked like the improbable combination of Victorian and twenty-first-century science fiction but has now expanded to invoke much broader recombinations and alternate histories. The steampunk tinkering impulse has consequently broadened our imagination about the homologies we may find. As Jacob writes (and as Westerfeld likely agrees), "Novelties come from previously unseen association of old material. To create is to recombine."[51]

The figure of the tinkerer invites us to think about recombined pieces that are enabled by affinities and perhaps reinforces our sense that the explanatory power of homologies for Darwin might be the same explanatory and liberatory power steampunks find in their hybrids. What's more, the tinkerer gives us a way to consider the question we began with. Beyond the "what" and the "how" of steampunk, we are interested in the "why" and the "why now." As tinkerers, steampunks use "what is available." To what end? As Jacob puts it, it "depends on the opportunities."

Tinkering is a response to a particular environment. Natural selection tinkers with the available physiological features to produce adaptations well suited to changed and changing environmental conditions. Steampunk's recombinant DIY ethos, in its commitment to using what is there, has hybridized centuries, technologies, and generic conventions as products of its tinkering impulse. But why the impulse in the first place? If tinkering, as a figure, invokes a relationship to an external environment and an awareness of opportunities, then we want to be attentive to the historicity of steampunk's tinkering.

To consider our "why" as well as what work is done by this genre of unexpected compatibilities, we turn one last time to *Origin of Species*, in which Darwin's recognition of chains of affinities underpinned the great explanatory power of his argument. The discovery of these similarities radiates through Darwin's prose as a profoundly inspirational insight. Repeatedly, he writes about the awe homologies inspire in him. Perhaps most memorable are the famous closing lines of *Origin of Species*, where he anticipates Wilberforce's arguments and assures his reader that "there is grandeur in this view of life." But there are many other instances in his treatise that invoke a similar sense of wonder at his discovery of so many homologies among so many different phenotypes. He writes, for example, "It is a truly wonderful fact—the wonder of which we are apt to overlook from familiarity—that all animals and plants throughout all time and space should be related to each other in group subordinate to group, in the manner in which we everywhere behold."[52] Similarly, later in the volume, he explains,

> When I view all beings not as special creations, but as lineal descendants of some few beings which lived long before the first bed of the Silurian system was deposited, they seem to me to become ennobled.... As all the living forms of life are the lineal descendants of those which lived long before..., we may feel certain that the ordinary succession by generation has never once been broken, and that no cataclysm has destroyed the whole world. Hence we may look with some confidence to a secure future of equally inappreciable length.[53]

In this passage, Darwin makes clear not only his awe and the ennobling import of interspecies affinities but also the profound comfort such affinities engender in him. This evidence of both common ancestry and the ability to evolve different but clearly compatible adaptive features assures Darwin that because life has to this point survived any cataclysm that may have threatened it, the clear evidence before him suggests that it will continue to do so.

Darwin's reference to life's persistence through cataclysm is a clear acknowledgment of the nineteenth-century debate about geology and the age of the Earth. Charles Lyell's uniformitarianism was only slowly replacing the prevailing notions of catastrophism and in that process facilitating intellectual revolutions like the one presented in *Origin of Species*. But Darwin's positioning of homologies as a salve—as having a profoundly comforting effect—can be explanatory beyond that specific context. These connections between creatures, the fact of their parts being so compatible and their thus having similar origins, assures us of resilience and of their ability to respond and adapt to a volatile and often hostile environment. We can contend, then, that much of the work and the appeal of steampunk—a genre characterized by blending—is its assurance that we not only share common roots and respond to common narrative but also that we are likely to carry on, through catastrophe and cataclysm. The mashing up of genres, centuries, apparel, and technologies highlights the commonalities that comfort us and trigger a sense of persistence and adaptability. In other words, it is not only the plot of steampunk texts or the features of retrofitted objects and fabricated creatures that thematize adaptation; instead, it is the nature of the mode itself.

This is not to suggest that steampunk is a Pollyanna genre, all sunshine and rainbows and optimism about the resilient future of civilization. Certainly the content of many steampunk novels and films is apocalyptic enough to dissuade us from that.[54] Indeed, steampunk seems often to expose paradigmatic problems within social structures without imagining alternatives. In part, we agree with Jess Nevins's observations that steampunk "rarely offers a solution to the problems it decries."[55] Its recurring subject matter and historical period present ample opportunity for commentary on ideological ills, but they present just as many opportunities for fetishism. Tom Easton describes steampunk as "a bit of a prettified cheat, for all that steampunk imagery is polished brass and wood and sexy leather, when anything to do with real steampower was marked by grease and soot.... Steampunk is retro. It's static and antiprogressive."[56] Writing in a special issue of *Locus* devoted to the genre, Liz Gorinsky remarks on its "potential as progressive literature," whereas Michael Moorcock sees its becoming increasingly "escapist nostalgia."[57] There is no shortage of debates about the politics of steampunk, and we aren't chiming in to act as boosters.

We do want to suggest, however, that the ethos of steampunk, with its insistence on hybrids and tinkering, seems oriented toward the notion of adapting to a changing environment, even sometimes a cataclysmic environment. If we want to push on to the "why now?" of the genre, we certainly must consider the "now" of its rise, and, given our focus to this point, the cataclysms associated with that "now." Before turning to our contributors, who answer this question in their own varied ways, we want to gesture toward one line for future exploration, one that considers 9/11, the form of trauma, and steampunk as a recursive genre.

Steampunk and 9/11, or Fort-Da in Brass

At the risk of sounding trite, it's fair to say that the attacks of September 11, 2001, changed everything. Such a statement is certainly true for the thousands who lost their lives or were injured in the attacks, as well as their families and friends. The events affected two of the largest metropolitan areas of the United States and destroyed some of their landmark structures. More than a decade later, New York City is still rebuilding what was destroyed in less than two hours. The extent of the destruction makes it clear why so many have described the events as "traumatic," and the term is a productive way to understand the attacks and their effects. While physicians consider trauma to be a wound to the body created by an outside object or source, the more frequent understanding of trauma in contemporary culture is a wound to the psyche. Psychological trauma can occur when a person "directly experience[s]" or "witness[es]" "actual or threatened death, serious injury, or sexual violence."[58] The events of 9/11 certainly provided ample opportunity for individuals in New York City and Washington, D.C., to be traumatized. Unsurprisingly, the *New York Times* reports that more than "10,000 firefighters, police officers and civilians" in New York City were diagnosed with post-traumatic stress disorder, or PTSD, after the attacks and "at least 3,600 of them still have symptoms" ten years later.[59] Other estimates put the number of New Yorkers traumatized by the attacks and their aftermath at more than 60,000.[60]

It is clear from these numbers that the attacks of 9/11 affected a larger group of people than, for lack of a better term, "ordinary" trauma. But the several thousands in New York and Washington who were directly affected by the terrorist attacks are just the beginning of the story. Thanks to twenty-first-century communications networks, the news of the first plane's impact at the World Trade Center was reported almost immediately—indeed, so quickly that live television caught the second plane hitting the second tower. Audio and video of the destruction at both locations traveled almost instantaneously around the world. While those who saw the attacks on television, heard about them on the radio or via cell phone, or read about them on the Internet weren't on the ground, they were still witnesses and therefore are also susceptible to traumatic stress. Indeed, as E. Ann Kaplan recounts in *Trauma Culture*, "most people encounter trauma through the media."[61] Although those who experienced mediatized trauma did not have the same experience as those in lower Manhattan, their trauma is still real.[62] Spectators to the attacks of 9/11—across the country or across the world—were confronted with images that could return to haunt them.

Our perception of the impact of those confrontations is perhaps made clear, somewhat ironically, in the revisions to the definition of PTSD in the 2013 fifth edition of the *Diagnostic Statistical Manual of Mental Disorders* (DSM). The DSM's fourth edition, text revision (2000), had included mediated experience as a possible criterion for PTSD: "The person experienced, witnessed or was confronted with an event or events that involved actual or threatened death or serious injury, or a threat to the physical integrity of others."[63] In comparison, the DSM-5 criteria rule out what it terms "indirect exposure" to life-threatening events, including that mediated by electronic media. We might understand this revision as a response to claims of PTSD on behalf of those who only had media exposure to the 9/11 attacks. The arguments that prompted this revision were, it seems, voluminous. A November 2001 study published in the *New England Journal of Medicine* of those who had not been present at the locations of the attacks found 90 percent of study participants displaying stress related to the attacks, but only 44 percent displaying significant stress three to five days after the attacks.[64] A 2009 article by Richard McNally explicitly calls for the DSM-5 to remove diagnostic criteria that allow indirect exposure to 9/11 to qualify a subject for a PTSD diagnosis.[65]

No one who lived through this period will be surprised to read of such high levels of stress. At the time, one could not avoid imagery and rhetoric that kept the attacks at the fore of one's mind. Flags and ribbons in support of victims and first-responders, enhanced security in public spaces, and merchandise urging us to "never forget" ensured that the impact of 9/11 was never far from sight. That impact of course extended far beyond the United States, in both geopolitical time and space. The swift terrorist strikes, compressed within a space of ninety minutes, produced long-lasting effects, including the military's entanglements in Iraq and Afghanistan in the pursuit of terrorists (and its concomitant distance, even a decade on, from other armed conflicts that are not connected explicitly with terrorism, such as Syria or Ukraine) to the proliferation of an NSA-powered surveillance state/theater legislatively enabled by the Patriot Act to prevent subsequent terrorist assaults. The actions of the United States and its allies has served as a multipronged reminder of international connectedness and vulnerability. Subsequent terror attacks in Madrid, London, and Mumbai, to name a few, have certainly heightened that sense of exposure.

Because of the wide circulation and ubiquity of images related to the 9/11 attacks; because of the heightened awareness of danger suggested by the now-defunct Homeland Security Advisory System; because of the response from the international community that legitimated the attacks as something beyond the pale; because of the dramatic changes in domestic and foreign policy that visibly and invisibly alter everyday interactions and thought patterns; and because of the ubiquitous and significant residue of the attacks, we might consider them as a source of cultural—in addition to individual—trauma. Such collective trauma, a relatively new concept in sociological and political discourse, is succinctly defined by Jeffrey C. Alexander: "Cultural trauma occurs when members of a collectivity feel they have been subjected to a horrendous event that leaves indelible marks upon their group consciousness, marking their memories forever and changing their future identity in fundamental and irrevocable ways."⁶⁶ Certainly this description applies to the events and sociopolitical aftermath of the 9/11 attacks. To this end, Neil J. Smelser specifically addresses the status of 9/11 as cultural trauma. Smelser begins by remarking, "If the screen industry's most talented scriptwriter had been asked to draft a scenario for the quintessential cultural drama, that script could not have surpassed the actual drama of September 11, 2001."⁶⁷ He goes on to discuss the features of this trauma, including the nation's initial reaction of shock and disbelief; widespread collective mourning; an immediate sense of the permanence of the trauma; and "a culminating sense that American identity had been altered fundamentally."⁶⁸

This paradigm is illuminating, and it certainly will ring true to most who experienced the attacks, either directly or indirectly. It expands on the previously existing model of trauma, which is generally figured as an individual disorder. This begs the question, then, of how traumatic symptoms might manifest themselves on the scale of an entire culture. Like most disorders, PTSD first attracted attention because of its symptoms. Physicians like John Eric Erichsen and psychiatrists like Jean-Martin Charcot and Sigmund Freud were surprised at how an individual could walk away from a railway accident unscathed but begin to suffer debilitating memories or dreams a short while thereafter. The return of these memories struck Freud in particular as curious in the context of dreams, which he believed to be a vehicle for wish fulfillment: "Anyone who accepts it as something self-evident that their dreams should put them back at night into the situation that caused them to fall ill has misunderstood the nature of dreams." Trauma, Freud observed, was a shocking interruption of the present by the past, one that "repeatedly bring[s] the patient back into the situation of his accident."⁶⁹ This temporal aberration is at the heart of trauma. As Cathy Caruth writes, "Trauma is not locatable in the simple violent or original event in an individual's past, but rather in the way that its very unassimilated nature—the way it was precisely *not known* in the first instance—returns to haunt the survivor later on."⁷⁰

In their discussions of cultural trauma, Smelser and his coeditors return frequently to this same trope: the haunting return of memories. In a large population, this irruption of the past often looks like a compulsive need to relive and reexperience the original event. The editors discuss memorials, reenactments, and the circulation of witness testimonies as examples of such reexperiencing. Although these events are understood as remembrance, they are often closer to what

Freud identified as "acting out," a form of repetition that, as a result of resistance on the part of the patient, actually replaces remembrance.[71] Such acting out takes place in cultural trauma as well as individual trauma, reinforcing the notion that the master trope of such disruption is recursivity or the uncontrollable cycle of repetition.

Just as we are drawn to the similarities of homology in Darwin's theories and hybridity in steampunk, so are we struck by the resonance between trauma's structure of recursive return and steampunk's cycling and recycling of time. If a genre of literature/culture can be said to resemble Freudian figures of trauma, steampunk is it. Steampunk traffics in startling anachronism, the sudden displacement of cultural and technological markers that interrupt history. The nineteenth century intrudes on the twenty-first—or vice versa—without warning, and the narratives that are produced depend precisely on the problems created by these temporal ruptures. In both cases, the past and the present are connected in a manner that occludes the specificity of each and in a way that frequently resembles a haunting. In its looping of time, steampunk cycles and recycles tropes that are unexpected and surprisingly out of place. In this way, steampunk functions as a model for trauma. It encapsulates the temporal oddities and juxtapositions spurred by an event that happens too soon.

This, then, might explain why steampunk has finally risen to prominence in the twenty-first century, after three decades of slow growth. It is a mode that speaks to our moment of cultural trauma in its presentation of time buckling in on itself, of a cultural revisiting past and present. If IBM predicted that steampunk would appear in "mainstream clothing, furnishings, and accessories" in 2014, then it was in part because we live in a moment when the time of steampunk—recursive, looping, repetitive—makes sense to a large, collective audience that lived through the cultural trauma of 9/11.

That said, another appeal of steampunk is that for many it is simply fun. It is fiction, and it is maker culture. While its content often includes postapocalyptic paradigms and tinkered-with World War I, it does not, as a matter of course, meditate on historical tragedy or contemporary violence. No one who has read a handful of steampunk novels or attended a convention would call it a mournful movement. We would not suggest that steampunk is acting out trauma in its every instance. Nor would we want to mount an argument that steampunk is only a direct response to 9/11.[72] That might be an interpretive move for some, but it is not ours.

But we do, to loop back on ourselves, locate the vast majority of steampunk's increasingly mainstream, meteoric rise within the twenty-first century, and we do agree with the scholars who regard one of the early events of that century to be a cultural trauma. Further, we see the tropes of trauma and steampunk overlapping in their recursive return. For us, this raises questions about the mode of reading/participation steampunk solicits and what it promises its enthusiasts. In answer, we return briefly to our readings of its nineteenth-century antecedents.

At the same time that it appears to be about discontinuities of time, steampunk participates in the nineteenth-century discovery about the continuity in time, as we have discussed elsewhere.[73] Steampunk is the ultimate uniformitarian genre. Relatedly, it revels in homologies and affinities, as we have discussed here. As such, it points to the persistence of life and the recovery from catastrophes. The recognition of similarities, between time periods and creatures, allows us to, to return to Darwin, "feel certain that the ordinary succession by generation has never once been broken, and that no cataclysm has destroyed the whole world. Hence we may look with some confidence to a secure future of equally inappreciable length." Darwin's comfort in the overlapping features he found throughout the ecosystem may also be our comfort when steampunk highlights compatibilities and similarities. Despite the sense of rupture, the feeling that a catastrophe like 9/11 represents an indelible change in the wake of which culture is fundamentally altered, homologies and affinities between features and moments remind us that "no cataclysm has destroyed the whole world." Steampunk's looping through time, its literalized Darwinian hybrids functioning as war technology, its grafting of Victorian aesthetics on new technologies, its overlaying the Industrial Revolution with a nanotechnology explosion—these imaginative recombinants entertain and intrigue us, but perhaps they also comfort us. Perhaps they remind us of compatibilities, of how ideologies and technologies have persisted through time, of the shared imaginative endeavors our makers and writers invest in. Perhaps steampunk appeals to so many at the moment it does because it promises to bridge gaps, to reassure us of the possibility of recovery from catastrophe.

Thus, though we may be immediately struck by the ways steampunk is structured like an acting out in response to trauma, we are ultimately persuaded to think of it more as a "working-through."[74] Freud understood working-through as what happens when a patient overcomes resistance to treatment by harnessing the pattern of remembering and repeating to move toward a goal of integration and acceptance. Steampunk seems anything but resistant to its repetitions; it feel celebratory, reveling in history's cycles and in the compatible structures among ages. Steampunk may, then, feel like a cultural salve in the wake of tragedies that are experienced as catastrophic ruptures. It speaks to those ruptures through its structure, but it also promises that they can be overcome through ingenuity and persistence. Indeed, if steampunk is the genre of ultimate tinkering, and if tinkering, as we noted above, is always and fundamentally a response to environment—making use of what's available—then we cannot ignore the cultural trauma of 9/11, so prominent in the environment during steampunk's rise to prominence.

It's important to be clear: steampunk was not birthed by the tragedies of the twenty-first century; after all, as Mike Perschon's essay in this volume shows, steampunk as we know it today has existed since the early 1970s in literature; the term came into existence in 1987. Nor is the rise of steampunk anywhere near the most important effect or outcome from the terrorist attacks in New York City or the ones that followed elsewhere in the world. Yet when one begins to wonder "Why steampunk now?" it is certainly worth considering that the decade that opens the twenty-first century begins not with a whimper but with a bang.

The Shape of Things to Come

The essays in this volume all engage the matter of steampunk's historicity to one degree or another, and can all be said to provide distinct answers to the question "Why steampunk now?" Further, the structural divisions within the volume elucidate the multiple valences of that question. We are obviously interested, as are our contributors, in the question of why steampunk rises to cultural prominence when it does. But we are also interested in staking the claim that steampunk is uniquely positioned, as a cultural and discursive phenomenon, to pave inquiries into the most productive academic fields of the twenty-first century. The volume's informing divisions of "Steampunk Spaces and Things," "Steampunk Bodies and Identities," and "Steampunk Reading and Revising" underscore the interventions that can be made in a wide range of scholarly fields—including disability studies, digital humanities, urban studies, postcolonial analysis, and gender and queer studies—from the vantage point of steampunk scholarship.

In "Steampunk Spaces and Things," the authors examine steampunk's specialized relationship to its urban locations and its DIY objects. David Pike and Catherine Siemann provide analyses of steampunk cities (drawing on authors that include H. G. Wells, Bryan Talbot, Cherie Priest, and China Miéville), with Pike focusing on the palimpsestic nature of London within the steampunk universe and Siemann more broadly examining the industrial and supernatural cataclysms that drive so many steampunk cities into dystopia. In this same section, Roger Whitson shifts us to a materialist approach, taking up the role of objects in defining the steampunk ethos. Whitson argues for critical making as the paradigm central to steampunk, suggesting an intersection with shifts in rhetoric that parallel the rise of digital humanities within academe.

In "Steampunk Bodies and Identities," our authors engage a range of texts that invoke steampunk corporeality and subjectivity, largely concluding that steampunk responds to and participates in a cultural shift toward more nuanced understandings of the relationship between body and identity. Kathryn Crowther brings disability studies to bear on steampunk, examining the role of prosthetics within steampunk and drawing connections to a contemporary culture of access. Stefania Forlini turns our attention to historically situated identities, particularly the figures of the aesthete and the dandy, and traces their relationship to steampunk culture. In so doing, she places the dandy and his attendant intellectualization of objects at the center of an analysis that situates critical making and surface adornment as both the ideological vectors that sustain identity, and as political responses to a changing environment. Politicized identities and their relationship to changing environments are the focus of Diana M. Pho's chapter, which examines steampunk performances and artists, arguing that the hybrid identities contained therein break the conception of a homogeneous national culture (and subculture) as much as steampunk dismantles historical narratives.

The volume's final section, "Steampunk Reading and Revising," links together authors for whom steampunk lenses have opened up already existing tropes and paradigms. Mike Perschon's "Seminal Steampunk" asks us to reconsider how we think of the rise of steampunk and the dominant themes of its various generations. Perschon repositions many of steampunk's major figures in a manner that invites us to question any totalizing ideology within the genre or its evolution. Lisa Hager's chapter examines the methodological approaches within Victorian studies to steampunk, focusing especially on literary representations of female sexuality and agency to illuminate contemporary tensions and ambivalence. Joseph Weakland and Shaun Duke find literary representations of steampunk technology applied in pursuit of enfranchising historically marginalized individuals.

None of these pieces offers a definitive answer to the question of "why steampunk now?"; likely none of the authors would accept a definitive answer from this historical vantage point. But all of the pieces offer insight into steampunk's relevance and rise. They examine its historicity, its material surfaces, and its ideological depths. All of these angles illuminate steampunk's place within maker and literary cultures; moreover, they all point our attention in various ways to the consumers of steampunk. As our contributors make clear, although the readers, the cosplayers, and the makers belong to a culture of fandom, it is a fandom that is well aware of the limitations and the shortcomings of steampunk. They are, it turns out, a very twenty-first-century set of enthusiasts.

NOTES

1. Howard Pousner, "Dragon Con Unveils Longer Parade Route Closer to Third MARTA Station," *AJC.com*, August 18, 2015, http://ajc.com.
2. Josh Jackson, "Steampunk Dog at the #dragoncon Parade," *Instagram*, September 1, 2012, https://instagram.com/joshjackson/.
3. "SteamCon VI—The Mechanical World," SteamCon, http://www.steamcon.org/.
4. "The Fairhaven Steampunk Festival," Bellingham Steampunk Society, http://www.bellinghamsteampunk.org/.
5. Ay-leen the Peacemaker [Diana M. Pho], "Steampunk Events for February 2015," *Tor.com* (blog), http://www.tor.com; "Steamathon 2—The Empire 2016," Steamathon, https://www.steamathon.com/.
6. "The Steampunk World's Fair," Jeff Mach Events, http://steampunkworldsfair.com/; "Watch Steampunk City Festival," Watch City Steampunk Festival and Downtown Waltham Partnership, http://www.watchcityfestival.com/.
7. Holly Cara Price, "New York City's First Ever Steampunk Weekend August 9, 10, 11 Kicks Off Tonight at Lincoln Center Out of Doors," *Huffington Post*, August 9, 2013, http://www.huffingtonpost.com; "New York City Steampunk Social Calendar," New York City Steampunk, http://www.nycsteampunk.com/.
8. "No. 15 Renwick Hudson Square Boutique Condos," http://15renwick.com/; see also Danielle Tcholakian, "Steampunk-Themed Luxury Project Aims to Draw 'Rich Hipsters' to Hudson Sq.," *DNAinfo*, December 2, 2014, http://www.dnainfo.com/.
9. Dr. Damon Molinarius, "European Steampunk Convention," *Strange Dreams—Steampunk Art and Fiction* (blog), April 25, 2012, http://drmolinarius-spartandfiction.blogspot.com/; "The Third Installment of EuroSteamCon," EuroSteamCon, http://aetherscope.eurosteamcon.com/.

10. Ay-leen the Peacemaker [Diana M. Pho], "Gearing Up for 2011: A Steampunk Convention List," *Tor.com* (blog), January 24, 2011, http://www.tor.com; Ay-leen the Peacemaker [Diana M. Pho], "Gearing Up for 2012: A Steampunk Conventions Listing," *Tor.com* (blog), January 16, 2012, http://www.tor.com; Ayleen the Peacemaker [Diana M. Pho], "Gearing up for 2013: A Steampunk Convention Listing," *Tor.com* (blog), January 10, 2013, http://www.tor.com.

11. Ay-leen the Peacemaker [Diana M. Pho], "Steampunk Events for January 2015," *Tor.com* (blog), December 31, 2014, http://www.tor.com.

12. Merle Ginsberg, "Gary Oldman, Garrett Hedlund, Jamie Bell and Willem Dafoe's Next Project: The Fall Prada Campaign," *Pret-a-Reporter* (blog), *Hollywood Report and Billboard*, June 5, 2012, http://www.hollywoodreporter.com/style.

13. John Yong, "Prada Menswear Goes Steampunk this Fall," *DesignTAXI* (blog), June 25, 2012, http://designtaxi.com; Stubby the Rocket, "Sci-Fi Actors Wearing Steampunk Clothes Designed by Prada," *Tor.com* (blog), June 25, 2012, http://www.tor.com; Joey Paur, "Prada Goes Steampunk with Oldman, Dafoe, Hedlund, and Bell," *GeekTyrant* (blog), July 5, 2012, http://geektyrant.com/. It's important to note that Numi Prasarn wrote an impassioned post on the *Steampunk Workshop*, arguing that "PRADA IS NOT STEAMPUNK (at least not in the way you say it is)"; Prasarn, "Steampunk Stahp! Or the Appropriation of Prada," *Steampunk Workshop* (blog), May 24, 2013, http://steampunkworkshop.com/.

14. Matt King, "The World of Steam," *Kickstarter*, https://www.kickstarter.com/. While it might seem that anything steampunk is a sure bet, there are reminders that this is not the case. Another Kickstarter project for a steampunk Web series, *Tinker*, failed to reach its goal of $20,000 to fund its pilot episode despite its promise to deliver "Dr. Who + Blade Runner + Firefly, all rolled together in a Film Noir, Victorian Futurism that would make Verne and Wells proud"; Containment Field Studio, "TINKER Steampunk Web Series Pilot," *Kickstarter*, http://www.kickstarter.com.

15. Matt King, "UPDATES!!! The Work and the World continues . . . ," for "The World of Steam," *Kickstarter*, February 13, 2016, http://www.kickstarter.com.

16. IBM, "IBM Social Sentiment Index Predicts New Retail Trend in the Making," *IBM News Room*, January 14, 2013, https://www.ibm.com.

17. Ibid.

18. IBM, "Birth of a Trend: Steampunk," *IBM Social Sentiment Index*, January 14, 2013, http://www.ibm.com.

19. David Cross, "The 50 Most Steampunk Cities in America," *Movoto Blog*, August 8, 2013, http://www.movoto.com/blog/.

20. See, for example, Diane Sadoff, *Victorian Vogue* (Minneapolis: University of Minnesota Press, 2009); and John Kucich and Diane Sadoff, ed., *Victorian Afterlife* (Minneapolis: University of Minnesota Press, 2010).

21. Jess Nevins, "Introduction: The 19th-Century Roots of Steampunk," in *Steampunk*, ed. Ann VanderMeer and Jeff VanderMeer (San Francisco: Tachyon, 2008), 3-12.

22. Rachel A. Bowser and Brian Croxall, "Introduction: Industrial Evolution," *Neo-Victorian Studies* 3, no. 1 (2010): 21.

23. The question of prescriptivism versus descriptivism in identifying steampunk is at issue for many of its scholarly critics and participants, as is frequently the case with newly emerging genres and subcultures. This oscillation may not always rise to the level of "an intense semantic and philosophical battleground" that Jess Nevins signals, but Nevins is correct that prescriptivist definitions often fail to encapsulate the full range of activities that are recognizable as steampunk; "Prescriptivists vs. Descriptivists: Defining Steampunk," *Science Fiction Studies* 38, no. 3 (2011): 513.

24. Bowser and Croxall, "Introduction: Industrial Evolution," 4-10.

25. Charles Darwin, *On the Origin of Species* (1859; repr., Cambridge, Mass.: Harvard University Press, 1964), 470.

26. Ibid., 479.

27. For a thorough discussion of instances in which the concept of homologies and hybridities preceded Darwin, see U. C. Knoepflmacher, "Introduction: Hybrid Forms and Cultural Anxiety," in *Victorian Hybridities: Cultural Anxiety and Formal Innovation*, ed. U. C. Knoepflmacher and Logan D. Browning (Baltimore, Md.: Johns Hopkins University Press, 2010), 1-10.

28. Samuel Wilberforce, review of *On the Origin of Species, by Means of Natural Selection; or The Preservation of Favoured Races in the Struggle for Life*, by Charles Darwin, *Quarterly Review* 108, no. 215 (1860): 231.

29. Bowser and Croxall, "Introduction: Industrial Evolution," 4.

30. Scott Westerfeld, *Leviathan* (New York: Simon, 2009), 66.

31. Ibid., 323.

32. Scott Westerfeld, *Behemoth* (New York: Simon, 2010), 102.

33. Westerfeld, *Leviathan*, 31-32.

34. Ibid., 71.

35. Ibid., 439-40.

36. Ibid., 387.

37. Ibid., 394.

38. Ibid., 399.

39. Ibid., 416.

40. Ibid., 430.

41. In this seizure of a paid-for ship, the events in Westerfeld's novel mirrors that of real events in World War I. The British navy refused to deliver the *Sultan Osman-ı Evvel* and a second ship, the *Reşadiye*, when they feared that the Ottomans would use them against the British. The first ship was renamed H.M.S. *Agincourt*, and Winston Churchill's fears about the Ottomans joining the Central Powers became a self-fulfilling prophecy.

42. Scott Westerfeld, *Goliath* (New York: Simon, 2011), 31.

43. "TESLA, AT 78, BARES NEW 'DEATH-BEAM': Invention Powerful Enough to Destroy 10,000 Planes 250 Miles Away, He Asserts. DEFENSIVE WEAPON ONLY Scientist, in Interview, Tells of Apparatus that He Says Will Kill without Trace," *New York Times*, July 11, 1934.

44. Westerfeld, *Goliath*, 513, 515.

45. Ibid., iv.

46. Westerfeld, *Leviathan*, 417.
47. Westerfeld, *Goliath*, 54.
48. Westerfeld, *Behemoth*, 92.
49. "Glass Armonica: An Instrument of Glass, Fingers, and Gears," *SteamPunk Magazine* 1 (2007): 8-9.
50. François Jacob, "Evolution and Tinkering," *Science* 196, no. 4295 (June 10, 1977): 1163-64.
51. Ibid., 1163.
52. Darwin, *Origin of Species*, 128-29.
53. Ibid., 578.
54. For examples of the apocalyptic and the horrible within steampunk, one might consider, for a start, fiction and films such as K. W. Jeter, *Morlock Night* (1979); William Gibson and Bruce Sterling, *The Difference Engine* (1990); Alan Moore and Kevin O'Neill, *The League of Extraordinary Gentlemen* (1999-); China Miéville, *Perdido Street Station* (2000); *Steamboy* (dir. Katsuhiro Otomo, 2004); and Cherie Priest, *Boneshaker* (2009).
55. Nevins, "Introduction: The 19th-Century Roots of Steampunk," 9.
56. Tom Easton, "A Post-Steampunk Manifesto," *New York Review of Science Fiction* 25, no. 6 (2013): 15-16.
57. Liz Gorinsky, "Steampunk," *Locus Magazine* 65, no. 3 (September 2010): 34; Michael Moorcock, "Steampunk Sans Punk," *Locus Magazine* 65, no. 3 (September 2010): 34.
58. American Psychiatric Association, *Diagnostic and Statistical Manual of Mental Disorders*, 5th ed. (Washington, D.C.: American Psychiatric Association, 2013), section 309.91.
59. Anemona Hartocollis, "Post-Traumatic Stress Disorder from 9/11 Still Haunts," *New York Times*, August 9, 2011.
60. Ibid.
61. E. Ann Kaplan, *Trauma Culture: The Politics of Terror and Loss in Media and Literature* (New Brunswick, N.J.: Rutgers University Press, 2005), 2.
62. See Katherine Harmon, "The Changing Mental Health Aftermath of 9/11—Psychological 'First Aid' Gains Favor over Debriefings," *Scientific American*, September 10, 2011, paragraph 17.
63. American Psychiatric Association, *Diagnostic and Statistical Manual of Mental Disorders*, 4th ed., text revision (Arlington, Va.: American Psychiatric Association, 2000), section 309.81.
64. Mark A. Schuster et al., "A National Survey of Stress Reactions after the September 11, 2001 Terrorist Attacks," *New England Journal of Medicine* 345, no. 20 (November 15, 2001). The authors surveyed, via random-dial telephone calls, a representative sample of 560 U.S. adults who were not present at the attack locations.
65. Richard McNally, "Can We Fix PTSD in DSM-V?," *Depression and Anxiety* 26, no. 7 (2009): 597-600.
66. Jeffrey C. Alexander, "Toward a Theory of Cultural Trauma," in *Cultural

Trauma and Collective Identity, ed. Jeffrey C. Alexander et al. (Berkeley: University of California Press, 2004), 1.

67. Neil J. Smelser, "Epilogue: September 11, 2001 as Cultural Trauma," in Alexander et al., *Cultural Trauma and Collective Identity*, 264.

68. Ibid., 266–67.

69. Sigmund Freud, *Beyond the Pleasure Principle*, in *The Standard Edition of the Complete Psychological Works of Sigmund Freud*, ed. James Strachey et al., vol. 18, *1920–1922: Beyond the Pleasure Principle, Group Psychology and Other Works* (1920; repr., London: Hogarth Press, 1955), 12.

70. Cathy Caruth, *Unclaimed Experience: Trauma, Narrative, and History* (Baltimore: Johns Hopkins University Press, 1996), 2–3.

71. See Sigmund Freud, "Remembering, Repeating and Working-Through (Further Recommendations on the Technique of Psycho-Analysis II)," in *The Standard Edition of the Complete Psychological Works of Sigmund Freud*, ed. James Strachey et al., vol. 12, *1911–1913: The Case of Schreber, Papers on Technique and Other Works* (1914; repr., London: Hogarth Press, 1958), 145–56.

72. That said, the third book of Westerfeld's Leviathan series does stage the fiery crash of an airship into a New York City building after its attack by German saboteurs. Other post-9/11 steampunk texts, such as *Steamboy*, stage massive battles in urban locations and pay particular attention to burning, towering buildings.

73. Bowser and Croxall, "Introduction: Industrial Evolution."

74. Freud, "Remembering, Repeating and Working-Through."

PART I
Steampunk
Spaces and Things

Steampunk and the Victorian City
Time Machines, Bryan Talbot, and the Center of the Multiverse

DAVID PIKE

> One may easily sail round England, or circumnavigate the globe. But not the most enthusiastic geographer . . . ever memorised a map of London. Certainly no one ever walks round it. For England is a small island, the world is infinitesimal amongst the planets. But London is illimitable.
> —FORD MADOX FORD, *The Soul of London*

To describe the steampunk city is very close to a truism: the steampunk city is, overwhelmingly, London, and it is, inevitably, Victorian. What is interesting about the steampunk city is what it does with that truism. Steampunk, and its rise in popularity over the past decade, have tended to be characterized (and rightly so) in terms of its nonlinear relationship to temporality and in terms of its simultaneously speculative and hands-on attitude toward technology.[1] The contemporary fascination with steampunk derives not only from the different ways it asks us to think about temporality and technology but also from how it uses urban space to visualize those differences and how it uses fantastic and otherwise reworked imagery of the nineteenth-century city to formulate alternative modes for thinking about urban history. Two propositions in particular run implicitly as threads through much of steampunk fiction: that the material spaces and spatial practices of the Victorian city itself are constitutive of our contemporary situation in the world and formative to the process of rethinking and transforming that contemporary situation; and that representations of the Victorian city constellate within themselves much that is important to the self-conception of steampunk.

This is a grandiose and sweepingly general pair of propositions, and a pair of propositions that is shot full of holes. And that is precisely my point: a key element to the allure of Victorian London for steampunk is its limitless capacity to contain not only the world, as the imperial narrative would maintain, but also the multiverse—this world, all alternative worlds, and all the holes, fissures, and folds in between. Note that this is no anachronistic retrojection from the twenty-first century; Ford Madox Ford may have given the idea its most elegant formulation (as in the epigraph above), but it was commonplace to consider London as an entity that had become "illimitable" in a world otherwise grown finite and knowable. What Ford expressed in terms of geography, however, steampunk elaborates in terms of time and technology. The space-time of London in steampunk figures as the still point or umbilicus of a multiverse that knows no limits—not physical, not epistemological, and not metaphysical. Take a novel like Cherie Priest's *Boneshaker* (2009), set in a beautifully rendered 1880s Seattle amid the western genre trappings proper to it—saloons, dusters, rifles, American Indians, Chinese immigrants. The steampunk twists on that setting—the polluted cityscape, the sealed-off ghetto, the abandonment of the surface for tunnels and rooftops, even the undead monsters and the psychotic übervillain—all derive from nineteenth-century London and its pulp literary traditions. However elastically the relationship may be conceived and however far it may be stretched, Victorian London constitutes perhaps the only constraints steampunk allows for its wild speculations.

It is this elasticity that leads me to define steampunk as a mode through which any text or cultural manifestation can be understood, expressed, and transmuted rather than more strictly as a genre or a movement. Defining a particular literary or cultural phenomenon as a mode helps to deflect the potential for navel-gazing and prescriptive arguments about what its genre qualities are and whether or not a certain text qualifies for inclusion in a genre canon.[2] Instead, it focuses attention toward analysis of the effects of the modality of steampunk on the genres and movements it appropriates and the changing meanings of that modality depending on the genre appropriated and the spatiotemporal moment of the appropriation (as, for example, in Mike Perschon's parsing in this volume of the very real differences in first-wave steampunk between Michael Moorcock's "radical, political doctrine" and the "whimsical, romantic" vision of Californians Tim Powers, K. W. Jeter, and James Blaylock). Much of the pleasure, fascination, and capacity for critique of this mode arise from the exquisite tension and play between the tight spatiotemporal constraint and the illimitable phenomena that simultaneously characterize Victorian London.[3] To define this tension and play in greater detail, I begin with a brief outline of what I consider its defining characteristic as a mode, a characteristic that underlies but is not limited to steampunk's familiar stylistic and technological flourishes: the peculiar historical situation of steampunk's time in relation to the nineteenth century and to changing late twentieth- and early twenty-first-century attitudes toward questions of temporality. I then address the broad topic of the Victorian city in terms of two specific examples within steampunk: the afterlife of H. G. Wells's *The Time Machine* (1895) and the neo-Victorian work of artist and writer Bryan Talbot.

The Victorian City in the Twenty-First Century

My starting point is a nineteenth-century trope that is in many ways anathema to the steampunk vision of history: the impossibility of thinking beyond one's own time. As Walter Benjamin, Giovanni Macchia, Lynda Nead, and others have argued, a primary mode for conceptualizing the nineteenth-century city was to see it in ruins; Macaulay's New Zealander on a broken arch of London Bridge is perhaps the most familiar image of a Victorian London understood in terms of its inevitable decline and fall.[4] In terms of the historical consciousness of the city and its built environment, even the future was imagined in terms of the past. When they found time to think about their own future, many inhabitants of London (or Paris, although my focus here is on London[5]), rather than foreseeing the endurance of their city, tended to write it out of existence.

A writer of speculative fiction such as H. G. Wells thus used the city to think about the future in primarily negative terms. Despite the assumptions of many of the novel's readers, it is never clarified whether the machinery tended underground by the Morlocks in *The Time Machine* is of Victorian provenance or a later invention, or even from which Victorian population, if any, the Morlocks may be descended. All that we know is that everything recognizable has vanished, with the possible exception of a South Kensington museum turned green and a river Thames that has shifted mightily in its banks. But even there, the only use the future will have for the past is as relics and ruins. The Time Traveller's tale covers the trajectory of his journey some 800,000 years into the future in a mere four paragraphs, only one sentence of which alludes to any actual cityscape, and then only the vague description of the "great and splendid architecture rising about me," referring, presumably, to the colossal and alien buildings that will later shelter the Eloi at night, void of any traces of human labor or evidence of how they came into existence.⁶ With the benefit of hindsight, we know now that Victorian apocalypticism would not in fact succeed in imagining the Victorian city out of existence. It was no more successful in doing so than the subsequent tabula rasa approach of the modernists, who did think about the future, who had a strong sense of the historicity of the cityscape, and who regarded the elimination of Victorian urban space, in particular its dense and tightly packed streets, as the necessary first step in creating a salubrious and rational metropolis.

Despite the modernists, and against the predictions of the Victorians, the built environment of the nineteenth-century city has endured not as ruins but as part of the intricate texture of contemporary urban space. It survives pretty much wholesale, for example, in the subterranean infrastructure of London's transport and drainage systems,

FIGURE 1.1. The nineteenth-century trope of the city in ruins. Gustave Doré, "The New Zealander," in *London: A Pilgrimage*, by Doré and Douglas Jerrold (London: Grant & Co., 1872), 188–89.

and more piecemeal in its street system, housing stock, and industrial buildings, damaged as they were by war, the decline of industry, and urban renewal projects. What interests me in this endurance is the way Victorian London has established itself over the past half century as an alternative way of visualizing the temporality of the cityscape in general, and in particular the possibility of uniting multiple times and places into a single, relatively stable space. In other words, from what was a nineteenth-century perception of a present problem to be resolved by some form of destruction or elimination of the past, the Victorian city, in its very status as belonging to the past of the twentieth century, has come to represent something of a still point in a moving world, a center of gravity toward which all history and prior cityscapes converged and from which everything we now think of as the urban will emerge. In *Dickens in Cyberspace,* Jay Clayton notes the consistency with which postmodernist theorists elided the nineteenth century in their leap from the Enlightenment to modernism.[7] But during the same decades in which postmodernism was at its height, popular culture and urban demographics were filling in that very gap, for what the "Victorian" city now provided was cheap alternative housing and a plethora of material culture, precisely the nuts and bolts that modernist art and architecture had not succeeded in eliminating and that postmodernist theory tended to pronounce as dead, along with history itself. By the 1960s, the Victorian had begun to assume a new identity as part of a discourse around traces of nonalienated, human-oriented culture that had survived the onslaught of modernism. This discourse was available to the full range of political viewpoints; what concern me here are ways in which it manifested itself in critical appropriations of the city's Victorian spaces. In London, as squatters took over the decaying remnants of the Victorian cityscape and social historians decried the loss of working-class sociability in the tower blocks that had replaced that cityscape in the East End, countercultural writers like Michael Moorcock and Bryan Talbot inaugurated, primarily in revisionist science fiction, the alternate neo-Victorianist history from which steampunk would eventually emerge. Rather than the locus of everything that was not modern, the Victorian became newly understood as an alternate modernity. Redefined as the crossroads of traditional forms of sociability, powerful new technologies, and modernist rationalization, the spaces of the Victorian city allowed an extended and fraught process of historical change to be grasped as a single moment in space and time; moreover, that single moment could be understood as ongoing in the present rather than fixed in a lost and inaccessible past. The mere fact that the Victorian city had survived into the late twentieth century leveled a reproach at the modernist narrative of progress and gave the lie to postmodernist claims for the end of history and a fluid present, and steampunk has proven to be the most influential mode for registering and making sense of this survival.

Time Machines and the Victorian Street

The Victorian street is by no means the best preserved of nineteenth-century traces in the twentieth-first century city, but in the very hybridity of its temporal blending of different periods and of the ersatz with the authentic, it has provided a spatial image well suited to conceptualizing the new relationship between the past and the present intrinsic to the steampunk mode. I unpack this image here through the ways a pair of Hollywood movies have visualized the Victorian cityscape of Wells's *The Time Machine:* first in 1960, directed by special effects maestro George Pal, and then in 2002, directed (rather poorly, it must be said) by Simon Wells, the great-grandson of the novel's author.[8] Both versions preserve the novel's notion of a cataclysmic rupture with the distant future, but both also add to the novel a transitional episode that establishes a historical continuity between the late nineteenth century of the Time Traveller and the subsequent century prior to that coming cataclysm, the present and near future of the films' original audiences. Both versions, as it were, carve out a bridge of time from the late twentieth century to a moment somewhere after the present day in the late twentieth or early twentieth-first century, respectively. And in both films, the setting of this bridging sequence is the Victorian street and the visual iconography is recognizably steampunk, for this sense of bridging is essential to steampunk's changed temporality. In the 1960 version, where the bridge lasts a full twenty minutes in duration and is the primary showcase of the movie's award-winning time-lapse special effects, the Time Traveller pauses his machine a number of times between 1900 and a nuclear apocalypse in 1966. The street outside his house displays in its mise-en-scène three defining features: a plate-glass shop window, a brick archway, and an Underground railway entrance.[9]

The movie identifies the street and its emblematic shop window as the locus of stability—the mannequin persists changeless through time, just as the Time Traveller (Rod Taylor) does—and of change—her fashionable garb is ceaselessly updated. But in his focus on the mannequin,

FIGURE 1.2. The persistence of the Victorian street and infrastructure in the shop window, archway, and Underground amid the modernism of 1966 London. *The Time Machine,* directed by George Pal, produced by Metro-Goldwyn-Mayer (1960; Atlanta, Ga.: Turner Home Entertainment, 2010), DVD.

the Time Traveller in fact neglects to observe that the shop window and certain other street features that frame her also remain the same through time, although the time-lapse effects emphasize this fact for the viewer. Like his iconic machine, the street features are enduring traces of the Victorian cityscape in the twentieth century, even into the apparently modern 1966. Now, both mannequin and shop front will eventually be destroyed in a nuclear war, but when the Time Traveller reaches the distant future, he will have carried the spatial memory of the street and the companionable desire for the mannequin with him. As protector of the young Eloi maiden Weena (played in mannequinish fashion by Yvette Mimieux), the Time Traveller locates where his house had been, marks out its dimensions on the grass, and makes a fire in the spot where his hearth was located, essentially remaking the Victorianist set in his (and our) imagination. He will eventually return to this future, presumably to rebuild his home there with her, bringing what was good from the past to redeem the future. The film closes on Filby, his closest friend among the party guests and the owner of the shop, in 1895 imagining the Time Traveller's actions in the same space, 800,000 years in the future. The desire born of the afterlife of the Victorian street provides a utopian supplement able to supplant the bleak vision of Wells's original. It is typical of the operation of postwar Hollywood narrative (and atypical of steampunk) that this desire must first be gendered and sexualized, then transplanted from the public space of the street to the private space of the hearth in order to be realized. But one of the mechanisms of the nineteenth-century street was to commodify desire, bringing the world to the city in the form of goods and promising the world to consumers through the spectacle of those goods. The 1960 film adds another element to this dynamic that would be important to the visual culture of steampunk, for the flicker effect to which it calls our attention with its stop-motion animation incorporates the mediatization of the street into its image. The Time Traveller is equally a proto-movie spectator, grasping the world in images of desire. The historical trajectory from 1895 to 1966 is also bridged by the invention of cinema, which, as many critics have observed, is itself first and foremost an instrument of time travel.

The 2002 version of Wells's novel transplants the setting to late nineteenth-century New York City and intensifies the motivation of desire in the journey through time. This Time Traveller is driven not by scientific curiosity but by the need to find a way to prevent the violent death of his fiancée. His machine is flashier, although no less Victorian in its accoutrements, and the scene of his experience of the next 130-plus years (about twelve minutes in full) is, once again, a city street and its signature shop window. The mannequins that open the sequence appear to be present as a vestigial reminder of the 1960 film and of the Victorian London streetscape before it. This Time Traveller is not distracted by spectacle, however; he has the weight of loss to deal with, until passing time steals from his clumsy hand the locket bearing the image of his beloved. Individual memories may fade, but the street endures. The flicker effect is no longer enough to signify motion picture technology, and so this film has new effects for us, pulling us out with vertiginous CGI all the way to a 2030 moon colony to inform us, with self-conscious irony, that "The Future Is Now." The mannequins themselves have been replaced by an advertising billboard, but their 2030 descendant is there on the street, sheathed in Lycra, sporting that Victorian invention the bicycle, lazily flirtatious, and hip enough to recognize in the Time Traveller his new identity as steampunk—"Nice suit, very retro." In 2030 New York, the late Victorian dandy is still (or once again) in fashion, along with his retro-cool machine, and the steampunk is self-consciously evoked as the mediating link between past and future.[10]

I don't want to attribute any attempt at cohesive argument to either of these scenes. It is enough to acknowledge that someone felt the need

FIGURE 1.3. The persistence of the Victorian shop window across space and time. *The Time Machine*, directed by Simon Wells (Burbank, Calif.: Warner Bros., 2002), DVD.

to insert these bridging sequences, whereas in 1895 Wells did not; to notice that the spatial image chosen for the bridging sequence between past and near future is the Victorian street; and to observe that the cinematic iconography is recognizably steampunk. What I take away from these two sequences is that something about the Victorian street is felt not only to connect the present to the past—for something in that street promises to sum up the nineteenth century along with everything that came before it—but also to provide us with whatever it is that we need in order to survive in whatever distant and alien future we may find ourselves. It is no accident that both films also close on images of the 1895 street rather than the distant future to which the Time Traveller has chosen to return. There is an implicit argument about modernity here: the nineteenth century would be the earliest time we instinctively recognize as our own and in which we feel comfortable. One might think that this would be an exclusively European argument if it weren't for all of the neo-Victorianist downtowns around the United States and the enduring stateside popularity of both heritage fiction and steampunk, the distinctive take on the latter in Japanese manga and the films of Miyazaki Hiyao and others, and the capacity of steampunk, as Diana M.

Pho writes, to create spaces that "explore the complicated intersections of racial and national hybridity."[11] The nineteenth-century street was arguably the first image capable of visualizing world networks of trade within the space of the city; to extend that image infinitely in all directions suggests that the present is rooted in that prior moment, but also that it has extended far beyond it. This image is essential to steampunk's predilection for London, since London was the heart of the century's most powerful empire and steampunk is fundamentally concerned with power in all of its forms and manifestations.

Steampunk Time Machines

Bowser and Croxall argue that a primary factor in the recent surge of interest in steampunk is the way it mediates technology differently than the "drive toward an aesthetic of technological invisibility" suggested by "invisible information flows and the unseen technology that made possible those flows and their navigation."[12] Victorian London is a focal point in this process not only because it provides evidence and imagery of "tangible," "dirty," and "rough-edged" technologies whose processes

FIGURE 1.4. Steampunk confronts sci-fi fashion in 2030. The shop window mannequins in the background subtly frame each choice. *The Time Machine*, directed by Simon Wells (Burbank, Calif.: Warner Bros., 2002), DVD.

of production are eminently visible but also, I would argue, because we can already see in it the beginning of today's "aesthetic of technological invisibility."[13] The iron-and-glass engineering that created the monumental architecture of industrial London along with the plate-glass shop fronts that lined its streets propose transparent, readily comprehensible building technology even as they display objects from which the traces of social relations and global trade have been neatly erased. The Time Traveller, his Time Machine, and their 1895 London origin provide a ready-made vehicle for the expression of this dialectic. In 1895, Wells deployed a handcrafted technological device to narrativize a sociopolitical debate and a philosophy of history. An imagined technology interacts with a known set of Victorian spatial practices to represent simultaneously their apocalyptic and their utopian potentials. The 1960 film overlays an imaginary technology now explicitly identified as past and Victorian—the protosteampunk burnished wood and brass of the machine (a lovingly crafted prop that threatens to upstage both Rod Taylor and his equally anodyne costar)—with cinematic effects also dating from the end of the nineteenth century and the looming specter of nuclear technology that obsessively preoccupied the Cold War present and through which the machine would have to travel in order to reach its (Victorianist) destination in the distant future.[14] In contrast, the 2002 film signals with typical fin de siècle knowingness its active participation in the culture of steampunk (or at least its awareness of that culture as a constituent of its target audience), by acknowledging its moment as one capable of misrecognizing the Time Traveller: for a few minutes in 2030, he is not a man out of time but a man of the present, styling himself (to our eyes, at least) as a steampunk. Surrounded by incomprehensible technology, his retrofuturistic machine and garb retain steampunk's promise of agency, even as that promise can be expressed only in degraded form as a stylistic choice in a throwaway moment of a forgettable movie.

Just as steampunk can range far afield from its neo-Victorian origins, so too can its appropriations of the Time Traveller and his machine range far afield from the familiar spaces of nineteenth-century London. In fact, they are a common trope used precisely to mark the extent of that distance without wholly severing the link. In Jeter's *Morlock Night* (1979), a loving ekphrasis of the London sewers and sewer workers drawn from Henry Mayhew's *London Labour and the London Poor* (1851) opens up into a vast underground sea, part of a global network of aquatic tunnels built by the ancient Atlanteans.[15] Having killed the

Time Traveller upon his ill-judged return to the future, the heretofore underestimated Morlocks have used the machine to follow a pathway carved through time back to 1892 London, their beachhead in a scheme for global conquest. Jeter frames the novel as the cosmic struggle between two transhistorical forms of Victorianism: an organic, medievalist vision of collective good and sacrifice embodied in an immortal Merlin, a cyclically reincarnated Arthur, and a magically powerful Excalibur, cast against a technologized, degenerate vision of cannibalistic evil. Both are irresistibly drawn to Wells's London as the stage of their metaphysical conflict. In Jeter's fictional transposition of the arguments of Thatcherite Victorianism, collectively mobilized advanced industrial technology is trumped by the timeless magic of Albion's traditional values.

Like the atomic bomb that looms so largely (if mostly invisibly) in pre-1989 steampunk, the destabilizing technology of the Time Machine represents a threat to the essential fabric of society. Unsurprisingly, the Time Traveller's agency is simply written out of the plot. In Joe Lansdale's exuberantly profane dime novel homage, *The Steam Man of the Prairie and the Dark Rider Get Down* (2000), that agency has also wrought nothing but chaos and destruction, but here he is an active participant, ruined by Weena's loss to the Morlocks' appetites. As the Dark Rider, he travels through time with his Morlock army, raping, pillaging, and torturing as he goes, bereft of even the slightest vestige of humanity. Moreover, his machine has rent the fabric of time, collapsing the known world into a tissue of growing rifts in the space-time continuum. Where Jeter retains the urban framework as part of his vision of the restoration of order in the traditional genre framework of the medieval romance, Lansdale's 1890s is an insanely wild Wild West from which all traces of order, logic, and urbanity have vanished. "All about," the narration concludes, "earth and sky resounded with the sounds of time and space coming apart."[16]

While Lansdale's Wild West seems to have taken over the world, Pynchon's sprawling *Against the Day* imbricates a capitalized but no less lawless West into a global urban modernity stretching from Los Angeles to New York, London, and Paris, and across Europe through central Asia and Shambhala to arrive at Irkutsk in an equally wild East. Wells and his Time Machine manifest in the central pages of the novel, first discovered in a "ramshackle" and "fiendish" secondhand contraption tucked away in a mad inventor's workshop under the Ninth Avenue El train in Hell's Kitchen, followed to its Midwestern origins in the annual Candlebrow University Convention on Time Travel, and reaching its nadir in the suitably decadent city of Bruges-La-Morte, where we happen briefly upon a "timeweapon" based on "the one force no one knows how to defeat, resist, or reverse."[17] Inspired by Wells's novel, and even attended by the master himself in its inaugural year some time soon after 1895, the First International Conference on Time Travel is at the center of a loosely interwoven plethora of folds, holes, pathways, technologies, and other means by which Pynchon pulls together the threads of a late nineteenth-century fascination with the fourth dimension.[18] Along with a wildly variegated popular genre pastiche, a cast of hundreds, and a sweeping geographical reach, the spatiotemporal instabilities and multiplicities signal the novel's refusal to accept the given path of history as written, arguing instead that the twenty-five-year period inaugurated by Wells's *The Time Machine* contains multitudes that exceed in imagination, potential, subversiveness, and sheer verve even the sucker punch of the Great War that conventionally put paid to them all.

Alan Moore and illustrator Kevin O'Neill's *League of Extraordinary Gentlemen* (1999–present) depicts a space-time that seems to have come apart as much as *Steam Man*'s has and pastiches as vigorously as Pynchon, but with a significant difference: in Moore's world, this has always been the case, but it was only in Victorian London that the fact was able to be widely recognized. As the serial moves out from its originary impetus in a band of late nineteenth-century pulp heroes (Wells's Invisible Man, Stevenson's Mr. Hyde, Stoker's Mina Harker, Haggard's Allan Quatermain, and Verne's Captain Nemo), the surviving core of Mina, Allan, and Orlando (an immortal character drawn from Virginia Woolf's eponymous 1928 time-traveling novel) becomes increasingly unstuck in time. Moore's conceit is to reshape conventional history as if it had been told by fiction and to reshape the world as if shaped by the fictions written in it: Gloriana was queen during Shakespeare's age, *The Third Man*'s Harry Lime runs the secret service, *1984* is the template for postwar Britain, and so forth. It's a self-consciously looking-glass strategy, using the tools of fiction and comics to make the world strange; it's also a self-consciously Victorianist strategy. The idea of the League emerges from the late nineteenth century; so too do the enduring presence of Mina and Allan, as well as the constant references back to their London, insist on its status as the moment on which an eternal process somehow turned.

The moment of that turning is first figured in "Allan and the Sundered Veil," a penny dreadful-style serial of which an episode concludes each of the six issues of the series' first volume.[19] This moment is figured as a profoundly traumatic and permanently scarring one, and it is figured with the Time Traveller and his Machine making a significant cameo appearance.[20] Of the baroquely convoluted plot, suffice it to say that Quatermain finds himself rescued from an attack by Morlocks and other horrors in the "shifting psychic landscape" of a "twilit realm" that is the natural habitat of the Time Traveller, a free agent who ranges "the phantom stream of decades . . . as an explorer."[21] The serial of the sundered veil as well as the entire first volume run of *League* (since the installments bring each issue to a close) conclude with Quatermain battling a Lovecraftian deity from Yuggoth, "a monstrous, alien threat from outside our familiar Universe," over possession of his body, which it has taken over as prelude to some kind of "infernal and unfathomable design" against the more familiar Universe. In his detailed analysis of "Sundered Veil," Jason B. Jones treats this episode and its imagery primarily in terms of their (highly disturbing) effect on Quatermain's body and as an expression of his desires.[22] I suggest that it can also be understood in terms of Quatermain's relationship to temporality and the nineteenth-century city. As often occurs in steampunk, Moore uses the extreme violation of the boundaries of self and body to figure the eruption of alternate modes of existence and of temporality into the linear and rational experience of space-time epitomized by the Time Traveller's late Victorian London.[23] The Time Traveller and his machine are simultaneously traces of London's space-time as the moment of eruption, the vehicle of that eruption, and the means of wresting meaning from it.

Even as the Time Traveller and his Machine signify the distance traveled from Victorian orthodoxy and familiarity as well as the strange things that happen "when the markers of various time periods are estranged from their contexts and made simultaneous,"[24] they also serve always to remind us of a tangible spatiotemporal bond, however tenuous, with whatever far-flung corner of the multiverse the fiction may have wandered into. For what these iterations of Wells's novel share with each other and with the original fiction, and what steampunk in general assumes with its Victorianist trappings, is a time—1895—and a place—London—as the still point where it—whatever *it* is—all began and to which it, somehow, like the Time Traveller and his Machine, always returns.[25] Wherever it may range in space and time, the multiverse that is steampunk finds its center of gravity and its raison d'être in the streets of the late Victorian city. Jeter sets the penultimate realization of the true identity of Arthur not in the London sewers or the Atlantean tunnels but under a gas lamp in the streets above. Even the wild ride of Lansdale's novella finds its epilogue in a suburban mother's Dodge Caravan, picking up two lost astronauts while pursued by a pack of velociraptors on a paved highway, rather than the irrational space-time flooding into that world through the Time Traveller's rips. Pynchon's mammoth novel concludes on the *Inconvenience,* the flying ship of the boys' own adventurers the Chums of Chance, itself metamorphosed with "updated engineering" into a "small city," with "neighborhoods," "parks," and "slum conditions" as it sails "remote stations . . . exceeding the usual three dimensions."[26] And Moore and O'Neill set the climactic reunion of Mina, Allan, Orlando, Fanny Hill, and Venus in the Blazing World, something like the utopian analogue of the dystopian chaos of "Sundered Veil," at a paved urban street crossing.[27] The Blazing World may be outside of time, its inhabitants may include nude eighteenth-century courtesans and Nyarlathotep, a shambling emissary from Yuggoth, and they may be rendered by O'Neill in psychedelic-toned 3-D, but its fundamental layout is recognizably urban and nineteenth century. Even League founder Prospero's exultant final proclamation, that "Here are brave banners of romance unfurled / to blaze forever in a blazing world," explodes from a pedestal with a backdrop of urban towers and, to his right, an elevated street.[28] These are willful traces of a Cartesian past—a welcome, familiar, and necessary link to the non-Cartesian present.

Bryan Talbot and the Nineteenth-Century Multiverse

Heavily indebted to psychogeography and true to its roots in the radical science fiction of Moorcock, Ballard, and others, British steampunk has tended toward a more explicitly oppositional sociopolitical agenda in its recourse to the past. Like Moore, Bryan Talbot's steampunk narratives argue not only that Victorian London was the heart of a highly conflicted empire but also that the entire universe, not to mention its myriad parallels, can somehow be conjured out of the image of its streets and its river. Talbot's influential Luther Arkwright comics—*The Adventures of Luther Arkwright* (1978–88) and *Heart of Empire* (1999)— take this conceit to its logical extreme, with London quite literally at the center of the multiverse. *Arkwright* opens and closes in the Crystal Palace of 1851, the exemplary Victorian image of London as center of the world and its modern streets as the conduits leading to and from that center.²⁹ However, in Talbot's vision, there are many Crystal Palaces in an infinity of parallel worlds in a multiverse through which the protagonist Arkwright, uniquely, is able to travel freely. London occupies the point of convergence of the parallels, and while Talbot borrows from other moments in history, it is the Victorian city, and especially its streets and squares, that provide his core iconography and identify the comic as early steampunk. Each parallel visited or glimpsed provides alternate permutations on the past century and a half of history, but each one is somehow rooted in the nineteenth century. Victorian London provides a fulcrum for the grand sweep of alternate history, an attempt simultaneously to exorcise and to rescue a notion of Britannia from its own abuses and negligences.

FIGURE 1.5. The Crystal Palace, still in Hyde Park in 1984, as the center of the multiverse. *The Adventures of Luther Arkwright* #1 (1978; Milwaukie, Ore.: Dark Horse, 1990), 4 (detail). By permission of the artist.

(a)

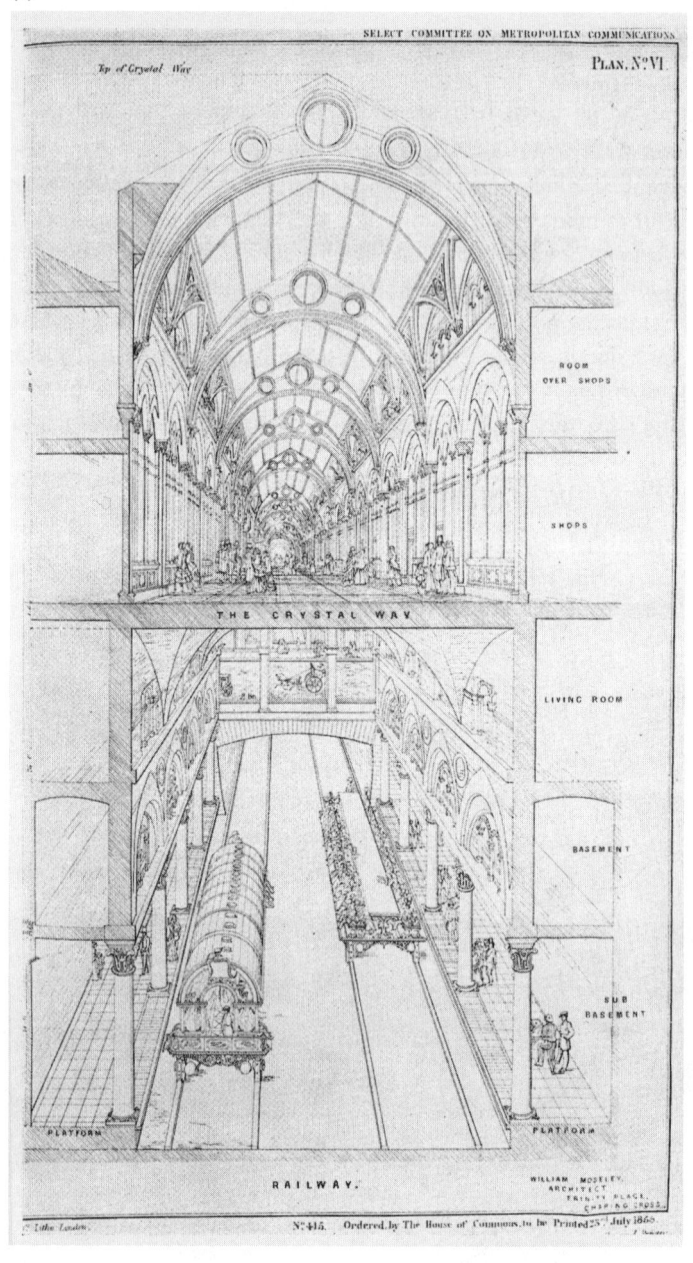

FIGURES 1.6. "London as it might have been." (a) William Moseley, *The Crystal Way*, "Report from the Select Committee on Metropolitan Communications." *Parliamentary Papers* (1854-55), vol. 10, plan no. 6. (b) Bryan Talbot, *Heart of Empire* (Milwaukie, Ore: Dark Horse, 1999), 63. By permission of the artist.

(b)

PARA 00.72.87
CHEAPSIDE, LONDON
THREE DAYS TO CATACLYSM
...ALL CROWNED BY THE NEW SAINT PAUL'S CATHEDRAL. IT'S HARD TO BELIEVE THAT THIS WHOLE SECTION OF LONDON WAS RAZED TO THE GROUND DURING THE FINAL, BLOODY STAGES OF THE CIVIL WAR, JUST OVER TWO DECADES AGO.
PUT TO THE TORCH ON THE DIRECT ORDERS OF NATHANIEL CROMWELL, "THE MAZE" WAS A CENTRE OF ROYALIST RESISTANCE FOR CENTURIES.

In typical science fiction fashion, London is the site of nefarious attempts to blow the multiverse to shreds: by the Disruptors in 1984 (*Arkwright*) and by an obscenely powerful mutant remnant of the queen's son, Henry, housed in St. George's Chapel, which has been rebuilt inside the Imperial Palace from the ruins at Windsor Castle, in 2007 (*Heart of Empire*). In equally typical fashion, it is also the site at which the attempts will be foiled. While Moore's London, like Wells's, provides the foundation for conceptualization and intertexuality, Talbot works, as it were, from the ground up, with his starting point the architecture and imagery of the Victorian city and what that city might have been. Thus the Cheapside Underground line of parallel universe 00.72.87, the splash page of the third issue, was directly inspired by William Moseley's 1854 scheme for a Crystal Way, a vast covered arcade that would in fact have followed Cheapside and extended to Oxford Street. The Kings Cross International Airway Station was inspired by architect Charles W. Glover's 1931 design for the Central Airport of London, erected atop the existing railway station.[30] Where the art for the Cheapside Underground closely follows Moseley's nineteenth-century sketch, only substituting the open air for the enclosed Victorian iron and glass, Talbot preserves solely the idea of Glover's modernist airport, reimagining it as a French outpost in London, a truncated Eiffel Tower base with one of Hector Guimard's Paris Métro entrance signs thrown in to complement the equally art nouveau style of the dragonfly tram wagon. In addition to figuring the links that connect Queen Anne's vast empire (we see, for example, the pope's envoy arrive in the city at Lambeth International Railway Terminal), Talbot's transportation network provides conduits between the real and the imagined city, as between the Victorian past of the network's origins and its steampunk future in 2007. The fecund seed of Victorian London proves capable of containing this world, all others, and any we can imagine, and its streets and transport networks provide the visual image of that capability.

The French influence would emerge as the central conceit of Talbot's alternate history steampunk graphic novel series, *Grandville* (2009–present), which imagines a roughly present-day Britain having lost the Napoleonic Wars and become "a small and unimportant country connected to the French empire by the Channel railway bridge."[31] Grandville is both the name of this world's Paris and the iconographic source of the animal characters, derived from the eponymous Parisian illustrator's volume of caricatures, *Scènes de la vie privée et publique*

FIGURE 1.7. "A small and unimportant country connected to the French empire by the Channel railway bridge." Bryan Talbot, *Grandville* (Milwaukie, Ore.: Dark Horse, 2009), 17. Image used by permission of the artist.

des animaux (1840-42). Explicitly steampunk (each volume boasts "Art Nouveau steampunk pattern" endpapers, adapted by Talbot from a 1900 German textbook of steam and electric technology), the series suggests, among other things, what steampunk might look like if it had taken Paris as its inspiration rather than London—if, in other words, the heart of empire had perchance been located on the Continent.[32]

Whereas Arkwright and his world derive from Moorcock's Jerry Cornelius and a British tradition of the effete and nearly amoral outsider antihero, as well as from space opera science fiction, *Grandville* and its no-nonsense badger protagonist, Scotland Yard detective inspector Archibald "Archie" LeBrock, have their roots in fantasy, caricature, art history, and hard-boiled detective novels. "Doughfaces" (humans) constitute the oppressed underclass, corruption runs rampant through the corridors of power, and sex and absinthe rule the night. Talbot incorporates visual homages to a gamut of fictional animal figures and continental comics that expand the series' range beyond the typical Victorianism of steampunk. His detective heroes, LeBrock and his refined partner, Roderick Ratzi, are loosely drawn from Badger and Ratty in Kenneth Grahame's 1908 fantasy of pastoral Englishness, as are Tope (Mole), a misguided inventor of automata murdered early on in the first volume, and the greedy industrialist Toad, who schemes in James Bond-ish supervillain style in the third volume to take over the newly installed republican government of Grandville by suppressing figurative art and releasing an army of murderous automata and automated dreadnoughts onto the city from Toad Hall, his secret stronghold beneath its streets. Talbot bluntly urbanizes and darkens the animals of children's literature—the first volume also features a cameo by an opium-addled Snowy/Milou, dreamily recalling memories of his departed master, Tintin—while at the same time incorporating them into the orbit of steampunk's themes and iconography.

Grandville uses that iconography to comment acidly on British Victoriana and contemporary global politics. As in *Arkwright*, battle lines are drawn between Republican and working-class anarchist rebels and between corrupt, reactionary imperialists and capitalists, who have blown up the Robida Tower (this world's Eiffel Tower) and are planning to use a British superbomb to destroy the Opéra, blaming both on British anarchists. LeBrock's father was one of the guerillas responsible for England's obtaining independence from France in the 1970s, and the badger's actions in the first volume lead to a revolutionary overthrow of Napoleon XII. Like the ultraviolent world of turn-of-the-century French pulp fiction, Grandville is irrational and dangerous, and its steam and compressed-air technology—airships, pneumails, and a wide variety of eccentric firearms—are no less deadly than their more familiar cousins. Each volume opens with a pretitles action teaser (two set in Paris, one in London) before introducing its hero at home in a London where French is the native language. LeBrock will then travel to Grandville, where the bulk of the plot unfolds. Much of the humor of the series derives from its very nineteenth-century play on the similarities and differences between the two metropolises and their inhabitants, spiced up by an endless series of multilingual puns on animal metaphors (for example, tuxedoed gorillas in "monkey suits") and Frenchified and Anglicized surnames—we encounter artists such as Gustave Corbeau and Auguste Rodent and locations such as the brothel of Madame River Horse (a hippopotamus) and the Agile Rabbit nightclub.

At the same time, Talbot's alternate history opens up the nineteenth-century competition between London and Paris into the global politics of the next century plus. The first volume unfolds as an alternate and highly paranoid version of the 9/11 bombings in New York City; the second volume rewrites its own history of the English resistance as a sordid narrative of betrayal by a bulldog prime minister caricaturing the features of Winston Churchill; and the third volume moves through the twentieth-century history of covert government support for abstract art and suppression of its figurative competition as passé and communist. The lightly sketched but unmistakable argument regarding what Nelson Rockefeller termed the "free-enterprise art" of the rooster "Jackson Pollo" and others suggests that Talbot has found in the nineteenth century not only a different approach to temporality and urban space-time but also a different visual iconography that bypasses twentieth-century modernism in favor of a popular figurative tradition running from Grandville and other caricaturists through underground and pulp comics into a renaissance of graphic composition that closely parallels the rise of steampunk.

While certainly not steampunk even in the broadest understanding of the mode, Talbot's masterpiece, *Alice in Sunderland* (2007), provides fascinating insight into a broader neo-Victorian context for steampunk's concern with temporality and the Victorian city.[33] An innovative work of urban history told in comics form, *Alice in Sunderland* takes the steampunk principle of the city as a generative matrix of universal space-time to perhaps its logical (or absurd) extreme. Figuring the Victorian city as his navel point, Talbot basically discovers the world in

Behind Monkwearmouth Station is *The Stadium of Light* – the city's football ground, its lasers visible for miles, playing in the Sunderland night.

Opened in 1997, it replaces the traditional home of the City's team at *Roker Park*, famous to soccer fans throughout Britain for the *Roker Roar* of the fans.

The team's nicknamed *The Black Cats*, after the lions on its coat of arms.

Here's a little known fact. Step this way.

This is Bilbao, in the beautiful *Basque Country* of Northern Spain.

It has the very first football team in Spain...

...started by Sunderland shipyard workers in the late 19th century.

Its roots are evident in its name, *Athletic Club Bilbao*, its ground, *The English Hill*...

...and its colours, the red and white stripes of Sunderland.

Sunderland's stadium is built on the site of *Monkwearmouth Colliery*, begun in 1826 and in its time the deepest in the world.

FIGURES 1.8. A broader neo-Victorian context for steampunk's concern with temporality and the Victorian city: discovering the world out of Sunderland. Bryan Talbot, *Alice in Sunderland* (Milwaukie, Ore.: Dark Horse, 2007), 168–69. Image used by permission of the artist.

the northern industrial metropolis of Sunderland, which had its heyday in the late nineteenth century but has since basically vanished from all but local knowledge. Using the medium of sequential art as his own time-traveling principle, on one page Talbot strides from Sunderland in 1997 to late nineteenth-century Bilbao and back to Sunderland in 1826, following the path of an early nineteenth-century mine down the next page back into the present of sculptor Graeme Hopper's monument to the long-gone miners who had originally created Sunderland's Victorian wealth and power. What is so compelling about this performance is that, as Talbot maintains at the end of the book, everything in it is true. Talbot's history of Sunderland ranges as far back as the dawn of life and as far forward as the future of the city's twenty-first-century revival. But its heart is in the nineteenth century, the period of the city's industrial strength and global reach, and also of its most famous son, Lewis Carroll; indeed, a good portion of the book is devoted to a literary detective tale of the repressed history of Carroll and Alice and the submerged subtext of Sunderland in the Alice books. While one Talbot is performing a hyperactive monologue cum PowerPoint on stage at the venerable Sunderland Empire music hall, another avatar is exploring the city with us on foot, all the while expatiating on his theory regarding the relativity of space and time. The wager of this extraordinary book is that any place on earth is so seamed with networks of information and parallels that you can unpack the world from it—or, at least, the wager is that this is the case with any Victorian place. The alternate historical imagination and urban space-time that define steampunk as a formal mode are both symptomatic and formative of changing attitudes toward a past newly liberated from the constraints of Cold War modernism. The opening up of a single nineteenth century into an infinite multiverse betokens a changed sense of possibility and a refusal to be locked into a single narrative of the past. At the same time, the talismanic mooring of that multiverse provides a constant reminder of its material origins; for unlike the heady time of postmodernism from which steampunk emerged, even its wildest forays out of the nineteenth century never quite relinquish their sense of connection and responsibility to the world from which it set out.

NOTES

1. Most every scholarly essay on steampunk at least touches on these two issues; in addition to the essays in the present volume, see, in particular, Stefan Hantke, "Difference Engines and Other Infernal Devices: History According to

Steampunk," *Extrapolation* 40, no. 3 (1999): 244-54; Rebecca Onion, "Reclaiming the Machine: An Introductory Look at Steampunk in Everyday Practice," *Neo-Victorian Studies* 1, no. 1 (2008): 138-63; and Rachel A. Bowser and Brian Croxall, "Introduction: Industrial Evolution," *Neo-Victorian Studies* 3, no. 1 (2010): 1-45.

2. Two seminal examples of effectively applying a modal approach to a vexed cultural form are Angus Fletcher's *Allegory: The Theory of a Symbolic Mode* (1964; repr., Princeton, N.J.: Princeton University Press, 2012) and James Naremore's *More Than Night: Film Noir in Its Contexts*, 2nd ed. (1998; repr., Berkeley: University of California Press, 2008).

3. Consequently, I see more going on in steampunk's appropriation of Victorian London than what Hantke terms a nostalgia for the authenticity of the nightmare of modernity ("Fond Memories of Alienation: Images of the City in Contemporary Victoriana," *EnterText* 5, no. 2 (2005): n.p.). Nor would I limit its scope to what Hantke calls an "allegorization of postmodernity," although I acknowledge the validity of regarding steampunk as the "repressed, chaotic, uncontrollable margin to the cultural center that postmodernity has undeniably become by now" ("Difference Engines," 253). Similarly, I agree with Shannon Lee Dawdy when she defines modernity as "a form of temporal ideology that valorizes newness, rupture, and linear plot lines" and characterizes steampunk as "embrac[ing] a knotted temporality" that repudiates modernity's assertion of rupture with the past followed by linear progress toward the future; "Clockpunk Anthropology and the Ruins of Modernity," *Current Anthropology* 51, no. 6 (2010): 762, 766. Nevertheless, I see in the specific investment of steampunk with the material space-time of Victorian London a recognition that we cannot wholly reject modernity's claim to rupture with the past and to ongoing progress any more than we can unilaterally accept it.

4. On the tradition of the New Zealander visiting London in ruins, see Lynda Nead, *Victorian Babylon: People, Streets and Images in Nineteenth-Century London* (New Haven, Conn.: Yale University Press, 2000), 212-15. On the consciousness of the nineteenth-century city in ruins, see Walter Benjamin, *The Arcades Project*, trans. Howard Eiland and Kevin McLaughlin (Cambridge, Mass.: Harvard University Press, 1999), 82-100; Giovanni Macchia, *Paris en ruines*, trans. Paul Bédarida (Paris: Flammarion, 1988), 362-63; and David Pike, *Subterranean Cities: The World beneath Paris and London, 1800-1945* (Ithaca, N.Y.: Cornell University Press, 2005), 273-78.

5. I have discussed at length elsewhere the vexed, complex, and complementary relationship between London and Paris in the nineteenth century. Although Paris has long dominated cultural studies approaches to the nineteenth century (primarily through the influence of Benjamin), London unquestionably reigns supreme in the steampunk world. There are a number of possible explanations for this fact; I touch on a few of them below in my discussion of Talbot's *Grandville*.

6. H. G. Wells, *The Time Machine: An Invention* (New York: Henry Holt, 1895), 43-44.

7. Jay Clayton, *Dickens in Cyberspace: The Afterlife of the Nineteenth Century in Postmodern Culture* (New York: Oxford University Press, 2003), 6–7.

8. A third adaptation, made for American television in 1978, is interesting for other reasons less relevant here, as it transplants the entire setting into the present day, eliminating Wells's Victorian London and any protosteampunk trappings in favor of *Doctor Who*–style time-travel adventuring.

9. My focus here is on the shop window. The Underground railway entrance appears in 1917 and then as a shelter entrance in 1940 and 1966; it raises a related but different set of issues that I do not have the space to elaborate on here.

10. That this is a problematic link, especially in the context of the digital technology and commodity culture of twenty-first-century Hollywood, is a question explored in Stefania Forlini's essay in this volume, "The Aesthete, the Dandy, and the Steampunk; or, Things as They Are Now."

11. Diana M. Pho, "Punking the Other: On the Performance of Racial and National Identities in Steampunk," this volume.

12. Bowser and Croxall, "Introduction: Industrial Evolution," 16.

13. Ibid., 17.

14. On the insertion of nuclear technology into Victorianist adaptations during the postwar period, see James W. Maertens, "Between Jules Verne and Walt Disney: Brains, Brawn, and Masculine Desire in *20,000 Leagues under the Sea*," *Science Fiction Studies* 22, no. 2 (1995): 223, and J. P. Telotte, "Science Fiction as 'True-Life Adventure': Disney and the Case of *20,000 Leagues under the Sea*," *Film and History* 40, no. 2 (2010): 68, 70.

15. K. W. Jeter, *Morlock Night* (New York: DAW Books, 1979).

16. Joe Lansdale, *The Steam Man of the Prairie and the Dark Rider Get Down: A Dime Novel* (2000), in *Steampunk*, ed. Ann VanderMeer and Jeff VanderMeer (San Francisco: Tachyon, 2008), 107–45.

17. Thomas Pynchon, *Against the Day* (New York: Penguin, 2007), 558.

18. On Pynchon's use of various theories of the fourth dimension during this period, see Justin St. Clair, "Borrowed Time: Thomas Pynchon's *Against the Day* and the Victorian Fourth Dimension," *Science Fiction Studies* 38, no. 1 (2011): 46–66.

19. When the original serial was reprinted in one volume, "Allan and the Sundered Veil" was pulled together as a single double-columned penny dreadful at the end of the "properly" graphic novel, complete with covers and endpapers, somewhat changing the dynamics of the nonlinear temporality established by "Sundered Veil." My analysis is based on the original serialization, while noting that the existence of distinct and distinctly destabilizing publishing formats is itself typical of Moore's neo-Victorianist literary strategies.

20. As is characteristic of Moore and O'Neill here, the Time Machine intertext is not straightforward. O'Neill bases his rendering of the Machine on Lou Cameron's artwork for the 1956 Classics Illustrated comic of *The Time Machine*. Although explicitly telling us that it takes place in "late-nineteenth-century London," the illustrator gives the machine the appearance of 1950s science fiction technology rather than straightforwardly neo-Victorianist wood, brass, and gears,

and he garbs the Time Traveller in a thin-tied gray flannel suit straight out of postwar England.

21. Alan Moore and Kevin O'Neill, *The League of Extraordinary Gentlemen*, vol. 1, no. 3 (La Jolla, Calif.: America's Best Comics, 1999), n.p.

22. Jason B. Jones, "Betrayed by Time: Steampunk and the Neo-Victorian in Alan Moore's *Lost Girls* and *The League of Extraordinary Gentlemen*," *Neo-Victorian Studies* 3, no. 1 (2010): 117-20.

23. Annalisa DeLiddo's monograph pays close attention to Moore's metafictional and self-reflective gestures as well as to tension between "crisis" in his "urban, local, regional, and national . . . identity as an Englishman" and discovery of "its most vital forces," although not always in full relationship to one another. *Alan Moore: Comics as Performance, Fiction as Scalpel* (Jackson: University of Mississippi Press, 2009), 133.

24. Bowser and Croxall, "Introduction: Industrial Evolution," 7.

25. The exception is *The Time Machine* (2002), which shifts the city to New York, although it retains the urban setting. Nevertheless, in choosing Wells's great-grandson, Simon, to be director, the film indirectly points to that same London origin, although in a biographical rather than directly geographical register.

26. Pynchon, *Against the Day*, 1084.

27. Moore and O'Neill, *The League of Extraordinary Gentlemen: Black Dossier* (La Jolla, Calif.: America's Best Comics, 2007), n.p.

28. Ibid.

29. Bryan Talbot, *The Adventures of Luther Arkwright* (1978; Milwaukie, Ore.: Dark Horse, 1990), and *Heart of Empire* (Milwaukie, Ore: Dark Horse, 1999). I discuss this argument in more detail in "World Streets and *Via Ferae*: The Nineteenth-Century Cityscape in Space and Time," *Studies in the Humanities* 45 (2015): 194-221. On the Great Exhibition in relation to commodity culture and alternate forms of "object relations," see Forlini, "The Aesthete, the Dandy, and the Steampunk."

30. Bryan Talbot, *Heart of Empire CD-ROM* (Milwaukie, Ore.: Dark Horse, 2001), annotation to page 63. Talbot cites here and elsewhere Felix Barker and Ralph Hyde, *London as It Might Have Been* (London: John Murray, 1992), as his source. Barker and Hyde discuss (and illustrate) Glover's plan (212) and Moseley's Crystal Way (137-38).

31. Bryan Talbot, *Grandville* (Milwaukie, Ore.: Dark Horse, 2009), 17. Further volumes include *Grandville Mon Amour* (2010), *Grandville Bête Noire* (2012), and *Grandville: Noël* (2012), with one more projected for 2017, *Grandville: Force Majeure*.

32. Stephen Baxter's story "The Unblinking Eye," in *Steampunk II: Steampunk Reloaded*, ed. Ann VanderMeer and Jeff VanderMeer (San Francisco: Tachyon, 2010), 50-56, also imagines England as a colony to the Frankish Empire since 1066. In Baxter's story, however, Frankish power pales in the face of the "Sunrise," the global expansion of the Inca Empire. Nevertheless, Baxter still chooses to open the story in Londrais and make his protagonist, Jenny Cook, a Londoner. My thanks to Rachel Bowser and Brian Croxall for this reference.

33. Bryan Talbot, *Alice in Sunderland* (Milwaukie, Ore.: Dark Horse, 2007).

How to Theorize with a Hammer; or, Making and Baking Things in Steampunk and the Digital Humanities

ROGER WHITSON

In a July 30, 2011, post on the blog *EPBOT*, an author identified as Jen presents a series of directions for "How to Make: Steampunk Goggles." Jen mentions that even though "there are about as many ways to make steampunk goggles as there *are* steampunk goggles," she "hope[s] this tutorial will help [her readers] get started." The goggles are made of "leather/vinyl," "a small buckle or vest clip," "1.5 inch plumbing coupler," "Plexiglas," and an *"optional . . .* 2-hole pipe strap." Steps for making the goggles include scroll sawing, painting, sewing, gluing, bolting, and screwing. The materials Jen describes on her blog cost around $15, not including the more expensive electric saws and sewing materials. *EPBOT* includes several tutorials in their archive, including a ray gun with electronic lights, steampunk costumes, and even a so-called steampunk dining room. Jen's description of the dining room credits a blog, the *Steampunk Home*, which describes the genre as "more than just brass and watchparts. It's finding a way to combine the past and the future in an aesthetic[ally] pleasing yet still punkish way. . . . It's taking the detritus of our modern technological society and remaking it into useful things."[1]

Jen's comment about remaking discarded things into useful artifacts underlines an ethic of repurposing that is common among steampunk fans, but it also combines the past and the present like an engineer would combine circuits to create a machine. I argue that this move rejects the notion that history is simply a set of narratives about culture, a concept that has dominated cultural approaches to steampunk criticism. In another chapter in this collection, Stefania Forlini suggests that the "opportunity to glimpse alternative object relations" offered by Victorian and steampunk objects is "ultimately obscured by our own immersion in commodity culture."[2] I think that there is a further but related problem for critics when confronting steampunk objects: scholarly immersion in a form of critical theory that is primarily cultural and textual conceals the tactile and material components making up objects as well as the processes surrounding the act of their making. If steampunk was ever exclusively a literary genre, it can no longer lay claim to that single identity. Of course, not everyone is happy about this change. In a January 11, 2014, response to a similar argument I made about steampunk and literature at that year's Modern Language Association conference in Chicago, Bruce Sterling (@bruces) tweeted, "Okay, fine, prof, #steampunk is no longer a literary movement. We lack such luxuries these days."[3] To me, the response underlined Sterling's cynicism about the complex digital world that is confronting us, but steampunk's dedication to objects also offers a unique opportunity to start examining this complexity. Approaches to steampunk that are primarily textual certainly lead to valuable scholarship, but they can also construct blind spots. The dominance of social analysis has obscured, for example, what Natalie Jeremijenko calls "the materiality of what actually works and the open endedness of how others interpret, receive, and use things."[4]

Take Bruno Latour's widely cited article, "An Attempt at a Compositionist Manifesto." "What performs a critique," according to Latour, "cannot also compose. . . . With a hammer (or a sledge hammer) in hand you can do a lot of things: break down walls, destroy idols, ridicule prejudices, but you cannot repair, take care, assemble, reassemble, stitch together."[5] Of course, anyone who has actually used a hammer knows this is not true. As many scholars of the nineteenth century know, sledgehammers were often used to pound railroad spikes into the ground when connecting ties. Working with tools can produce a more tactile understanding of how things work together, similar to how Levi Bryant describes bodies adapting themselves to hammers. "The perpetual hammering on the metal of an anvil produces corporeal changes in the smith's body," Bryant argues. "His muscle structure, bone structure, and the way of holding himself change over time. This is not the result of expression or signs."[6] Richard Sennett calls this nonexpressive realm "material consciousness" and suggests that developing this consciousness "requires us to care about the qualities of cloth or the right way to poach fish." The specificities of such haptic analysis are often not considered in cultural criticism, according to Sennett, which "slights cloth, circuit boards, or baked fish as objects worthy of regard in themselves, instead treating the shaping of such physical things as mirrors of social norms, economic interests, religious convictions—the thing in itself is discounted."⁷

I believe we can appeal to steampunk to understand making as developing a form of critical material consciousness. Steampunk offers a space where the study of culture intersects with ideas about making and the repurposing of objects. In the introduction to *What Is Media Archaeology?*, Jussi Parikka mentions that steampunk fans combine "the punk-influenced spirit of tinkering" to their historical curiosity for "mad science, experimental technologies and the curiosity cabinets that such worlds offer."⁸ In the words of Joshua Tanenbaum, Karen Tanenbaum, and Ron Wakkary, steampunk has become a "design fiction" in which objects "are created largely as an exercise in seeing what is possible."⁹ If science fiction inspired the creation of new scientific methods and technologies, such as the January 2013 development of a *Star Trek*-inspired tractor beam by a team of scientists working at the University of St. Andrews in Scotland, then the anachronistic ethos of steampunk can help us imagine alternative relationships between humans and technology.¹⁰ Steampunk making is an exercise in critical theory as a result of the genre's tendency to help designers and writers repurpose history and imagine alternatives.

Focusing on the critical making practices of steampunk can give us a better understanding of the kinds of knowledge that are used in the act of making; it can also argue for the importance of a maker-centered knowledge in critical theory. I thus suggest that whatever we say about the politics, economics, or sociology of the making of steampunk objects, the act of making those objects yields us a different epistemological dimension than reading and writing about culture. "Critical Making," as defined by practitioners like Matt Ratto and Stephen Hockema, "is an elision of two typically disconnected modes of engagement in the world—'critical thinking,' often considered as abstract, explicit, linguistically-based, internal and cognitively individualistic; and 'making,' typically understood as material, tacit, embodied, external, and community-oriented."¹¹ Considering the importance of objects within steampunk communities, the genre can act as a powerful tool for theorizing critical making. Here I examine how-to essays from steampunk fans to show how methods of making translate into critical perspectives on culture. By focusing on the genre of the how-to guide, I demonstrate continuities between traditionally textual forms of critical theory and a notion of critical knowledge embedded within objects and making practices.

How to Make Theory

The genre of the how-to article has a particular resonance to the DIY maker movement, especially in the magazine *Make*. *Make* is published by O'Reilly Media and focuses on complex projects that can be made with relatively cheap materials.[12] In an interview with Jake von Slatt, Gareth Branwyn calls steampunk "a kind of carrier wave for holding people's interest in the art of making things."[13] Branwyn's comment likens steampunk to an energy oscillation that pulls people toward maker culture while also articulating their otherwise amorphous creative interest in the genre's objects and stories. Yet *Make Magazine*'s investment in steampunk has also affected the genre's popularity. Twenty-four of the thirty-four issues published by *Make* since 2005 mention steampunk at least once. Authors interview prominent steampunks and fans, review products and books, and outline how-to pieces for making flair and gadgets.

The "Rediscover Lost Knowledge" issue has how-to articles on imagined steampunk artifacts and real nineteenth-century technologies. Molly Friedrich's "The 'Discreet Companion' Ladies' Raygun" is manufactured out of a torch-style cigar lighter and ornamented with brass lamp washers, decorating rivets, and a hall-tree hook. According to the introduction, the ray gun was "invented in 1885 for use by the daring ladies of the Cloud Frontier" and has "been a staple of purses and garter belts ever since."[14] Of course, a cultural critic might point out that the Ladies' Raygun, along with its description, signifies a concerningly heteronormative sense of femininity. Why, for instance, aren't small ray guns appropriate for men or transgendered steampunk fans as well? The photograph further underscores the intended audience: it features Friedrich posing with the demure gun, readying herself for battle.

Despite these problems, the article demonstrates an awareness of materiality often lacking in accounts of steampunk that are more focused on its social context. In particular, it gives users an impressive amount of practice with molding Victorian materials to create the gun. We see how different materials might react to the various methods described by the article. "Don't worry if the edges bend a little," Friedrich explains. "This is normal. When you're done cutting, use your pliers to flatten out the edges again."[15] There is a concern in Friedrich's piece with understanding the material aspects of each piece of the ray gun. The steampunk how-to manual is materialist in the strictest sense. It is concerned, first and foremost, with forming a relationship between the person constructing the artifact and the material qualities of the object itself—the way a thin brass sheet might bend when cut by metal pliers, the trickiness of squeezing locknuts, washers, and bolts through the holes formed by the pliers. Friedrich acknowledges the difficulty, then directs the user: "Pressing in on the sides of the gun body at the bolts (friction will help keep them in place), navigate the bolts into the holes on the base of the B&M hall tree hook, aka ray gun handle."[16]

In the *Maker Magazine*-produced book *Vintage Tomorrows*, Kimric Smythe conceptualizes the relationship between an object's materials and the physical qualities of the maker by appealing to the strange experience of manipulating metal while welding. Smythe laments the increasing appearance of industrially produced steampunk artifacts while offering a powerful account of how making is central to understanding steampunk. "When you weld something," he explains, "you feel it writhing around when you're welding it. As the bead pulls around it's a weird quasi-organic material and most people have never experienced that."[17] We might call the knowledge involved in Smythe's experience a form of what Stephen Ramsay has identified as "thing-knowledge" or what Forlini has called the "mutual constitutivity in which humans make and are made by technological things."[18] More fundamentally, though, the how-to manual instructs on a proprioceptive or haptic level. It constructs an interface between the body and the material, illustrating how the body can manipulate itself to embrace the properties of a physical object. The proprioceptive characteristics of DIY maker culture are a form of materialist collaboration or interface where users experience the physics of working with certain materials.

This materialist power of critical making is embodied by the mixing of present and past in steampunk, using current tools to create objects from the nineteenth century or combining nineteenth-century designs with twenty-first-century tools. More difficult projects in the *Make* magazine catalog illustrate this mixed effect. Jim Shealy's "Teacup Stirling Engine," from the same issue of *Make* as the Ladies' Raygun, uses "the heat from tea, coffee, or candles" to power a piston.[19] Stirling engines were frequently used in the nineteenth century. According to C. S. Vineeth, Robert Stirling patented the engine in 1816 despite the existence of designs for a similar and earlier "caloric machine" by Sir George Cayley.[20] The Stirling engine produces work for a piston by translating the heat given off by liquids undergoing a thermodynamic cycle into energy. Stirling engines are efficient because the mechanism loses much less energy in heat transfer than regular steam engines when powering the piston. A set of displacer plates, pictured as the black plates in Figure 2.1, alternately expand and contract the gas inside the compressor between them as a result of a temperature differential. The bottom plate is warmed by steam escaping from the tea, while the top plate remains at room temperature. Stirling engines are considerably cheaper to produce than other types of engines, making it potentially attractive as an alternative energy source. X. Q. Kong, R. Z. Wang, and X. H. Huang demonstrated in 2004 that the Stirling engine "saves fuel resources and has the assurance of economic benefits" compared to conventional independent cooling, heating, and power systems.[21] For Shealy, the Teacup Stirling Engine is about exploiting useful energy that often remains hidden to most people. "Whether it's hot coffee on a cold day, light from the sun, scented candles, waste heat from electronics," Shealy proclaims, "there's power to be had! How about we turn it into useful power?"[22] The alternative technological interface required to power the Stirling engine requires the maker to imagine different mechanical ways of producing power and thus different ecologies of heat and energy. Building the Stirling engine is also quite complex. *Make* magazine lists the project as "difficult," and Shealy includes a troubleshooting guide at the end of the article. In fact, these problems help to explain why the Stirling engine lost out to the comparatively easier-to-produce steam engine. Shealy notes that "leaks" and "friction" often ruin most Stirling engines.[23] We know from technology scholars like Donald Cardwell that the metal manufactured in the early twentieth century could not withstand the heat generated by the Stirling engine's thermodynamic cycle to work within automobiles or boats; further, lubricants did not advance quickly enough to provide enough protection for the moving parts.[24] Stirling engines also require a large temperature differential. Shealy mentions that the displacer plates should have a differential of at least 200 degrees Fahrenheit and that builders should "try putting ice on the cold plate."[25]

Shealy's project combines a materialist approach to history—that is, a historical stance based on a physical relationship with epoxies, brass, and hacksaws—with a hacker ethos that focuses on machinic effects. For him, the idea is to recreate history by eliciting a machinic process. Critical making forces the theorist to engage in kinds of knowledge that are related to the functioning of objects. These temporalities include what Wolfgang Herst calls "zeitkritik," or time criticality, in which

FIGURE 2.1. Using heat differentials, a Stirling engine can be powered by something as small as steam coming from a teacup. Photograph by Michele M. Ferrario; used under the terms of a Creative Commons Attribution Share-Alike (CC-BY-SA) license.

narrative understandings of history are complicated by the operational life span of machines. "A radio built in Germany during the National Socialist regime," Ernst elaborates, "receives radio signals when operated today because the stable technological infrastructure of broadcasting media is still in operation."[26] The difference between World War II and the contemporary world in which the device continues to function relies on a narrative history that the machine does not recognize. Ernst rejects the notion of a historical "difference in the functioning of the apparatus now as compared to then," arguing that technological infrastructure creates "a media–archaeological short circuit between otherwise historically clearly-separated times."[27] Likewise, the act of repurposing older but still operational technologies illustrates a link between the material tinkering occurring in maker communities and the historical tinkering occurring in steampunk.

How to Bake Theory

If quirky technology is the focal point of steampunk enthusiasts, then reviving and remixing older forms of Victorian baking comes in a close second. Victorian scholars often resurrect nineteenth-century recipes to express their enthusiasm for the period. *The Journal of Victorian Culture*, for instance, hosted a Victorian bake-off in February 2013 and presented links to digitized versions of Victorian cookbooks like *Nelson's Home Comforts* (1892) and *The Lady's Own Cookery Book and New Dinner-Table Directory* (1844).[28] Contemporary Victorian baking competitions have largely been described as meaningless fun by scholars used to examining textual sources, yet I argue that steampunk takes the popularity of reviving older recipes and remixes it with new tastes and anachronistic environments as a form of engaging in critical theory. Tim Morton has argued that "ideology is externalized in food." I would add that the act of cooking in steampunk reveals the practice as a critical intervention into culture.[29]

Gastronomic shows depicting traditional Victorian food often make interventions into culture by meshing together older diets with contemporary bodies in order to show their incompatibility. In many cases these shows are not self-consciously steampunk, but their whimsical anachronism parallels the tinkering ethos found in the culture as well as its emphasis on material knowledge. Anachronistic effects are often registered in the bodily experience of its stars. For instance, the BBC show *The Supersizers Go* . . . follows Giles Coran and Sue Perkins as they eat diets from different historical periods for a week and are analyzed by a doctor to determine the food's effect on their health. The show takes inspiration from Morgan Spurlock's documentary *Super Size Me* (2004), in which Spurlock eats McDonald's food exclusively for a month. The episode dealing with the Victorian period featured a Christmas dinner of three courses. The first included Brown Windsor soup, potato croquettes, baked cod's head; the second had cold game pie, boiled red cabbage, roast goose, and stuffing; and the third incorporated plum pudding, bird's custard, furmity, and mince pies. The cold game pie is of particular note for its large size, and the fact that it was filled with "8 types of game bird, ham, chicken, bacon, and tongue."[30] Part of the humor of the show emerges from historical differences in cuisine coupled with social expectations surrounding eating. The centerpiece of Coran and Perkins's dinner on the first night of their week was a boiled calf's head, in which the brains were scooped out and cooked with a butter-and-herb sauce and the ears were fried and served with tomatoes. During the dinner, the narrator mentions that Victorian women did not show their hunger or eat large portions because "a healthy appetite for food suggested a healthy appetite for sex."[31] Perkins

FIGURE 2.2. As Sue Perkins serves cold game pie to Giles Coran on the "Victorian" episode of *The Supersizers Go* . . . (London: BBC, June 3, 2008), the differences between nineteenth- and twenty-first-century eating are visible. Screen shot used according to fair use guidelines.

appeals to this ideology to excuse her from eating the calf's head. "This is the lucky decade for me," she jokes. "To me, that big ol' head just says 'power,' 'look at me,' 'macho man,'" indicating that Coran has to eat the head to prove his masculinity.[32] Despite not being forced to eat the calf, Perkins's body had difficulty adapting to the Victorian diet. During her visit to the nutritionist at the end of the show, the narrator reports, "In the last week Perkins had 20,000 calories, she's downed 14 liters of booze, and eaten countless animal heads."[33] The doctor reports that she's gained nearly an inch on her waist and seven pounds in weight. The physical effects of anachronism are stark here. As a result of habituating to smaller diets and less meat, a twenty-first-century body literally does not have the stomach to process the food displayed on the Victorian episode. Scientific instruments used by the nutritionist and filmed by the producers become gauges for the effects of ideology. *The Supersizers Go . . .* uses anachronism to highlight appetite and weight gain as physical effects of colliding food ideologies between the Victorian period and now.[34]

Steampunk chefs experiment with this gastronomic anachronism in order to create new tastes and experiences. In an article for the cooking magazine *Toque,* Erika Kotite notes parallels between steampunk and cooking: "Many of Steampunk's tenets—to celebrate the history of mechanical ingenuity and its aesthetics, to appreciate the high tech of a lower tech era—are lived out every day in restaurant kitchens and food service laboratories."[35] Kotite sees steampunk as a genre that perfectly captures the experimental attitude of many chefs. If fusion restaurants represent the mixing of different national cuisines, then steampunk chefs show that the same can be done with historical periods. Aaron Eagan, the self-proclaimed "First Chef of Steam," argues in the tagline of his blog *Steampunk Cookery,* "If you can sew a steampunk wardrobe, write a steampunk story, and create a steampunk computer . . . why shouldn't you cook steampunk food?"[36] Steampunk is not a visual aesthetic for Eagan. It reflects instead a culinary philosophy emphasizing experimental fusion. In the introduction to *The Steampunk Cookbook,* Elizabeth Stockton also notes the centrality of fusion to steampunk cuisine. "There are no transistors here, no boilers to explode at inconvenient moments, no sky piracy," but, Stockton argues, "if [mechanical steampunk] was an undulating concave pillow of brass, steel, steam, and mixed metaphors [this book is] a mix of the culinary science of steampunks."[37]

Eagan's recipes illustrate this philosophy of experimental fusion.

For his first "Monthly Steampunk Feast," he notes that his goal is to "fuse modern techniques with an older approach to food and service," and he repeats the lessons of *The Supersizers Go* . . . by emphasizing that portions were much larger in the Victorian period than they are today.[38] "We in the American/French tradition," Eagan explains "serve plates with a single protein, a sauce, a vegetable, and a starch—or some variation thereupon—because that's how cooking has evolved in the last hundred years or so."[39] He outlines several other differences: that Victorians served hors d'oeuvres not simply at the beginning of the meal but made them available throughout each course; that an entrée originally meant a small yet full-flavored dish that preceded the main course; and that after the entrée came the main, larger roast followed by two or three smaller meat courses called *relevés*. According to Eagan, these were followed by an ice or sorbet (for cleansing the palate); a vegetable course (he argues that vegetables were not served with meat courses); a first dessert course called an *entremet* that included sweet and savory dishes like flavored porridge or puddings; and a final dessert course that was not sweet but often included "a fruit and cheese course served with port, cordials, cigars, and coffee."[40]

Eagan's redesign of the Victorian feast into something appropriate for steampunk is made necessary by the very different diets of contemporary people and those living during the Victorian period. He aims, he says, to "combine our modern understanding and the older understanding into something harmonious." For instance, he reduces the three meat dishes during the *relevés* to one; makes the Victorian raw cucumber appetizer recipe more complex for a modern palate by adding a Parmesan crisp, microgreens, and goat cheese mousse; and steams instead of blanches asparagus for the vegetable course. The materialism of this approach to steampunk and gastronomy plays on physical differences in appetite and taste in order to remix and repurpose "classic modalities and recipes." Yet the materialist approach of steampunk cookery differs, I'd argue, from those producing textual critique about the social and political contexts of food. In *Food Studies: An Introduction to Research Methods*, Jeff Miller and Jonathan Deutsch say that their field "is not really the study of food" but "the study of the relationships between food and the human experience."[41] Producing steampunk food requires an understanding of this relationship, to be sure, but it also requires knowledge of specific palates in different historical periods and a willingness to bring those periods together in the service of creating new tastes.

How to Remake Theory

Common to both critical making practices I have outlined—engineering and cooking—is a commitment to touch, process, and experimentation. These commitments have at least two consequences. First, the act of making gives us a tactile approach to the production and destruction of objects. Cultural approaches to objects often treat them as a single, complete whole that signifies a concept, to the detriment of understanding objects in the process of change. This tendency may be due to the role of modernist art in helping to shape the ideas of mid- and late twentieth-century cultural theory.[42] Glenn Adamson has shown how much of modernist art criticism saw process and craft as a "supplement to the work of art," that the "physical consideration [of artistic production] has been consistently sidelined so that other qualities—opticality, transcendence, aesthetic resolution, conceptual depth—can take center stage."[43] While many cultural critics have been skeptical of ideas like resolution and transcendence, the study of cultural criticism remains tethered to the analysis of concepts largely practiced through discursive modalities and assuming an already produced artifact as a primary source. We have a small, but not nonexistent, understanding of how objects come into being. As Ian Bogost questions in *Alien Phenomenology*, "Can we even imagine a dramatic serial that delves deeply into the compression heat of a diesel engine combustion chamber, or the manner by which corn or sugar additives increase the alcoholic content of malt, or the dissolution of heroin in water atop the concave surface of a spoon?"[44] Steampunk enthusiasts are already engaging with these dramas when they link making methods to larger alternative historical fantasies. I see making practices in steampunk offering a powerful complement to the dominant, almost exclusive, focus on concepts as shaping the material of theoretical analysis.

Consider the emerging ethos of making in the digital humanities community characterized by an unofficial THATCamp motto: "more hack, less yack." Natalia Cecire criticized the phrase for its "zero sum logic" that "strictly demarcate[s] the construction of knowledge through writing (i.e. discursively) as different in kind from the construction of knowledge through (for instance) building a database."[45] Adeline Koh labeled the distinction as based on a modular and lenticular logic, following Tara McPherson's discussion of 1970s UNIX programmers who relied on hyperspecialized approaches to programming rather than questioning the larger ideological context of their work.[46] Much of the theory about making in the digital humanities, particularly work by

Stephen Ramsay, Geoffrey Rockwell, Tom Scheinfeldt, and Bethany Nowviskie, relies on what Cecire calls a "difficult and elusive" definition of haptic or tacit knowledge.[47] Steampunk making practices connect narrative and object, requiring a more nuanced understanding of how making practices extend discursive forms of knowledge. Procedural knowledge, modding, and repurposing contribute to an embodied history that links ideological criticism to objects, technologies, and foods. Feeling the effects of ideology as it results in an upset stomach complicates the separations between nature, technology, and culture that often motivate the divide between hacking and yacking. Makers learn that ideology can be tasted on the tongue, probed in circuits, and felt in a mechanism's backlash.

Further, making enables us to rethink how a different combination of methods and practices could create different gadgets, experiences, and histories. Critical making is a materialist practice that holds creativity to be a central part of its methodology. Making is not simply a way of understanding; it is also an investigation of what could have been. This practice creates, compared to more traditional historicisms, a kind of alternative historicism that rearranges the objects making up our world to imagine a different kind of past. For Trevor Owens, alternative historicism shows how "strange and contingent the past is," that it "is only inevitable in hindsight."[48] The making of objects or food from alternative histories provides us with an opportunity to see how, for example, colonialism might have played out differently with a different set of economic, technological, or sociological circumstances. In contrast to what Bruno Latour describes as "a privileged access to the world of reality beyond the veils of appearances," the alternative historicism of steampunk offers a wealth of different possibilities for the past.[49] Traditional historicisms stop at unveiling the conditions for historical events. Alternative historicisms intervene in political disparities by giving people the opportunity to recompose their own history. Two other essays in this collection show that the act of recomposing history has its own political and social complexities. Diana M. Pho, for example, identifies in the phenomenon of steampunk performance a juxtaposition between the subversively motivated inclusion of minoritarian identities and the mythologization of a homogeneous (British) national identity.[50] Likewise, Joseph Weakland and Shaun Duke suggest that while some steampunk novels return to the nineteenth century with a critical awareness, individual works of steampunk fiction naturally vary in their level of critical engagement with Victorian ideologies.[51]

I think it is telling that neither Pho nor Weakland and Duke do not automatically equate critical engagement with historicism. Historicism places scholars in a curatorial role as keeper of a past that is imagined as whole, complete, and unchanging. Steampunk scholars complicate this history by contrasting our image of the Victorian past with fictional and design fantasies. Steampunk's "counterfactual knowledge" allows humanist scholars to see history, in the words of Kari Kraus, "as alterable rather than immutable; as possibility spaces rather than rigid, inherited structures."[52] Of course, all possibility spaces have the potential for participating in microaggressions against marginalized groups just as much as they can give those same groups the opportunity to construct historical alternatives.[53] Still, the stakes of alternative historicism are different from traditional historicism. Bruce Sterling suggests that steampunk's interest in alternatives is motivated by the idea that "the way we live has already died"—or, in the words of Joshua Tanenbaum, Audrey Desjardins, and Karen Tanenbum, "our technological infrastructures are rapidly becoming irrelevant."[54] How can we combat a vision of our technological future dominated by the limitless spying capabilities of the seemingly omniscient National Security Agency? In what ways will the repealing of the 2013 Voting Rights Act by the Supreme Court or the dismantling of unions by Republican governors produce new forms of very familiar Southern racisms? Refusing to see the present as inevitable transforms the critical mission of the humanities from describing an oppression assumed to belong to the past to using critical making as a means of combating oppression in the ever-changing present.

Further, the focus on method, process, tactility, and materiality in steampunk makes relevant a broader set of cultural practices. The how-to manual rhetorically invites readers to participate in the act of making rather than, as in novels or critical scholarship, relying on an established author to represent a specific group. The steampunk object expresses a particular ideological perspective, but this perspective is often complicated by a dizzying array of different materials from different regions by a process of making that is a combination of techniques from different historical periods and by a set of specifically nonhuman concerns from alien organisms and inorganic objects. The politics of making in steampunk are overwhelmingly vast—something more akin to the weird realism of interdimensional predators, hive mind artificial intelligences made of trash, and cross-species sexuality in China Miéville's *Perdido Street Station* than any single appeal to a stable history or reality populated by humans and their discursive apparatuses.[55] Steampunk shows us that nothing is predictable, that everything is in the process of making and being remade, and that alternate worlds, alternate histories, and alternate lives are always possible.

NOTES

1. Jen, "How To Make: Steampunk Goggles," *EPBOT: Geekery, Girliness, and Goofing Off* (blog), July 30, 2011, http://www.epbot.com/.
2. Stefania Forlini, "The Aesthete, the Dandy, and the Steampunk; or, Things as They Are Now," this volume.
3. Bruce Sterling, Twitter post, January 11, 2014, 11:38 AM, http://twitter.com/bruces.
4. Garnet Hertz, "Natalie Jeremijenko: Interview by Garnet Hertz," in *Critical Making: Conversations* (Hollywood, Calif.: Telharmonium Press, 2012), 14.
5. Bruno Latour, "An Attempt at a 'Compositionist Manifesto,'" *New Literary History* 41, no. 3 (Summer 2010): 475.
6. Levi Bryant, "A Brief Note on Incorporeal Machines," *Larval Subjects* (blog), December 5, 2012, http://larvalsubjects.wordpress.com/.
7. Richard Sennett, *The Craftsman* (New Haven, Conn.: Yale University Press, 2008), 7–8.
8. Jussi Parikka, *What Is Media Archaeology?* (Boston: Polity, 2012), 1.
9. Joshua Tanenbaum, Karen Tanenbaum, and Ron Wakkary, "Steampunk as Design Fiction," in *CHI: Conference on Human Factors in Computing Systems 2012 Proceedings* (New York: ACM, 2012), 1585.
10. See O. V. Brzobohatý et al., "Experimental Demonstration of Optical Transport, Sorting and Self-Arrangement Using a 'Tractor Beam,'" *Nature Photonics*, no. 7 (2013): 123. The authors "present a geometry to generate . . . a 'tractor beam,' and experimentally demonstrate its functionality using spherical microparticles of various sizes, as well as its enhancement with optically self-arranged structures of microparticles."
11. Matt Ratto and Stephen Hockema, "Flwr Pwr: Tending the Walled Garden," *Walled Garden* (Amsterdam: Virtueel Platform, 2009), 52. See also Garnet Hertz, *Critical Making*, http://conceptlab.com/criticalmaking/. For Hertz, critical making blends and extends "the fields of design, contemporary art, DIY/craft and technological development. It also can be thought of as an appeal to the electronic DIY maker movement to be critically engaged with culture, history and society." He continues the critical focus in Garnet Hertz, "Introduction: Making Critical Making," *Critical Making* (Hollywood, Calif.: Telharmonium Press, 2012). Here Hertz mentions "hacker work," "tactical media," "circuit-bending work," "media archaeological work," or "people that are into making custom 'bespoke' things like lowrider cars or bikes" (4).
12. Several prominent scholars interested in the Maker movement have criticized the apolitical tendencies of *Make Magazine* as capitalizing on the enthusiasm surrounding maker culture while obfuscating its hacker origins. Perhaps the

most succinct is Garnet Hertz's satirical "Made Magazine: Technology on Affluent Leisure Time," in *Critical Making*. This vinyl sticker features a father and his child launching a self-made rocket flanked by several satirical article titles and callouts. The most prominent of the latter urges readers to "Join the Arduino Revolution!" and then qualifies it with, "But Avoid Civil Disobedience!" Other articles announce, "Open Source Secret Revealed: Everyone Just Buys the Kit!," "101 DIY Gadgets for White Males," and "How to Use a MakerBot to Create a Three-Cent Piece o' Plastic."

13. Gareth Branwyn, "Romancing the Steam," *Make Magazine*, no. 17 (2009): 12.

14. Molly Friedrich, "The 'Discreet Companion' Ladies' Raygun," *Make Magazine*, no. 17 (2009): 76.

15. Ibid., 77.

16. Ibid., 79. B&M (Bargain Madness) is a furniture company based in Blackpool, England, that also distributes furniture parts like knobs and handles. The tree hook has multiple branches used to hang articles of clothing or handbags, and these are repurposed in Friedrich's article as the ray gun handle.

17. James H. Carrott and Brian David Johnson, *Vintage Tomorrows: A Historian and a Futurist Journey through Steampunk into the Future of Technology* (Sebastopol, Calif.: Maker Media, 2013), 264.

18. Stephen Ramsay, "On Building," *Stephen Ramsay* (blog), January 11, 2011, http://stephenramsay.us; Stefania Forlini, "Technology and Morality: The Stuff of Steampunk," *Journal of Neo-Victorian Studies* 3, no. 1 (2010): 81.

19. Jim Shealey, "The Teacup Stirling Engine," *Make Magazine*, no. 17 (2009): 68.

20. C. S. Vineeth, *Stirling Engines: A Beginner's Guide*, rev. ver. (2012), 3, http://www.vineethcs.com/pdf/Stirling%20Engines-A%20Begineers%20Guide_rev_2.pdf.

21. X. Q. Kong, R. Z. Wang, and X. H. Huang, "Energy Efficiency and Economic Feasibility of CCHP Driven by Stirling Engine," *Energy Conversion and Management* 45, no. 9–10 (2004): 1433.

22. Shealey, "Teacup Stirling Engine," 69.

23. Ibid., 75.

24. Donald Cardwell, *Wheels, Clocks, and Rockets: A History of Technology* (New York: Norton, 2001), 244.

25. Shealey, "Teacup Stirling Engine," 75.

26. Wolfgang Ernst, "Media Archaeography: Method and Machine versus the History and Narrative of Media," in *Digital Memory and the Archive*, ed. Jussi Parikka (Minneapolis: University of Minnesota Press, 2013), 57.

27. Ibid.

28. For more information about the contest, see Lucinda Matthews-Jones, "Let's Bake Victorian Style! Comic Relief and This Year's JVC Bake Off," *Journal of Victorian Culture Online*, February 12, 2013, http://blogs.tandf.co.uk/jvc/.

29. Tim Morton, *The Poetics of Spice: Romantic Consumerism and the Exotic* (Cambridge: Cambridge University Press, 2000), 11.

30. "Victorian," *The Supersizers Go* ... (London: BBC, June 3, 2008).

31. Ibid.
32. Ibid.
33. Ibid.
34. For a similar use of humor to underscore gastronomic difference, see Sarah Lohman, "Drink Like a Colonial American Day," *Four Pounds Flour* (blog), January 5, 2012, http://www.fourpoundsflour.com. Lohman began her day drinking like a colonial American by sipping bitters, then had eleven ounces of hard cider for breakfast, two ounces of brandy during midmorning, and another twelve ounces of cider with lunch. She quit after the lunch cider, so she did not consume the additional brandy on a midafternoon break, another cider for supper, or a final drink of "spirits" meant to finish the day. On the following day, Lohman underscores her appreciation for the late nineteenth-century temperance movement. "I feel like the temperance movement has always gotten a bad rap," Lohman observes, "particularly recently with the boom in books and documentaries about prohibition. But considering in 1830 we were drinking five gallons of distilled spirits per person per year, and a decade later that number was down to two—that's pretty incredible."
35. Erika Kotite, "Steampunk Cuisine," *Toque* (blog), July 9, 2012, http://www.toquemag.com/.
36. Aaron Eagan. "Monthly Steampunk Feast No. 1," *Steampunk Cookery* (blog), December 14, 2010, http://cookingsteampunk.blogspot.com/.
37. Elizabeth Stockton, *Fuel for the Boiler: A Steampunk Cookbook* (lulu.com, 2008), 2.
38. Eagan, "Monthly Steampunk Feast No. 1."
39. Ibid.
40. Ibid.
41. Jeff Miller and Jonathan Deutsch, eds., *Food Studies: An Introduction to Research Methods* (Oxford: Bloomsbury Academic, 2009), 3.
42. The links between cultural criticism and modernist art can be traced through several different thinkers and texts. A few examples include Gilles Deleuze's appeal to the Francis Bacon's paintings in *The Logic of Sensation* (Minneapolis: University of Minnesota Press, 2004); Walter Benjamin's invocation of Paul Klee's *Angelus Novus* in "Theses on the Philosophy of History," in *Illuminations*, ed. Hannah Arendt, trans. Harry Zohn (New York: Schocken, 1969), 253–64; and Lev Manovich's discussion of how avant-garde aesthetic practices were embedded into film and digital media in *The Language of New Media* (Cambridge, Mass.: MIT Press, 2002).
43. Glenn Adamson, *The Invention of Craft* (Oxford: Bloomsbury Academic, 2013), xix.
44. Ian Bogost, *Alien Phenomenology, or What's It Like to Be a Thing* (Minneapolis: University of Minnesota Press, 2012), 115. Bogost's call for a new focus on "carpentry" in the humanities is a big influence on the way I describe steampunk making practices. Bogost says that the notion of carpentry "entails making things that explain how things make their world" and act as "earnest entries into philosophical discourse" (93).

45. Natalia Cecire, "When Digital Humanities Was in Vogue," *Journal of the Digital Humanities* 1, no. 1 (Winter 2011), http://journalofdigitalhumanities.org.

46. Adeline Koh, "More Hack, Less Yack? Modularity, Theory, and Habitus in the Digital Humanities," *Adeline Koh* (blog), May 21, 2012, http://www.adelinekoh.org/.

47. See Stephen Ramsay and Rockwell, "Developing Things: Notes toward an Epistemology of Building in the Digital Humanities," in *Debates in the Digital Humanities*, ed. Matthew K. Gold (Minneapolis: University of Minnesota Press, 2012), 75-84; Tom Scheinfeldt, "Where's the Beef? Does Digital Humanities Have to Answer Questions?," in Gold, *Debates in the Digital Humanities*, 56-58; and Bethany Nowviskie, "Don't Circle the Wagons," *Bethany Nowviskie* (blog), March 4, 2012, http://nowviskie.org/.

48. Trevor Owens, "Playing Pastwatch 1: Fracturing the Inevitability of the Past," *Play the Past* (blog), August 2, 2011, http://www.playthepast.org.

49. Latour, "Attempt at a 'Compositionist Manifesto,'" 475.

50. Diana M. Pho, "Punking the Other: On the Performance of Racial and National Identities in Steampunk," this volume.

51. Joseph Weakland and Shaun Duke, "Out of Control: Disrupting Technological Mastery in Michael Moorcock's *The Warlord of the Air* and K. W. Jeter's *Infernal Devices*," this volume.

52. Kari Kraus, "Introduction—Rough Cuts: Media and Design in Process," *The New Everyday*, July 28, 2012, http://mediacommons.futureofthebook.org/tne/.

53. For a definition of microaggressions, see Derald Wing Sue et al., "Racial Microaggressions in Everyday Life: Implications for Clinical Practice," *American Psychologist* 62, no. 4 (May-June 2007): 271-86. Sue et al. define microaggressions as "brief and commonplace daily verbal, behavioral, or environmental indignities, whether intentional or unintentional, that communicate hostile, derogatory, or negative racial slights and insults toward people of color" (271). Microaggressions can be directed toward any marginalized group.

54. See Bruce Sterling, "The User's Guide to Steampunk," *SteamPunk Magazine* 1, no. 5 (2009): 33; Joshua Tanenbaum, Audrey Desjardins, and Karen Tanenbaum, "Steampunking Interaction Design," *Interactions* 20, no. 3 (May-June 2013), http://interactions.acm.org/.

55. China Miéville, *Perdido Street Station* (London: Macmillan, 2000). *Perdido Street Station* takes place in the alternate steampunk fantasy world of Bas-Lag and includes such creatures as the slake moth, an interdimensional insect that mesmerizes human victims and feeds off their conscious minds; the construct council, a group of artificially intelligent hive-mind robots; and the khepri, an insectoid race whose females have humanoid bodies. For Miéville's understanding of weird realism, see his "Weird Fiction," in *The Routledge Guide to Science Fiction*, ed. Mark Bould et al. (London: Routledge, 2009), 510-16. Miéville identifies his work as one that "allows swillage of the awe and horror from 'beyond' back into the everyday—into angles, bushes, the touch of strange limbs, noses, etc." (511). I suggest that a deep concern with the nonhuman and the inorganic turns the strange realities described by Miéville into a humanistic methodology.

The Steampunk City in Crisis

CATHERINE SIEMANN

Steampunk is, in its most recognizable form, an urban genre. Its hallmarks are its simultaneous inhabiting of two historical moments; its resultant connection of the industrialization and urbanization of the nineteenth century to the postindustrial economy of the twenty-first places its concerns solidly in the urban sphere. This urban space may be the London whose existence has been reshaped by the steam-driven computing of William Gibson and Bruce Sterling's *The Difference Engine* (1990) or the postcatastrophe Seattle of Cherie Priest's *Boneshaker* (2009); it may be the government oppression and civil unrest evident in China Miéville's imaginary city-state, New Crobuzon, in *Perdido Street Station* (2000). Steampunk fiction may focus variously on depictions of technologies, the politics of empire, labor conditions and the lives of the poor, or even the social whirl of the leisured classes, but its central themes tend to revolve about the metropolitan center. Most frequently, the steampunk city presents itself as a sketchily defined backdrop, the generic gaslit surroundings of an alternative historical London or its analogue. However, the steampunk city that comes vividly to life on the page, that transcends the generic, is also a city in crisis, a place where imagined, steam-powered technologies create or address social problems and environmental disasters that echo historical ones.

That sense of crisis resonates as an integral component of the steampunk novel and about the urban space in which it takes place. Franco Moretti, writing about the nineteenth-century novel, claims that "without a certain kind of space, a certain kind of story is simply impossible."[1] Writing about science fiction, Frederic Jameson similarly suggests that "spatial representation" has a "deeply constitutive relationship" for the genre.[2] Since steampunk is perhaps most easily explained as a fusion of the nineteenth-century novel and science fiction, it is not surprising that the speculative space of the steampunk city should enable certain stories to be told. The steampunk city appears most vividly in the subgenre I have defined elsewhere as the steampunk social problem novel, a genre that, echoing Victorian novels of purpose by authors like Charles Dickens and Elizabeth Gaskell, engages in an "examination or rewriting of nineteenth-century social issues [and] speaks to contemporary audiences, who see in them a reflection of our own concerns."[3] The social problem novel was inevitably framed as an urban novel, set in Dickens's cosmopolitan London or Gaskell's industrial Manchester; the steampunk social problem novel is also set in a city. These steampunk cities provide a staging ground for stories in which speculative technologies and a dense and diverse population allow for an examination of issues of concern in the past as well as in either the present or an imagined future.

Each of the steampunk cities I consider below highlights the urban anxieties that arise out of technologically created disasters, and each novel infuses its city with a vivid sense of place: a physical location with specific geographic, architectural, and infrastructural features, and a community of people who are undergoing a significant trauma engendered by the plot crisis. While steampunk is often (and sometimes rightly) accused of uncritical nostalgia for a system implicated in imperialism and racial inequalities,[4] it can also be a site for the critical exploration of an urban past whose specters we encounter in our present. Many of these dystopian steampunk texts center around the damage done by imagined steam-based technologies, and it is in the urban environment where the impact of these technologies gone wrong comes to a crisis, leading to environmental and infrastructural problems as well as attendant social unrest. Each of these texts centers on a city in crisis and examines it in a way for which steampunk, with its dual temporality, is uniquely suited.

History and Alternate History: Steampunk Urban Crises in The Difference Engine

William Gibson and Bruce Sterling's *The Difference Engine* is steampunk in its most alternate historical form. Extrapolating outward from the development of computing in the nineteenth century, it considers resulting differences in industry, society, and politics. It contains two different types of urban crisis: the social upheaval that would result from an earlier automation of means of production, law enforcement, and so forth, and the actual environmental consequences of the Industrial Revolution and increasing urban population that remain the same, as represented here by the Great Stink.

Although not the earliest steampunk novel, *The Difference Engine* was arguably a watershed moment for the genre, attracting attention as the work of two of cyberpunk's most prominent writers. Its *New York Times* review by Thomas Disch introduced the novel and steampunk to a broader, nongenre audience.[5] The novel shifts steampunk's technological speculations from the playful imaginings of K. W. Jeter, James Blaylock, and Tim Powers, as described by Mike Perschon in this volume, to a grittier and more technological cyberpunk aesthetic. It considers what might have happened if Charles Babbage's never-completed early nineteenth-century protocomputers, the Difference Engine and the Analytical Engine, had been successfully constructed, thus bringing computing onto the scene in the heyday of the British Empire, in the early 1800s.[6] This early start on computing, however, does not lead to a technoutopia; rather, for every problem this technology solves, it creates another; ultimately it only advances the onset of a cyberpunk dystopian future. The novel's plot centers around the Modus, a computer program of great strategic value, through the eyes of three successive viewpoint characters: Sybil Gerard, a prostitute drawn into the world of espionage through a client who recognizes her as more than what she seems;[7] Edward Mallory, a paleontologist and explorer inadvertently involved thanks to his chivalrous rescue of Ada Byron, the gambling-addicted programmer and daughter of the prime minister,[8] from the clutches of a racetrack tout who is really the leader of the neo-Luddites; and Laurence Oliphant, an agent for the British government who is seemingly the only one to fully understand the potential consequences of the Modus program. While the government, ever more reliant on its own computing systems, plots to disable France's rival Grand Napoleon computing system, London is also threatened by an imminent crisis: an oncoming popular uprising in the form of a revived Luddite movement.

London is at the very heart of *The Difference Engine;* as the capital city of the politically and economically dominant British Empire, it is also the center from which this technological change radiates. While Gibson and Sterling's London differs little in many respects from Dickens's, and the characters' movements could be traced on a map of mid-nineteenth-century London, it is clearly a steampunk city; the presence of the functioning Babbage engines has led to substantial differences in its culture and technology. While many steampunk works contain fanciful, even ornamental elements, *The Difference Engine*'s speculations are extrapolated from the construction of the Babbage engines and from the technological, political, and social consequences that arise from bringing computing onto the scene over a century early. Its portrayal of London is not full of steampunk's iconic airships (they do turn up in a 1905 flash-forward), featuring instead multiple steam-powered computer mainframes and the steam-driven vehicles that have replaced horses in the races at Epsom.

Gibson and Sterling's London is a city in crisis for reasons both historical—an ecological catastrophe created by an increase in urban population combined with new sanitation technology—and sociological—the aforementioned neo-Luddite movement. Patrick Jagoda notes that "as a steampunk novel, *The Difference Engine* itself, of course, both *is* and *is not* a representation of nineteenth-century London and the empire that extends outwardly from it. It both is and is not an exploration of the effects of computing technologies on our own history."[9] In some ways, Gibson and Sterling's novel is the most uncanny—in the Freudian sense—of the texts I am examining. Although it is solidly grounded in both history and geography, that history and geography are deeply defamiliarized by the presence of mid-Victorian computer mainframes and their concomitant consequences. It does what steampunk does best: it creates and examines a nineteenth-century crisis that echoes the concerns, in this case technological, of the moment in which it is written. Sterling remarked in a 1992 interview, "*DE* is about the 1990s . . . It's our disease projected onto a lab animal of the nineteenth century."[10]

The London of *The Difference Engine* is a city under siege by the Great Stink, which came about as the result of an extended period of hot and dry weather, combined with an infrastructure overwhelmed by London's rapidly increasing urban population and new sanitation technology.[11] Although it resembles something out of an apocalyptic novel, this environmental catastrophe is not invented by Gibson and Sterling, nor is it the direct result of the steampunk technologies in the book. It was an actual historical occurrence, a by-product of the Industrial Revolution, which increased both urbanization and population in Britain. The invention of the flush toilet overwhelmed London's sewer system, which had originally been created as a system for storm runoff, while human waste was collected manually by night soil men, who disposed of it in cesspits. Instead the waste was now being dumped directly into the Thames, described here as "a putrid, disease-ridden tidal sewer,"[12] which, combined with the increased industrial pollution resulting from the flourishing manufacturing economy of the period, made London an unhealthy place to be. The upper classes retreated to the countryside, while the urban poor had nowhere else to go. Where the novel differs from history is that the Great Stink stokes the urban unrest that simmers throughout until it reaches a flash point.[13] Edward Mallory wends his way in the early morning through the aftermath of the urban violence that has arisen as a result of the appalling conditions:

> More by luck than design, he emerged on Commercial Street, ordinarily a thriving Whitechapel venue. Deserted now, its smooth tarmac was spread with fountained shards of shop-front glass. . . . There was scarcely a window intact. Cobbles, grubbed up from side-streets, had been flung right and left like a shower of meteors. A seeming whirlwind had descended on a nearby grocery, leaving the street ankle-deep in dirty snow-drifts of flour and sugar. . . . Scatterings of damp flour showed a stampede of men's brogues, the small bare feet of street-urchins, the dainty trace of women's shoes, and the sweep of their skirt-hems.[14]

Gibson and Sterling's choice to show traces of looting in its aftermath, rather than engaging with the scene directly, is a curious one. The crisis is only depicted at second hand, reduced to the footmarks participants have left behind. Mallory, who will later take up arms against the neo-Luddites, is here posed as the flaneur, the detached urban observer. Still, the scene contributes to a sense of the city as a complex mechanism that is breaking down.

How, then, is that breakdown positioned within the novel's semihistorical, semifictional universe? Since the major ecological catastrophe is not driven by the Babbage engines or the other advanced technology, it might at first seem that the impact of this new computer age has been all to the good. The Rad Lords (members of the Industrial Radical Party), under the leadership of Lord Byron, have replaced rule by hereditary wealth with an industrial-technological meritocracy. Whitechapel, a poverty-stricken district in the East End of London, has transformed itself entirely. Instead of the "infernal space of darkness" and "urban jungle" that it was historically perceived as,[15] it is now full of upwardly mobile strivers. Whitechapel resident Sybil Gerard, prostitute and daughter of an executed Luddite revolutionary, reflects on the changes this technology has brought to her surroundings:

> The place was full of bettering-blokes, really: shopkeepers and store-clerks and druggists, with their tidy wives and broods. In her father's day, such people, Whitechapel people, had been angry

and lean and shabby, with sticks in their hands, and dirks in their belts. But times had changed under the Rads, and now even Whitechapel had its tight-laced scrubfaced women and its cakey clock-watching men, who read the *Dictionary of Useful Knowledge* and the *Journal of Moral Improvement,* and looked to get ahead.[16]

It seems here that improved technology has brought upward mobility for Whitechapel's population, with better living conditions and a decrease in violence, into the heart of urban darkness.[17]

But technological progress benefits the population only selectively; the East End gentrifies, but artisans and workers are thrown out of work, and a neo-Luddite movement arises under the leadership of Wilkie Collins, aka Captain Swing, the name historically attached to a series of rural riots surrounding the increasing mechanization of farming in the 1830s. The novel's Swing is rallying the disaffected and unemployed under the banner of his antitechnology forces, intent on striking back against what he terms the "vampyre capitalist" and the "Moloch steam."[18] But Swing and his neo-Luddite ideas are defeated with surprising ease by Mallory and a small band of followers, with the help of the advanced technology that the Luddites are opposing. The middle class reasserts its control over the dangerous masses in the typical triumphal form of the Victorian novel.[19] As critic Jay Clayton notes, the text's most surprising omission is the absence of "sympathetically portrayed workers or rioters motivated by unendurable injustice."[20] Swing's defeat demonstrates that there is no viable alternative to the rising technoculture and that those who do not adapt are left with nothing.

The consequences of the neo-Luddites' failure are a decisive step forward in the ultimate rise of the machines. According to Gibson, "One of the things that [the novel] does is to disagree rather violently with the Whig concept of history, which is that history is a process which leads to us, the crown of creation."[21] By the time *The Difference Engine* reaches the present day, there is no "us." The technological head start of mid-Victorian computing leads inexorably to the nightmare of the closing paragraphs, in which an alternate 1991 London has devolved into a cyberpunk dystopia, with nothing remaining but a central cybernetic consciousness, the All-Seeing Eye. There are no longer any individuals but rather "paper-thin faces [that] billow like sails . . . human faces that are borrowed masks, and lenses for a peering Eye."[22] From the flawed and filthy but vibrant and diverse London of 1855, in all its culture and its commerce, its kinotropes and its Palaces of Paleontology, its East End whores and its Queen of Engines, we have reached a sterile present day. The *Matrix*-like surveillance state portrayed in the closing paragraphs represents the ultimate devolution of society, a city as hive mind. The apparently triumphant technological advantages of steampunk have led us, in fact, to a present-day catastrophe, using a city in crisis to foretell a future of ongoing urban crisis. The defeat of Swing and his Luddites is therefore ultimately the defeat of humanity in this dystopian take on steampunk.

The nightmare of the final pages is prefigured by the panoptical government engines of the Quantitative Criminology Office, which have instituted the beginnings of a surveillance state based on record keeping:

> Behind the glass loomed a vast hall of towering Engines—so many that at first Mallory thought the walls must surely be lined with mirrors, like a fancy ballroom. It was like some carnival deception, meant to trick the eye—the giant identical Engines, clock-like constructions of intricately interlocking brass, big as rail-cars set on end, each on its foot-thick padded blocks. The white-washed ceiling, thirty feet overhead, was alive with spinning pulley-belts, the lesser gears drawing power from tremendous spoked flywheels on socketed iron columns. White-coated clackers, dwarfed by their machines, paced the spotless aisles.[23]

The size and scale of the Engines, so vast that Mallory cannot at first perceive them as anything but a visual trick, gives a sense of the immensity of the endeavor. Nicholas Spencer describes them as a "vast informational panopticon [that] is ostensibly under society's utilitarian control" but that "actually has become a monolithic and terrifying entity."[24] And it is the precursor of the nightmare of the book's closing pages:

> It is London. Ten thousand towers, the cyclonic hum of a trillion twisting gears, all air gone earthquake-dark in a mist of oil, in the frictioned heat of intermeshing wheels . . . It is *not* London—but mirrored plazas of sheerest crystal, the avenues atomic lightning, the sky a super-cooled gas, as the Eye chases its own gaze through the labyrinth, leaping quantum gaps that are causation, contingency, chance.[25]

The first image, which "is London," is steampunk imagery intensified to the outermost extremity, where the gears and towers of the government Engines, the Industrial Revolution–esque technology, is pushed beyond the functional to the all encompassing. While the 1860s engines evoke a now-familiar steampunk visual aesthetic, with their "clock-like constructions of intricately interlocking brass,"[26] their gears and flywheels, the image of the depopulated "*not* London" is also *not* steampunk, analogous to what Rachel A. Bowser and Brian Croxall call the "aesthetic of technological invisibility."[27] Bowser and Croxall use recent Apple products and their minimalist design as the prime examples, while in the All-Seeing Eye's domain,[28] machinery has become elemental—crystal, lightning, gas.

The Difference Engine gives us a London that is a city in crisis on many levels: the ordinary technological, the steampunk technological, an alternate past, a glimpse of a cyberpunk dystopian future (the time of which aligns with the reader's present). The Great Stink reminds the reader of both the limitations and complications of the existing technology of the era—the limitations of the London sewer system and the complications emanating from improvements in home sanitation and plumbing—as well as the larger-scale impact of the intensified urbanization of the Industrial Revolution. The fictional steampunk crisis—the negative effects of the steam-powered computing of the text—leads to significant social unrest in the novel's time frame and to an accelerated rise of the machines in its future. This combined catalyst for crisis—the real and the imagined technologies in the urban center of the fictional universe—suggest an urban critique embedded in this staple of the steampunk canon. Gibson and Sterling present a vibrant and diverse metropolis that both drives the need for new technologies and fails to absorb the impact they inevitably generate.

The Destruction and Rebirth of the City in the Clockwork Century

Technology and the resultant environmental and social catastrophes are also central to *Boneshaker* and *The Inexplicables,* the novels in Cherie Priest's Clockwork Century series that take place in Seattle. Here, however, they are magnified to an apocalypse in the moment rather than, as in *The Difference Engine,* looming a century and a half hence. Steampunk technology has led to the city's downfall while at the same time allowing a hardy remnant of Seattle's population to live among its ruins.

The Clockwork Century series takes place in North America in an alternate historical timeline in which political and technological differences have kept the Civil War going into 1880. The series spans much of the North American continent, with episodes in Richmond, Virginia; St. Louis, Missouri; New Orleans, Louisiana; and Washington, D.C. Priest's series is largely Western and Southern oriented, but it is also firmly urban, with a ruined Seattle the primary setting of *Boneshaker* (2009) and *The Inexplicables* (2012), the first and fourth novels in the series. The books center on a technologically driven environmental catastrophe with serious social consequences: in Seattle, an industrial accident involving Dr. Leviticus Blue's Incredible Bone-Shaking Engine,[29] a steam-powered motorized megadrill designed to mine Arctic ice in the Yukon gold rush, has led to the release of a gas known as Blight, which causes those exposed to devolve into rotters, zombielike creatures that seek to devour any humans they encounter. These rotters serve as the common crisis across the five novels and two novellas in the series. At the conclusion of the final novella, *Jacaranda* (2015), we learn that by 1895, fifteen years after the main action of the series, the plague of rotters has finally come to an end, with only a few of these unfortunates remaining in the wilderness.

Although in *Boneshaker* the Seattle disaster area has been physically contained, enterprising individuals are shipping the Blight gas and yellow sap, a highly addictive drug distilled from it, throughout North America, threatening to spread rotters across the continent. While this growing problem, and the way people adapt to it, is the common thread of the series, the most centralized crisis is in Seattle, where the gas and rotters were first unleashed. The Boneshaker has destroyed Seattle when an out-of-control test run undermines the structure of the city. The Seattle that Dr. Blue has destroyed was a vibrant urban landscape, a frontier boomtown in the process of transforming itself into a major city. The Boneshaker's "course took it under the earth and down the hills, gouging up the land beneath the luxurious homes of wealthy mariners and shipping magnates, under the muddy flats where sat the sprawling sawmill, and down along the corridors, cellars, and storage rooms of general stores, ladies' notions shops, apothecaries, and yes . . . the banks."[30] The path of destruction included a broad range of urban districts, from the residential to the commercial of every sort. Perhaps most emblematic of the destruction caused by the drill is the palatial and almost-completed King Street Station, abandoned before it had ever been used for its proper purpose.[31]

Here, as in *The Difference Engine*, steampunk echoes the crises of the real world, which are themselves often brought about by technology. The crisis in Seattle is at once the product of technology—Dr. Blue's

Bone-Shaking Drill—and nature—the Blight gas that has been released from under the city. The catastrophic physical nature of the crisis echoes the fires and earthquakes that leveled nineteenth-century cities, such as the San Francisco earthquake of 1906, the Great Chicago Fire of 1871, and others in Boston, New York, London, and Glasgow, as well as the subtler and more pervasive crises that arose with industrialization, the result of a laissez-faire system that provided no regulation on the conditions of production. Priest's Seattle struggles with apocalypse rather than pollution as the outcome of industrial catastrophe, but the deadly contamination of air and water through newly developed technologies was historically also a characteristic of industrialized cities, such as London's Great Stink. Instead of becoming zombies, workers faced the potential of workplace-generated diseases such as black lung and phossy jaw, not to mention death from machinery-related accidents. Here, as in *The Difference Engine,* the city is under siege as a result of the unthinking or callous acts of human agency.

The disaster area has been contained within the city limits of Seattle. Since the Blight gas was "a thick, slow-moving substance that killed by contamination, [which] could be generally halted or stilled by simple barriers," ultimately "the entire downtown area was surrounded by an immense brick, mortar, and stone wall . . . stand[ing] approximately two hundred feet high . . . [and] averag[ing] a width of fifteen to twenty feet . . . containing an area of nearly two square miles."[32] Inside this wall, the city becomes a ghost town, with a diminished population living and working in an area known as the Outskirts, much like the so-called doughnut cities of the latter half of the twentieth century, where a crumbling urban core is surrounded by suburban residential and commercial districts.[33] Surprisingly, however, the city center is not completely uninhabited. The walled city, accessible only by airship or through concealed tunnels, is inhabited by a hardy breed of urban pioneers. They live in sealed underground environments, salvaged largely from former bank vaults, and protect themselves with gas masks as they traverse the city's sunken streets and buildings.[34] The sense of a city under siege is made literal here, but the city in decline also sets the stage for a resurgence.

David Pike argues that although *Boneshaker* is "set in a beautifully rendered 1880s Seattle amid the Western genre trappings proper to it . . . the steampunk twists on that setting . . . all derive from nineteenth-century London and its pulp literary traditions."[35] While the down-and-outers who live behind Seattle's containing walls and scavenge a living in an economy that is part salvage, part industrial, and part survival bear a certain resemblance to the East End of London's urban poor—those "angry, lean and shabby" Whitechapel inhabitants whom Sybil Gerard recalls[36]—Seattle also represents a reversal of the so-called civilizing narrative of Western expansion. While the ruined city contains the remnants of urban civilization (those banks and ladies' haberdasheries), it has reverted to the frontier aspects that the disaster has left as its sole remaining characteristics. The population is composed primarily of former prisoners and others whose predisaster social and economic status was already marginal, including a large group of Chinese immigrants.

The series demonstrates the life of a city in crisis and the persistence of its inhabitants, with the aid of the steampunk technology that makes their lives underground possible—weapons, specialized gas masks, mechanical limbs, and the like. Priest's novel makes the standard tropes of the steampunk subculture functional, putting the omnipresent goggles to good use in detecting Blight gas, for example. While in *Boneshaker* the existence of Seattle's human population is unknown even to the inhabitants of the Outskirts, by the time of *The Inexplicables*, set a few years later, the residents of the underground city are looking forward to an improved airship terminal, a telegraph, and regular postal service.[37] In *Boneshaker*, the town is run in large part by drug kingpin Dr. Minnericht; thereafter, authority splits between his successor, Yaozu, and the forces of order in the person of Sheriff Briar Wilkes, the widow of Leviticus Blue. The resilience of the city is evident; here, rather than urban wasteland, it becomes a true community, if a deeply flawed one. The final full-length novel in the series, *Fiddlehead* (2013), ends in December 1880 with Ulysses S. Grant looking out the White House window at an electrified fence keeping the rotters at bay, but the mood is triumphant overall because the Civil War has finally ended. By 1895, when *Jacaranda* is set, the crisis has passed. We don't return to Seattle (the novella is set in a haunted hotel on Galveston Island in Texas), so we don't know exactly how things have resolved there, but the absence of the Blight gas and the near extinction of the rotters presumes a hopeful future. We might, then, characterize the conflict at the center of Priest's novels as an urban catastrophe that has grown out of an uncontrolled technology. More so than in *The Difference Engine*, this catastrophe grows specifically out of singularly steampunk technology. Further, this series differs from Gibson and Sterling's novel in that it shows a promise of containment rather than an inevitable degeneration into a dystopian historical present.

The Crisis and the Crisis: The Dysfunctional City in Perdido Street Station

Although it is the single wholly imagined city I address here, New Crobuzon, the steampunk city in which China Miéville's *Perdido Street Station* is set, is so richly portrayed that the city, its history, and its immediate crises seem as real as Priest's vastly changed Seattle or Gibson and Sterling's more subtly steampunked London. While the novel's plot centers on a fairly standard monster movie crisis, as an infestation of slake moths, giant multidimensional creatures that feed on human minds, threatens the city, New Crobuzon is a city always already in crisis—a city with millennia-long history of decay and corruption, described by a new arrival as "this dusty city dreamed up in bone and brick, a conspiracy of industry and violence, steeped in history and battened-down power."[38] The city is in the midst of political turmoil; an oppressive government suppresses dissent with deadly force and seeks profit over the well-being of its citizens.

A magical-retro steampunk technology plays a major role, both supporting the mechanisms of the state and defeating the rampaging creatures that threaten it. While there is no overt ecological catastrophe in New Crobuzon like the Great Stink of London or the collapse of Seattle, the first impressions we are given on a journey upriver into the city include the results of industrial pollution. The narrator of this passage, an outsider, perceives a river that "smears slime on its brick banks" with a "stinking rainbow of impurities, effluents and chymical slop, making it sluggish and unsettling."[39] The spelling of "chymical," with its suggestion of alchemy in the setting of industrial pollution, creates a sense of otherness while echoing that historical moment where Sir Isaac Newton simultaneously practiced alchemy and laid out many of the principles of modern science. The technology of the Bas-Lag novels is part steampunk and part magical; it at once involves relatively simple firearms, household-cleaning robots or "constructs," steampunk-inflected trains and airships, and biotechnology.

The slake moths are both natural and uncanny, operating in more than one dimension. They are believed to have come from the Fractured Lands, the origin place of the Cacotopic Stain, a catastrophe of mysterious origins that sent waves of mutating energy over a significant portion of the world of Bas-Lag, in a disaster of far greater proportions than the blight gas of Priest's Seattle.

There is a strong element of steampunk Foucauldian imagery in the structure from which Miéville's *Perdido Street Station* takes its name. It is an architectural nightmare, steampunk style:

> An industrial castle, bristling with random parapets. The westernmost tower of the station was the militia's Spike, that loomed over the other turrets, dwarfing them, tugged in seven directions by taut skyrails. But for all its height the Spike was only an annex of the enormous station . . . Five enormous brick mouths gaped to swallow each of the city's trainlines. The tracks unrolled on arches like huge tongues. Shops and torture chambers and workshops and offices and empty spaces all stuffed in the fat belly of the building, which seemed, from a certain angle, in a certain light, to be bracing itself, taking its weight on the Spike, preparing to leap into the enormous sky it so casually invaded.[40]

The station's architect went mad, a condition that the text clearly links to his creation; it contains the embassy of Hell; and more practically, it provides a transportation hub and economic center for the vast city whose center it has become. Most importantly, its tallest tower, the Spike, is the home of the militia; it serves as the panopticon from which the entire enormous city is under surveillance. The city-state of New Crobuzon is under the shadow of an oppressive government that will ultimately drive the novel's protagonists into exile. Workers will strike, unifying across species boundaries, but the government will put their strike down. Dissidents will be hunted down and tortured, quite possibly in the station itself.

The city in which all this takes place is one of the most thoroughly conceived urban spaces in steampunk fiction. New Crobuzon provides the industrial city its ultimate mirror, a steampunk antiutopia: the docks where human and nonhuman workers join together to strike; the hidden offices of a dissident newspaper beneath a factory in the Mayhewian slum of Dog Fenn; alien immigrant enclaves inhabited by insect and cactus people; the train station that broods over the sprawling, decaying city.[41] David Pike, in his study of steampunk London, points out that London "was the heart of the century's most powerful empire, and steampunk is fundamentally concerned with power in all of its forms and manifestations."[42] It is perhaps not surprising that Londoner Miéville's imagined city is, like his hometown at various points in history, a port city, an industrial powerhouse, a hub for immigration, and the center of a politically oppressive state.[43] It is home to both the immediate crisis, the slake moth rampage, and a longer-term malaise that manifests itself in images of entropy and oppression.

The slake moths, which were imported by the government for undetermined reasons, possibly to be weaponized, have been kept in a high-security lab. The government, unable to put them to productive use, sells its specimens to a drug kingpin: the moths feed their larvae on psychic "milk" that can be cut with other materials and turned into "dreamshit," which in humans acts as a potent hallucinogen. Just as the drug lord seeks to profit on a large scale, an underpaid clerk seeks to profit on a smaller one: he sells one of the caterpillars to an independent researcher, and this unidentified and unsecured specimen eventually frees its siblings. By hypnotizing humans and other sentient beings with the patterns on their wings, the slake moths feed on their victims' consciousness, draining them of memory and personality and leaving a still-living husk. Their keepers wore complicated steampunk helmets that enabled them to view the moths through attached mirrors; to gaze on the moths directly is to succumb to them. The moths move about the city freely, finding their prey throughout the city and its inhabitants. The novel's protagonists eventually destroy them through a complicated maneuver involving possibility physics and a mechanical-sentient collective called the Construct Council, but they make enemies of both the government and the crime syndicates along the way.

The government's collusion in willingly making the slake moths available as a source for illicit drugs shows how deep its corruption goes. Its oppressive nature is similarly exemplified in its response to the Kelltree dockworkers' strike. The strike is notable for an unprecedented solidarity of purpose between the humans and the amphibious dockworkers, two often conflicting groups putting aside their differences to form an alliance for the greater good. It is a vibrant scene, with counterdemonstrations and public shows of support.[44] Pamphlets from both strikers and antistrike nativists circulate freely, and "the event is marked by a vociferous free exchange of ideas"[45] until government troops attack via a steampunk technological mélange of musketry, airships, and giant biologically engineered Portuguese man o' war jellyfish. While it parallels the historical London dockworkers' strike of 1889 in its goals and size, that strike was successful. Miéville's outcome instead more closely recalls the Peterloo massacre of 1819, where government troops opened fire on a group of demonstrators in St. Peter's

Square, Manchester, as they advocated for better wages and expanded suffrage.[46] Both the Kelltree strikers and those in Peterloo are seen as a threat to the existing order and are dealt with accordingly, despite the peaceful nature of their protests.

Though the novel's protagonists are victorious over the immediate crisis in New Crobuzon (the reality-distorting slake moths), they voluntarily go into exile, one step ahead of their enemies both within and without the city's power structure. As Christopher Palmer states, "The city is saved, but it has not been the scene of any transformative political action . . . Instead, there is complex disillusionment."[47] The slake moths have been destroyed, but nothing has really changed. The oppressive government is still in power; the dissident voice of the newspaper *Runagate Rampant* is still silenced. Miéville suggests, particularly with the ending of his third and final Bas-Lag novel, *Iron Council* (2004), that the struggle for the city—whether in the midst of attacks by monstrous, inexplicable creatures or neighboring states; between the people and the government; or against the entropy we see in the landscape all around us—goes on. Individual crises come and go, but the city is eternally the site of crisis. Like *The Difference Engine,* the novel foregrounds how crises are not caused so much by technologies as by the social structures in which those technologies find themselves. It is not the fantastical elements of extrapolated nineteenth-century technologies that lead to the New Crobuzon being under siege. Instead it is the extrapolated social structure of the Victorian period, with its industrialization, ideals of discipline and punishment, and rise of incapacitating bureaucracy producing the crisis in *Perdido Street Station*. Unlike Priest's Clockwork Century series, Miéville's novel gives no hint of possible redemption. Instead, it presents a picture of a city that is always already in crisis, where rampaging monsters or warfare are merely intervals in an internal history of conflict and oppression.

Conclusion: Why the Steampunk City Now?

While Walter Benjamin calls Paris "the capital of the nineteenth century," one could more readily posit, as David Pike does in this collection, that London is the capital of steampunk. If, borrowing from Benjamin, we call New York City the capital of the twentieth century, the shock waves from the crisis with which we began the twenty-first century might shape the very image of our city in the present moment. In their introduction to this volume, Rachel A. Bowser and Brian Croxall argue that "we cannot ignore the cultural trauma of 9/11, so prominent in the environment during steampunk's rise to prominence."[48] If this is true, then the city generally, if not New York City specifically, proves itself the most vital location for working through a notion of urban crisis that finds its ultimate manifestation at ground zero.

I do not agree wholly with this reading—two of my three texts demonstrate that the steampunk city faced crisis before the terrorist attacks of September 11, 2001, and London was under siege in early steampunk works by Jeter and Blaylock before that time as well. The environmental, technological, and political situations that arise in the steampunk urban crises are almost wholly dissimilar to the events of that day.[49] However, it can be argued while dystopian steampunk cities both before and after that watershed tend to be dark, troubled places, there are more potentially redemptive possibilities in the later stories. Gibson and Sterling's novel, published in 1990, ends with a future apocalypse of sorts, and Miéville's, published ten years later, closes with the voluntary exile of the protagonists who have saved the city from its immediate crisis, with the oppressive government still very much in place.

As Jeff VanderMeer and S. J. Chambers have suggested, there has been a major increase in steampunk's popularity in the last ten years, and this newer steampunk fiction draws from the steampunk subculture, itself a vibrant and diverse community.[50] Where post-2001 steampunk contains overt social critique, more optimistic endings are the general rule. Such endings could be read as a working through of crisis, similar to Bowser and Croxall's notion that steampunk's tinkering can be used recursively to address problematic issues in the past and present with answers more palatable to the modern reader. Here, I have examined Priest's *Boneshaker*, published in 2009, which premises the collapse of a city, as suddenly and unexpectedly as the collapse of the towers on 9/11, but ends with the return of law and order in the underground city of Seattle in the person of the new sheriff, Briar Wilkes. This is true of other works as well, such as S. M. Peters's *Whitechapel Gods* (2008), where supernatural-mechanical deities who have conquered a portion of London are defeated, and Gail Carriger's popular Parasol Protectorate series (beginning with *Soulless*, published in 2009), a significant part of which takes place in London, and which combines adventure and romance with lighthearted social satire. Steampunk of the last decade characteristically contains assertive heroines who engage in technological careers in the setting of advanced technology that solves more problems than it creates. As Diana M. Pho demonstrates in this volume, contemporary steampunk attempts to engage with the legacy of racism and colonialism—and, of course, it examines urban crisis. The texts I have analyzed here each engage with resistance or rebellion. The peaceful labor protestors and alternative press of New Crobuzon, the Luddites of *The Difference Engine*'s London, and the urban pioneers of postcatastrophe Seattle all resist a more dominant and better-equipped power. There have been more directly proactive steampunk connections with modern city-centered protest movements as well: for example, musician Painless Parker (Noam Berg) and performance artist Steampunk Emma Goldman (Miriam Roček) entertained the Occupy Wall Street protesters in New York's Zuccotti Park in 2011-12, and *SteamPunk Magazine* has strong anarchist leanings, featuring articles like Miriam Roček's "The New Orleans General Strike of 1892 Laughs at Your Shitty Attempts to Divide the Working Class with Racism"[51] and stories like the Catastrophe Orchestra's "Mother of the Dispossessed."[52] While this is only one strand of the steampunk subculture, it is a substantial and persistent one.

In the twenty-first century, the post–World War II move to the suburbs seems to be reversing itself, as there is a "major cultural and demographic shift away from suburban sprawl" and "young workers and retiring Boomers are actively seeking to live in densely packed, mixed-use communities,"[53] despite the urban trauma of 9/11. That said, the city still seems to be a place of crisis, as we have recently seen from urban protests in Ferguson, Missouri, Baltimore, Maryland, and Staten Island, New York, over the deaths of young African American men at the hands of police officers. These crises are obviously far removed from the fictional steampunk crises discussed in this essay, but the prevalence of urban problems in 2015 highlights why steampunk might be interested in considering urban crises in a past that is like our present in so many ways. Steampunk offers us a vision of how we might avoid these crises—or, in some cases, what we might face if we cannot undo them.

NOTES

1. Franco Moretti, *Atlas of the European Novel: 1800-1900* (London: Verso, 1999), 100.

2. Frederic Jameson, *Archaeologies of the Future: The Desire Called Utopia and Other Science Fictions* (London: Verso, 2007), 306.

3. Catherine Siemann, "Some Notes on the Steampunk Social Problem Novel," in *Steaming into a Victorian Future*, ed. Julie Anne Taddeo and Cynthia Miller (Lanham, Md.: Scarecrow Press, 2013), 3.

4. See, for example, the blog of Diana M. Pho (writing as Ay-leen the Peacemaker), *Beyond Victoriana* (http://beyondvictoriana.com/), and Jaymee Goh's blog *Silver Goggles* (http://silver-goggles.blogspot.com/). See also Jeff VanderMeer and S. J. Chambers, *The Steampunk Bible: An Illustrated Guide to the World of Imaginary Airships, Corsets and Goggles, Mad Scientists, and Strange Literature* (New York: Abrams, 2011), 212–15; and Ann VanderMeer, introduction to *Steampunk III: Steampunk Revolution*, ed. Ann VanderMeer (San Francisco: Tachyon, 2012). These characteristics can be found in a wide range of steampunk works, ranging from the steampunk military history of S. M. Stirling's *Peshawar Lancers* (2002) and the revised adventures of Victorian explorer Sir Richard Francis Burton in Mark Hodder's *Expedition to the Mountains of the Moon* (2012) to the alternative history of an England only recently freed from Mongol rule in Meljean Brook's *The Iron Duke* (2010) and the blithe airship tourism of Gail Carriger's *Prudence* (2015).

5. Thomas Disch, "Queen Victoria's Computers," review of *The Difference Engine*, by William Gibson and Bruce Sterling, *New York Times*, March 10, 1991.

6. For a more playful view of the same, see Sydney Padua, *The Thrilling Adventures of Lovelace and Babbage* (New York: Pantheon, 2015).

7. Sybil is an adaptation of a character created by Benjamin Disraeli in his eponymous novel (1845); Disraeli himself appears in *The Difference Engine* as a writer, having kept to his original profession rather than entering politics—though since Byron and Shelley have become politicians, Keats a cinematographer, and Wilkie Collins a revolutionary, they have left plenty of room in the literary profession for him.

8. Lord Byron has turned to politics, as the leader of the Industrial Radical party, a meritocracy of engineers and manufacturers who have displaced the old ruling class. In this alternate history, Ada has not become Lady Lovelace.

9. Patrick Jagoda, "Clacking Control Societies: Steampunk, History, and the Difference Engine of Escape," *Neo-Victorian Studies* 3, no. 1 (2010): 61.

10. Daniel Fischlin, Veronica Hollinger, and Andrew Taylor, "'The Charisma Leak': A Conversation with William Gibson and Bruce Sterling." *Science-Fiction Studies* 19 (1992): 5–6.

11. Johanna Lemon, "The Great Stink," *Cholera and the Thames*, City of Westminster Archives, http://www.choleraandthethames.co.uk.

12. William Gibson and Bruce Sterling, *The Difference Engine* (New York: Bantam, 1991), 194.

13. The Great Stink does not seem to have been a direct cause of urban violence. It was closely connected to the cholera epidemics of the period and was the event that led to the modernizing of London's sewage system; see Lemon, "The Great Stink."

14. Gibson and Sterling, *Difference Engine*, 238.

15. Joseph McLaughlin, *Writing the Urban Jungle: Reading Empire in London from Doyle to Eliot* (Charlottesville: University Press of Virginia, 2000), 2.

16. Gibson and Sterling, *Difference Engine*, 34.

17. This reading makes the presumption, perhaps incorrectly, that these are Whitechapel residents whose position has improved as a result of the new tech-

nology and relative egalitarianism under the Rads. However, the text does not state that certainly, and Whitechapel may instead be undergoing gentrification.

18. Gibson and Sterling, *Difference Engine*, 273. Swing's imaginative rhetoric and scheming may arise in part because he is *The Difference Engine*'s version of Victorian novelist Wilkie Collins (see Fischlin, Hollinger, and Taylor, "Charisma Leak," 9), author of both sensation and social problem novels and hence an appropriate figure to be cast as a sensational villain in a novel centering on urban crisis.

19. See, for example, Charles Dickens's *Barnaby Rudge* (1841) and Charlotte Brontë's *Shirley* (1849).

20. Jay Clayton, "Hacking the Nineteenth Century," in *Victorian Afterlife: Postmodern Culture Rewrites the Nineteenth Century*, ed. John Kucich and Dianne F. Sadoff (Minneapolis: University of Minnesota Press, 2000), 115.

21. Fischlin, Hollinger, and Taylor, "Charisma Leak," 7.

22. Gibson and Sterling, *Difference Engine*, 428.

23. Ibid., 137.

24. Nicholas Spencer, "Rethinking Ambivalence: Technopolitics and the Luddites in William Gibson and Bruce Sterling's *The Difference Engine*," *Contemporary Literature* 10, no. 3 (1999): 418. Herbert Sussman, in the earliest published scholarly piece on *The Difference Engine*, argues that the text "rejects the Foucauldian model of a seamless, invincible panoptical power"; Herbert Sussman, "Cyberpunk meets Charles Babbage: *The Difference Engine* as Alternative Victorian History," *Victorian Studies* 38, no. 1 (Autumn 1994): 5. However, it is difficult to read these vast engines, in their oppressive scale, as rejecting the panoptical. Patrick Jagoda also supports the Foucauldian reading in "Clacking Control Societies," 51.

25. Gibson and Sterling, *Difference Engine*, 428–29.

26. Ibid., 137.

27. Rachel A. Bowser and Brian Croxall, "Introduction: Industrial Evolution," *Neo-Victorian Studies* 3, no. 1 (2010): 16.

28. There's even an unintentional and anachronistic pun here, with Apple's famous i-prefix.

29. Blue's Bone-Shaking Engine echoes the contraptions in early steampunk works by James Blaylock and K. W. Jeter; its very name evokes the steampunk aesthetic.

30. Cherie Priest, *Boneshaker* (New York: Tor, 2009), 17–18.

31. Railway stations seem to be common landmarks in steampunk novels; as we shall see, Miéville's eponymous Perdido Street Station looms significantly over the novel to which it gives its name. In the Clockwork Century sequence, the King Street Station becomes the headquarters of Seattle's drug kingpins. In reality, it serves twenty-first-century Seattle as an Amtrak station.

32. Priest, *Boneshaker*, 19.

33. Andalusia Center for Contemporary Art, "Doughnut City," *Atributos Urbanos*, http://www.atributosurbanos.es/en.

34. The buried city is inspired by the Seattle Underground, in the Pioneer Square area, the heart of the original settlement. The actual Seattle Underground is a more limited area than what Priest has created for her text and is the result

of city planning in the wake of the Great Seattle Fire of 1889. In the rebuilding process, the street level was raised eight or nine feet, but because business was booming thanks to the Yukon Gold Rush, an underground level was constructed to serve temporarily until the raised streets were completed; see "A Little History," *Bill Spiedel's Seattle Underground Tour,* http://www.undergroundtour.com.

35. David Pike, "Steampunk and the Victorian City: Time Machines, Bryan Talbot, and the Center of the Multiverse," this volume.
36. Gibson and Sterling, *Difference Engine,* 34.
37. Cherie Priest, *The Inexplicables* (New York: Tor, 2012), 365.
38. China Miéville, *Perdido Street Station* (New York: Ballantine Books, 2000), 4.
39. Ibid., 2-3.
40. Ibid., 64.
41. Referencing Miéville's Marxist politics, William J. Burling writes, "The city is thus for fantasist Miéville, as it was for realist Dickens, the precise and only setting by which to depict and to critique the unrepresentable capitalist totality"; "Periodizing the Postmodern," *Extrapolation* 50, no. 2 (2009): 333.
42. Pike, "Steampunk and the Victorian City," this volume.
43. Sherryl Vint has referred to New Crobuzon as "one vision of Victorian London transformed by Gothic sensibilities and curious, scientifically rigorous magic," thus reinforcing Pike's argument that the steampunk city inevitably relates back to Victorian London; Sherryl Vint, "Introduction: Special Issue on China Miéville," *Extrapolation* 50, no. 2 (2009): 197.
44. Miéville, *Perdido Street Station,* 297.
45. Siemann, "Some Notes," 9.
46. In New Crobuzon, only the wealthiest have a guaranteed right to vote. For the remainder, "the illusion of democracy is created by a lottery in which a certain number of ordinary citizens get the vote each year"; Siemann, "Some Notes," 8.
47. Christopher Palmer, "Saving the City in China Miéville's Bas-Lag Novels," *Extrapolation* 50, no. 2 (2009): 229.
48. Rachel A. Bowser and Brian Croxall, "It's About Time: Reading Steampunk's Rise and Roots," introduction to this volume.
49. It is notable, however, that toward the end of Miéville's *Iron Council* (2004), Perdido Street Station is targeted by a revolutionary who tries to destroy it with an explosives-laden train. The militia detonates the train short of its target, causing damage to the city's transportation infrastructure but not the station itself. The attempt is incidental to the main plot of the novel.
50. VanderMeer and Chambers, *Steampunk Bible,* 63.
51. Miriam Roček, "The New Orleans General Strike of 1892 Laughs at Your Shitty Attempts to Divide the Working Class with Racism," *SteamPunk Magazine* 9 (2013): 32-37.
52. Catastrophone Orchestra, "Mother of the Dispossessed," in *SteamPunk Magazine: The First Years* (New York: Combustion Books, 2011), 17-21.
53. Ania Wieckowski, "Back to the City," *Harvard Business Review,* May 2010, http://hbr.org/.

PART II

Steampunk
Bodies and Identities

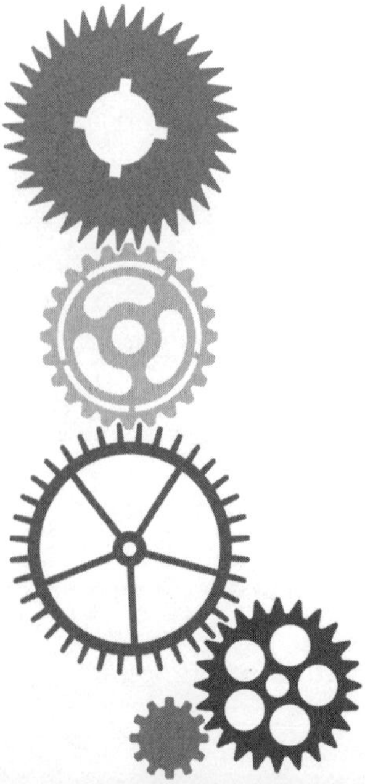

From Steam Arms to Brass Goggles
Steampunk, Prostheses, and Disability
KATHRYN CROWTHER

> At Waterloo he lost an arm,
> Which gave him pain and great alarm;
> But he soon got well, and grew quite calm,
> For a shilling a day was a sort o' balm.
>
> The story goes, on every night
> His wife would bang him left and right;
> So he determined, out of spite,
> To have an arm, cost what it might.
>
> He went at once, strange it may seem,
> To have one made to work by steam,
> For a ray of hope began to gleam,
> That force of arms would win her esteem.
>
> —ANONYMOUS, "The Billy-Cock Hat, New Comic Song,
> Singing Nightly with Applause and Also the Following Popular Songs"

In "The Steam Arm," the song excerpted above, a veteran who lost his arm at Waterloo obtains a prosthetic steam-powered arm that not only replaces his missing limb but gives him, via the double entendre, the "force of arms" to stand up to his bullying wife.[1] The steam arm proves too powerful, however, and ends up striking his wife to the floor, killing the police who come to arrest him, and knocking down the walls of the prison in which he is imprisoned. By the end of the song, the soldier has tried in vain to control the arm, but he is fully at its mercy: "His arm keeps moving with two-horse might."[2] The story of the steam arm might at first glance seem to be a creation of the contemporary steampunk imagination: a retrofuturistic technology (an advanced prosthetic yet powered by steam) that fuses with the body and serves as both a replacement and an enhancement. However, "The Steam Arm" is actually a Victorian popular song dating from 1833 or 1834, and thanks to its recuperation by Kirstie Blair, we can read it as a Victorian commentary on the very anxieties that steampunk projects back into the nineteenth century. This is, as Blair writes, "an exciting text for steampunk enthusiasts, because it seems to justify steampunk retrofutures, to give them historical credibility."[3]

Certainly the song does bolster the standard argument of steampunk theorists that steampunk takes its inspiration from the Victorian era because the period marks the emergence of the modern subject's fascination with technology, which mirrors our own contemporary ambivalence toward technology.[4] While the soldier's arm gives him power and restores his masculinity, his own autonomy is threatened by the power of the technology and the blurring of the boundaries of man and machine via his prosthesis. Yet it is also a story of disability; the historical reality of the nineteenth-century amputee whose lived experience with a body that is supplemented by technology is overshadowed by the metaphorical ramifications of this relationship. In Blair's detailed close reading of "The Steam Arm," she identifies numerous social and political contexts that undergird the song, from the emergent anxiety about the power of technology to override human agency to the liberatory potential of technology to empower the working classes (when the protagonist overcomes the force of law), yet she never considers the context of disability. While it could be argued that the song itself pays little attention to the notion of disability (notably the arm gives a superability in the same way that much contemporary steampunk portrays prosthetics), it certainly engages with the sociohistorical context of disability: the prevalence and visibility of veterans and factory workers with prostheses, their inability to find gainful labor (the protagonist of the song receives only "a shilling a day"), the material reality of prosthetics as manufactured objects, and the disempowerment and emasculation of men with disabilities. Blair's elision of perhaps the most obvious function of the prosthetic in the song—a marker of the historical reality of disability and prosthetic use—mirrors the absence of a discussion of the steampunk prosthetic and disability in contemporary theorizations of steampunk. This absence is both surprising and troubling, given the current prominence of the field of disability studies and its critical imperative to not only theorize the presence of disability in literature but also to address its historical and material specificity.

The steampunk prosthetic (steam arm, robotic hands, artificial eyes) and assistive technologies (the steam-powered wheelchair, the ubiquitous brass goggles) have become a common motif in steampunk literature and film as well as in the cultures of steampunk crafting and

FIGURE 4.1. Image of G. D. Falksen in an arm mechanism created by Thomas Willeford. Photograph by Tyrus Flynn; this image is used under the terms of a Creative Commons Attribution Share-Alike (CC-BY-SA 3.0) license.

cosplaying. Indeed, the prevalence of the steampunk prosthetic seems to be ever increasing; while the occasional prosthetic appears in the early novel-length works and the stories anthologized in *Steampunk* (2008), they appear with increasing frequency in the works of more recent steampunk authors (Cherie Priest, Gail Carrigan, Scott Westerfeld) and in a striking number of the stories in the most recent anthology, *Steampunk III: Steampunk Revolution* (2012). Similarly, in films such as *Wild Wild West* (1999), *Steamboy* (2004), and *Casshern* (2004), prosthetics play a significant role in the story line. Just as steam-driven or clockwork prosthetics have become a hallmark of steampunk fiction, they have also become a common artifact in the world of making and modding and a popular accessory in the world of steampunk cosplay.[5]

Despite its seeming ubiquity in steampunk literature and culture, little critical attention has been paid to the literary or the material steampunk prosthetic. This lack of theoretical inquiry is a troubling gap, especially considering the considerable attention devoted to the other ideologies and social constructs critiqued (or punked) in steampunk.[6] When Steffen Hantke describes how "identities . . . begin to slip and slide" in steampunk, he only includes "gender, race, or social class" in his examples.[7] Catherine Siemann examines a wide range of steampunk fiction that addresses social issues and accumulates an impressive list including "imperialism, racism, workers' rights," "the plight of women," "working-class unrest, press censorship, voting inequalities," "the plight of the poor," and "the legacy of colonialism" but never mentions disability.[8] Indeed, most critiques of steampunk literature and culture completely disregard the fact that prosthetics are, as material objects with a contemporary and historical specificity, most often a direct signifier of disability.

As both a material representation of the supplementation of the human body with technology and an historical reference to the prevalence of prosthetic limbs in the nineteenth century, the steampunk prosthetic clearly opens itself up to a range of critical interpretations. However, little theoretical attention has been paid to either its symbolic or historical role in steampunk literature and culture or as a material marker of the lived experience of disability. Depictions of steampunk prosthetics in literature and film, along with the practitioners of steampunk who build them, tend to present prosthetics as simply an extension of the contemporary fascination with technology and the way it augments and enhances our own abilities (the metaphor of technology as prosthesis). In this interpretation, the prosthetic loses its material presence as a marker of disability and becomes merely a symbolic representation of a web of posthuman concerns about technology, the body, and the definition of what makes us human.

However, while the symbolic function of the prosthesis and its relationship to the blurring of the body and technology is a compelling theorization, it fails to account for the historical specificity of the prosthetic, its nineteenth-century roots, and the reality of living with a prosthetic. This gap between a theorization that details the symbolic qualities of the steampunk prosthesis versus one that attends to the materiality of the prosthetic and the lived experience of disability mirrors the gap between the figurative nature of steampunk literature and the material focus of the maker culture, which Roger Whitson addresses in this volume.[9] Given the prevalence of the prosthesis in steampunk literature and culture, it is vital that theorizations of steampunk address the prosthetic and its relationship to the history of disability, amputation, and technology in the nineteenth century. In doing so, we must draw on the significant body of work from Victorian studies on nineteenth-century disability and from contemporary disability theory and seek to understand the significance of the steampunk prosthetic in this larger context.

In the first part of this essay, I examine several works of steampunk fiction in which prosthetics play a central role and unpack the multiplicity of meanings that the prosthetic can bear. I next look at the material history of the prosthetic in the nineteenth century and use the lens of disability theory to reflect upon the lived experience of prosthetic use that is both represented and elided in contemporary representations of the steampunk prosthetic. Finally I consider the subversive potential of the fetishized materiality and purposeful visibility of the steampunk prosthetic, as well as the potential of steampunk culture to make inclusion and access part of its reimagining of history and consequently of our present moment and future.

Steampunk Prosthetics in Literature and Film

Steampunk prosthetics appeared in the literature long before they were built and worn in steampunk culture. However, while early steampunk fiction does contain examples of prosthetics, they generally appear as small anatomic replacements that serve to distinguish a particular character (usually a villain) or fully fledged automatons. William Gibson and Bruce Sterling's seminal steampunk novel, *The Difference Engine* (1991), features a clockwork automaton but no characters with prosthetics. In Paul Di Filippo's 1991 novella *Victoria*, the evil Lord Chuting-Payne wears "a prosthetic silver nose" made from the family's sterling silver after his is blown off in a duel. While the prosthetic shows sophisticated design ("the simulacrum was a marvel to behold"), its only function is to replace the original nose and excite "the most jaded of women."[10] Another 1991 short story, Ian MacLeod's "The Giving Mouth," inhabitants of a bleak feudal kingdom, Castleiron, use a contraption called an "eater machine" fashioned of "liveiron" that is strapped to the face like a muzzle and was designed for people "who wished to avoid the effort of working their throat and jaws as they ate."[11] The eater machine represents more of an assistive device than a prosthetic, and its role in the story, while pivotal, is related more to fantastic notions of regeneration than of ability or disability. Both of these stories appear in the first *Steampunk* anthology, which, noticeably, contains many stories with automatons but, aside from the artificial nose and mouth of Di Filippo and McLeod's stories, features no other significant prosthetics.

However, by the time of the publication of *Steampunk III: Steampunk Revolution* in 2012, many of the stories feature some kind of prosthetic, and the majority make the relationship between the body and technological replacement and enhancement the central engagement of the text. Melissa Kent's "The Heart Is the Matter" (2012) highlights the modern anxiety around the definition of what it means to be human. Set in nineteenth-century France, the story describes a world in which prosthetics and "half-humans" are common.[12] The protagonist, Sophie, has a prosthetic that she hides under her long sleeves: a metal heart that she holds and continuously pumps with her hand. The mechanical heart replaces the missing organ that she donated to her sister to keep her alive—an act of selfless love that the "heart" of the title literally and figuratively represents. Despite her obvious humanness, Sophie ends up imprisoned in a glass case on display at the Great Exhibition as an example of scientific progress. When humans integrate technology into their bodies, where, the story asks, is the line between human and machine? How do we balance scientific progress with concerns about our humanity? Yet the story reminds us that the body is itself a machine and the heart is the only "completely automatic organ. . . . The heart is the closest thing to a machine of perpetual motion known to man."[13] If the heart is a machine, the story posits, then the body/machine boundary becomes impossible to demarcate.

Also featured in *Steampunk III* is Nick Mamatas's 2012 story "Arbeitskraft." It is clear from the title that the story uses the rhetoric of Karl Marx's *Das Kapital* (1867) to highlight the plight of the Victorian working class. The story deftly intertwines traditional steampunk tropes: an urban nineteenth-century setting in a recognizable Victorian England, historical personages engaged in fictional plotlines, anachronistically advanced technology, and a focus on industry and the problems of the laboring class. "Arbeitskraft" is narrated by Friedrich Engels, who is covertly building a Dialectical Engine to communicate with the dead Karl Marx. The success of Babbage's Difference Engine has brought unimagined efficiency to the production of all forms of steam technology, and now automaton "steam-workers" perform the majority of labor-intensive tasks, including producing more steam-workers to expand the labor force. As Engels strives to continue the work of Marx and produce a revolution of the proletariat (who are now being forced out of jobs by the steam-workers), he encounters a group of young women match makers who are still employed because they perform work that is too delicate for the steam-workers. Remarkably, the girls have had their mandibles removed as a result of phossy jaw (a real nineteenth-century phenomenon wherein the match makers' jaws were contaminated with the white phosphorous they worked with and literally rotted away) and replaced with prosthetic stainless steel jaws. As he fights to keep the girls employed, Engels discovers that the new automaton steam-workers are actually humans encased in metal bodies, which gives them the strength of machines but the brains and dexterity of humans. Outraged, he screams his realization: "Replace the body of a man with a machine, encase the human brain within a cage, and dead labour lives again!"[14] The steam worker has become a fully fledged cyborg, guaranteeing the full enslavement of the working class. Mamatas's story is another meditation on the consequences of the merging of the modern human with the technology that he produces and consumes. However, the fearmongering of the story is clearly tongue in cheek and reveals a much more rigorous critique of postmodern anxiety itself than of actual technology.

Finally, Lev Grossman's story "Sir Ranulph Wykeham-Rackham, GBE, a.k.a. Roboticus the All-Knowing" (2011) pushes the symbolic function of prosthesis beyond its imaginable limits. After winning medals for gallantry in early World War I battles, the eponymous protagonist suffers a devastating injury when white phosphorus burns away his body from the hips down and a German sniper blows away most of his face. With the help of his family fortune and brand new prosthetic technology, Wykeham-Rackham's lower body is rebuilt with stainless steel controlled by hydraulics and rubber tubing, and his face is reconstructed using "a mask made of paper-thin galvanized copper" upon which a painted enamel reproduction of his features is bonded.[15] Famous artists compete to produce the best mask, and ultimately Wykeham-Rackham has twelve to choose from. With his prosthetic body, Wykeham-Rackham becomes both a celebrity and a work of art. As his human parts age, they begin to look incongruous with his unchanged prosthetics, so he is persuaded by Andy Warhol to become completely synthetic. He undergoes a final surgery to replace "his skull with a steel casing, and his brain with a large light bulb."[16] Abandoned by Warhol and sold to a traveling carnival, Wykeham-Rackham becomes a fortune-telling machine who, despite many adjustments to his settings, only predicts the death of those seeking a fortune. Like the "The Heart Is the Matter," the central concern of this story is the line between artifice and humanness, the complicated blurring of technological prosthesis and subjectivity; in his final synthetic form, it is hard to tell whether any of the original man remains. The story aligns technology and craft in typical steampunk fashion: Wykeham-Rackham is both cyborg and an art object. The story ends with an Oscar Wilde quotation, "A mask tells us more than a face," implying that perhaps the technology we choose to adopt says more about us than any of our inherent human qualities.[17]

In contrast, steampunk films such as *Wild Wild West*, *Steamboy*, and *Casshern* feature prosthetics as enhancements that endow their wearer with augmented power. In *Wild Wild West*, the iniquitous Dr. Arliss Loveless use a steam-powered wheelchair to move around, and in *Steamboy*, the mad scientist, Edward, wears a prosthetic eye covering and a mechanical hand to replace the parts he lost in an experiment.[18] Notably, both of these characters are villains, and it certainly seems to be the case in film (and often in fiction) that prosthetics mark a character as malevolent as they use their augmented powers for evil. However, they are not figured as fully nonhuman or automatons and still retain human qualities: both Loveless and Edward are vain and proud and are motivated by a desire for wealth, fame, and revenge. In the Japanese film *Casshern*, the hero, Tetsuya, is killed in battle, then resurrected by his scientist father. His body is encased in full armor that endows him with superhuman abilities.[19] Tetsuya is fighting an army of resurrected humans called neosapians who also have augmented powers. The line between using technological enhancement for good or ill is more uncertain in *Casshern*, but the film still clearly represents the trope of the prosthetic as dangerous superpower. While many steampunk films, like much steampunk literature, feature elaborate prosthetic devices, these films fail to connect the prosthetic with the concept of disability. Instead, the prosthesis stands in symbolically for larger questions about the modern subject's relationship to technology.

The Nineteenth-Century History of Prosthetics and Disability

Collectively, these stories and films feature a steampunk prosthetic representative of a specific set of anxieties about the agency of the body and how we can identify and quantify humanness when a body is integrated with technology. The prosthetic functions symbolically in these texts rather than representing a person living with a disability or the material reality of a prosthetic worn to supplement the body. As the work of disability theorists like Rosemarie Garland-Thomson, David T. Mitchell and Sharon L. Snyder, Jennifer Esmail, and Christopher Keep have observed, the very transformation of disability in literature into a representation of something else, a "narrative prosthesis," undermines an understanding of disability as lived experience.[20] Disability studies as an academic discipline began with a social constructivist model for understanding and defining disability, positing that

> the meanings attributed to extraordinary bodies reside not in inherent physical flaws, but in social relationships in which one group is legitimated by possessing valued physical characteristics and maintains its ascendancy and self-identity by systematically imposing the role of cultural or corporeal inferiority on others.[21]

In this way, "extraordinary bodies" serve to actually uphold a mythical idea of a normal body (or a "normate" body, as Garland-Thomson terms it). Disability theory also works to dismantle the idea of the figure of the normate, focusing instead on the ways that disability is actually a construction of a society and physical environment designed to accommodate the normate body and in which "people deemed disabled are barred from full citizenship because their bodies do not conform with architectural, attitudinal, educational, occupational, and legal conventions based on assumptions that bodies appear and perform in certain ways."[22]

While much important work continues to be done analyzing and deconstructing how disability is societally created and defined, some disability theorists have shifted to what Garland-Thomson calls material analysis. Rather than focusing on symbolic representations of disability, material analysis focuses on "how the material aspects of social categories such as race, gender, class and—in particular—disability play out in the material world."[23] Similarly, in their introduction to a special journal issue on Victorian disability (with a special section on prostheses), Jennifer Esmail and Christopher Keep note that while scholarship on the Victorian era has examined the historical and social frameworks that structure nineteenth-century discourse on disability, a turn to "materiality and an attention to the cultural products of marginalized peoples, has much to offer the study of disability."[24] They argue that because disability "has often been problematically read as a straightforward metaphor for lack," there has been a "tendency to efface the material specificity of what it means to live in a society largely governed by ableist assumptions about which bodies matter and which do not."[25] Thus, while the literary prosthetic offers a compelling representation of the interconnectedness of the modern human subject with technology, it is a reading that elides both the historical specificity of the nineteenth-century prosthetic as an object worn by an individual with a material existence and the role that technology played in actually causing the types of injuries and amputations that required prosthetics. Given that the visibility of prosthetics dramatically increased during the nineteenth century and that the discourse on disability (especially as it related to larger social norms and definitions of work) became a frequent part of cultural and political debates, it is clear that the correlation between steampunk prosthetics and steampunk's Victorian roots offers rich sociohistorical readings beyond the symbolic relationship of body and technology.

The Victorians would not have deployed the word "disability" as the broad (albeit unstable and indefinable) term we use today. Blindness, mental disability, and physical infirmity all fell into different categories, and people were more generally evaluated on how their "affliction" affected their ability to participate in social and work-related contexts.[26] The use of prosthetics to restore a body to its former functioning was not only a part of the medical realities of the nineteenth century but also constitutive of a larger social dynamic that defined all bodies by their ability (or inability) to be a useful part of society and an effective laborer. By the nineteenth century, significant advancements in prosthetic technology produced prosthetic arms and legs with articulating and locking joints, and although they were not always readily available for the working classes, who might have to make do with a temporary or rudimentary wooden device, there were sophisticated devices available for those who could afford them.[27] Further, there was an increasing need for them: as more people survived amputations as a result of advancements in surgical techniques, and as more amputations were performed as a result of war and factory accidents, the sight of the amputee became a fairly common one. In America, veterans of the Civil War were often amputees; indeed, amputations constituted three quarters of the surgeries performed on wounded soldiers, and despite the still-high mortality rate, an estimated 15,000 amputees survived the war.[28] In a literalization of the blurring of the boundaries between the human and the machine, as factory machines and modernized warfare took limbs from workers and soldiers, technology also provided prosthetic replacements.

Most of the amputees were men, and their disabled bodies invoked a new discourse of rehabilitation that would return damaged bodies back to productivity in the burgeoning industrial society.[29] In most cases, productivity meant the ability to work in a factory. Such work was repetitive and dangerous; dismemberment was not uncommon as a result of getting caught in the machinery. The repetitive, precise motions of the workers who spent twelve to fourteen hours a day on the same machine often caused irreparable damage to the body, twisting limbs and creating deformities, as well as injuring the lungs from breathing in toxic chemicals and other substances. As Erin O'Connor describes, "Industrial disease remade the worker's body in the image of his trade. Jobs involving repetitive mechanical movements, for instance, tended to cause unusual orthopedic problems, generating joint deformities, permanent flexures, and even paralyses that embodied the adaptive subordination of body parts to specific tools and machines." In this way, "physical disability marked the worker's complete appropriation by the activity and apparatus of labor."[30]

For all people requiring prostheses, whether they were injured in an accident or born with congenital deformities, access to good prosthetic technology was dictated by class and income. While the upper class could expect a sophisticated artificial leg, which was made to order and fitted with articulating joints, working class amputees often had to settle for a wooden peg or metal hook.[31] The Victorians viewed those with prosthetics as cripples, and as such, amputees were alternately treated with pity, charity, or distaste; in the case of severe disabilities, they were placed in hospitals and sanatoriums. The possibility that amputees with more modern prosthetics could pass as nondisabled was highly significant in a time in which social norms, including normative standards for the body, meant that visible bodily difference led to discrimination, unemployability, and often poverty and destitution. The figure of the poor amputee was common in Victorian literature, and authors like Charles Dickens often included characters with prostheses. Indeed, Adrienne E. Gavin describes Dickens's fascination with artificial legs, pointing out that nearly all of Dickens's novels contain a character with a wooden leg.[32] As Gavin remarks, this is a reflection on the relative prevalence of wooden legs, although it must be noted that Dickens generally endowed his more villainous characters with a disability or deformity, aligning character with physical traits according to traditional literary symbolism. Dickens's most notable character with a wooden leg is Silas Wegg in *Our Mutual Friend* (1865). Wegg's peg leg is a marker of his lower-class standing and unemployability: he is a street ballad seller "who is unable to secure regular employment with a nearby house, probably because of the limited physical capacities that were associated with limb-loss and prosthesis use."[33]

Well-designed prostheses, then, could not only hide visible difference but could also allow an individual to remain employable and productive in a society that valued work, individuality, and uniformity. The workers, while evaluated by their fitness and ability to work, performed labor that was broken down into small sequences, so laborers were ultimately reduced to the parts needed to perform the task. Henry Ford famously describes the process:

> Of [7,882 different jobs at the factory,] 949 were classified as heavy work requiring strong able-bodied . . . men, 3,338 required men of ordinary physical development and strength. The remaining 3,595 jobs were disclosed as requiring no physical exertion . . . and could be performed by the slightest weakest sort of men [or] satisfactorily filled by older women or children. [Of these,] 670 could be filled by legless men, 2,637 by one-legged men, two by armless men, 715 by one-armed men and ten by blind men.[34]

Although Ford's example is striking, it was not the norm; most workers were evaluated on the integrity of their body and their ability to perform backbreaking labor for twelve to fourteen hours a day. In fact, the repetitive labor of the factory reduced workers to just their bodies, and "the body of the average worker," Lennard J. Davis writes, "becomes the new measure of man and woman."[35] The standardization of work became tied to the standardization of the body, which in turn contributed to increasingly narrow definitions of "normal" bodies. Commensurately, the body itself, as merely a part in the larger functioning of the factory and a synecdoche of itself (the hands of the factory), became representative of the mechanical labor it performed. Each body was a cog in the larger machine of the factory. In his *On the Economy of Machinery and Manufactures* (1832), Charles Babbage (a seminal figure in steampunk) envisions the factory system as a way to augment and extend human power, figuring machines as "hand[s]" and "giant arms" and the humans who work them as part of this larger machine body.[36] Thus, as body/machine discourse slid toward defining bodies as machines that could be repaired and extended with prostheses, so too were machines figured as bodies, with hands, arms, and an organic system.[37] Thus, in its literalization of the merging of body and technology, prostheses became a visible marker not only of the specificity and materiality of the individual worker's body but also of the body's machine-like functioning and thus a metaphor for the nineteenth-century man/machine relationship. In this way, the material slips into the figurative and the figurative is literalized in the material: the prosthetic, it seems, despite our efforts to excavate its material and historical specificity, always exceeds that material specificity and inevitably becomes a symbol of the human's relationship to technology.

Critiques have produced compelling analyses of how this nineteenth-century figuration of the man/machine relationship as a prosthetic one is inextricably linked to discussions of capitalism, labor, and the modern subject.[38] In a capitalist economy, workers are both highly embodied (in the literal way their bodies are damaged by repetitive labor and by machines) yet simultaneously disembodied into an abstraction as part of the larger discourse of economics. Machines are figured as prosthetic attachments to laboring bodies, and bodies are figured as prosthetic parts of a larger machinic whole. It is not surprising, then, that in an era in which humans became increasingly defined by their relationship to technology, the prosthetic became both a literalization and a metaphor for this relationship.[39] Thus, as Herbert Sussman and Gerhard Joseph describe, "Prosthetic extensions of the organic body, whether seamlessly sutured to that body or not, became a figure for discussions of subjectivity and human identity," and consequently, "the mid nineteenth century thus not only marked the birth of the form we recognize as technological modernity, but also became the basis for what has become one of the defining conceptual formations of the modern, the notion of prosthesis as both a figure for and materialization of a perfectly realized mode of production of things."[40]

Steampunk's Material Turn

Thus, it seems that even when we turn to the nineteenth century for an account of the prosthetic and its relationship to disability, we find that discussions of the prosthetic always seem to slide away from materiality and into metaphor. Yet despite the metaphorical nature of the steampunk prosthetic in literature and film, the homemade steampunk prosthetic is most determinedly material. For many steampunk theorists, the material culture of steampunk—the making, modding, and cosplaying—truly defines the genre, and the steampunk prosthetic is notably one of the most common handcrafted artifacts. If the prosthetic in steampunk film and literature stands in figuratively for our fascination with (and concerns about) the blurring line between technology and the body, then we must ask what work the material steampunk prosthetic is doing. Significantly, just as disability theory pushes us to move away from disability as representation to investigate the material lived experience of disability, so also have some steampunk critics called for more critical attention to the maker culture of steampunk and the material artifacts they produce.[41] Steampunk's turn to material culture and disability theory's turn to material analysis line up and allow us to examine the relationship between the prosthetic, disability, and the individual body.

Steampunk practitioners build machines and artifacts using cogs, brass, hydraulics, and, of course, steam to create modern objects with a nineteenth-century aesthetic. These steampunk artisans push back against the uniformity of mass-produced technology and reject the idea that technology should be inaccessible to the individual craftsman. Computers retrofitted to a nineteenth-century style, steam-driven machines, and earrings made of tiny cogs—these steampunk products proudly display their components, rendering visible the inner workings that modern contemporary technology hides beneath smooth surfaces. Rachel A. Bowser and Brian Croxall write about this modern "sleek" aesthetic, noting that with the advent of laptops, pocket-size devices, and wireless technologies, "technological objects have tried to become invisible. . . . It is a drive toward an aesthetic of technological invisibility."[42] Steampunk thus pushes against the ethos of invisibility that characterizes contemporary technology. Rebecca Onion applies this theory to the steampunk prosthetic via the figure of the steampunk cyborg, countering that

> Though steampunk cyborgs provoke the same kinds of questions about bodily modification as do more contemporary computerised cyborg objects, they tend, through their visual appearance, to remind the viewer of what used to be conceptualised as the mechanical nature of the human body. The moving parts of the machine are analogous to the moving parts of the body, making visible what, in the actual flesh, remains hidden behind a smooth, iPod-like surface. This visibility empowers the human mind, which seeks to be reassured that the functions of the body have a visible, comprehensible (and thus medically controllable) logic of their own.[43]

Unlike the posthuman cyborg, who seeks to hide its technology under the "smooth" surface, the steampunk cyborg proudly displays its prosthetic extensions.[44] In this way, the subversive potential of steampunk pushes into view both the mechanical nature of the body and also the way it can be damaged, modified, extended, and enhanced. Similarly, as the body is revealed as a machine, machines in steampunk are humanized. In their steampunk manifesto, the Catastrophone Orchestra and Arts Collective writes, "Steampunk machines are real, breathing, coughing, struggling, and rumbling parts of the world. . . . [They are] the hulking manifestations of muscle and mind, the progeny of sweat, blood, tears, and delusions. The technology of steampunk is natural; it moves, lives, ages, and even dies."[45] In this way, the body is reconceptualized as a machine. But this body is not the uniform, mass-produced object of the postindustrial age; instead, it is an individual, fallible body that we can tinker with and modify. This fallible body returns us to disability theory and Garland-Thomson's assertion that extraordinary bodies, "demand a reckoning with the messiness of bodily variegation, with literal individuation run amok . . . in an era governed by the abstract principle of universal equality, disability signals the body that cannot be universalized."[46] The handmade, crafted steampunk prosthetic and the disabled body foreground the same unreliability and variability of the body and unsettle the idea that bodies are whole, seamless, and uniform.

While steampunk prosthetics emphasize the fallibility and uniqueness of the body, they also emphasize its possibilities: amputation and disability are often figured as lack, but steampunk emphasizes the malleability of the body and its potential to be enhanced and improved. When fictional characters such as the veteran in "The Steam Arm" and Edward Steam, the evil father in the film *Steamboy*, are augmented with prosthetics, their abilities become superior to ordinary humans: rather than being disabled, they instead become extraordinarily abled (though it is significant to note again that these powers are often used for evil rather than for good). Similarly, contemporary cyborgs like athletes Oscar Pistorius and Aimee Mullins challenge the very notion of disability by threatening to surpass normate ability with their augmented bodies. Steampunk prosthetics not only make disability visible but also often endow their wearer with specific advantages.[47] As one blogger writes:

> With a steampunk prosthetic, the wearer isn't seen as disabled. In fact, the wearer becomes imbued with many attractive and even super-human traits. First, there is the visual appeal of steampunk gear, the brass and clockworks, which makes a nice addition not just to clothing but to the body itself. And second, the implication is often made that a steampunk prosthetic makes the wearer stronger or faster, or in some way better than a "normal" person. I think there's a wonderful implication here. We've discovered that technology, even if it doesn't resemble the human form, can still be so beautiful and capable in its own ways that we would willingly (or even eagerly) integrate it into our own bodies.[48]

If steampunk prosthetics transform disability into superability, then it is possible to critique this as a positive subversion of disability.

Notably, both Pistorius and Mullins have made the design and look of their prosthetic legs a significant part of their athletic—and, in the case of Mullins, fashion—personae. Mullins, in addition to being a runner, is a model and actress; she performs on the catwalk wearing different designer prosthetic legs specially commissioned and tailored for her. Traditionally prostheses have been designed to be invisible—to closely mimic the body and to be hidden beneath clothing. Steampunk prosthetics, however, are stylized, aesthetically pleasing pieces intended to be on display, and they often push the boundaries of prosthetic design. As Roger Whitson observes, the how-to culture of steampunk maker movement encourages steampunk artisans to post plans and blueprints for the objects they build and mod and to post step-by-step pictures of their process.[49] Several steampunk blogs and websites document making prosthetics for amputees and provide detailed descriptions of the process. One artisan posted step-by-step instructions that describe how he built an Iraq war veteran "a golden mechanical hand. Not to replace the hand he lost so much as to replace the empty air that occupied that space now [and to make] . . . an exhibition hand. Something to get people's attention."[50] The desire to draw attention to the prosthetic hand works to counter traditional discourse on disability which encourages people to conceal their disabilities and pass as nondisabled. Thus, steampunk prostheses, rather than being sleek and seamless, are visible and clunky; disability in steampunk becomes a coveted superability rather than something shameful and marginalized.

The steampunk maker ethos fetishizes materiality; further, the steampunk prosthetic is prized for the types of materials used to construct it, its aesthetically pleasing appearance, and, most significantly, its functionality. Interestingly, the one genre of steampunk literature that captures the material culture's fetishization of the prosthesis is steampunk romance and erotica—actually a large portion of fiction produced in the steampunk genre. In her blog post, "Amazing and Bizarre Prosthetics in Steampunk Romance," Heather Massey inventories ten

FIGURE 4.2. A steampunk prosthetic hand that draws attention to the functionality and aesthetics of a disability accommodation. ArtificerMade [Christopher Bright], "Steampunk Prosthetic Hand—Step Four: Phalanges," *Instructables*, http://www.instructables.com/. Photograph by ArtificerMade and used with his permission.

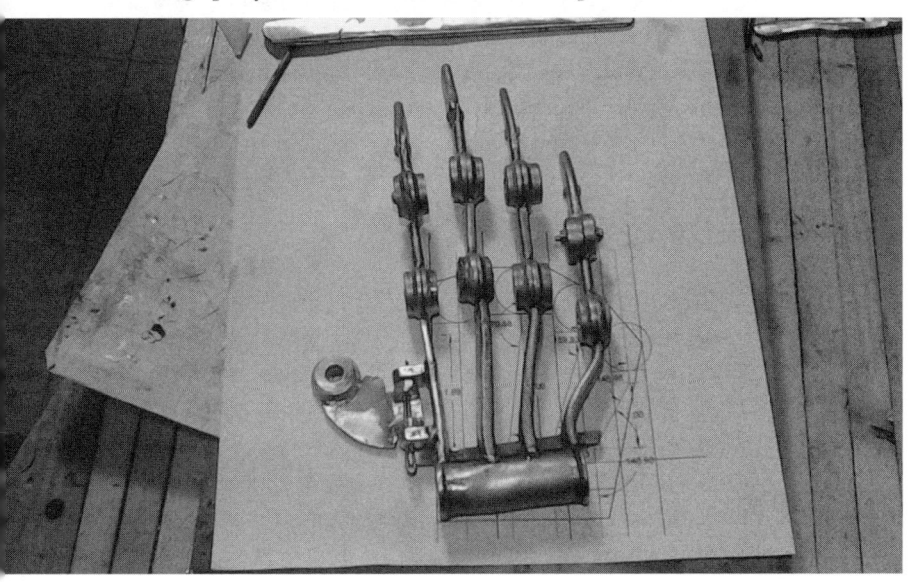

steampunk novels that can be categorized as romance or erotica that contain prosthetics, including Meljean Brook's *Here There Be Monsters* (2010), Sheryl Nantus's *Wild Cards and Iron Horses* (2010), and S. M. Peters's *Whitechapel Gods* (2008).[51] These novels figure the prosthesis as an erotic object, and in many cases, the sex scenes highlight the prosthesis as the source of desire and arousal.[52]

In one such story, published in 2007, "The Steam Dancer (1896)," by Caitlín R. Kiernan, the protagonist, Missouri Banks, wears a prosthetic arm, leg, and eye and performs on stage as an exotic dancer. The story highlights the beauty of her prosthetic parts and eroticizes their materiality:

> She thinks that she has grown to be a very beautiful woman, and sometimes she believes the parts she wasn't born with have only served to make her that much more so and not any the less. Missouri smiles and gazes back at her reflection, admiring the high cheekbones and full lips (which were her mother's before her), the glistening beads of sweat on her chin and forehead and upper lip, the way her left eye pulses with a soft turquoise radiance. Afternoon light glints off the galvanized plating of her mechanical arm, the sculpted steel rods and struts, the well-oiled wheels and cogs, all the rivets and welds and perfectly fitted joints.[53]

When she dances, Missouri feels more alive than if she were only made of flesh: "The piston rods in her left leg pump something more alive than blood, and the flywheels turn on their axels. She is muscle and skin, steel and artifice."[54] The story transforms prosthesis and disability into an eroticization of the beautiful blending of the human body with artfully designed technology: "Other women are only whole, she thinks. Other women are only born, not made. I have been crafted."[55] Even her own desire is tied to her prostheses; in a sex scene with her husband, Missouri feels "his fingertips lingering at the sensitive bolts where her prosthetics attach. She likes that best of all, that faint electric tingle."[56] Significantly, this story pays attention not only to the beauty and erotics of the prosthetic but also to the lived reality of being a prosthetic wearer. When she slips as a result of her prosthetic leg and burns her other leg, Missouri laments having to use crutches to get around while the prosthesis is repaired. But despite the inconvenience, she looks at her legs and sees the fallibility of both of them: "Injured meat and treacherous, unreliable metal. Machines break down, she thinks, and the flesh is weak. *Ain't nothing yet conjured by God nor man won't go and turn against you, sooner or later.*"⁵⁷ This story highlights not only the ways that prostheses can supplement the human body but also the beauty and sensuality of the blended body and machine. In the same way that traditional romance fiction eroticizes the physical body, steampunk romance fiction eroticizes the mechanized body and therefore resists the turn to metaphor found in most steampunk literature.

The fetishization of prosthesis in steampunk romance fiction and steampunk material culture argues for the visibility and even desirability of the technologically enhanced body. The visibility of the steampunk prosthesis, and the idea of dressing up and display (which is a large part of the visual pleasure of attending and participating in steampunk conventions), work in opposition to the general desire to hide or disguise physical disability. However, it is important to note that most steampunk prostheses are not worn by amputees but rather by steampunks who use them as part of their costume when they attend steampunk conventions.⁵⁸ Thus, what is missed in any subversive critique that steampunk fiction and culture mounts against the socially constructed notion of disability is the real intersection of disability and steampunk—that is, when people with disabilities participate in steampunk culture. Although Elsa Sjunneson, Jaymee Goh, and Diane Pho have begun conversations on this issue, it has been otherwise absent from conversations of minority identity, access, and inclusion in steampunk, which usually focus on gender, race, and sexual normativity (especially the problematic notion of assuming nineteenth-century attitudes and prejudices while role-playing).⁵⁹ Theoretically, the steampunk community, with its emphasis on nonconformity, can be a welcoming place for those with disabilities. However, if steampunk is to live up to its ideological nature, then playing at having a disability at a con should go hand in hand with designing a convention experience that is accessible to everyone. When Jaymee Goh surveyed the steampunk community, she was overwhelmed with responses from steampunks who consider themselves disabled describing their positive and negative experiences within the steampunk community.⁶⁰ Goh argues that addressing access should be a priority of steampunk culture. She writes, "Steampunk favours visible technology, and people with physical disabilities can lay claim to that, to raise their own visibility, and assert their right to participate in public spaces without obstacle. . . . Any steampunk revolution must be wheel-chair accessible."⁶¹

If the steampunk revolution is here, then there is a reason why it has found its moment now. Steampunk allows us not only to reimagine the past but also to reconfigure the future. As participants in an alternative history, world-rebuilding genre, steampunks are free to envision the world as it might have become. Indeed, Joshua Tanenbaum, Karen Tanenbaum, and Ron Wakkary consider steampunk as constituting a design fiction that "provides an explicit model for how to physically realize an ideological and imagined world through design practice [and] that the practices of DIY and appropriation that are evident in Steampunk design provide a useful set of design strategies and implications for HCI [human–computer interaction]."[62] With its focus on the material beauty of body and machine, along with the subversive critique it launches at all types of identity politics, steampunk culture is well positioned to redefine standards of normativity and to provide a model of inclusion and accessibility. However, while steampunk fiction and culture bring visibility and desirability to the prosthetic, more critical attention needs to be paid to the lived experience of those who wear prostheses rather than the metaphorical and symbolic meanings they accrue.

NOTES

1. Kirstie Blair cites the source as *The Billy-Cock Hat, New Comic Song, Singing Nightly with Applause and also the following Popular Songs* (London: P. Macdonald, n.d. [1860–63]), Bodleian Library, Harding A777, 1; Kirstie Blair, "'The Steam Arm': Proto-Steampunk Themes in a Victorian Popular Song," *Neo-Victorian Studies* 3, no. 1 (2010): 196-207.
2. *Billy-Cock Hat*.
3. Blair, "Steam Arm," 196.
4. As Rachel A. Bowser and Brian Croxall describe, "The emphasis on technology within steampunk suggests that the genre's popularity says something about our experiences of, unease with, and desires for technology in the present"; "Introduction: Industrial Evolution," *Neo-Victorian Studies* 3, no. 1 (2010): 16.
5. I use the word "accessory" intentionally here; most steampunk prosthetics are designed as accessories to be worn as part of a steampunk costume. For example, prosthetics in *1,000 Steampunk Creations* are included in the category of "Hats and Accessories"; Dr. Grymm [Joey Marsocci] and Barbe Saint John, *1,000 Steampunk Creations: Neo-Victorian Fashion, Gear, and Art* (Beverly, Mass.: Quarry Books, 2011), 202-3.
6. For a more detailed discussion of the much-debated claim that steampunk offers a subversive critique of certain ideologies, see Diana M. Pho's "Punking

the Other: On the Performance of Racial and National Identities in Steampunk" and Mike Perschon's "Seminal Steampunk: Proper and True," this volume.

7. Steffen Hantke, "Difference Engines and Other Infernal Devices: History According to Steampunk," *Extrapolation* 40, no. 3 (Fall 1999): 251.

8. Catherine Siemann, "Some Notes on the Steampunk Social Problem," in *Steaming into a Victorian Future: A Steampunk Anthology*, ed. Julie Anne Taddeo and Cynthia J. Miller (Lanham, Md.: Scarecrow Press, 2013), 6, 7, 9, 10.

9. Roger Whitson, "How to Theorize with a Hammer; or, Making and Baking Things in Steampunk and the Digital Humanities," this volume.

10. Paul Di Filippo, *Victoria* (1991), in *Steampunk*, ed. Ann VanderMeer and Jeff VanderMeer (San Francisco: Tachyon, 2008), 263.

11. Ian MacLeod, "The Giving Mouth" (1991), in *Steampunk*, ed. Ann VanderMeer and Jeff VanderMeer (San Francisco: Tachyon, 2008), 58.

12. Melissa Kent, "The Heart Is the Matter" (2012), *Steampunk III: Steampunk Revolution*, ed. Ann VanderMeer (San Francisco: Tachyon, 2012), 69.

13. Ibid., 73.

14. Nick Mamatas, "Arbeitskraft" (2012), in VanderMeer, *Steampunk III*, 121.

15. Lev Grossman, "Sir Ranulph Wykeham-Rackham, GBE, a.k.a. Roboticus the All-Knowing" (2011), in VanderMeer, *Steampunk III*, 57.

16. Ibid., 60.

17. While these short stories clearly engage with questions about how to define humanness when the body can be adapted and transformed by technology, a significant number of steampunk stories simply feature prosthetics as a representation of the mechanical world the characters inhabit rather than as a central theme. For example, in Cherie Priest's *Boneshaker* (New York: Tor, 2009), Lucy O'Gunning uses her clockwork arm and hand to lend a literal and figurative helping hand to the protagonist, Briar Blue, but the prosthetic plays no larger role in the story.

18. *Wild Wild West*, directed by Barry Sonnenfeld (1999; Burbank, Calif.: Warner Home Video, 1999), DVD; *Steamboy*, directed by Katsuhiro Otomo (2004; Culver City, Calif.: Sony Pictures Triumph Films, 2004), DVD.

19. *Casshern*, directed by Kazuaki Kiriya (2004; Tokyo: Casshern Film Partners, 2007), DVD.

20. For a discussion of the term "narrative prosthesis," see David T. Mitchell and Sharon L. Snyder, "Introduction: Disability Studies and the Double Bind of Representation," in *The Body and Physical Difference: Discourses of Disability*, ed. David T. Mitchell and Sharon L. Snyder (Ann Arbor: University of Michigan Press, 1997), 1–5, 47–64.

21. Rosemarie Garland-Thomson, *Extraordinary Bodies: Figuring Physical Disability in American Culture and Literature* (New York: Columbia University Press 1997), 7.

22. Ibid., 46.

23. Rosemarie Garland-Thomson, foreword to *Victorian Freaks: The Social Context of Freakery in Britain*, ed. Marlene Tromp (Columbus: Ohio State University Press, 2008), ix–xi.

24. Jennifer Esmail and Christopher Keep, "Victorian Disability: Introduction," *Victorian Review* 35, no. 2 (Fall 2009): 47.

25. Ibid.

26. There were charitable bodies for the blind, the "deaf and dumb," "lunatics," "idiots," "epileptics," and "the deformed." See "The Daily Life of Disabled People in Victorian England—Community, School and Charity," *Historic England*, http://historicengland.org.uk; see also Martha Stoddard Holmes, "Working (with) the Rhetoric of Affliction: Autobiographical Narratives of Victorians with Physical Disabilities," in *Embodied Rhetorics: Disability in Language and Culture*, ed. James C. Wilson and Cynthia Lewiecki-Wilson (Carbondale: Southern Illinois University Press, 2001), 27-44.

27. Hunter Oatman-Stanford, "War and Prosthetics: How Veterans Fought for the Perfect Artificial Limb," *Collectors Weekly* (blog), October 29, 2012, http://www.collectorsweekly.com/; see also Vanessa Warne, "'To Invest a Cripple with Peculiar Interest': Artificial Legs and Upper-Class Amputees at Mid-Century," *Victorian Review* 35, no. 2 (Fall 2009): 83-100.

28. David D. Yuan, "Disfigurement and Reconstruction in Oliver Wendell Holmes's 'The Human Wheel, Its Spokes and Felloes,'" in *The Body and Physical Difference: Discourses of Disability*, ed. David T. Mitchell and Sharon L. Snyder (Ann Arbor: University of Michigan Press, 1997), 71.

29. Ibid., 71-72.

30. Erin O'Connor, *Raw Material: Producing Pathology in Victorian Culture* (Durham, N.C.: Duke University Press, 2000), 7.

31. Warne, "To Invest a Cripple," 84.

32. Adrienne E. Gavin, "Dickens, Wegg, and Wooden Legs," *Our Mutual Friend: The Scholarly Pages* (Santa Cruz: Dickens Project, 1998), http://omf.ucsc.edu/.

33. Ryan Sweet, "Our Mutual Friend," *Nineteenth-Century Disability: Cultures and Contexts*, http://www.nineteenthcenturydisability.org.

34. Henry Ford, *My Life and Work* (New York: Doubleday, 1923), 108, quoted in Sarah S. Jain, "The Prosthetic Imagination: Enabling and Disabling the Prosthesis Trope," *Science, Technology, and Human Values*, 24, no. 1 (Winter 1999): 34.

35. Lennard J. Davis, "Nude Venuses, Medusa's Body, and Phantom Limbs: Disability and Visuality," *The Body and Physical Difference: Discourses of Disability*, ed. David T. Mitchell and Sharon L. Snyder (Ann Arbor: University of Michigan Press, 1997), 54.

36. Charles Babbage, *On the Economy of Machinery and Manufactures* (1832; repr., Fairfield, N.J.: Augustus M. Kelly, 1986), 35-36, quoted in Tamara Ketabgian, *The Lives of Machines: The Industrial Imagination in Victorian Literature and Culture* (Ann Arbor: University of Michigan Press, 2011), 32.

37. See Ketabgian, *Lives of Machines*, 17-46.

38. Marx argued that rather than workers using tools, the factory's monstrous machinery uses the workers "who are incorporated into it as its living appendages"; Jessica Kuskey, *The Body Machinic: Technology, Labor, and Mechanized Bodies in Victorian Culture* (PhD diss., Syracuse University, 2012), 54, *Syracuse University Surface*, http://surface.syr.edu/.

39. As N. Katherine Hayles describes, the body is "the original prosthesis we all learn to manipulate, so that extending or replacing of body parts with other prosthetic devices becomes the continuation of a process that began before we were born"; *How We Became Posthuman: Virtual Bodies in Cybernetics, Literature, and Informatics* (Chicago: University of Chicago Press, 1999), 3.

40. Herbert Sussman and Gerhard Joseph, "Prefiguring the Posthuman: Dickens and Prosthesis," *Victorian Literature and Culture* 32, no. 2 (2004): 618.

41. See Whitson, "How to Theorize with a Hammer."

42. Bowser and Croxall, "Introduction: Industrial Evolution," 16.

43. Rebecca Onion, "Reclaiming the Machine: An Introductory Look at Steampunk in Everyday Practice," *Neo-Victorian Studies* 1, no. 1 (2008): 149.

44. The cyborg, as Donna Haraway describes, is "a hybrid of machine and organism, a creature of social reality as well as a creature of fiction"; Donna Haraway, "A Cyborg Manifesto: Science, Technology, and Socialist-Feminism in the Late Twentieth Century," in *The Haraway Reader*, ed. Donna Haraway (New York: Routledge, 2004), 7. The figure of the cyborg haunts much contemporary fiction and film and represents the same set of concerns about the merging of humans and technology, specifically the fear that we will be unable to define what is human (which is indeed a central thread of steampunk short stories) and about the possibility that we will lose control of the technology that we have integrated into our lives and our bodies (as we saw in "The Steam Arm"). One way this fear is manifested is the idea that the cyborg moves among us unseen: equipped with microtechnologies, implanted devices, and prosthetics that can pass for human limbs under clothing, cyborgs "are everywhere and they are invisible"; Hayles, *How We Became Posthuman*, 12.

45. Catastrophone Orchestra and Arts Collective, "What, Then, Is Steampunk? Colonizing the Past So We Can Dream the Future," *SteamPunk Magazine* 1 (March 2007): 4.

46. Garland-Thomson, *Extraordinary Bodies*, 22–24.

47. Disability studies warns us to be careful of the supercrip myth, however. As Rosemarie Garland-Thomson writes, the supercrip is a rhetorical mode deployed as a way to frame disability: "The supercrip ... amazes and inspires the viewer by performing feats that the nondisabled viewer cannot imagine doing.... By making the disabled figure exceptional rather than ordinary, the wondrous can estrange viewer from viewed and attenuate the correspondence that equality requires"; "The Politics of Staring: Visual Rhetorics of Disability in Popular Photography," *Disability Studies: Enabling the Humanities*, ed. Sharon L. Snyder, Brenda Jo Brueggemann, and Rosemarie Garland-Thomson (New York: MLA, 2002), 61. After amputee Oscar Pistorius was accused of murdering his girlfriend, his loss as a hero in the world of disability led many to redeploy the supercrip narrative, figuring him as a lost hero or alternatively as a dangerous cyborg gone rogue; see Leslie Swartz, "Oscar Pistorius and the Melancholy of Intersectionality," *Disability and Society* 28, no. 8 (2013): 1157–58, http://doi.org/10.1080/09687 599.2013.808085.

48. Joseph Robert Lewis, "Steampunk Prosthetics: Rebuilding Our Humanity,"

Xerposa, June 2012, http://xerposa.com/5881/steampunk-prosthetics-rebuilding-our-humanity (site discontinued).

49. Whitson, "How to Theorize with a Hammer."

50. AtificerMade [Christopher Bright], "Steampunk Prosthetic Hand for a Wounded Warrior [Now More Pics]," *Instructables*, http://www.instructables.com/.

51. Heather Massey, "Amazing and Bizarre Prosthetics in Steampunk Romance," *Heroes and Heartbreakers* (blog), March 7, 2012, http://www.heroesandheartbreakers.com/.

52. For a detailed discussion of the different ways technology features in steampunk romance, see Dru Pagliassoti, "Technology and Human Relationships in Steampunk Romance," in Taddeo and Miller, *Steaming into a Victorian Future*, 65–87.

53. Caitlin R. Kiernan, "The Steam Dancer (1896)" (2007), in *Steampunk II: Steampunk Reloaded*, ed. Ann VanderMeer and Jeff VanderMeer (San Francisco: Tachyon, 2010), 68.

54. Ibid., 70.

55. Ibid., 68.

56. Ibid., 74.

57. Ibid., 72, emphasis in original.

58. The idea that steampunk prosthetics are props for steampunk costuming and role-playing invokes the ethically troubling notion of playing at having a disability and ignores the very real obstacles people with those actual disabilities face. Elsa Sjunneson writes about steampunk and disability: "Ableism isn't just about using words like 'cripple'; it isn't just about how the bulk of able-bodied society assumes that we are all helpless; it's also about taking disability and acting like it is a cool thing that we can just take off at the end of the day"; "A Word about Eyepatches: A Personal Essay," *Beyond Victoriana* (blog), June 12, 2011, http://beyondvictoriana.com.

59. Both Jaymee Goh and Diana M. Pho write about issues of diversity and inclusion on their blogs, *Silver Goggles* (http://silver-goggles.blogspot.com/) and *Beyond Victoriana* (http://beyondvictoriana.com/), respectively.

60. For more on the types of barriers people with disabilities face within steampunk culture and as attendees at steampunk conventions, see Jaymee Goh, "With This Steam Powered Prosthetic Arm I Could Be as Strong as . . . a Normal Person," *Tor.com* (blog), October 28, 2009, http://www.tor.com/.

61. Jaymee Goh, "From Airships of Imagination to Feet on the Ground," in VanderMeer, *Steampunk III*, 395.

62. Joshua Tanenbaum, Karen Tanenbaum, and Ron Wakkary, "Steampunk as Design Fiction," in *CHI: Conference on Human Factors in Computing Systems 2012 Proceedings* (2012), 1583. See also http://www.bespokeinnovations.com/content/gallery for examples of prosthetics inspired by steampunk and other aesthetics.

The Aesthete, the Dandy, and the Steampunk; or, Things as They Are Now

STEFANIA FORLINI

> A virtual past is the best we can hope for.
> —HAYDEN WHITE, *The Fiction of Narrative: Essays on History, Literature, and Theory, 1957–2007*

> Like seeds around which an elaborate crystal can suddenly congeal, things in a supersaturated cultural solution can crystallize ways of thinking, feeling, and acting. These thickenings of significance are one way that things can be made to talk.
> —LORRAINE DATSON, *Things That Talk: Object Lessons from Art and Science*

In the second issue of *SteamPunk Magazine,* photographer and designer of wearable art Libby Bulloff and illustrator Colin Foran suggest possible modes of dress for different types of steampunks.[1] Although Bulloff emphasizes that her designs are meant to incite the imaginations of readers (and not to prescribe specific steampunk identities or sartorial codes), her designs nonetheless embody some of the key values of steampunk as it is defined in the pages of this magazine of steampunk "Lifestyle, Mad Science, Theory & Fiction." The Tinkerer/Inventor's "utilitarian garb," complete with "protective eyewear," is meant to accommodate his love of experimenting with technology and science; the Street Urchin/Chimney Sweep's style is "the most 'punk' of steampunk" and "nods smugly to the lowest classes of Victorian and steam society"; the Explorer is characterized by tailored military-influenced garments and flying goggles that speak to her preparedness to explore unknown worlds; and perhaps most interestingly, the Dandy/Aesthete flags steampunk's commitment to aesthetics more explicitly than any of the other styles.[2] Bulloff and Foran's representations of the steampunk dandy/aesthete work to dissociate the figure from its aristocratic roots, reinventing it as a representative of what Bulloff calls "anachrotechnofetishism."[3] For Bulloff, the steampunk dandies/aesthetes are "simply pretending to be high-class, whilst cloaking their absinthe addictions with heavy perfumes and flamboyant gestures." She imagines "fellows in nicely rendered Victorian and Edwardian suits, brainstorming infernal devices over cigars and brandy, and . . . ladies in high-button boots who dabble as terrorists when they aren't knitting mittens."[4] Clearly there is more to the dandy/aesthete than meets the eye: she embodies one of the seemingly more problematic aspects of steampunk.

As is often repeated in the pages of *SteamPunk Magazine* and elsewhere, steampunk is an aesthetic, but as some of the magazine's contributors are quick to add, it is not just an aesthetic. It is apparent that some contributors worry that too much emphasis on the aesthetic aspects of steampunk would be mistaken for mere nostalgia, neo-Victorianism, or,

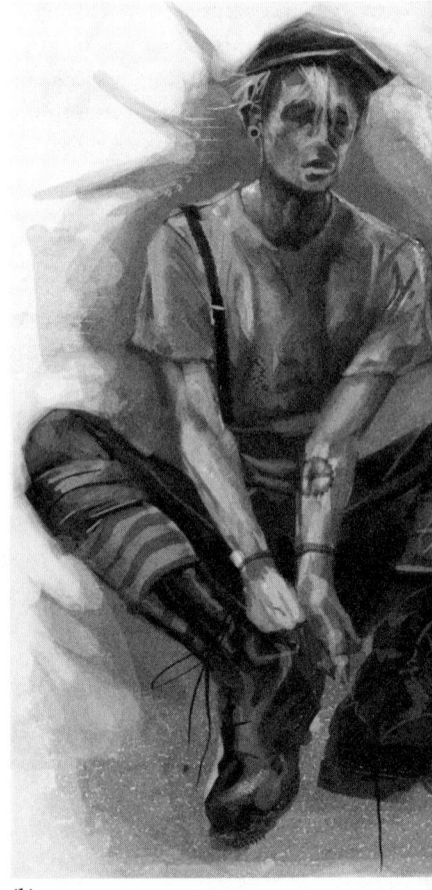

(a) (b)

worse, an easily imitated and co-opted look. Other contributors, however, remain adamant that even if the steampunk aesthetic seems to be a thing of surfaces, and even if the look is being co-opted by mainstream culture, "aesthetics have power" nonetheless.[5] The ambivalence about aesthetics and whether or not they can be radical (to borrow Isobel Armstrong's term) is what I explore here by considering the dandy/aesthete in both Victorian and steampunk contexts. It is this tension between aesthetics

FIGURES 5.1. These illustrations by Colin Foran first appeared in the second issue of *SteamPunk Magazine* (2007) and showcase selected steampunk personalities, including the (a) "Tinkerer/Inventor," (b) "Street Urchin/Chimney Sweep," (c) "Explorer," and (d) "Dandy/Aesthete." Images reproduced with the kind permission of Colin Foran.

(c)　　　　　　　　　　　　　　　　　　　　　　　　(d)

and politics that I hope to explore more closely in light of the recent renewed interest in aesthetics.[6] If the dandy/aesthete is a contradictory figure then as now (particularly in its complex relationship to industrialism, consumerism, and political activism), it is nonetheless a compelling one that continues to attract critical attention[7] and is often specifically invoked in the steampunk imagination.

Even before Bulloff and Foran suggested the dandy/aesthete as part of the steampunk zeitgeist, the Catastrophone Orchestra and Arts Collective's steampunk manifesto, featured in the first issue of *SteamPunk Magazine,* situated steampunks as "stand[ing] with the traitors of the past"—traitors that include "aesthete dandies."[8] Bruce Sterling, co-author with William Gibson of *The Difference Engine* (1990), perhaps the best-known example of steampunk fiction, traces steampunk to John Ruskin, the Pre-Raphaelite Brotherhood, William Morris, and Aubrey Beardsley in his "User's Guide to Steampunk."[9] In the May 2013 issue of *SteamPunk Magazine,* one contributor explicitly reclaims Oscar Wilde, the best-known aesthete dandy, for steampunk. James H. Carrott argues that of all Victorians, Oscar Wilde would best appreciate steampunk attempts to "punk the past."[10] The article begins with an epigraph from Wilde: "The past, the present, and the future are but one moment. Time and space, succession and extension, are merely accidental conditions of thought. The imagination can transcend them." After a brief discussion of Wilde's own life, the article concludes with a quotation that (anachronistically) shows Wilde's inner steampunk: "Our one duty to the past," Wilde writes, "is to rewrite it."[11]

Although both contemporary steampunk and Victorian aestheticism have been accused of superficial self-indulgence in needless ornamentation, both movements nonetheless attempt to make beauty political and to call attention to the materiality of things and their existence in complex economies of meaning and value. When Wilde and other aesthetes famously proclaimed that "all art is quite useless" and that the most useful things are "ugly," they emphatically objected to the standards by which their culture assigned value.[12] Steampunks similarly object to contemporary standards of value by attempting to recover an appreciation for the beauty and materiality of things, which are easily overlooked in this age of ephemeral information and fast-paced consumption of mass-produced, disposable goods. By examining popular Victorian representations of the aesthetes, alongside the self-conscious attempts of steampunks to define themselves and their movement through a materialist aesthetic, I will examine what is at stake in steampunk and its invocation of Victorian-era aestheticism. Both movements emphasize embodied modes of knowledge as they attempt to navigate a difficult line between popularizing beauty and feeding into the consumerism they hope to critique. What becomes apparent is that for steampunks, as for Victorian aesthetes, bodies and identities are fully enmeshed with material things in complex and provocative ways that not only challenge the tendency in Western thought to separate people from things[13] but also help confirm some of the most important insights of the material turn in the humanities.[14]

The Importance of Seeing Things as They Are Not

During the Great Exhibition at the Crystal Palace in 1851, Britain, "the workshop of the world," put on display the products of industry from around the globe. Although critics have often looked to the 1851 exhibit as exemplifying commodity culture and its culture of display (famously described by Guy Debord), Elaine Freedgood has suggested that it may be time to revise this compelling narrative. She argues that if one considers the range of things displayed (everything from oats to objects of interior decor) and the fact that "after long debate, price tags were banned" from the exhibit, this same exhibit also speaks of the possibility that Victorians had alternative object relations that were obscured by the emergence of commodity culture.[15] Freedgood argues that although "the most influential criticism of Victorian commodity culture relies on" the idea that somewhere around the mid-nineteenth century the commodity "completes its colonization of social life," that colonization is unlikely to have been as totalizing, as critics have suggested.[16] Freedgood proposes that a Victorian "thing culture" competed with and was ultimately obscured by commodity culture and that "other kinds of object relations . . . may have preceded and survived it."[17] For Freedgood, "the process of commodification—abstraction, alienation, and spectacularization—were achieved . . . slowly rather than suddenly, unevenly rather than consistently or finally."[18] In other words, if all critics see in the Great Exhibition are commodities on display, it is in part because of our own immersion in commodity culture; just as we may have misconstrued the range of Victorian object relations, so also we may be overlooking alternative object relations in our own time.

Following Freedgood, we could imagine the Great Exhibition "as the emblematic and epic face-off between thing and commodity culture," noting that even if the Great Exhibition indulged in spectacular display, there was also "a significant showing of the mundane, the everyday, the distinctly and perhaps definitely unspectacular," and that based on the Great Exhibition catalog and the large body of nineteenth-century literature about processes of industrial production, Victorians likely had significantly different relations to things that are not easily intelligible to those immersed in commodity culture.[19] Freedgood calls on us to be open to allowing for "residual or resistant modes of object relating in commodity culture," both then and now.[20] This means becoming attentive to the ways that material things are not necessarily abstracted into the commodity fetishism famously described by Marx. I suggest that one of the "residual or resistant modes of object relating" can be found in the materialist aesthetics of both the aesthetes and the steampunks.

Although accounts of aestheticism do not typically begin with the Great Exhibition, it is nonetheless important to note that the Exhibition helped shape aesthetic sensibilities and may have inadvertently spurred some aesthetes to action. In introducing wide segments of the population to many examples of "craftsmanship and technical sophistication" from around the world, Charlotte Gere argues that the Exhibition helped spread the "interest in the arrangement and embellishment of the home" from "within a cultured and moneyed elite into the prosperous—and increasingly influential—middle-classes."[21] If the Great Exhibition helped promote an interest in the beautiful interior, however, it did so in a roundabout way for some—not because it displayed and invited attentiveness to beauty in everyday life but rather because it displayed and helped spread ugliness and thus spurred some aesthetes to help remedy the situation. The comments of both William Morris and Oscar Wilde on the Great Exhibition are telling in this respect. William Morris "remarked to his mother that it was all 'wonderfully ugly.'"[22] Ten years later, he would help found the design firm Morris, Marshall, Faulkner & Co. and display his beautiful things at the 1862 Exhibition. Oscar Wilde claimed, "The public clung with really pathetic tenacity to what I believe were the direct traditions of the Great Exhibition of international vulgarity, traditions that were so appalling that the houses in which people lived were only fit for blind people to live in. Beautiful things began to be made, beautiful colours came from the dyer's hand, beautiful patterns from the artist's brain, and the use of beautiful things and their value and importance were set forth."[23] Of course, the interest in the house beautiful is but one facet of aestheticism, which became increasingly associated not only with art for art's sake but also with the idea that one should dedicate one's life to art and beauty, especially strange beauty. Despite the socialist leanings of some of its most important figures, it is not difficult to see how aestheticism would become associated with elitism and wrapped up in a consumer culture that depends on the pleasures of consumption.[24] In fact, even in their own time the aesthetes came to be associated with a deviant kind of materialism.

For instance, throughout the 1870s and 1880s, *Punch* cartoons invariably depict the aesthete as a physically depleted person engrossed in the aesthetic contemplation of a beautiful object and neglecting other forms of sustenance such as food or contact with the outside world (Figures 5.2 and 5.3). In these and in all other cases, the aesthetes have dark circles under their eyes and often look emaciated or exhausted, as if consumed by their consumption of beautiful things. By the end of the century, in all seriousness, physician Max Nordau reads the aesthetes' attraction to things as symptomatic of the degeneration that he believes threatens all of civilization. His notorious and widely disseminated study, *Degeneration,* begins with a chapter entitled "The Symptoms," in which he lists articles of clothing, fashion accessories, objects of interior decor, and forms of aesthetic entertainment.[25] In very different kinds of publications (the satirical periodical *Punch* and the pseudomedical treatise *Degeneration*), the aesthetes are noted for what we might call, borrowing a phrase from Scott Herring, "aberrant object conduct," but it is not entirely clear what exactly might be at stake in their material deviance[26] and/or their intense acts of aesthetic contemplation until we situate the aesthetes' object practices in what Gillian Beer famously called the open fields of Victorian knowledge.[27]

Although the aesthetes have been known to upset a few normative social boundaries, many critics have read the aesthetes' object practices as ultimately implicated in the rise of consumer culture, which emphasizes and promotes the pleasure of consumption as an end in itself.[28] As convincing as such arguments continue to be, however, if we keep Freedgood's suggestion of a Victorian thing culture in mind, I argue that the aesthetes offer one opportunity to glimpse alternative object relations ultimately obscured by our own immersion in commodity culture. The aesthete's materialism is inflected with scientific discourses that helped to keep this thing culture alive for the aesthetes, effectively interfering with the abstraction of things inherent in Marx's commodity fetishism.[29] Aestheticism (although it arguably helped produce and was co-opted by the consumer culture it sought to critique) was key in

FIGURES 5.2 AND 5.3. Two illustrations from *Punch* magazine that showcase aesthetic appreciation as an aberrant object practice: "An Æsthetic Midday Meal" (1880, left) and "What It Has Come To" (1881, right).

WHAT IT HAS COME TO.

Mrs. Muggles. "Well, Doctor, I don't know as what's the matter with Marier since she come from her last Siterwation in Lunnon. There she sits all Day a-staring at an old Chiney Dish, which she calls a-going in for *Asthletix!*"

promoting aesthetic experience as a mode of embodied knowledge that promoted contact with the alterity of things.

If aestheticism and the aesthetes have been seen as apolitical and even solipsistic, it is in part because of their insistence on artistic freedom (art for art's sake was meant to free art from the constraints of morality, utility, and the marketplace) and because of their intense sensual indulgence. In paying so much attention to things, they seem to be prime examples of what Freedgood calls "the bad materialism of commodity culture."[30] However, if we consider the ways that aesthetes based their understanding of aesthetic experience on physiological processes as they were then understood, we can see that aesthetes might be placed among writers (including Dickens and Marx) that Freedgood argues did not see materialism as bad but that rather made "profound arguments for the problematic disconnection between subjects and objects, the ways in which industrial culture makes it difficult for human beings to know things and to know each other by or through things."[31] In effect paying attention to things, especially their material qualities and their impact on the material body, the aesthetes' materialism becomes a kind of resistance to the abstractions of commodity fetishism. For the aesthetes, I argue that attentiveness to things (and their sensual properties) is political precisely because it involves a self-conscious regulation of the senses to attend to the very properties that literally connect us to things—and remind us that we are made of the same stuff (matter). Some of the key theorists of aesthetic experience of the time emphatically promoted certain ways of perceiving and interacting with the material environment (which involved both the regulation of the senses and certain kinds of object practices) often viewed by others as aberrant but ultimately resisting normalized object relations based on utility and productivity.

When Walter Pater infamously invited his readers to "burn always with [a] hard, gem-like flame," some readers believed that he was advocating for a life of sensual intensity and pleasure—hence the controversy and subsequent removal of the conclusion from the second edition of *The Renaissance*.[32] However, it is important to consider that Pater's controversial conclusion was embedded within a particular critical project that depended, and indeed insisted, on the attentive regulation of the senses through its interactions with beautiful things. As I have argued elsewhere, if Pater seems to emphasize that each one of us experiences a "whirlpool" of impressions and that "each mind [keeps] as a solitary prisoner in its own dream of a world," his perspective is nonetheless grounded in scientific understanding, as other critics have also noted.[33] He remains self-conscious of what the physiologically based psychology of his time was showing empirically: that all experience is mediated through the senses and the nervous matter (brain and nervous system) of our bodies.[34] As Pater shows in his 1885 historical novel, *Marius, the Epicurean* (intended to explain more clearly the potentially misleading conclusion), the training of the senses through commerce with beautiful things is meant to help the individual explore different modes of being in the world.

The conclusion that appears at the end of a work of impressionistic criticism, for which Pater is now famous, belies a materialist impulse that is part of a larger empirical project that governed many different branches of knowledge in the nineteenth century, as Pater himself acknowledges. In the preface to the same work, Pater announces that his critical project is indebted to both John Ruskin and Matthew Arnold. Pater explicitly invokes a long critical tradition and its empirical impulse by echoing Ruskin's suggestion in *The Stones of Venice* (1851) that the critic must be like "a chemist" and work to see into "the depth of things" and by reiterating Arnold's 1864 suggestion that the aim of all criticism (and indeed the aim of all branches of knowledge, including aesthetic knowledge) is "to see the object as in itself it really is."[35] For Pater, "seeing the object as in itself it really is" becomes knowing one's neurologically mediated impressions as they really are—something that probably leads Wilde to claim years later in "The Critic as Artist" (1891) that the "primary aim of the critic is to see the object as in itself it really is not."[36] Wilde, much like Pater, understands aesthetic experience as a fundamentally embodied one, perhaps best exemplified in the character of Dorian Gray, who cultivates a temperament of openness to influence, including the influence of beautiful things. Douglas Mao, in his study on the Victorian belief in the healthful benefits of aesthetic environments, convincingly reconstructs the history of Victorian aesthetic thought to show how it becomes bound up in physiological understandings of the impact of environmental stimuli on the development of individuals.[37]

Although Mao does not consider the work of Vernon Lee (Violet Paget, 1856-1935), a well-respected intellectual and disciple of Pater, Lee's work theorizes aesthetic experience in even more explicitly materialistic terms and is thus worth examining more closely. Working within a complex field of physiological aesthetics,[38] Lee emphasizes how our interactions with things shape not only individuals but also the human species as a whole. A self-described evolutionist, Lee hypothesizes that the aesthetic sense evolved from the habitual making and shaping of things as simple as arrowheads, and that the very practice of aesthetic perception connects us not only with the aesthetic memories of the human race but also with our own lifetime of weaving "between ourselves and the things which surround us" numerous "webs of association" that remain recorded in our nervous systems and continue to connect us to our material environments and imbue our everyday lives with meaning and pleasure.[39] Well before French biologist François Jacob would suggest that evolution "behaves like a tinkerer who, during eons upon eons, would slowly modify his work, unceasingly retouching it,"[40] given the materials and opportunities that happen to present themselves, Lee recognized that the process of interacting with the material environment was a profoundly transformative one—that part of what humans crafted when they crafted things was themselves. We make and are made by our things. But Lee goes even further. She argues that our aesthetic instinct is an evolutionary achievement that primes us for ethical behavior by creating in us an openness to otherness. Indeed, for Lee, the process of aesthetic perception (the intense engagement with beautiful things ridiculed in *Punch* and diagnosed in *Degeneration*) is an embodied, active engagement with alternative "modes of being" through which we "live . . . the life of all things" and feel ourselves "consubstantial with the universe."[41] The aesthetic experience is an experience of equalization in which we recognize our connectedness to human and nonhuman others with whom we share a common substance: matter.[42]

For Lee, evolution and life in increasingly urbanized centers have trained us to respond quickly and increasingly automatically to our material environment, but beautiful things are those that can arrest our attention and give us pause to discern more carefully—to engage more critically and more creatively with our material environments and thus avoid what she calls "the dangers of over rapid and uncritical inference."[43] As with Pater, the aesthetic project is tied into a critical one that insists on embodied knowledge and is ultimately tied to developing ethical ways of being in the world.

This larger field of scientifically inflected aesthetic thought complicates the view of aesthetes as commodity fetishists and accomplished (and/or deviant) consumers. Certainly for Lee, who was finely attuned to the implications of evolutionary theories, the embodied interaction with the material world (its environments and objects) is no sterile, solipsistic moment of consumption; rather, it is an inherently productive interface in which humans participated in the making of themselves and the fashioning of the future of the species. For Lee, the aesthetes engaged in intense contemplation of beautiful things are not consuming so much as they are producing—producing themselves and an openness to otherness. Although we glimpse here an old tradition that seeks to associate the beautiful and the good as well as a nineteenth-century tradition of believing in the humanizing powers of art in the face of industrialization, for the aesthetes, with their finely tuned sense of the possible transformations elicited by things, art was not meant to preserve us so much as to help us continue becoming human through the aesthetic commerce with things.

The Matter of Steampunk

In one of her earliest works on aesthetics, Lee claimed that beautiful things speak to everyone in the same language of form, a language our senses have slowly evolved to appreciate through repeated acts of perception and making. Lee claims that this universal language of form is part of the pleasure beauty gives, but even beyond this democratic vision of aesthetics, Lee sees things (even everyday things like doors and chairs) speaking to us in other ways as well, through what she calls "a half-articulate and irrational language," a "mumble-jumble language" that she believes is "more dear to us than all the eloquence and poetry which our soul hears from a great work of art."[44] Such a view of the "eloquence" of things can only come about because for Lee every act of perception leaves its traces in the very materiality of our bodies, and as such, every new perception calls up and renews earlier aesthetic experiences already recorded in our neurological pathways, thus linking each aesthetic experience to previous ones across a lifetime but also across our species' history—a kind a pleasurable, interminable reverberating haunting. When she claims that things speak, she means that they speak through us, through our bodies as they elicit sensations and perceptions, playing us like instruments.[45]

If things speak, it must be said that what Victorian things may have said to Victorians (or what they may say to us, for that matter) remains as multifarious as it is ultimately unknowable. Not only would every human being have developed over the course of her own lifetime (through her very specific combination of embodied experiences) her own unique "half articulate language," as Lee's theory suggests, but also discursive formations and technological networks help shape (and are shaped by) everyday experiences in ways that, as N. Katherine Hayles has shown, fundamentally alter our embodied experiences and cognitive and affective development.[46] In engaging with the aesthetes and their dandyism of the senses, I have presented a speculative but historically plausible interpretation of what things may have meant to the aesthetes, and as we turn our attention to the steampunk dandy/aesthete, I will highlight some parallels while also necessarily acknowledging the many differences that separate us from historically distant Victorian texts and contexts.[47] Ultimately I hope to cultivate a sense of historical relativity in order to engage critically (and self-consciously) with the changing (that is, historically specific) meanings of material things, and indeed of matter and materialism itself.

If the Victorian aesthetes adapted scientific materialism to understand and cultivate their relationships to things and to demonstrate forms of value not encompassed in the exchange value of commodity culture, steampunk aesthetes adapt a kind of craft materialism to combat what they see as a pervasive devaluation of materiality inherent in the hyperconsumption of disposable goods and the "airy" technologies of the digital age.[48] Even as steampunks feel the weight of the growing wreckage of disposed things that threatens environmental sustainability in the era of planned obsolescence, they deplore the loss of "physical culture" that comes with digital media and the apparent dematerialization of technology as it tends toward "invisibility."[49] If, as Rebecca Onion has persuasively argued, steampunks attempt to "re-access what they see as the affective value of the material world of the nineteenth century," it is because they seek to fight what they perceive as the depreciation of materiality with a new kind of materialism that emphasizes the affective qualities and what one steampunk calls "the inherent dignity of created objects."[50] As I hope to show, steampunks strive to cultivate certain kinds of object practices (making, tinkering, repurposing, experimenting) specifically intent on defamiliarizing normalized object practices in order to displace "disposable culture" with a craft culture and "the overly analytical abstractness of cybernetics" with "machines we can see, feel, and fear."[51] Using Freedgood's terms, we might say that steampunks seek to rediscover the object relations and alternative modes of value of thing culture to help combat what they see as some of the most disturbing ongoing trends of the present commodity culture. But steampunks are not only seeking examples of alternative object relations; they are also actively promoting them through making. As Roger Whitson argues, steampunk making can be read as an exercise in critical theory, a way of moving toward alternative object relations and "alternative relationships between humans and technology"; it is a form of speculative design that looks to the past and its science fiction to model and build possible futures.[52] This means that, as with many Victorian aesthetes, the aesthetic project is simultaneously a critical one.

SteamPunk Magazine is powered by a grassroots community led by retrofuturists who draw from the "moth-eaten tomes of forgotten possibilities" the inspiration to model and build a future alternative to the rather bleak ones promised by contemporary unsustainable practices.[53] In a sense, steampunks work toward discovering what Hayden White has referred to as the "utility" of the past for the present.[54] As it is defined in the steampunk manifesto of *SteamPunk Magazine*'s inaugural issue, steampunk is an explicitly political "aesthetic technological movement" and "vibrant and viable philosophy or culture."[55] Steampunks reenvision the past "with the hypertechnological perceptions of the present," but they are not faithful to either the past or the present as they "stand with the traitors of the past as [they] hatch impossible treasons against [their] present."[56] Clearly committed to moving steampunk beyond its origins as a subset of science fiction, the manifesto claims that steampunk embraces the kind of creative license that steampunk writers took with an imagined Victorian past but insists on putting this creative license to use in the real world where it can perform some cultural/political work. This involves not only bringing steampunk "off the page" but also, as editor Margaret P. Ratt insists, off-line—to make imaginative engagement with the past a means of intervening in the present and future: "rebuilding yesterday to ensure our tomorrow."[57] But this imaginative engagement is necessarily materially instantiated. As Ratt states in the introductory note, "Along with the death of physical media comes the death of physical culture," and it is precisely the "physical nature of SteamPunk" that is valued. It must be off-line because it is the loss of material culture and the loss of respect for "the concrete reality of technology" that steampunks oppose.[58] They are fighting with their own specific kind of materialism the devaluation of materiality at the basis of both disposable culture and the digital age.

That the manifesto defines the movement as targeting technology specifically is not surprising because technology and its commodification are in part driving what they perceive as the loss of "physical culture" and because technology is what historically has helped us make things. However, the movement (at least according to *SteamPunk Magazine*'s manifesto) is emphatically "a non-luddite critique of technology" because it does not reject technology altogether.[59] Instead, it opposes certain kinds of technology and technological design: "the overly analytical abstractness of cybernetics" and "the airy intellectual fairies of algorithmic mathematics."[60] The steampunk is thus a "mad scientist" who "refuses to be caged in by the ever-growing cage of specialization," suggesting that both people and things suffer at the hands of "those technocrats who drain [technology] of both its artistic and real qualities, who turn the living monsters of technology into the simpering servants of meaningless commodity."[61] Machines and their makers must be liberated, and steampunks hope to lead the way. In their "living dream," technology would be "neither slave nor master, but partner in the exploration of otherwise unknowable territories of both art and science."[62] They champion creativity with the past and creativity with making material things that display the marrying of "engineering and art," "rendering fashion and function mutually dependent," and "creating a seamless paradox between the practical and the fanciful."[63] With its emphasis on the critique of technology, its wrestling the process of making away from the overly specialized technocrat interested in producing only meaningless commodities, steampunk, the manifesto claims, is certainly not "dressed-up, reactionary nostalgia."[64]

Steampunks practice a kind of creative borrowing from a past that they imagine had a more robust, or at least substantially different, kind of material culture, one that might not only inspire but defamiliarize present material realities. Their emphasis on "putting the punk back into steampunk" (the title of the first issue) comes with the "aggressive, do-it-yourself ethic" that is sustained throughout subsequent issues.[65] It is this making and the values embedded in this making that become key to the movement as it is defined by *SteamPunk Magazine*; this is part of the materialism they use to reject the boring monotony of contemporary technological design and with it disposable culture with its planned obsolescence and other unsustainable practices.[66] In its eighth issue, *SteamPunk Magazine* goes so far as to align itself with the Occupy Wall Street Movement, calling on its readers to "Occupy Steampunk: Learn, Share, Craft."[67]

It is the learning, sharing, and crafting that is perhaps the most important aspect of steampunk according to *SteamPunk Magazine*. Every issue features DIY articles that insist on sharing knowledge of making while reusing, recycling, and repurposing materials. Such work is necessarily imaginative, as one must learn to see discarded things as things that are not devoid of function but rather as things whose function has changed.[68] Articles frequently encourage readers to insert their own creative touches (especially in articles advocating certain fashionable accessories). These articles clearly identify steampunks as *bricoleurs* or tinkerers who insist on working "with what is available" while often displaying an environmental, economic, and aesthetic consciousness in the choice of materials for crafting.[69] Some, for instance, specify that materials should be procured from Goodwill, thrift stores, or even "scrap at a construction site," "a roadside 'junk' shop," and through "dumpster diving."[70] The sharing of ways of making not only underlies the desire for the democratization of technological mastery but also wards against the will to individual mastery expressed by some steampunks, which threatens to undermine the movement's otherwise posthuman approach to technology.[71]

But the DIY articles also promote the value of experimentation and of imperfection. From its first issue, *SteamPunk Magazine* DIY articles emphasize "trial and error," suggesting that one may "wind up with something completely different than [one] set out to create," and in some cases writers even explicitly tell readers that they should "not expect this to work!"[72] The second issue in particular—subtitled "A Journal of Misapplied Technology"—emphasizes the importance of making things that may not work or that may not work as intended. Issue editor Margaret P. Killjoy calls on readers to "misapply" or "misappropriate" technology, to "be diverse and inefficient," claiming that current uses of technology serve "as a buffer between us and wonder" and that those who "are not afraid to significantly demean their efficiency" can "fill their lives with wonder."[73]

The object practices modeled in the pages of *SteamPunk Magazine* clearly invite engagement with the unpredictable processes of making, with an obduracy of materials and limits of one's skills that cannot but call forth a reconsideration of the value of made things—not simply as objects of utility or increased efficiency or profitability, but as objects in what Lorraine Datson calls a supersaturated cultural solution that "crystallize ways of thinking, feeling, and acting," and, I would add, modes of being akin to those sought by some Victorian aesthetes.[74]

If, in the surfaces of Gothic architecture, Ruskin saw (and asked his readers to see) the depth of freedom and creativity of the workers who made those imperfect structures, insisting that the imperfection itself spoke of the freedom of the workers' imaginations, steampunk in a sense asks us to read things as Ruskin did—to see the worker (her freedom and creativity and thus dignity) in the thing and to support certain kinds of making over the perfection of machine-made disposable goods. But they also, like William Morris (who was much indebted to Ruskin's thought and helped inspire the Arts and Crafts movement), ask us to craft things—to become producers, not just consumers. According to philosopher Jacques Rancière, the Arts and Crafts movement "developed an idea of furniture—in the broad sense of the term—for a new community"; in other words, its things were meant to crystallize alternative forms of labor, of community, of value.[75] The value such a movement placed on beauty and on beautiful surroundings effected an important displacement of barriers between "works of pure art and the ornaments made by the decorative arts," between the activities called work and the activities called aesthetic practices, between labor and pleasure.[76]

Indeed, aestheticism's cult of beauty, championed by aesthetes and dandies (and numerous aesthetic theorists, including Ruskin, Morris, Pater, Wilde, and Lee), "presupposes a revalorization of the abilities attached to the very idea of work."[77] This revalorization is in effect a "recomposition of the landscape of the visible, a recomposition of the relationship between doing, making, being, seeing, and saying."[78] To be sure, for Rancière, all artistic practices are "ways of doing and making that intervene in the general distribution of ways of doing and making as well as in the relationships they maintain to modes of being and forms of visibility."[79] Art is necessarily political because it is "a practice of dissensus" that "creates a fissure in the sensible order by confronting the established framework of perception, thought, and action with the 'inadmissable.'"[80] Moreover, art "disrupt[s] the relationship between the visible, the sayable, and the thinkable without having to use the terms of a message as a vehicle."[81]

This is where even the surfaces of things can be political—not because they enlist people in a particular cause through their messages but rather because they exist through a refusal of the implicit social consensus that partitions out makers from consumers and workers from pleasure seekers, art from ornament, and the practical from the fanciful. When steampunks invoke the aesthete/dandy of an earlier time and point (as they did) to the importance of embodied interactions with material things, they offer glimpses into alternative modes of value, alternative modes of being that are everywhere otherwise entirely discouraged or entirely invisible, insensible, inadmissable. The steampunks are right in claiming the aesthete/dandy as among the traitors of the past, as they betrayed (and displaced) what Rancière calls "the distribution of the sensible" that governed their time. Steampunks are traitors too, especially in "refus[ing] to be caged in by the ever-growing cage of specialization" and in refusing to let both people and technology suffer at the hands of "those technocrats who drain [technology] of both its artistic and real qualities, who turn the living monsters of technology into the simpering servants of meaningless commodity."[82] They refuse planned obsolescence, nontinkerable black box technologies, and the unquestioned values of utility and profitability that are almost exclusively measured in economic terms (as if this is the only form of value we recognize). In the midst of a forward-looking technophilic society, steampunks emphatically look back and dare to revive long-lost ideas, visions, and material practices.[83] They go so far as to echo a suggestion made by Thomas Pynchon in 1984 that it might, after all, be "O.K. to Be a Luddite," or at the very least to be a little "techno-suspicious," as one reader suggests.[84] Of course, Luddites here are not (as is often implied) irrational, nostalgic haters of scientific and technological progress. Rather, they are technophiles who want to have a say in "the pace and direction of technological change."[85]

Conclusion: Aesthetic Experience and Contemporary Technogenesis

In considering the guiding question of this volume of essays—why steampunk now?—*SteamPunk Magazine* offers a number of answers: steampunk now because in the midst of "airy" technologies and the planned obsolescence of our things, steampunks believe we must reconnect with materiality. They propose their own kind of deviant materialism that works to defamiliarize the normal (unsustainable) materialism of the present moment. If their whimsical approach goes so far as to celebrate the making of things that are inefficient, misapplied, and even nonfunctional and superfluous, we might recall Théophile Gautier's defiant claim that he is "one of those to whom superfluity is a necessity" and that utility (much like beauty) is relative.[86] Why reinvent the Victorian aesthete (and all her contradictions) in times of austerity? Because it is precisely in times of austerity that it becomes difficult, not to say impossible, to voice the need for something else. Some Victorian aesthetes looked to the medieval period for inspiration when attempting to revitalize ways of making in their own time. Today steampunks look back to the Victorians. In both cases, an imagined past provides the kind of historical relativity that might help put things in perspective while challenging commonplace understandings of what is and is not necessary, desirable, and valuable.

In *How We Think: Digital Media and Contemporary Technogenesis*, N. Katherine Hayles argues for a model of technogenesis that would help us historicize technological change and show how humans and technics coevolve. In her words, "contemporary technogenesis is about adaptation, the fit between organisms and their environments, recognizing that both sides of the engagement (humans and technologies) are undergoing coordinated transformations."[87] These coordinated transformations between humans and their technologies are certainly not unique to the present time (as Hayles shows through her examination of human interactions with the telegraph, for example), but it is at the present moment that many studies are revealing profound changes in cognitive modes that seem to be related to human use of digital technologies. Specifically, Hayles shows that one of the most profound changes we are witnessing is the shift in modes of attention from "the deep attention characteristic of humanistic inquiry [and 'close reading'] to the hyper attention characteristic of someone scanning webpages."[88]

Interestingly, Lee similarly notes a change in attention that affected the perceptive abilities of persons in her time, arguing that both the process of evolution and life in increasingly fast-paced urban centers have trained the human sensorium to respond quickly and increasingly automatically to its material environment. The value she places on beautiful things is in part due to the ways she believed they could interrupt sensory and perceptive automatisms of everyday life. Beautiful things, she believes, are those that can arrest our attention and give us pause to discern more carefully—that is, to avoid what she calls "touch-and-go" perceptions and "the dangers of over rapid and uncritical inference" for more critical and creative modes of engagement with our material environments.[89]

If some critics today continue to consider this experience of pause or momentary arrest of our attention as a defining characteristic of aesthetic experience, then it would seem that such experiences may be needed more than ever given the move toward increasingly hyper modes of attention.[90] However, the studies Hayles discusses also give one pause to consider whether with the changes in attention we may be losing access to different kinds of perceptual, critical, and affective modes.

When Hayles reports that studies have found that those who read online become less capable of reading print-based works (and thus less capable of close critical reading),[91] one wonders what kinds of experiences, modes of thought, and being are becoming increasingly less accessible and what others are becoming increasingly available—that is, one wonders how the use of new technologies helps to reconfigure Rancière's distribution of the sensible. Perhaps it is now becoming apparent that technology and art are joined in unexpected ways in their contributions to the partitioning (and repartitioning) of the perceptible. And perhaps, like the aesthete, the dandy, and the steampunk, we might reconsider cultivating embodied interactions with beautiful things and flirting with alternative modes of being. At the very least we should examine critically the ways in which sensible experience has been, and continues to be, regimented, and we should remember that alternative ways of partitioning the sensible remain possible.

NOTES

1. Libby Bulloff and Colin Foran (illustrator), "Steam Gear: A Fashionable Approach to the Lifestyle," *SteamPunk Magazine* 2 (2007): 8-13.
2. Ibid., 10, figs. 5a–d.
3. Ibid., 12.
4. Ibid.
5. James Schafer and Kate Franklin, "Why Steampunk (Still) Matters," *SteamPunk Magazine* 8 (2012): 15.
6. See, for example, Elaine Scarry, *On Beauty and Being Just* (Princeton, N.J.: Princeton University Press, 1999), Isobel Armstrong, *The Radical Aesthetic* (New York: Wiley-Blackwell, 2000), Peter de Bolla, *Art Matters* (Cambridge, Mass.: Harvard University Press, 2001), Denis Donoghue, *Speaking of Beauty* (New Haven, Conn.: Yale University Press, 2003), Jonathan Loesberg, *A Return to Aesthetics: Autonomy, Indifference, and Postmodernism* (Stanford, Calif.: Stanford University Press, 2005), and especially Jacques Rancière, *The Politics of Aesthetics*, trans. Gabriel Rockhill (New York: Continuum, 2011 [first published in French by La Fabrique-Éditions, 2000]), and *Aesthetics and Its Discontents*, trans. Steven Corcoran (Cambridge: Polity Press, 2009 [first published in French by Editions Galilée, 2004]). There are also a number of edited collections worth noting, such as George Levine, *Aesthetics and Ideology* (New Brunswick, N.J.: Rutgers University Press, 1994), John J. Joughin and Simon Malpas, *The New Aestheticism* (Manchester: Manchester University Press, 2003), and Pamela R. Matthews and David Bruce McWhirter, *Aesthetic Subjects* (Minneapolis: University of Minnesota Press, 2003).
7. I am thinking here of recent studies on the dandy, including Susan Fillin-Yeh, *Dandies: Fashion and Finesse in Art and Culture* (New York: NYU Press, 2001),

Miranda Gill, *Eccentricity and the Cultural Imagination in Nineteenth-Century Paris* (Oxford: Oxford University Press, 2009), and Monica L. Miller, *Slaves to Fashion: Black Dandyism and the Styling of the Black Diasporic Identity* (Durham, N.C.: Duke University Press, 2009), as well as the March 2013 Northeast Modern Language Association panel "The Dandy after Wilde."

8. Catastrophone Orchestra and Arts Collective, "What, Then, Is Steampunk? Colonizing the Past So We Can Dream the Future," *SteamPunk Magazine* 1 (2006): 5.

9. Bruce Sterling, "The User's Guide to Steampunk," *SteamPunk Magazine* 5 (2009): 30–33.

10. James H. Carrott, "Punking the Past: The Politics of Possibility," *SteamPunk Magazine* 9 (2013): 70.

11. Oscar Wilde, "De Profundis" (1897), quoted in Carrott, "Punking the Past," 70; Oscar Wilde, "The Critic as Artist" (1891), quoted in Carrott, "Punking the Past," 71.

12. This well-known line concludes Wilde's famous preface to *The Picture of Dorian Gray* (1891) and echoes Théophile Gautier's claim that "there is nothing beautiful but that which can never be of any use whatsoever; everything useful is ugly"; Théophile Gautier, preface to *Mademoiselle de Maupin*, trans. Jacques Barzun (New York: Heritage Press, 1944, first published in French in 1835), xxx. Not all supporters of aestheticism would agree, of course. Ruskin and Morris, for instance, would insist that all things should be beautiful, even everyday useful things. In fact, Ruskin and Morris would go so far as to suggest that useless things should not be made at all, as their making can degrade the laborer. Perhaps more important than individual positions, however, are the very debates about what counts as useful and the place of the beautiful in everyday life, which are fundamental to writers associated with aestheticism.

13. Igor Kopytoff explains the West's "predisposition" to separate "people from things"; "The Cultural Biography of Things: Commoditization as Process," in *The Social Life of Things: Commodities in Cultural Perspective*, ed. Arjun Appadurai (Cambridge: Cambridge University Press, 1986), 84. Bruno Latour also discusses the problematic separation of people and things in Western thought in *We Have Never Been Modern*, trans. Catherine Porter (Cambridge, Mass.: Harvard University Press, 1993, originally published in French in 1991). In "The Berlin Key" and elsewhere, he insists that in fact we cannot consider one without the other: "Consider things, and you will have humans. Consider humans, and you are by that very act interested in things"; Bruno Latour, "The Berlin Key, or How to Do Words with Things," in *Matter, Materiality and Modern Culture*, ed. P. M. Graves-Brown (London: Routledge, 2000), 20.

14. The so-called material turn has been ongoing for some fifteen years or more and can be characterized by a shift from subject-focused to object-focused criticism in a wide range of fields that investigate (among other things) the "co-performance of sociality and materiality"; Dick Pels, Kevin Hetherington, and Frédéric Vandenberghe, "The Status of the Object: Performance, Mediations, Techniques," *Theory, Culture, and Society* 19, no. 1 (2002): 2.

15. Elaine Freedgood, "Commodity Criticism and Victorian Thing Culture: The Case of Dickens," in *Contemporary Dickens*, ed. Eileen Gillooly and Deirdre David (Columbus: Ohio State University Press, 2009), 155.

16. Guy Debord, *The Society of the Spectacle* (1967), quoted in Freedgood, "Commodity Criticism and Victorian Thing Culture," 152.

17. Freedgood, "Commodity Criticism and Victorian Thing Culture," 153. For more on what Freedgood calls Victorian "thing culture," see the coda to her book-length study, *The Ideas in Things: Fugitive Meaning in the Victorian Novel* (Chicago: University of Chicago Press, 2006).

18. Freedgood, "Commodity Criticism and Victorian Thing Culture," 154.

19. Ibid.

20. Ibid., 153.

21. Charlotte Gere with Lesley Hoskins, *The House Beautiful: Oscar Wilde and the Aesthetic Interior* (Aldershot, U.K.: Lund Humphries in association with the Geffrye Museum, 2000), 35-36.

22. William Morris, quoted in ibid., 42.

23. Oscar Wilde, "The Soul of Man under Socialism," in *The Complete Works of Oscar Wilde*, vol. 4, *Criticism*, ed. Josephine M. Guy (Oxford: Oxford University Press, 2007), 260.

24. According to Regenia Gagnier, "An aesthetic and economics of pleasure became salient at the *fin de siècle*, having competed with ethical, political-economic, and evaluative models"; "Productive Bodies, Pleasured Bodies: On Victorian Aesthetics," in *Women and British Aestheticism*, ed. Talia Schaffer and Kathy Alexis Psomiades (Virginia: University Press of Virginia, 1999), 285. Gagnier associates this aesthetic with "pleasured bodies whose taste established their identities" (274). It should be noted that although it was caught up in the consumer culture it sought to critique, aestheticism took a number of forms, including, as Diana Maltz has shown, philanthropic aestheticism, which sought to introduce beauty into the lives and surroundings of the working classes; see Maltz, *British Aestheticism and the Urban Working Classes, 1870-1900: Beauty for the People* (New York: Palgrave Macmillan, 2006).

25. *Degeneration* was first published in German in 1892 and translated into English in 1895. It was translated into several languages and went through many editions in a number of European countries; George L. Mosse, "Max Nordau and His *Degeneration*," introduction to *Degeneration*, by Max Nordau, trans. Mosse (New York: Howard Fertig, 1968), xvi.

26. In his examination of the A&E television series *Hoarders* (2009-present), Scott Herring works toward a theory of "material deviance" and "queer objecthood" that would allow us to interrogate the ways that "object pathology" or "aberrant object conduct . . . can upset normative social boundaries"; "Material Deviance: Theorizing Queer Objecthood," *Postmodern Culture* 21, no. 2 (January 2011): n.p., http://doi.org/10.1353/pmc.2011.0009. I argue that Victorian aesthetes' materialism is akin to the scientific materialism of their time, which was associated with atheism and radical thought.

27. See Gillian Beer *Open Fields: Science in Cultural Encounter* (Oxford: Oxford

University Press, 1999). Situating the aesthetes in the scientific culture of their time means attending to the interactions between literature and science for which the period is well known.

28. See especially Gagnier, "Productive Bodies, Pleasured Bodies," and Kathy Alexis Psomiades *Beauty's Body: Femininity and Representation in British Aestheticism* (Stanford, Calif.: Stanford University Press, 1997).

29. Although materialism in the late nineteenth century "was not a coherent doctrine—its most fundamental proposition being simply that nothing exists independently of matter—the term was nevertheless deployed frequently in Victorian Britain as a pejorative label that could be used to tarnish the reputation of those who challenged the old tradition of natural theology and instead insisted on a naturalistic, though not necessarily a materialistic, understanding of the universe"; Gowan Dawson, *Darwin, Literature, and Victorian Respectability* (Cambridge: Cambridge University Press, 2007), 52. It refers, in other words, to the "allegedly materialist epistemology of contemporary science" (38), the subject of much debate. For some scientists, all natural phenomena could be reduced to material mechanism, but others worried that this insistence on explaining natural phenomena through the mechanical laws of physics was a dangerous and misleading practice, for it left no room for God and seriously undermined the basis of morality, leading inevitably to "selfishness" (41). As such, materialism came to be associated with radical beliefs (atheism and agnosticism, as well as the equalizing of all things organic and inorganic) and with antisocial/antiethical tendencies. Dawson shows how scientists guarded themselves against accusations of materialism and of being associated with the materialism of certain artists associated with aestheticism. I am suggesting that while scientists may have guarded against materialism, some artists daringly explored its imaginative implications.

30. Freedgood, "Commodity Criticism and Victorian Thing Culture," 153.

31. Ibid., 163.

32. Walter Pater, *The Renaissance: Studies in Art and Poetry*, ed. Adam Phillips (Oxford: Oxford University Press, 1986), 152.

33. Ibid. As I discuss briefly in "The Difference an Object Makes: Conscious Automaton Theory and the Decadent Cult of Artifice," in *Bodies and Things in Nineteenth-Century Writing and Culture*, ed. Katharina Boehm (London: Palgrave, 2012), Pater mentions science twice in his conclusion and recognizes elsewhere that the relativism he adopts "has been developed in modern times through the influences of the sciences of observation"; Charles S. Blinderman, "Huxley, Pater, and Protoplasm," *Journal of the History of Ideas* 43, no. 4 (1982): 478. For discussions that link Pater's work to the natural sciences, see also Helen Hawthorne Young, *The Writings of Walter Pater: A Reflection of British Philosophical Opinion from 1860 to 1890* (Lancaster: Lancaster Press, 1933); David J. DeLaura, *Hebrew and Hellene in Victorian England: Newman, Arnold, and Pater* (Austin: University of Texas Press, 1969); Philip Appleman, "Darwin and Pater's Critical Dilemma," in *Darwin*, ed. Philip Appleman (New York: Norton, 1970); Gerald Monsman, *Walter Pater* (Boston: Twayne, 1977); Billie Andrew Inman, "The Intellectual

Content of Walter Pater's 'Conclusion,'" in *Pater: An Imaginative Sense of Fact*, ed. Philip Dodd (London: Frank Cass, 1981); and George Levine, "Two Ways Not to Be a Solipsist: Art and Science, Pater and Pearson," *Victorian Studies* 43, no. 1 (2000).

34. For more on the underacknowledged importance of physiologically based psychology grounded in the emerging study of nineteenth-century neurology, see Anne Stiles's edited collection, *Neurology and Literature, 1860-1920* (New York: Palgrave Macmillan, 2007).

35. Pater, *Renaissance*, xxi; Matthew Arnold, "The Function of Criticism at the Present Time," *National Review* (1864), quoted in Pater, *Renaissance*, xix. In *The Stones of Venice* (Boston: Aldine Book Publishing, 1851), Ruskin claims that, like "the chemist," who "defines his mineral by two separate kinds of character; one external, its crystalline form, hardness, lustre, &c.; the other internal, the proportions and nature of its constituent atoms," the critic must examine both the surface and the depth of things (154). Matthew Arnold, in "The Function of Criticism at the Present Time," in *The Works of Matthew Arnold in Fifteen Volumes* (New York: Macmillan, 1903), argues that the aim of all criticism (and of all branches of knowledge) is "to see the object as in itself it really is" (1).

36. Oscar Wilde, "The Critic as Artist," in Guy, *Complete Works of Oscar Wilde*, 4:159.

37. See Douglas Mao, *Fateful Beauty: Aesthetic Environments, Juvenile Development, and Literature, 1860-1960* (Princeton, N.J.: Princeton University Press, 2008).

38. While Grant Allen (and through him Herbert Spencer and Alexander Bain) is most often taken to be exemplary of physiological aesthetics, historian of science Robert Michael Brain rightfully reminds us that "physiological aesthetics assumed almost as many guises as physiology itself"; "The Pulse of Modernism: Experimental Physiology and Aesthetic Avant-Gardes circa 1900," *Studies in the History and Philosophy of Science* 39 (2008): 405, http://doi.org/10.1016/j.shpsa.2008.06.011. Brain continues, "The diversity of the new field was reflected in a variety of names applied to it: along with the English 'physiological aesthetics,' there were German terms such as *Kunstphysiologie* or *experimentelle Aesthetik*, and French appellations including *ésthétique scientifique* and *critique scientifique*" (405).

39. Vernon Lee, *The Beautiful: An Introduction to Psychological Aesthetics* (Cambridge: Cambridge University Press, 1913), 95; Vernon Lee, *Belcaro: Being Essays on Sundry Aesthetical Questions* (London: W. Satchell & Co., 1881), 283.

40. François Jacob, "Evolution and Tinkering," *Science* 196, no. 4295 (June 1977): 1164.

41. Vernon Lee, "Art And Life, III," *Contemporary Review* 70 (July/December 1896): 69, 71.

42. In 1897, together with her partner, Clementina Anstruther-Thomson, Lee published an extended article, "Beauty and Ugliness," in which she theorizes the mechanism of aesthetic experience. Unlike other physiologically based theories, Lee and Anstruther-Thomson argue that aesthetic experience is not primarily a function of the higher senses; rather, in one's encounter with an object (whether

a jar or a cathedral), one experiences changes in breathing, balance, the musculature and of the body, and even the large viscera as one unconsciously mimes the shape of the object. Diana Maltz has read this process as one in which "sexual passion" between women is projected onto the object. This remains a convincing reading, but Lee's passion also explicitly moves beyond human others; Diana Maltz, "Engaging 'Delicate Brains': From Working-Class Enculturation to Upper-Class Lesbian Liberation in Vernon Lee and Kit Anstruther-Thomson's Psychological Aesthetics," in *Women and British Aestheticism*, ed. Talia Schaffer and Kathy Alexis Psomiades (Charlottesville: University Press of Virginia, 1999), 222. For Lee, aesthetic experience allows one to experience alternative "modes of being" that are accompanied by "the sense of serenity and fellowship with the non-ego"; Vernon Lee and Clementina Anstruther-Thomson, "Beauty and Ugliness I," *Contemporary Review* 72 (July/December 1897): 565. In *Beautiful*, Lee expands on this theory, arguing that aesthetic experience is a form of empathy with things.

43. Lee, *Beautiful*, 90.

44. Lee, *Belcaro*, 283.

45. It should be mentioned that Lee's approach to aesthetics changed across her writings. For a concise overview of her shifting views, see Sondeep Kandola, *Vernon Lee* (Tavistock, U.K.: Northcote House Publishers, 2010). However, I would agree with Carolyn Burdett, who shows that despite shifts in her aesthetic theory, Lee's aesthetics remain tied to the body and its materially instantiated experiences. See Burdett, "'The subjective inside us can turn into the objective outside': Vernon Lee's Psychological Aesthetics," *Interdisciplinary Studies in the Long Nineteenth Century*, no. 12 (2011), http://doi.org/10.16995/ntn.610.

46. Lee, *Belcaro*, 283. See, for example, Hayles's analysis of the telegraph as a case study showing "the connections between epigenetic changes in human biology, technological innovations, cultural imaginaries, and linguistic, social, and economic changes"; N. Katherine Hayles, *How We Think: Digital Media and Contemporary Technogenesis* (Chicago: University of Chicago Press, 2012), 123. I say more about aesthetics and contemporary technogenesis below.

47. Stephen Calloway, "Wilde and the Dandyism of the Senses," in *The Cambridge Companion to Oscar Wilde*, ed. Peter Raby (Cambridge: Cambridge University Press, 1997), 34.

48. Steampunks are not alone in noting the current devaluation of matter and materiality. As political theorist Jane Bennett argues, our excessive consumption and wastefulness is based on seeing matter as inert, as everywhere available for human use and disposal; see *Vibrant Matter: A Political Ecology of Things* (Durham, N.C.: Duke University Press, 2010). Hayles has famously shown how information technologies gave rise to dangerous fantasies of a bodiless posthuman that risk perpetuating a devaluation of material bodies and environments; see *How We Became Posthuman: Virtual Bodies in Cybernetics, Literature, and Informatics* (Chicago: University of Chicago Press, 1999).

49. Margaret P. Ratt, "Introduction: Putting the Punk Back into Steampunk,"

SteamPunk Magazine 1 (2006): 2; Rachel A. Bowser and Brian Croxall, "Introduction: Industrial Evolution," *Neo-Victorian Studies* 3, no. 1 (2010): 16.

50. Rebecca Onion, "Reclaiming the Machine: An Introductory Look at Steampunk," *Neo-Victorian Studies* 1, no. 1 (Autumn 2008): 138; Professor Calamity, "My Machine, My Comrade," *SteamPunk Magazine* 3 (2007): 25.

51. Ratt, "Introduction: Putting the Punk Back into Steampunk," 2.

52. Roger Whitson, "How to Theorize with a Hammer; or, Making and Baking Things in Steampunk and the Digital Humanities," this volume.

53. Catastrophone Orchestra and Arts Collective, "What, Then, Is Steampunk?," 5. For a discussion of the many apocalyptic scenarios that steampunks project from current unsustainable practices, see issue 3 of *SteamPunk Magazine*, "The Sky is Falling!," as well as Margaret P. Killjoy, *The Steampunk Guide to the Apocalypse* (2007).

54. Hayden White, "Literature Against Fiction: Postmodernist History," *Torre* 2, no. 4–5 (1997): 207.

55. Catastrophone Orchestra and Arts Collective, "What, Then, Is Steampunk?," 5, 4. This manifesto remains *SteamPunk Magazine*'s go-to guide to understanding steampunk. Readers who might be wondering what steampunk is are repeatedly referred to this manifesto in most subsequent issues, including issues 2, 3, 4, 8, and 9.

56. Ibid., 4, 5.

57. Ratt, "Introduction: Putting the Punk Back into Steampunk," 2; Catastrophone Orchestra and Arts Collective, "What, Then, Is Steampunk?," 5.

58. Ratt, "Introduction: Putting the Punk Back into Steampunk," 2.

59. Note that although putatively non-Luddite, *SteamPunk Magazine* does consider the historical Luddites as possible role models in their pre–Industrial Revolution issue, in which one contributor even argues, "The decision of groups other than those in power to influence the pace and direction of technological change is, far from being a misguided and ultimately pointless attempt to stop the inevitable, a reasoned and legitimate mode of participation in an open and democratic society"; Carolyn Dougherty, "The Luddites," *SteamPunk Magazine* 6 (2009): 13.

60. Catastrophone Orchestra and Arts Collective, "What, Then, Is Steampunk?," 4.

61. Ibid.

62. Ibid., 5.

63. Ibid., 4, 5.

64. Ibid., 4.

65. Ibid., 5.

66. As detailed in "The Sky Is Falling," or apocalypse, issue (#3, 2007). Libby Buloff, "The Chronabelle, an Interview Conducted by Libby Bulloff," *SteamPunk Magazine* 5 (2009): 19; Schafer and Franklin, "Why Steampunk (Still) Matters," 10–15.

67. David Z. Morris and Tommy Poirier-Morisette (illustrator), "Never-Mind the Morlocks, Here's Occupy Wall Street!," *SteamPunk Magazine* 8 (2012): 93.

68. Dylan Fox, "My Dear Punks of Steam," *SteamPunk Magazine* 7 (2010): 2.
69. "Glass Armonica," *SteamPunk Magazine* 1 (2006): 9.
70. "Electrolytic Etching Adapted from the Esteemed Mr. von Slatt," *SteamPunk Magazine* 1 (2006): 38; Thomas Truax, "Thomas Truax, an Interview," *SteamPunk Magazine* 1 (2006): 52, 55.
71. I discuss this posthuman approach to technology and the dangers of the desire for individual mastery in "Technology and Morality: The Stuff of Steampunk," *Neo-Victorian Studies*, 3, no. 1 (2010).
72. Truax, "Thomas Truax," 52; "The Pyrophone," *SteamPunk Magazine* 1 (2006): 7.
73. Margaret P. Killjoy, "Introduction: A Journal of Misapplied Technology," *SteamPunk Magazine* 2 (2007): 3. Onion has rightfully noted the importance of the danger of technology for steampunks; see "Reclaiming the Machine."
74. Lorraine Datson, introduction to *Things That Talk: Object Lessons from Art and Science*, ed. Lorraine Datson (New York: Zone Books, 2004), 20.
75. Rancière, *Politics of Aesthetics*, 15.
76. Ibid.
77. Ibid., 45. William Morris's work is perhaps most relevant here, as he argued explicitly for rethinking work and its pleasures (see especially "Useful Work Versus Useless Toil," 1885), and claimed that the cause of the people (of labor) and of art were one and the same because in reconnecting with different kinds of making, we could revitalize art and work (see especially "Art and Socialism," 1884).
78. Rancière, *Politics of Aesthetics*, 45.
79. Ibid., 13.
80. Rancière, *Aesthetics and Its Discontents*, 96; Rancière, *Politics of Aesthetics*, 85.
81. Rancière, *Politics of Aesthetics*, 63.
82. Catastrophone Orchestra and Arts Collective, "What, Then, Is Steampunk?," 4.
83. To be clear, steampunk's commitment to dissensus and to foregrounding alternative modes of value is no more free from the possibility of co-optation or commercialization than the Victorian aesthetes were. Certainly one can think of numerous examples of mainstream appropriation of the steampunk look—not least of which is Guy Ritchie's blockbuster Sherlock Holmes films (2009, 2011). Clearly flaunting (and banking on the popularity of) the steampunk aesthetic—through the visible, clanking building of large things such as London Bridge, large ships, the underground railway (nothing "airy" here), the mad scientist and tinkerer (the "ginger midget" of the first film), Holmes's own experiments in his apartment (often to the detriment of his dog) and the evil machinations of Dr. Moriarty (an evil genius who happens to be a scientist), as well as the dramatic display of the inner cogs and wheels inside numerous technological devices—the films nonetheless preserve a desire for the object relations of Freedgood's thing culture, as the watching of detectives is one of a number of practices she lists in which "personal, random value trumps exchange value [and] apparently

meaningless things can suddenly become legible, or luminous, or life-altering. Freedgood, "Commodity Criticism and Victorian Thing Culture," 157.

84. See Thomas Pynchon, "Is it O.K. to Be a Luddite?" *New York Times*, October 28, 1984; Johnny H. Payphone, "An Open Letter to Jake von Slatt and Datamancer," *SteamPunk Magazine* 4 (2008): 5.

85. Carolyn Dougherty, "The Luddites," *SteamPunk Magazine* 6 (2009): 13.

86. Gautier, preface to *Mademoiselle de Maupin*, xxx.

87. Hayles, *How We Think*, 81.

88. Ibid., 69.

89. Lee, *Beautiful*, 90.

90. See de Bolla, *Art Matters*.

91. See Hayles, *How We Think*, especially chap. 3, "How We Read: Close, Hyper, Machine."

Punking the Other

On the Performance of Racial and National Identities in Steampunk

DIANA M. PHO

The pervasive Anglophilia associated with steampunk subculture often results in the impression from outside observers that steampunk promotes a singular racial and national narrative: white Britishness.[1] Additionally, the steampunk genre has been charged with romanticizing nineteenth-century Western history and culture, and some have interpreted steampunk subculture as promoting white supremacy.[2] Indeed, steampunk has the requisite ingredients to seem laudatory of and nostalgic for Western imperial domination. Given the increasing sensitivity to the legacy of that domination, we might productively examine the genre with an eye to its use of that legacy.[3] Many (including critiques by science fiction writers Charles Stross and Catherynne Valente) have turned a skeptical eye to steampunk's treatment of this heritage of oppression, dismissing the transgressive potential in its "punk" moniker and seeing instead a romanticized and hegemonically controlled glorification of oppression, passed off under the guise of rebellious subcultural expression.[4]

Historically, white subjects have enjoyed the privilege of appropriating from minority cultures in order to identify as a subcultural other, taking on the mantle/characteristics of oppressed identities without suffering from actual systemic violence. Dick Hebdige notes in his seminal 1979 book *Subculture: The Meaning of Style* that middle-class white "ethnicity" created punk and other subcultural styles influenced by working-class and Afro-Caribbean populations of British urban centers.[5] Punk used the stylings of the other to develop a deviant subcultural voice, Hebdige argues, and then used that subculture for empty, nihilistic gestures against the dominant culture. The minority groups that they aesthetically replicated, however, had contrasting reasons for keeping their distinctive styles: as a form of cohesive community building in opposition to oppressive political and social forces, which bell hooks describes as speaking from the "margins."[6] Though yearning to express the social isolation and frustrations felt by white youth and minority groups alike, subculture participants frequently refuse to sympathize with the plight of the marginalized. Instead, styles like punk, mod, and hipster create an alternate identity onto which adherents can project their own feelings of dissatisfaction: "Just as the mod and the skinhead styles had obliquely reproduced the 'cool' look and feel of the West Indian rude boys and were symbolically placed in the same ideal milieux (the Big City, the violent slum), so the punk aesthetic can be read in part as a white 'translation' of 'black ethnicity.'"[7] Might this be, many critics have wondered, an appropriative phenomenon to which steampunk, given its subject matter, is especially vulnerable? In its progression from a literary or art movement into a sociopolitical one, the steampunk community is developing an ideology by blending modern and past sociopolitical ideals. Much like how steampunk objects juxtapose modern and nineteenth-century styles in order to reveal technological commonalities between them, steampunk as an ideology transgresses temporalities in order to question historical parallels. Beyond simple designations of nostalgia or subversion, however, steampunk participants frequently (but not always) explore the complicated intersections of racial and national hybridity, fracturing any notions of a homogenous national culture and dismantling historical narratives.[8]

As people from marginalized backgrounds increase their presence in the steampunk community, many have worked toward disrupting steampunk's default identity of Eurocentric whiteness. Some attempts simply create a global cultural showcase of material objects, as with Jeni Hellum's *Multiculturalism for Steampunk* blog.[9] Advocates for a non-Eurocentric view of steampunk tend to categorize this as multicultural steampunk, though the use of multiculturalism can fall prey to uncritical interpretations. As Ella Shobat and Robert Stam point out, advocating solely on the basis of representation may create a shallow overview of diversity without questioning the greater institutions of inequality: "Multiculturalism without the critique of Eurocentrism runs the risk of being merely accretive—a shopping mall boutique summa of the world's cultures."[10] Others actively decenter whiteness, such as Jaymee Goh, Balogun Ojetade, Suna Desi, and my own work with *Beyond Victoriana*.[11] Using tactics and insights gained from postcolonial thought, these minority participants recognize how the historical blending of steampunk can critique the Victorian era, British identity, and the problematic developments of modernity.[12]

A postcolonial view of steampunk posits the reexamination of dominant historical narratives in the Western canon to embrace cultural hybridity and challenge the traditional power dynamics of national identity. It asks, "What groups are seen as part of the 'nation'?" and "Who gains the rights and privileges of citizenship?," questions that have been increasingly defined against racial and cultural difference. As Jaymee Goh writes about postcolonial interpretations of the genre,

> By using anachronism to tamper with timelines, a writer of color can also tinker with how migration, assimilation, segregation, and other such cultural movements occur; this makes visible how identities are shaped by such histories, and how they could be shaped otherwise. This tampering also allows us to think through the process of colonization and methods of empowerment.[13]

Thus, steampunk's retrofuturistic appeal stems from the desire for an artistic reinterpretation of history to seek a remedy for real-world historical traumas, a concept that Mike Perschon describes as "social retrofuturism": integrating today's progressive attitudes into an imagined past.[14] Certainly the present upheavals felt in our post-9/11 world cannot be divorced from the global history of industrialization and Westernization—and the West's interference in the non-West through its imperialist and colonialist endeavors.

The "White Man's Message": Chap-hop by Mr. B the Gentleman Rhymer and Professor Elemental

"Chap-hop"—a form of popular music in steampunk that infuses hip-hop with attitudes, tastes, and preoccupations of white Britishness—exemplifies the tensions within the steampunk subculture: one that appropriates minority experience while also allowing participants to grapple progressively with a history of oppression. Chap-hop is "quintessentially British," as Jamieson Ridenhour aptly describes: "A chap-hop performance may contain rapping about cricket, smoking a pipe, and taking high tea."[15] Hip-hop by white rappers or about British culture isn't strictly appropriative but linked to the evolution of hip-hop as it reaches global audiences. The Wu-Tang Clan's blackness mixed with martial arts, the white (and Jewish) Beastie Boys, and of course the trailer park raps of Eminem, to name several examples, all came before chap-hop.

Because this content occurs within a subculture, one I am reading as predominantly resistant to culturally dominant narratives, the idea of default whiteness within steampunk thus becomes paradoxically exposed and challenged in chap-hop. In Western hegemonic spaces, white people often claim that they have "no culture" when in fact white culture's pervasiveness renders it invisible to these members. In steampunk, whiteness becomes associated with the British imperial narrative. While other examples of steampunk music—such as Abney Park or Vernian Process—focus on retrofuturistic or science fictional tropes, chap-hop is steampunk through the remix of form and function: a modern, black-originated musical style focusing on white culture. More than including lyrical references to goggles and gears, chap-hop's ideological message winkingly pokes fun at Britishness, and more importantly white Britishness, while simultaneously lauding it and genuinely mourning its former splendor. Professor Elemental and Mr. B the Gentleman Rhymer's songs reflect the complexities of reestablishing a progressive national identity linked to Britain's imperialist past.

Mr. B's songs, for example, herald "the chap," a romanticized figure of historical white masculinity. In "All Hail to the Chap," for instance, he mourns how the passing of "The age of the Corinthian" (the classical Greek age) and "the plunger and the dandy / Had given way to that of the prig and the bore."[16] He frames his polished lifestyle as a neoclassical aspirational ideal, and he wages criticism against a perceived uncouth "millennial malaise" that affects the general populace. Mr. B encourages others to join him in a "dandy revolution" and then names his own commandments in the "Chap Manifesto." They include wearing tweed, not smoking from pipes made of briar, and treating the ladies with courtesy, all while maintaining "an air of Zeus with a dash of Hades." This longing for material refinement and manners is nostalgia for a bygone era, an era marked by colonialization of the global south and east. His songs rely on his dogged determination to protect British identity from foreign contamination and vault his nativist nostalgia despite using a non-British musical form, as expressed in his music videos "Let's Get This Over and Done With" and "Straight Outta Surrey."[17]

"Let's Get This Over and Done With" teasingly demonizes non-Anglo culture (specifically the World Cup) as an encroaching force upon British life. Unlike his usual hip-hop music, the song's melody is a riff of "The Great Escape," emphasizing Mr. B's need to escape the forces of foreign influence. He wants to get this international sporting event "over and done with / Then we can get back to the cricket." He is captured by two men in black, taken to FIFA headquarters, and forced to consume productions of American mass culture: McDonald's fries, Coca-Cola, and Budweiser. His lyrics protest the state of modern English life, one that is sartorially clueless, money obsessed, and not Anglo-centric: "This nouveau riche nightmare / Plagued by oligarchs and young guttersnipes." The other that Mr. B rejects is the specter of foreign influence, propagated through mass consumerism and globalism. Rather than pushing his critiques beyond the level of disgust about the culture of today's Everyman, Mr. B, ever the gentleman, stays away from heavy politics. Instead he retreats into a rose-colored national dream: enjoying English goods at summer picnics while playing cricket: "We can show these clanknappers that money is not our god / We live for the joy of the summer sun and the crack of leather on willow." Mr. B's national identity is associated with cultural products linked to Britain's history of imperialism: cricket, a sport created in England and taught in subjugated territories, and tea, a drink made from leaves harvested in India but frequently identified with the East India Company instead. As scholar Ian Baucom notes in his work on the postcolonial construction of British identity, cricket was a sport that came to symbolize necessary Anglo-oriented municipal training as the game spread across the Empire:

> In the final, and robustly imperial, decades of the nineteenth century . . . the cricket field was the place where boys were taught the virtues of loyalty, obedience, discipline, and conformity which were held to be the characteristic virtues of the English "gentlemen," but that in acquiring these virtues they were also quite consistently being outfitted for the responsibilities of imperial rule.[18]

Britain's loss of national pride through the insidiousness of foreigners pushing their cultural products upon society plays as tongue-in-cheek commentary when coming from a citizen of a former worldwide empire that perfected the machine of cultural imperialism. Mr. B's cultural nostalgia has political undertones, whether intentional or not. In the video's resolution, Mr. B succeeds slightly in resurrecting his ideal world by converting his captors to the English way of life: he spies a pot of tea, and they all sit down for a nice cuppa. His message is a solid rallying cry to protect his idea of authentic British culture, although his use of humor—both in presenting his lovable, bubbling self and his equally mild-mannered enemies—dilutes the nativist sting.

Mr. B's content may ally him with the dominant (if fading) paradigm, but his typical musical form of choice—hip-hop—and his appreciation of it aligns him with a more progressive identity. In fact, much of Mr. B's work lies in paying tribute to hip-hop's roots by educating the listener about the canon (which he does with an air of amused elitism). For instance, Mr. B's "Chap-Hop History" schools the audience in "Thirty years of hip hop history in five minutes / Featuring myself and my banjolele," featuring "Rapper's Delight" by the Sugarhill Gang, "King of Rock" by RUN-DMC, Beastie Boys' "Fight for Your Right," Public Enemy's "She Watch Channel Zero," and ending with the industry-changing Eminem.[19] An underlying thread of racial tension exists in his lyrics, however, which are his direct lyrical responses to the life experiences of his black sources. While his deep respect for the musical genre is undeniable, his parodies frame his white, middle-class identity as superior to black hip-hop and gangsta culture, such as in "Straight Outta Surrey," his riff on N.W.A.'s "Straight Outta Compton." While his disdain could be interpreted a satire, much like in "Let's Get This Over and Done With," the humorous value nonetheless hinges on the stark contrast between his whiteness and the black origins of the song he parodies.

"You are about to witness the extent of my cricket knowledge," he begins as the video pans over a cricket field's green pastures, Mr. B's boom box emitting the chords of his banjolele. Shaky-cam shots of Mr. B's Surrey "hood" pop up—clean, empty streets and monolithic suburban housing—as the musician's head bobs in an imitation of rappers before him. Mr. B sings wearing his cricket whites as he responds line for line to the original rap lyrics, explaining the need for elegance, politeness, and humility, in opposition to N.W.A.'s brutal life experiences. Mr. B is friendly toward the police ("The constabulary popped in for a swift tea"), berates the use of foul language ("You embarrass yourself when you bumble / Going on about your mother like that"), and frowns over boasts about violence ("Talk of murder, that's so tawdry"). He brags about his cricket skills and how his polished manner and athleticism win him success. Mr. B maintains this sense of mastery over N.W.A.'s song through his white and middle-class advantages, which enable him to mock the struggles of impoverished thug life, one plagued by police brutality, drugs, street crime, and gang warfare.

Mr. B's cutting remark about gaining the admiration of a "Hottentot" because of his "charm" ("I'll charm her with wits / And with her blouse signed she'll leave ecstatic") reveals the extent of his musical appropriation. Much as the word "Hottentot" evokes a reference to the degrading history of South African woman Sarah Baartman as a Victorian sideshow and scientific specimen, Mr. B "charmingly" exploits N.W.A.'s lyrics for entertainment value. The overall effect shows the triumphs of his white Britishness while glossing over the power differentials behind the thrust of his critiques. Here, both contrasting potentials of steampunk—progressive acceptance of cultural hybridity and the nostalgic leanings toward white supremacy—is instantiated in Mr. B's acknowledgment of the deteriorating power of British national identity while also disparaging non-Anglo black culture.

Unlike Mr. B's praise of the Victorian gentleman as an ideal, fellow chap-hop rapper Professor Elemental stomps on that image. In his music video "I'm British," Elemental defines British identity as being confused but exaggeratedly white, and he acts both celebratory and remorseful about being British.[20] Professor Elemental trots through a sunny field with his gorilla companion, Geoffrey (Elemental's dependable servant who is mentioned occasionally in his songs and who at times feels uncomfortably close to a racialized stand-in for people of color), toward a crowd of revelers. He praises British pride not because of its triumphs but because of its failures: "See we used to have an empire but we got a little cocky / Like 'Ha ha, Johnny foreigner, I'd like to see you stop me!' / And sure enough, the rhubarb crumbled." Elemental, a remorseful but retrospective citizen, struggles to reconcile the crimes of his country with his yearning to regain his nationalism. Though modern life deprives the younger generation of any ideals ("in every town the drunk teens stumble"), Elemental calls this a beneficial history lesson ("rather glad really, it made us more humble"). Properly chastised by their fall from geopolitical supremacy, this humbleness—as opposed to the Empire's triumphant past—reconstitutes Britannia's greatness, so he "won't mumble" when declaring his background.

The survivors of the fall then appear: a sea of pale faces cheerfully announcing, "I'm British." Professor Elemental praises their stoic strength in light of their failure as colonizers, not acknowledging the formerly colonized citizens of today's multiracial Britain. Elemental compares himself to people and items that are typically white: "clotted cream tea," "Morris dancer," and literary figures "Wodehouse, Orwell, Welles, and Poe." He profusely apologizes for things the British did, listing a myriad of items viewed as created by white Anglo culture: "Simon Cowell, Jim Davidson, fox hunting, black pudding, racism." His remorse, while humorously justified, satirically places the present-day mantle of victimhood on the Anglo Brit, discomforted by the distasteful by-products of their culture. "I'm British" thus equates their national identity with white guilt writ large. By stating that white people are the ultimate victims of racism, "I'm British" encompasses the contrarian stance of steampunk: superficially acknowledging issues of oppression as a mark of progressive modernity while simultaneously dismissing the historical impact felt by minorities.

When the foul reality of British history is a source of its identity crisis, Elemental claims the only way to navigate past white guilt is through self-deprecating humor. Apprehensiveness around identity is his joke, and steampunk is the vehicle he uses to express this flippancy. For Tor.com, he describes the subgenre this way: "Imagine a comic convention and a fetish night had a baby. In Victorian times. In the future. That baby is Steampunk."[21] By unmistakably fronting his satire and lighthearted attitude, his songs' unabashed praising of British whiteness reveal his caricature of it.

Unlike Mr. B's self-glorifying parodies—which bring to light the appropriative exploitation of his music—Elemental's mostly original songs paint a loveable, cartoonish picture of the Victorian self that expose nationalism's flaws that nevertheless also strive to uplift Britishness. He obsesses over tea in his best-known song, "Cup of Brown Joy," goes on an exaggerated and failed quest à la Monty Python in "The Quest for the Golden Frog," and mocks sport hunters by including an interview about one who shoots hunters and mounts their heads over his fireplace in "Hunting Season."[22] Hence, Professor Elemental's satire of historical anxieties entertains on multiple levels. White Brits put on the mantle of the oppressed yet keep a stereotypical stoic (or even apathetic) stiff upper lip in their contriteness. Some may equate their white guilt to historic trauma or even laugh at the self-conscious hand-wringing that Elemental performs. Trading British pride in exchange for the British buffoonery is the root of Elemental's popularity—and acceptability. As opposed to being sincerely apologist, Professor Elemental and Mr. B manage to simultaneously celebrate and denigrate British culture, demonstrating the possibilities of hybridity as the other whiteness itself. Both musicians transform themselves into nationalist mascots that expose the myth that white people in a hegemonic society have no culture. This feat is accomplished by treating hip-hop as a comedic othered musical framework, through which they examine the changing meaning of British identity.

Speaking from the Margin in Theory and in Praxis

Many people of color are drawn to steampunk subculture as a site of resistance against hegemony. To use the words of bell hooks, steampunk's relationship to history from the minority perspective is "a politicization of memory that distinguishes nostalgia . . . that longing for something to be as once it was, a kind of useless act, from that remembering that serves to illuminate and transform the present."[23] For the marginalized, sharing steampunk stories can be a reclaiming act over positions of cultural autonomy and a method of finding allies. More than just the dynamic of appropriation and assimilation, minorities in steampunk subculture appropriate the signs and symbols of the genre in order to disrupt the current and historical power structure between hegemony and the marginalized.

How minority viewpoints are treated in steampunk have been debated since Jaymee Goh (as Jha) wrote "The Intersection of Race and Steampunk: Colonialism's After-Effects and Other Stories from a Steampunk of Colour's Perspective."[24] To her, racially subversive artistic performances and artworks—both online and off—are key to changing perceptions of whiteness in the steampunk imaginary: "Do I appropriate Victorianism as someone who's clearly a minority? . . . How do we take the trappings of the enemy and use it against them without simply assimilating into the imperialist's culture?" In response to steampunk's Eurocentrism, Goh imagines the Steampunk Magistrate, her own persona based on her Chinese diaspora heritage, in collaboration with Jeanette Ng.[25] Thus, steampunk provides the artistic license for people of color to transmute traumatic cultural histories onto an empowering subculture identity, an artistic/political survival method that bell hooks emphasizes as "speaking from the margins."[26] Reimagining—a concept not new to steampunk ideology—when viewed through a minoritarian lens defends against the notion that the genre and its community exist in an escapist vacuum, untouched by political realities.

Speaking from the margins endows steampunk minority artworks with a sense of empowerment that feels more hard-earned and exploratory than whimsical. Elizabeth Lameman's film *The Path without End* (2011) envisions Native space travel, for example, inspired by Grace L. Dillon's scholarship on Indigenous futurism and the need to combat assumptions about native technology.[27] Monique Poirier also developed the persona of the Native steampunk scientist to counteract stereotypical perceptions of indigenous people lacking sophisticated technology and to challenge the current assumption of the disadvantaged

FIGURE 6.1. Jaymee Goh as the Steampunk Magistrate. Photograph by Diana M. Pho.

Native American. On her blog *Moniquilliloquies*, she writes about how her steampunk setting is rooted in historical, scientific, nature-oriented speculation:

> By the 19th century in my alternate timeline, Turtle Island has a thriving, technologically advanced pan-Indian culture, a collective of independent nations with distinct regionalisms that has a UN-like organization to engage with the global community. A group of nations that meets Europe as equals and trades technology and cultural influences as such.[28]

Anger, rage, and dystopian resentment also form part of the affective milieu of minority performances as responses to historical pain. Anna Chen's *Steampunk Opium Wars* (2012), a one-act play inspired by her past as Chinese British punk rocker, educates and entertains viewers about a dark time of Chinese and British history to the three-chord tunes of the electric guitar and the rhythms of slam poetry.[29] On her website of the same name, Chen and her cast combine anachronistic styles, dressed in a mix of Qing dynasty historical clothing, metal spikes, safety pins, goggles, and black eyeliner. What all these examples have in common is the accessible empowerment steampunk provides for the marginalized. Oppressed and the oppressor, appropriated and appropriator, people of color in steampunk wrestle with the complexity of existing in multiple realities: subcultural, mainstream, physical, and imaginary.

Steamfunk: Fears of a Black Retrofuturism

As seen with chap-hop, white participants adopt signs of the other, but their identification is not necessarily a mind-set based on empathy across difference as much as a subsuming of it. Thus, people of color work to carve their own spaces within the steampunk community. Steampunks from the African diaspora share a history of resistance related to decolonization and the fight for cultural and social autonomy. bell hooks expresses this need to "resist from the margins," and she encourages the need for minorities to find their own artistic space: "Spaces can be real and imagined. Spaces can tell stories and untold histories. Spaces can be interrupted, appropriated, and transformed through artistic and literary practice."[30] The steamfunk movement, strongly propagated by authors and "steamfunkateers" Balogun Ojetade and Milton Davis, is one response to the hegemonic whiteness of the subculture.

The steamfunk movement's inception started in online conversations

FIGURE 6.2. Marcellus Shane Jackson's cover for *Steamfunk!*, edited by Milton Davis and Balogun Ojetade; image used by permission of the publisher.

among black authors in 2009 about why black characters weren't seen much in the genre; as a result, Maurice Broaddus wrote the first steamfunk story, "Pimp My Airship," for *Apex* magazine.[31] Since then, the steamfunk movement has spread its mission to recognize historical African/African American experiences in speculative fiction. In the introduction to the *Steamfunk!* anthology, Ojetade defines the movement's goals:

> The Steamfunk Movement is not a political party or interest group, nor is it a mass fad or trend. The Steamfunk Movement can be thought of as an organized, yet informal, social entity that is oriented toward the goal of cultural and historical awareness, enrichment and appreciation through Steamfunk—a philosophy or style of writing that combines the African and/or African-American culture and approach to life with that of the steampunk philosophy and/or steampunk fiction.[32]

Though advocating for blackness, Ojetade does not call for segregation of the steampunk community along racial lines or categorizes all steamfunk participants as black. On his blog, *The Chronicles of Harriet*, he clarifies that "Steamfunk is not 'Black Steampunk'; no more than Steampunk is, well, White Steampunk. Steamfunk offers a look at Steampunk through a different set of goggles."[33] Unlike chap-hop's loving exploitation of hip-hop, steamfunk pushes ideologically in reverse, appropriating the neo-Victorian science fiction interests of steampunk and infusing it with the aesthetics and sociopolitical concerns of blackness. While steamfunk artworks always focus on the goal of racial representation, many examples also addresses stereotypes and autonomy over the black body, such as Theoretics's "Jekyll & Hyde" and Nicki Minaj in the David Guetta song "Turn Me On."[34]

The casting of multiracial rap group Theoretics ambiguously plays with the racial stereotypes when a black Mr. Hyde rap-duels opposite a white Dr. Jekyll. This modern music video has a lush steampunk aesthetic with top hats, goggles, and clockwork lab mechanics galore; their storytelling is straightforward, but their demonization of blackness dances between laughable exaggeration and discomforting reinforcement of current racist thinking. The opening scene finds a white male passerby witnessing an attack on another white man by a shadowy figure: "Right there in front of me; it was one of the more horrible things I've ever seen," the witness confesses to the constable. He finds the attacker's cane, which names Henry Jekyll as the culprit, but the constable states that the witness's description doesn't match him at all. The next clip shows Henry Jekyll (played by singer Mark Hoy) being booed by an audience when he declares his new findings, and in the next scene, he gets rejected by performer Miss Shania. Growling, his rage peaking, Jekyll enters his laboratory and uses his newfound science to transform into Mr. Hyde (Chimaroke Abuachi). Stevenson's classic horror story is racialized, with Hyde recast as an uncontrollable black man: Hyde storms into Miss Shania's theater and terrifies onlookers (especially hysterical white women), transforms his personality-formula investors into their evil selves by having him drink the potion, and dances animalistically with a howling team of dark-skinned cohorts. Before the video's abrupt end, Hyde destroys the lab, raging: "Drink! Release the beast inside, show what you Hyde! / Bend, rip, tear those who dare oppose / Rawr! Break, crash, wreck, claw, bend, bite, crush!" Much like how chap-hop rappers expound upon their white identities, Theoretics's "Jekyll & Hyde" uses steampunk's pulpy style as an othered framework to display how blackness remains demonized today.

Similarly, Nicki Minaj uses the stylings and tropes of steampunk to present a layered take on assimilation and rebellion against societal norms in the Sanji-directed music video for David Guetta's "Turn Me On." Unlike most steampunk music—which usually emphasizes narrative speculative storytelling in its lyrics—Guetta's song is a typical club tune that has little relevance to the video's plot except as a dynamic contrast to the action. Yet when Minaj sings how her "body needs a hero, come and save me" and pleads for a "doctor" to "make me come alive," the black-sheathed, stallion-riding Minaj inspires an automaton uprising. The cognitive dissonance while viewing her video may be intentional: while the song's damsel in lustful distress waits for a man to motivate her, Minaj's authoritative physical performance represents her feminist counternarrative against a track she only pays lip service to. Just as the examples from chap-hop and Theoretics emphasize visual, musical, and lyrical contrasts to establish racial commentary, her video performance is undeniably steamfunk, even if the music is not. It engages in anachronistic technology (clockwork automatons) and science fictional tropes (the mad inventor, the rebellious creation), and its social retrofuturism centers black women in both a musical genre (hip-hop) and an aesthetic (steampunk) that has typically steered them to the wayside.

The introductory scene to the "Turn Me On" video objectifies Minaj, an automaton built at the hands of a white inventor (David Guetta). The singer, remarkably more lifelike than the other automatons around town, strides into view in an elaborate black gown and her signature pink hair. Her robotic compatriots' plastic bodily features remain obvious despite their neo-Victorian garb (the range of skin tones displayed by these automatons also racializes them). Minaj is also an instigator, first on horseback and later standing, self-possessed, amid male nude automatons who seem to pose on her command. Jealous of her superior human facade and suspicious about the identity of their engineer, three female automatons break into his lab, confront the inventor, and strip him to reveal his true metallic self—he is even less human than his creations. His role as the mechanical inventor represents, then, the cultural machine that demands minorities to assimilate in order to gain access to "honorary" human (and white) privilege. The inventor's exposure can also be interpreted as a rejection of the politics of respectability that often comes up in discussions about race: that marginalized individuals have to conform to an acceptable standard before being granted sociopolitical equality and respect. The song ends powerfully as the three female machines, liberated and nude, run into the streets. In light of the historical treatment of people of color as coolies, slaves, sharecroppers, migrant workers, house nannies, and maids, the message is clear: though the rights of personhood are dependent on the powerful, the minority should not have to conform to dominant expectations in order to recognize their own worth—and only the oppressed can demand their own freedom in the face of the oppressor. The steamfunk movement thus builds an imaginative politicized discourse on the gear-encrusted shoulders of steampunk.

Unfortunate Imitations? Minority Performances of Hegemony

While art can be the performance of protest, not all minority performances are clearly defined as countering hegemony; cross-cultural expressions may even become complicit with the overarching system of oppression governed by white supremacy. The works and identity performance of Vietnamese French cosplayer Maurice Grunbaum and Savan Gupta as A Count Named Slick-Brass, for instance, complicate arguments surrounding ethnicity, racial critiques, and identity politics.

Maurice Grunbaum's artistic work involves dystopian interpretations of multicultural steampunk that he labels "DARKsteam." In an online interview, he acknowledges embracing one's heritage in steampunk but divorces the genre from historical accuracy: "To me steampunk has nothing to do with history. It is Science-fiction, Alternate History, or Dystopian!"[35] Controversy follows Grunbaum when he explains that he left the French steampunk community because of their criticism of his "offbeat" style, which Grunbaum calls out as coded racist language since "there are so few non-Caucasian people in the French steampunk community. There is a white domination with a Victorian and Belle Époque style put forward which is perfectly natural! But it is not natural not to accept that there are other influences (and that's where I come up with my multiculturalism)." Outrage poured from several French steampunks in response, including one poster who wrote, "I am very disappointed myself, when I read that according to you, the French steampunk community is a bunch of racist bastards who never promoted multiculturalism."[36] Grunbaum's accusation of racism is complicated, however, by the neo-Nazi connotations of his cosplay performance as the "Black Hussar (Hussar of Death)." In the French steampunk community, where military paraphilia is avoided, Grunbaum wears the Iron Cross, a skull symbol reminiscent of the insignia worn on the hats of the Schutzstaffel (S.S.), and other German military symbols. Grunbaum states that his work is dystopic and doesn't glorify fascist regimes, alluding to his Jewish German ancestry as defense: "Don't forget that I have a Jewish-German surname (GRUNBAUM), my grandfather is German from Bavaria and I am not racist nor communist nor fascist."[37] A cognitive leap of faith must be made when Grunbaum says his work is apolitical while also evoking the historical and political trauma in his family history. Grunbaum privileges the other in a way unique from white chop-hop rappers and black steamfunkateers—as an other in temporality and history rather than an other of race/minority. He declares, "I do not support any moustachio'd or bearded malfeasant of the past or present century. I am Steampunk and I live in a different world! In alternate history! Very far from the reality of our history!"[38] His conflict is one answer to the questions Goh asks: do minority performances evoking historical trauma committed by hegemony further reinforce dominant power? Or do they defy the hegemony by exposing that traumatic break? For Grunbaum, reimagining from the margins is a radical act that does more than expose historical trauma; it provokes it with an artistic social amorality for the sake of innovation.

Cross-cultural minority steampunk performances may also fail to dismantle hierarchies if they have an insufficient critique of dominant paradigms of power, and, as Shohat and Stam point out, "[run] the risk

FIGURE 6.3. Maurice Grunbaum as the Hussar of Death. Photograph by Bernard Rousseau; image used by permission of the photographer.

of simply inverting the existing hierarchies rather than profoundly rethinking and unsettling them."[39] In the United States, Savan Gupta portrays another other as "A Count Named Slick-Brass," a steampunk version of Katt Williams's character "A Pimp Named Slick Back"; Gupta's performance attempts to subvert whiteness but flounders outside the source materials' context. Williams' pimp originated in his stand-up comedy routine but gained notoriety for his role on *The Boondocks* (2005–10), a television show created by Aaron McGruder. While Gupta embraces the steamfunk movement, his Count does not represent black empowerment. Gupta's aesthetics—a combination of leopard fur, leather, brass, and Prussian military gear—marks A Count Named Slick-Brass as European. Performance-wise, however, Gupta impersonates William's black pimp. A Pimp Named Slick-Back advocates for "slapping a ho" to resolve marital disputes, sells his female entourage for dates, and dresses garishly in a bright purple zoot suit and large-feathered matching fedora. Similarly, Gupta's A Count Named Slick-Brass runs an airship called the A.S.S. *Titilus*, which parallels his actual entertainment company Steam-Funk.com. Gupta's Slick-Brass parrots Slick-Back's mannerisms, makes misogynistic insults, offers unwanted sexual advances, and parades himself as the ultimate salesman at conventions and in Steam-Funk.com-produced media.

Many in the steampunk community do not question Gupta's character choices as Slick-Brass and in fact joyfully welcome him at steampunk events and in online media. For example, A Count Named Slick-Brass stars in the popular 2013 steampunk video parody of Psy's 2012 hit "Gangnam Style," produced by himself and steampunk maker Thomas Willeford.[40] Titled "Steampunk Style," Slick-Brass is the focus character, first daydreaming of gyrating white female bodies before pursuing them while living "steampunk style." Unlike Psy's original video, which served as a playful commentary of the lifestyle of the Korean nouveau riche, "Steampunk Style" lacks political drive and argues for the conflation of fandom life with real life, destroying any separation between Gupta's intentions and that of his character.

In the midst of these metaphysical arguments concerning art and life, Gupta interprets his character as a satirical commentary about race relations in Western countries:

> I find that my definition of steampunk is at odds with many, but that also ties back to certain conflicts of ideology in East Meets West. For instance, most Western civilization sees things—and apologies for the generalization—in black and white terms, espe-

cially in America. While I'm a moral imperialist, aesthetically, I tend to see in shades of gray (and color). I enjoy discourse and contradictions within to expand everyone's definition thereof.[41]

Unfortunately, outside the context of *The Boondocks*, Gupta's performance is ineffective satire. *The Boondocks* is a biting comedy concerned with political and social issues of African American life by black creators with a black audience in mind. On the other hand, steampunk subculture, which already faces issues concerning racial representation and romanticized historicity, does not provide the same cultural context for A Count Named Slick-Brass to exist as a satirical figure in the same way that A Pimp Named Slick-Back does. Appropriated from *The Boondocks* and situated in a white-dominant, Eurocentric subcultural space where other steampunks uncritically celebrate the stereotype that A Count Named Slick-Brass represents, Gupta's performances, instead of being antiracist, further promote antiblack racism. Furthermore, his performance is problematized by a long social history of antiblack racism within the Asian American community. According to progressive political advocacy group ChangeLab's report about Asian America's views on race, while

> Asian Americans do not think about race generally, they have also internalized a sense of superiority over other peoples of color, particularly Black people. Interviewees attributed this to structural forces that reinforce pejorative ideas of blackness, and positive ideas of whiteness, along with the prevalence of the model minority myth, which casts Asian Americans as "honorary whites" and encourages a sense of racial pride.[42]

The effect of Gupta's performances, despite his stated intent, works in collusion with the white supremacist framework that U.S. minorities struggle against. Thus, minority artworks are not inherently radical and can even be complicit in promoting ideas that their creators reject.

Conclusion: Toward a Polycentric Multiculturalism

What do all of these steampunk performances propose? To condense, expressions of national and racial identity are complicated in a world where both identities have been destabilized. Within steampunk subculture, however, all adherents develop a subcultural kinship created through Internet forums, convention gatherings, and shared interests. Yet while both white and minority participants are attracted to otherness, each arrives at this identity through different understandings: minorities draw on lived experiences of institutionally enforced oppression, while whites project these experiences onto themselves. A simplistic assumption, however, would be to argue that steampunk genre creates a level playing field as both groups grapple with the legacies of the oppressor and the oppressed. Their historical narratives are recognized as intertwined, but appropriation runs rampant, even if marginalized groups are able to control images of themselves to an extent in subcultural media.

I suggest that perhaps the shared presence of these conversations will build toward what Shohat and Robert Stam call "polycentric multiculturalism," or a discourse that "has to do less with artifacts, canons, and representations than with the communities 'behind' the artifacts" that result in "a profound restructuring and re-conceptualization of the power relations between cultural communities."[43] Polycentric multiculturalism in steampunk would reinforce the importance of the ethical implications of creative endeavors. This methodology aims for more than the glorification of art for art's sake; it aims for its contextualization. The beginnings of polycentric multiculturalism have already taken root in the accountability that steampunks hold each other to in discussions about race, culture, and historic oppression and in attempts toward global interactions. The latest endeavor is an online international blogging carnival called Steampunk Hands Around the World. Initiated by American steampunk Kevin Steil, this event ran during February 2014 and involved the participation of eighty-six bloggers from twenty-one countries across eleven languages with the goal of showcasing the contributions of a global community and addressing topics such as the arts, community spotlights, and discussions about race, multiculturalism, and colonialism.[44] The steampunk community is slowly recognizing the need to address historical grievances in conversations that go beyond a "Kumbaya" sing-along celebrating difference. Whether a radical definition of difference will take hold in steampunk subculture's evolving identity—one that delves further into the complexities of identifying and creating otherness—remains to be seen.

NOTES

1. The most prominent conversation about steampunk and whiteness still on record occurred on the *Steampunk Empire* in a thread that began on January 24, 2010, and ran over sixteen pages long with hundreds of comments; Crimean Palais, "SteamPUNK = A domain only for the WHITE ? +++ Is SteamRAP upcom-

ing soon?" *Steampunk Empire* (forum), January 24, 2010, http://www.thesteampunkempire.com/forum/.

2. See Bryan C. Sawyer, "Steampunk!—A White Aesthetic Movement," *Stormfront Forums*, September 21, 2008, http://www.stormfront.org/forum/t524908/. This thread started in 2007 and remained active several years later, with nineteen pages of comments, the last dated August 2012 from Kaiser Corax: "I've always been a big fan of steampunk, especially when set in realistic, earthly settings. I like the idea of the British and other European Empires crushing the rest of the world with steam powered, wood and brass robots."

3. Diana M. Pho, "Objectified and Politicized: The Dynamics of Ideology and Consumerism in Steampunk Subculture," in *Steaming into a Victorian Future: A Steampunk Anthology*, ed. by Julie Anne Taddeo and Cynthia J. Miller (Lanham, Md.: Scarecrow Press, 2013), 185–210.

4. Charles Stross, "The Hard Edge of Empire," *Charlie's Diary* (blog), October 27, 2010, http://www.antipope.org/charlie/; Catherynne Valente, "Here I Stand, with Steam Coming Out of My Ears," *Rules for Anchorites* (blog), November 3, 2010, http://catvalente.livejournal.com/.

5. Dick Hebdige, *Subculture: The Meaning of Style* (New York: Routledge, 1979), 64.

6. bell hooks, "Marginality as Site of Resistance," in *Feminist Theory: From Margin to Center* (Boston: South End Press, 1984), 203.

7. Hebdige, *Subculture*, 64.

8. Though this article will address whiteness as the dominant identity of North America and Western Europe, I do recognize that there are different levels of identification in play in how whiteness and Anglo-British identity are treated in Western culture. The Anglophilia of both the United States and Canada depends on a British other that is (naturally) not present in the British understanding of their own national identity. I do not wish to conflate them. Nevertheless, the dominant national understanding of both global areas centers whiteness as the racial default and speaks of British identity in the same manner, which is what I refer to when I talk about the hegemonic, Eurocentric white identity in steampunk subculture.

9. Jeni Hellum, *Multiculturalism for Steampunk* (blog), last modified January 21, 2013, http://thesteamerstrunk.blogspot.com.

10. Ella Shohat and Robert Stam, *Unthinking Eurocentrism: Multiculturalism and the Media* (New York: Routledge, 1994), 359.

11. Jha [Jaymee Goh], "The Intersection of Race and Steampunk: Colonialism's After-Effects from a Steampunk of Colour's Perspective," *Racialicious* (blog), June 24, 2009, http://www.racialicious.com/; Balogun Ojetade, *Chronicles of Harriet* (blog), http://chroniclesofharriet.com; Suna Desi, *Steampunk India*, http://www.steampunkindia.com; Ay-leen the Peacemaker [Diana M. Pho], *Beyond Victoriana* (blog), http://www.beyondvictoriana.com.

12. I also note that race relations play out differently outside of the geographic scope of North America and Western Europe, though the ramification of these conversations can still be witnessed by the rest of the world. Here I limit myself

to analysis of the West's relationship to otherness through steampunk. How steampunk, race, and identity function in non-Western, nonwhite steampunk communities (such as the Japanese steampunk community) are outside the scope of this article. Nonetheless, performance of identity in this ahistorical subculture highlights how different performers process the systematic and institutional acts of violence of the nineteenth century through their own specific racial and nationalist lenses.

13. Jaymee Goh, "Toward Chromatic Chronologies: Using the Steampunk Aesthetic for Postcolonial Purposes" (master's thesis, McMaster University, 2012), 14.

14. Mike Perschon, "The Steampunk Aesthetic: Technofantasies in a Neo-Victorian Retrofuture" (doctoral dissertation, University of Alberta, 2012), http://hdl.handle.net/10402/era.29133.

15. Jamieson Ridenhour, "'Anything Is Possible for a Man in a Top Hat with a Monkey in a Monocle': Remixing Steampunk in Professor Elemental's *The Indifference Engine*," in Taddeo and Miller, *Steaming into a Victorian Future*, 90.

16. Mr. B the Gentleman Rhymer, "'All Hail the Chap' by Mr. B the Gentleman Rhymer. Latitude Festival 2011. Sky Arts," YouTube, 3:41, July 16, 2011, http://www.youtube.com/watch?v=aUzTWJnHeDE.

17. Mr. B the Gentleman Rhymer, "Mr B the Gentleman Rhymer 'Let's Get This Over and Done With,'" *YouTube*, 2:46, June 13, 2010, http://www.youtube.com/watch?v=Wx4qZiiz7Cc; Mr. B the Gentleman Rhymer, "Straight Outta Surrey by Mr. B the Gentleman Rhymer," *YouTube*, 3:00, July 18, 2008, http://www.youtube.com/watch?v=Bj7J7vXCf5w.

18. Ian Baucom, *Out of Place: Englishness, Empire, and the Locations of Identity* (Princeton, N.J.: Princeton University Press, 1999), 147.

19. Mr. B the Gentleman Rhymer, "'Chap-Hop History' by Mr. B the Gentleman Rhymer," *YouTube*, 5:31, October 21, 2009, http://www.youtube.com/watch?v=6t28COxEp2k.

20. Professor Elemental, "Professor Elemental—I'm British (Dir: Moog Gravett)," *YouTube*, 3:18, November 27, 2012, http://www.youtube.com/watch?v=FkF_XpA5P48.

21. Professor Elemental, "Professor Elemental Defines Steampunk (or, At Least Tries To)," *Tor.com* (blog), October 1, 2012, http://www.tor.com.

22. Elemental and Tom Caruana, *Rebel Without Applause*, 2008, digital album, http://professorelemental.bandcamp.com/.

23. bell hooks, *Yearnings: Race, Gender, and Cultural Politics* (Boston: South End Press, 1989), 295.

24. Jha, "Intersection of Race and Steampunk."

25. Jeanette Ng, "Commission: Steampunk Magistrate," *Costume Mercenary* (blog), March 6, 2011, http://costumemercenary.blogspot.com.

26. hooks, *Yearnings*, 209.

27. Elizabeth Lameman, "#97 The Path Without End: An Anishinaabe Steampunk Film—Guest Blog by Elizabeth Lameman," *Beyond Victoriana* (blog), December 11, 2011, http://beyondvictoriana.com/.

28. Monique Poirier, "Musing about Native Steampunk," *Moniquilliloquies* (blog), May 18, 2011, http://moniquill.tumblr.com/.

29. Anna Chen, "The Steampunk Opium Wars," *Anna Chen* (blog), http://www.annachen.co.uk/the-steampunk-opium-wars/.
30. hooks, *Yearnings*, 209.
31. Maurice Broaddus, "Pimp My Airship," *Apex Magazine*, August 3, 2009, http://www.apex-magazine.com/.
32. Milton Davis and Balogun Ojetade, eds., *Steampunk!* (Fayetteville, Ga.: Mvmedia, 2013), 7.
33. Balogun Ojetade, "Steamfunk Is . . . ," *Chronicles of Harriet* (blog), 2013, http://chroniclesofharriet.com/2015/04/24/is/.
34. Theoretics, "Theoretics—Jekyll & Hyde (with Mark Hoy, Chimaroke Abuachi)," *YouTube*, 4:45, October 29, 2011, http://www.youtube.com/watch?v=nphr6QGiYrg; David Guetta, "David Guetta—Turn Me On ft. Nicki Minaj (Official Video)," *YouTube*, January 31, 2012, http://www.youtube.com/watch?v=YVw7eJovGfM.
35. Maurice Grunbaum, interview by Diana M. Pho, "Beyond French Steampunk: Multiculturalism with Maurice Grunbaum," *Beyond Victoriana* (blog), April 21, 2013, http://beyondvictoriana.com/.
36. Ibid.
37. Maurice Grunbaum, e-mail message to the author, May 21, 2013.
38. Ibid.
39. Shohat and Stam, *Unthinking Eurocentrism*, 359.
40. Savan Gupta and Thomas Willeford, "Psy–'Gangnam Style' Parody—Steampunk Style," *YouTube*, March 21, 2013, http://www.youtube.com/watch?v=TWY-59yGH6k.
41. Savan Gupta, personal interview with the author, February 26, 2012.
42. ChangeLab, "Left or Right of the Color Line: Asian Americans and the Racial Justice Movement," *ChangeLab*, 2012, http://www.changelabinfo.com/research.
43. Shohat and Stam, *Unthinking Eurocentrism*, 47.
44. Kevin Steil, "Steampunk Hands Around the World—Official Link List," *Airship Ambassador* (blog), February 1, 2014, http://airshipambassador.wordpress.com/2014/02/01/steampunk-hands-links/.

PART III

Steampunk
Reading and Revising

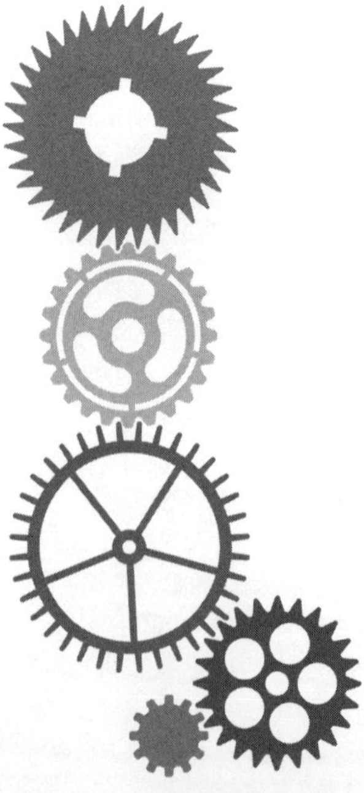

Seminal Steampunk

Proper and True

MIKE PERSCHON

On May 2, 2013, as I began in earnest to work on this chapter, Diana M. Pho's "Beyond Victoriana" Facebook page posted a link to an article with this intriguing tagline: "Over on the Steampunk Workshop, @Jonathan Greyshade talks about the nine novels that define steampunk and yes, how the punk element was *always* there."[1] Greyshade's article never overtly argues for the perennial presence of punk in steampunk, though the sentiment could easily be inferred. In "The Nine Novels That Defined Steampunk," Greyshade argues that steampunk has fallen from the heights of its origins, currently wallowing in a mire of unreflective clichés and tropes.[2] He arrives at this conclusion by briefly examining the early steampunk writing of K. W. Jeter, Tim Powers, James Blaylock, and Michael Moorcock, as well as William Gibson and Bruce Sterling's *The Difference Engine* (1990). The argument is emblematic of a common thread I've encountered in genealogies of the genre: it attempts to prove that modern steampunk lacks some sort of punk core—that is, a profound, political, perhaps countercultural message—that these seminal texts possessed. Until this volume, no sustained academic attention has been given to seminal steampunk in America, and misconceptions are becoming increasingly pervasive about the content of these early steampunk texts. Without any wish to quell current interest in steampunk being politically charged, I hope to give a brief survey of key seminal texts in steampunk, along with investigations of their ostensible deeper meaning, to counter the charge that steampunk has always been punk and that it should consequently remain so.

The now politically charged suffix *-punk*, terribly difficult to put to rest, is the proverbial chestnut of steampunk discussion, producing seemingly endless ruminations on the absence or presence of a countercultural punk attitude in steampunk. In issues 1 and 7 of *SteamPunk Magazine*, articles advocating "putting the punk back into steampunk" suggested punk had been there at the outset and had subsequently disappeared.[3]

Such fixation on the "punk" half of steampunk led Rebecca Onion to speculate on its origin: "Many of the people who participate in this subculture see reading, constructing, and writing about steam technology as a highly libratory countercultural practice . . . hence the addition of the word 'punk.'"[4] Where Onion and others err is in mistakenly assuming intentionality on K. W. Jeter's part in coining the term in 1987. This is arguably the product of the rift between what the subculture currently imagines as the values of steampunk and what Jeter as unintentional neologizer never meant to say. Nevertheless, our discussion began with appeals to original authorities, so clarification about what Jeter meant remains necessary. Jeter, with characteristic tongue in cheek, reveals his apolitical motivation: "My coining back in 1987 of the word *steampunk* originally might have been more of a humorous jab at a tendency going around those days, of labelling any two genre writers with more in common than bipedal locomotion as the '[insert word here]-*punk*' movement."[5]

Despite this whimsical origin for the "punk" in steampunk, articles and forum threads continue to appeal to the -*punk* suffix, conflating it with political activism and postcolonialism, or in certain cases "self-declaredly radical and openly anarchistic North American branches" of the steampunk subculture.[6] My issue is not with the appropriation of the "punk" in steampunk for political or ideological ends. Instead, I take umbrage with how these arguments sometimes appeal to the authority of literary origins, citing Michael Moorcock as the crucial example of early steampunk writers espousing countercultural ideologies, then attempting to jam Blaylock, Jeter, and Powers into that mold with a crowbar. While it is undeniable that Moorcock's Nomad of the Time Streams series (1971-81) expresses his anarchist views, it requires a series of hermeneutic contortions to force the California trio to express anything but entertaining tales with their early steampunk.

This presumption about punk politics clouds the steampunk scholar's inquiry, as evidenced by Onion's erroneous and potentially unintentional inference that the "punk" in "steampunk" is the result of a conscious decision on Jeter's part to associate the term with political activism. If a steampunk scholar were to proceed without engaging in extensive primary research, as though this "agenda setting, first wave criticism" was correct, she would likely find herself in error.[7] Nor is this association with steampunk and politics limited to peer-reviewed scholarly explorations of steampunk subculture. Most conspicuously,

Jess Nevins betrays a negative bias toward second-wave steampunk by denouncing it for abandoning the politics of the seminal works:

> Steampunk, like all good punk, rebels against the system it portrays (Victorian London or something quite like it), critiquing its treatment of the underclass, its validation of the privileged at the cost of everyone else, its lack of mercy, its cutthroat capitalism.... But most second generation steampunk is not true steampunk—there is little to nothing "punk" about it. The politics of the punk position have largely disappeared from second generation steampunk, and most of it is more accurately described as "steam sci-fi" or, following John Clute, "gaslight romance."[8]

Nevins's argument that "second generation steampunk" has not been "true" to the original vision of the genre has been influential: Brian J. Robb tacitly accepts Nevins's conflation of steampunk with punk rebellion, perpetuating the idea without questioning its pedigree.[9] Perpetuation is exacerbated by conjecture: despite a lack of explicit examples of what is meant by first-generation steampunk, Margaret Killjoy assumes Nevins meant K. W. Jeter, James Blaylock, and Tim Powers.[10] Only a few, like Dru Pagliosotti, appear to have any familiarity with seminal steampunk to dispute Nevins's claim.[11] Perhaps consequently, the work of Jeter, Blaylock, and Powers has become conflated with serious steampunk, or as Killjoy puts it, "steampunk proper," which, in his estimation, is political.[12]

Nevins endorses a prescriptivist approach to steampunk, where an expert determines what the "true" expression is—in this case, Peter Nicholls's definition in the *Encyclopedia of Science Fiction and Fantasy*, based on K. W. Jeter's coining of the term in April 1987—and dictates this idea to others.[13] If some homogeneity existed in the seminal steampunk texts of the first generation of steampunk, then an original ideology to steampunk could be conceded. But first-generation steampunk does not possess such ideological uniformity. As Sarah Ferguson has noted, Nevins is positing steampunk as a "once-'authentic' and homogeneously oppositional subculture" that, upon reaching critical mass, "is infiltrated by the media, and abandons its political edge."[14] To accept this requires the acceptance of two premises: first, that steampunk was intrinsically political at one time, and second, that it has ceased to be so. It turns out, however, that both of these assumptions are incorrect. I am aware of no second-generation steampunk that explicitly commits the sins Nevins attributes to it: "With its steam machines used against the American natives in Westerns, and steam-powered war machines being used in the service of the British army conquering Mars."[15] Many second-wave steampunk works contradict Nevins's accusations, with Ferguson noting how, ironically, "Nevins' assessment is . . . somewhat undone by its placement," given that several of the works in the VanderMeers' anthology are primarily second wave and punk in their politics.[16] Yet while Ferguson identifies this weakness in Nevins's argument, she assumes he is correct in the statement that all seminal steampunk was also intentionally ideological. She states that first-wave steampunk "is characterised by texts which adopt the framework of alternative history to explicitly condemn nineteenth- and twentieth-century systems of power and domination," adding that, despite fantastic elements, these works' "socio-political targets are nonetheless unmistakeable and relatively unambiguous."[17] However, like so many other critics, she cites only Moorcock's *Warlord of the Air* (1971) as an example. While Moorcock's steampunk is admittedly political, it is but one of many early steampunk works and—contrary to Killjoy's estimation that "there have always been radical politics at the core of steampunk"—arguably in the minority given its serious and intentional engagement with postcolonial criticism.[18]

By the time Jeter was inadvertently labeling not only his own "Victorian fantasies"[19] but (as it would come to pass) all Victorian fantasies, there were numerous examples to apply the term "steampunk" to. Kelly Link and Gavin J. Grant, for instance, address the indeterminacy of steampunk's beginnings: "Depending on whom you believe, steampunk has been exploding into the world for the last hundred years (thank you, Monsieur Jules Verne) or maybe the last twenty-five (when the term was first used by K. W. Jeter in a letter to *Locus* magazine)."[20] While Verne and Jeter are popular starting points for steampunk, others posit alternate and less well-known beginnings: Polish comic book writer Krzysztof Janicz, webmaster of *Retrostacja*, begins his steampunk chronology with Keith Laumer's alternate history novel *Worlds of the Imperium* (1962). In a list of steampunk works "written before a word existed to describe them," the *Encyclopedia of Fantasy*'s earliest inclusion is Joceyln Brook's *The Crisis in Bulgaria, or Ibsen to the Rescue!* (1956).[21] At the 2009 Eaton Science Fiction conference, SF author Greg Bear offhandedly suggested Harper Goff's design of the *Nautilus* in Disney's *20,000 Leagues Under the Sea* (1954) as the birth of steampunk.[22] The discussion surrounding these books is more an investigation of first instances of Victorian fantasy in the twentieth century and less an examination of the influential critical mass of texts and films that lead to Jeter's offhand creation of the term "steampunk." While I readily concede any of these works as potential antecedents and inspirations to steampunk, it seems counterproductive to seek a period earlier than the 1970s for steampunk's inception because such open-ended retrospeculation leads inevitably to debates about whether Jules Verne and H. G. Wells should be considered steampunk writers.[23] Whatever fuzzy boundaries one constructs for the origins of steampunk, a rising number of narratives written in homage, parody, or pastiche of Victorian and Edwardian scientific romances emerged in the 1970s, preceding Jeter's coinage of "steampunk."

Steampunk begins in the United States with James Blaylock's "The Ape Box Affair" (1978) and K. W. Jeter's *Morlock Night* (1979), which the *Encyclopedia of Fantasy* incorrectly describes as the "first genuine steampunk tale."[24] Here I focus on the four writers most frequently associated with what has largely been considered seminal steampunk: Michael Moorcock, K. W. Jeter, James Blaylock, and Tim Powers. For purposes of concision, I have further confined my attentions to the key texts that are often cited in arguments about the original punk ideology within steampunk.[25] Given the aforementioned dearth of treatment of the Californian steampunk writers, I discuss Jeter's *Morlock Night* extensively but deal with *Infernal Devices* (1987) only in passing, as that is dealt with at length elsewhere in this volume.[26] I have included all of Blaylock's early steampunk, with the exception of the short fictions of "The Idol's Eye" (1984) and "Two Views of a Cave Painting" (1988), since Blaylock's work is arguably the least supportive of the idea that seminal steampunk is serious and political. Finally, while Powers's inclusion in any discussion of steampunk should remain contentious, I briefly address *The Anubis Gates* (1983) because it is often cited as a work of early steampunk, but I do not include *The Stress of Her Regard* (1989) because it is rarely accepted as steampunk.

Michael Moorcock: The Warlord of the Air

Moorcock is arguably the first major SF writer of the 1970s to write what Jeter would later call "Victorian fantasies" with *The Warlord of the Air* in 1971. The novel tells the story of Captain Owen Bastable, a loyal English army officer, traveling seventy years into the future to an alternate 1973 where the British Empire still holds sway. What is immediately notable from the cover of the book's first edition is the distance between Moorcock's steampunk vision and the marketing machine of the day—something that should remind us that twenty-first-century steampunk cannot be seamlessly conflated with its twentieth-century roots. The cover of the first edition features sleek, silver air vessels that do not resemble lighter-than-air ships at all: they share greater kinship with the supersonic aircraft of the Cold War era than zeppelins or dirigibles. Although the first airship Bastable sees in the future does have an envelope "constructed of some silvery metal," it is clearly still an airship with a gondola and four triangular wings at the stern: a rigid airship such as the zeppelins of the early twentieth century. Later Moorcock describes the *Rover*, an airship that the novel's protagonist finds himself aboard after his removal from the British air force, which shares even fewer similarities with the glossy vessels on the first edition's cover:

> She was battered and needed painting, but she was as brightly clean as the finest liner. She had a hard hull, obviously converted from a soft, fabric cover of the old type. She was swaying a little at her mast and seemed, by the way she moved in her cables, very heavily loaded. Her four big, old-fashioned engines were housed in outside nacelles which had to be reached by means of partly-covered catwalks, and her inspection walks were completely open to the elements. I felt like someone who had been transferred from the Oceanic to take up a position on a tramp steamer.[27]

This Old World aesthetic is reflected better by White Wolf's omnibus release of Moorcock's Bastable books, *A Nomad of the Time Streams*, which features artwork by Chris Moeller, acting as the hand in the sketchbook of Bastable himself. His cover captures a number of the retrofuturistic concepts behind *Warlord of the Air* perfectly, as a fleet of airships from countries all over the globe drop lines of bombs, while Bastable stands in the foreground, looking pensively into the distance, dressed in a red uniform evocative of British colonial militarism.

This retrofuturistic, postcolonial gaze has led some to offer *Warlord of the Air* as evidence for the presence of the countercultural "punk" in seminal steampunk. While protagonist Captain Oswald Bastable begins his tale as a loyal servant of the British Empire, his journey eventually makes him an antagonist of it. Once he learns that "the Indian starves so that the Briton may feast," he finds himself gaining sympathy with the rebels within Dawn City, an "international settlement" containing "exiles from every oppressed country in the world." His conversion comes as a surprise, not so much to the reader as to himself: "I don't know when I had come to identify myself with bandits and revolutionists—and yet there was no mistaking the fact that I had. I refused to join them, but I hoped that they might win."[28]

Moorcock artfully delivers the impetus for Bastable's change via his decision to make a fin de siècle British citizen travel through time to a neo-Victorian 1974, so that the oft-used trope of "modern man travels into the past" is turned on its head, perhaps in homage to H. G. Wells.[29] Bastable's manners and loyalty to the crown are anachronistic enough to the modern reader, yet Moorcock takes the extra step of placing this anachronism within an alternate late twentieth century, so that the reader finds the familiar just as defamiliarized as Bastable does:

> And for the first time I had a sense of loss. I felt I was leaving behind everything I had come to understand about this world of the 1970s, embarking on what for me would be a fresh voyage of discovery. I felt a bit like one of the ancient Elizabethan navigators who had set off to look for the other side of the planet.[30]

The familiar is made even stranger by Moorcock's choice of the nationality behind the rebellion against Empire, given that Bastable ultimately chooses to side with the rebels, and the novel's eponymous warlord, who is Chinese. It is difficult for modern readers to remember that in the 1970s, it was still normative in mass media to imagine Asians largely as villains; Bruce Lee and the martial arts hero was the exception, not the rule. Consequently, contemporary 1970s-era global politics concerning the Vietnam War likely made Moorcock's novel a radical statement. The warlord of the air, Shuo Ho Ti, also known as General O. T. Shaw, strikes the reader as sympathetic in his acts of terrorism as Verne's Captain Nemo.

Warlord of the Air reads well as a straight adventure story until the final chapters, where Moorcock's political commentary switches from subtext to narrative thrust: in its final pages, Hiroshima is the target of the Warlord's new weapon: an atomic bomb. In Moorcock's alternate history, "The Great Powers are using the big airship yards at Hiroshima as their main base."[31] Within the narrative, destroying this colonial asset represents a considerable tactical gain for the Warlord; as metacommentary, dropping an atomic bomb on Hiroshima as politically postcolonial act is complicated, and Moorcock renders it so, with Bastable caught in the blast rising from the same city it did in real history, thirty years later.

> There was a strange noise, like a single, loud heartbeat. There was darkness and I knew I was blind. I burned with unbearable heat. I remember wondering at the intensity of the explosion. It must have destroyed the whole city, perhaps the island. The enormity of what had happened dawned on me.
>
> "Oh my God," I remember thinking. "I wish the damned airship had never been invented."[32]

Even as Moorcock sets the Warlord up as a postcolonial hero, he complicates this heroism with this act of monstrous violence. Perhaps it is done to show the horror of the end of the Pacific war to a 1970s readership that still believed without reservation in the need for the atomic bomb. Perhaps it is a counterfactual investigation of the question whether changing historical events changes human nature or the destiny of certain nationalities or communities. Before the bombing run commences, one character muses about the ramifications of choice: "There are an infinite number of possible societies. In an infinite universe, all may become real sooner or later. Yet it is always up to mankind to make real what it really wishes to be real. Man is a creature capable of building almost anything he pleases—or destroying anything he pleases."[33] These ruminations are borne out in the character of O. T. Shaw, the Warlord: he is both the builder of the utopian Dawn City, haven of oppressed revolutionaries, and the destroyer of Hiroshima in atomic fire.

This political aspect makes Moorcock's *Warlord of the Air* valuable to the study of steampunk: because his books are early in the progression of steampunk, they potentially validate the belief that "true" steampunk is engaged with political subtext and commentary. Moorcock continues this postcolonial conversation in *The Land Leviathan* (1974), the sequel to *Warlord*. Echoing O. T. Shaw's lecture on the rise of the opium trade in China as impetus for the "ruin of China," *The Land Leviathan*'s frame narrative finds a fictional Michael Moorcock (supposedly the author's grandfather) traveling through China in the first decade of the twentieth century, meditating on the disparity between the wealth of the West and the poverty of the East, the horrors of war, and the corruption of the opium trade.[34] Killjoy is unarguably correct in his estimation of Moorcock insofar as the punk/political roots of steampunk.[35] But finding political critiques in Moorcock's seminal steampunk is not particularly surprising, given how he has fostered a persona characterized by gestures toward "radical social transformations" and self-avowed anarchism.³⁶ Admittedly, it would be foolish of me not to concede that Moorcock's steampunk writing is a foundation for the punk/political aspects of steampunk. However, Killjoy is dead wrong in his conflation of "serious" steampunk with the writings of K. W. Jeter, James Blaylock, and Tim Powers. Turning our attention to the United States and the three Californian writers associated with steampunk's beginnings, the political subtext appears far less intentional—if there is indeed any political subtext to be found.

K. W. Jeter: Morlock Night

Because K. W. Jeter is heralded as the man who invented steampunk, readers likely have high expectations concerning his first steampunk work, *Morlock Night* (1979). Further, if one's steampunk expectations are influenced by Nevins or Killjoy, which is to say that steampunk is inherently political, we consequently expect *Morlock Night* to be among the most radical of steampunk texts. Perhaps one might also expect it to foreshadow the seriousness of cyberpunk, because of Jeter's early cyberpunk novel, *Dr. Adder* (1984), ignoring the obvious temporal distance between the two. Jeter is the only seminal steampunk writer who also wrote cyberpunk, but given his status as the man who invented steampunk, the association is likely further reason for the regular and misguided conflation of steampunk with cyberpunk: Nevins calls steampunk the "half-brother" of cyberpunk, despite few cyberpunk writers producing steampunk until the 1990s.³⁷ Since cyberpunk is often perceived as serious and political, *Morlock Night* is likewise assumed to be serious and political. Readers of H. G. Wells's *The Time Machine* (1895) have a further reason to raise the bar of expectation because *Morlock Night*'s original cover boasted an explanation for "what happened when the Time Machine returned."³⁸ Regrettably, fans of Wells's serious social commentary are likely disappointed to discover that Jeter's novel is largely escapist, page-turning entertainment. One of his characters self-reflexively warns the Wellsian faithful to avoid taking things too seriously here—after all, it's only a story: "My good fellow, don't get so excited over a mere story! Divert yourself with whatever sequels you care to imagine, but save such passion for reality."³⁹ The conversation surrounding this statement clearly indicates that Jeter is diverging from *The Time Machine*'s agenda. *Morlock Night* is a sequel to *The Time Machine* in plot and action, not politics or ideology.

The plot is relatively simple: *Morlock Night* picks up precisely where *The Time Machine* ends, with the attendees to the Time Traveller's story dispersing, wondering at the outcome of the open-ended tale. Among these attendees is Edwin Hocker, who meets a mysterious stranger on his walk home from the Time Traveller's. This stranger, who turns out to be Merdenne—the Arthurian Merlin—cryptically warns Hocker of an impending peril to the future of Britain and Christendom. This peril arrives in the form of the Morlocks, who have ostensibly done away with the Time Traveller and stolen his machine, and are using the machine to invade London. Merdenne sends Hocker on a quest to retrieve Excalibur, which holds the key to defeating the Morlock hordes. Hocker discovers his true identity as the reincarnated King Arthur, and in a final and fatal battle, he defeats the Morlocks. In "Parenthetically Speaking," his afterword to the collected *The Adventures of Langdon St. Ives* (2008), Blaylock states that Jeter's *Morlock Night* was written not only as a sequel to *The Time Machine* but also as part of a series "that would involve the reincarnation of King Arthur throughout history."[40] Although the series was scrapped, Jeter found a home for *Morlock Night* with DAW paperbacks. Readers unaware of this origin may be surprised to discover Jeter's Merlin using magic without any concession to steam or punk, and to learn that ultimately Merlin's goal is to save, not trouble or overthrow, Christendom and by extension Britannia. Before my first reading of Jeter, informal discussions with steampunks had lead me to believe that steampunk was SF not fantasy, was political, and was likely of an anarchic stripe—because that is the way original steampunk literature was. Yet there I was, reading "original" steampunk with closer affinities to C. S. Lewis's *That Hideous Strength* (1945) than anything by Moorcock.

Admittedly there are sections of *Morlock Night* that could be read politically, such as the denunciation of the British Empire by an old man initially suspected to be the reincarnation of King Arthur:

> "Did I live and die all those times so that a few children of England could grow fat while the many sweat out their drab lives in the dark holes of the cities?" His trembling hand flew toward the window, from which the dark shapes of the tenements could be seen. "And beyond our shores," he said with weary disgust. "Did I defend England so that other lands could be made to suffer our will, their people ground beneath our heel for our profit? Oh, how

tarnished our English honor has become! How strong the armor that covers a rotted heart!"[41]

But passages such as these must be balanced against the response of Hocker, the true reincarnation of Arthur, who refuses the old man's blanketing of the people of England as complacent: "England's light is buried, but not gone out. . . . Englishmen will fight and die without you, no matter how lost the cause."[42] Here the ideological distance between Wells's science fiction and Jeter's steampunk is considerable: in *The Time Machine* and *The War of the Worlds* (1898), Wells was criticizing English entitlement and complacency,[43] while Jeter repeatedly imagines Britain as possessing an essential messianic and mythic power, as evidenced in these statements by Merdenne/Merlin, seeking to convince Edwin Hocker to answer the dangerous call to adventure:

> There is a certain spiritual power . . . inherent in the English blood and soil. An embodiment of the highest Western values. This power, of course, gets perverted or eclipsed from time to time. A lot of this jingo nonsense in the name of Empire isn't much of a credit to the English race. But still, it's only a temporary lapse of memory. *The power remains,* however tarnished or neglected it becomes. And I have, shall we say, an interest in preserving that. For if it should die, the world would darken and lapse into brutishness.[44]

While Jeter engages in what I've called social retrofuturism—the insertion of contemporary values anachronistically into fiction set in the past—as Merdenne/Merlin worries over those oppressed by the boot of Empire, the statement is primarily about how there is something inherently good and arguably better about the English than the rest of the world: "King Arthur is reborn every generation in time to intercede against the direst threat facing the cherished Christian and human ideals that are embodied in England more than any other place. It's a commentary on humanity's penchant for mischief, inasmuch as there's always a threat to Christendom."[45] This valorizing of English and Christian ideals is delivered with deadpan seriousness, and overtures to problematizing Empire and the problem of the poor in English are largely paid lip service. This is clearly not the postcolonial critique of Moorcock.

Beyond the authorial expectations that surround Jeter as the inventor of the term "steampunk" and the writer of serious cyberpunk, it has become more widely known that Jeter and his compatriots based their writing on a nineteenth-century documentary text accurately chronicling the life of the impoverished and unfortunate in Victorian London. Consequently, Johnathan Greyshade states without qualification that, on the basis of their use of Henry Mayhew's *London Labour and the London Poor* (1851), the work of Jeter, Powers, and Blaylock, "portray[s] poverty frequently and unflinchingly."[46] The influence of Mayhew on *Morlock Night* is undeniable, at its most obvious in the overt correspondences between the section "Of the Sewer Hunters" from the second volume of *London Labour* and the account of Rich Tom in *Morlock Night*.[47] Consider Mayhew's account of how the Sewer Hunters, or "toshers," as they called themselves, could better their situation, based on the value of the objects they discovered discarded into the London sewers:

> With their gains, superior even to those of the better-paid artizans [*sic*], and far beyond the amount received by many clerks, who have to maintain a "respectable appearance," the shoremen might, with but ordinary prudence, live well, have comfortable homes, and even be able to save sufficient to provide for themselves in their old age. Their practice, however, is directly the reverse. They no sooner make a "haul," as they say, than they adjourn to some low public-house in the neighbourhood, and seldom leave till empty pockets and hungry stomachs drive them forth to procure the means for a fresh debauch. It is principally on this account that, despite their large gains, they are to be found located in the most wretched quarter of the metropolis.[48]

Now compare the testimony of Jeter's Rich Tom, an amalgam of one of the "peculiar nickname[s]" Mayhew's sewer hunters are known by— Long Tom—and an unnamed interviewee, whom Mayhew describes as "really an active intelligent man."[49] Here Jeter imagines that Long Tom, "one of the people he interviewed back in '49 or '50," has taken Mayhew's written advice to eventually become Rich Tom:

> Ah, well, there's the kindness Mr. Mayhew did me. The calling *does* pay well, for all manner of objects is lost into the sewers for the finding of those that know the ways. But most toshers spend their earnings on drinks and suchlike sprees as fast as they can get it. Mr. Mayhew, bless his memory, was the one who pointed out to me the folly of such rude practices, and how fast a little put by from one's findings would soon amount to a tidy sum. I followed his

advice, though Lord! I got thirsty at times, and now the people in this district hereabouts call me "Rich Tom."[50]

Yet such references, frequent or not, are hardly "unflinching" gazes at poverty. The way Jeter and, as we shall see, his fellow California steampunk writers engage with the impoverished of London shares more of the romanticism of Charles de Lint, who imagines the homeless of his fictional contemporary city of Newford (1990–2009) in a decidedly romanticized light. Jeter's steampunk toshers are simply a way to allow the heroes of *Morlock Night* to take their quest to the sewers of London, which take on an aspect of the watery catacombs beneath the Paris opera house in film versions of *Phantom of the Opera*. Rich Tom is a tosher who has, in a short bit of alternate history, taken advice Mayhew's interviewed toshers seem never to have taken. An unflinching look at Mayhew's toshers would have kept Tom a slave to drink, a guide more akin to Gollum than Jean Valjean or Abel Magwitch. This bit of wishful thinking on Jeter's part seems very much the flinch.

The romanticized influence of Mayhew on *Morlock Night* is further seen in the idea of the Grand Tosh, based on Mayhew's interviewee's description of "more than two or three hundred weight all rusted together, and plenty of money among it too," which he deemed "too heavy to carry out."[51] Jeter alternates between paraphrasing and sometimes nearly quoting the interviewee when Rich Tom tells Edwin Hocker of the likely location of one of the four copies of Excalibur in a Grand Tosh: "In that hidden magnetic lode of all that's most precious and lost—there is the place you'll find the Excalibur that was thrown into these sewers."[52] What Mayhew uses as proof of the potential riches available to the sewer hunters is turned into the reason for moving Hocker's quest for Excalibur into the sewers of London, which even Mayhew admits as a space that presents "an adventure of no small risk."[53]

Angry Robot Books released a new edition of *Morlock Night* in an omnibus with Jeter's other steampunk classic, *Infernal Devices*, in 2011. The omnibus features cover art by steampunk favorite John Coulthart, one for each story: *Infernal Devices*, which is arguably the superior work, on the front and, despite being chronologically first in publication date, *Morlock Night* on the back. Coulthart's beautiful cover is fascinating in how it continues to promulgate a horizon of expectation for *Morlock Night*. Julie Anne Taddeo and Cynthia J. Miller call the Californian steampunk books "darkly atmospheric novels" set in "a London darker and wilder than anything imagined by Dickens," an estimation matched by Coulthart's cover.[54] And while Coulthart's approach is visually pleasing, it would have been more accurate to have been able to commission *Morlock Night*'s first-edition artist, the late Josh Kirby, to produce another of his dizzyingly dense, madly crowded covers in the style he is famous for from Terry Pratchett's Discworld novels (1983–2015). It certainly would have indicated the tone of *Morlock Night* better. *Morlock Night* does not contain dark themes; it is a romantic adventure story filled with nineteenth-century tech and medieval magic.

James Blaylock: The Adventures of Langdon St. Ives

While *Morlock Night* is lighthearted in comparison to Jeter's other early works, it is the epitome of seriousness compared to fellow Californian James Blaylock's steampunk writing. Like Jeter, Blaylock made good use of Mayhew as source material, most clearly in *Homunculus* (1986) and particularly in the character of Bill Kraken. Kraken's wanderings and occupations read like a who's who from Mayhew: he is introduced in *Homunculus* as a peapod man, one of many costermonger occupations Mayhew catalogs in the first volume of *London Poor*.[55] He picks up one of Langdon St. Ives's soggy and discarded cigars, a possible reference to Mayhew's "cigar-end finders . . . who collect the refuse pieces of smoked cigars from the gutters."[56] Kraken is later revealed to have been employed in several other low-income trades, including squid hawker, a variation of street sellers of fish, though Mayhew makes no mention of squid or carp (the fish that figures so crucially to the action in *Homunculus*) in his cataloging of the kinds of fish sold by London costermongers; and grave robber.[57] At first glance, Kraken appears to be Blaylock's version of Dick Van Dyke's jack-of-all-trades, Bert, from Disney's *Mary Poppins* (1964). But Kraken is more accurately a jack-of-all-Mayhew-trades: to read Mayhew and *Homunculus* in tandem allows one to see how Kraken allows Blaylock to explore a number of the trades Mayhew chronicles in the first volume of his *London Poor*. It is true that Blaylock artfully describes impoverished areas of Victorian London and the people who inhabit them. Nevertheless, *Homunculus* is no more social commentary than is Jeter's *Morlock Night*. In truth, many of its vignettes are long-form versions of scenes of mistaken identity from Blaylock's 1978 short story, "The Ape Box Affair," the first steampunk work written in the United States, as it precedes Jeter's *Morlock Night* by a year.

In brief, the story is about an orangutan crashing in St. James Park in an experimental spherical flying ship, where he is promptly mistaken for an alien. Hilarity ensues in the intersections between the orangutan's adventures and an attempt to deliver a jack-in-the-box to a child. It's easy to imagine "The Ape Box Affair" as silent film played at high speed. The story has physical slapstick of the Keystone Cops variety, but is also riddled with dry, ironic statements about how Victorian Londoners might react to an alien invasion. Contrast H. G. Wells's "Exodus of London" in *War of the Worlds* with this line about the Lord Mayor's response to the alien in St. James' Park: "He rather fancied the idea of a smoke and a chat and perhaps a pint of bitter later in the day with these alien chaps and so organized a 'delegation,' as he called it, to ride out and welcome them."[58]

The most telling line of "The Ape Box Affair" comes halfway through the story, after high jinks and shenanigans have already reached a fever pitch: "It was at this point that the odd thing occurred"—as though an ape landing in St. James Park lacked oddity.[59] This is the style of Blaylock's steampunk, utterly lacking a serious political subtext. Blaylock is not looking into the past to say something about the present. He looks to the past as a fun place to play, a place where aliens arriving in London are met with the hope for a smoke, a chat, and a pint of bitter, rather than the London of today, where an alien might be met by the military. In short, Blaylock's steampunk is a world where whimsy rules.

There is no better example of the sovereignty of whimsy in Blaylock's oeuvre than "A Hole in Space," written in 1977 but left unpublished until the release of *The Adventures of Langdon St. Ives*. Blaylock openly admits Lewis's Space Trilogy as an influence on his work, and while reading "The Hole in Space," I recalled what Lewis said about technology in science fiction: "I took a hero once to Mars in a space-ship, but when I knew better I had angels convey him to Venus."[60] Blaylock takes the middle ground between angels and astrophysics, imagining the sort of solution to a black hole an eight-year-old boy might, especially the sort disposed toward plugging up dikes. The origin of "The Hole in Space" is a favorite anecdote of Blaylock's at public appearances:

> So there we were at O'Hara's Pub, talking about something vital. . . . K. W. [Jeter] rolled his eyes at something I'd said (something involving "science") and suggested that given my curious notions of that subject I'd be likely to write a story in which someone plugged a black hole with a Fitzall Sizes cork. After a momentary

silence I asked him whether, with all due respect, he was willing to let me have that idea or whether he wanted it for himself. He said I was welcome to it, and I went home and wrote "The Hole in Space."[61]

Here at the genesis of steampunk, as today, there is a decided absence of interest in real physics or astronomy. The technology here is far from the hard SF espoused by John W. Campbell Jr. Blaylock describes the operations of St. Ives's spacecraft with the same degree of rigor as his Fitzall Sizes Cork solution to black holes: "There were gyros to ameliorate and fluxion sponges to douse." When it is finally time to lift off, the Professor jabs buttons and heaves on "a bloody great anti-something-or-other-crank with silver wires sprouting from it like tentacles."[62] As such, Blaylock remains a wonderful monkey wrench in the great brass gears of those who decry modern steampunk as not being serious enough. Clearly one of steampunk's ostensible originators lacked this requisite seriousness.[63]

But even as critics like Greyshade and Killjoy are squeezing Blaylock into a preconceived notion about what true steampunk is, their lack of attention to whimsy or the romantic treatment of Mayhew is ancillary when one considers the other thread that runs through so much of Blaylock's long-form fiction. While steampunks are happy to trumpet the anarchist tendencies of Moorcock, they are far more reticent about the spiritual battles between good and evil in Blaylock's urban fantasies, which constitute much of his writing. I have joked that if Jeter, Blaylock, and Powers are really "steampunk proper," as Killjoy says, it might be more accurate to argue steampunk as inherently Christian in its ethos: Tim Powers is a Catholic, Jeter's *Morlock Night* is about a battle to preserve Christendom, and James Blaylock, in addition to citing Christian writers C. S. Lewis and Charles Williams as inspirations,[64] primarily writes theodicies. While this tendency is more obvious in his California novels such as *The Last Coin* (1988), *The Paper Grail* (1991), and *All the Bells on Earth* (1995), it is also present in his steampunk novels. The petty evil of the Un-man toward Ransom in C. S. Lewis's *Perelandra* (1943), "a black puerility, an aimless empty spitefulness content to sate itself with the tiniest cruelties," is more likely to be found in Blaylock's villains than some great, cataclysmic master plan.[65] Likewise, the acts of goodness and heroism are those of normal people, tempered by the mundane. There are no heroes of Arthurian mettle in Blaylock's steampunk. In the moral universe of *Lord Kelvin's Machine* (1992), Langdon

St. Ives's greatest act is not thwarting his nemesis, Narbondo, but showing him compassion. As Roz Kaveney notes, when St. Ives is faced with the opportunity to kill the villain as a child, his decision "to give alms to Narbondo's mother rather than to commit infanticide" is "typical" of Blaylock's writing.[66] St. Ives seeks to change the past to save his wife, Alice, but in the process ends up saving the young Ignacio Narbondo from meningitis. His act of compassion changes St. Ives as well, healing the bitter wound left festering from believing Alice's death occurred because of Ives's indecision. After a series of time traveling misadventures in which he vainly seeks to change the past, he finally succeeds in thwarting Alice's murder. However, despite wanting to stay in that moment in time with his wife, forcing his past self out of the picture, his misadventures have matured him, causing him to realize that he cannot remain in that past:

> He looked out into the street, where his past-time self lay invisible in the water and muck of the road. You fool, he said in his mind, I earned this, but I've got to give it to you, when all you would have done is botch it utterly. But even as he thought this, he knew the truth—that he wasn't the man now that he had been then. The ghost in the road was in many ways the better of the two of them. Alice didn't deserve the declined copy; what she wanted was the genuine article.
>
> And maybe he could become that article—but not by staying here. He had to go home again, to the future, in order to catch up with himself once more.[67]

This is a beautiful speculative reflection on the nature of identity and potential: St. Ives is no longer the man whose hesitation cost him his wife. He is no longer the man who stood and watched her die. He is another man—a man no longer driven by revenge upon his nemesis but tempered by compassion, knowing the origins that may have driven Narbondo to the life he led. The passages where St. Ives visits the fitfully sleeping child Narbondo are heartbreaking, given how villainous Blaylock renders Narbondo in *Homunculus* and more recently *The Aylesford Skull* (2012). St. Ives cannot conflate the criminal with the child. Near the end of *Lord Kelvin's Machine*, the moment when he traces the young Narbondo's spine for its characteristic hump is particularly touching because it echoes the touch of a parent checking his own child for injuries. St. Ives changes the past by curing the child's ailment, but more importantly, he changes himself. Blaylock's St. Ives, through the fictional novum of time travel, undoes even the fixed nature of the character in a play or novel, countering Luigi Pierandello's argument in *Six Characters in Search of an Author* (1921) that character is inevitably set, always cursed to play out the same actions. As St. Ives realizes in between one of his time traveling jaunts, "he had come back to a different world than he had left."[68] Changing the past through time travel is not only St. Ives's game but is also Blaylock's; he is rewriting St. Ives's past in this novel by giving him a wife. And while we, in the real world, are unable to make such massive changes arbitrarily, we can, like St. Ives, change the world around us through the sort of compassion shown Narbondo as a sickly child. It is an act that does not change Narbondo so much as it changes St. Ives. If oppositional politics are an essential part of true steampunk because they are found in Moorcock, then why do we not see the suggestion that charitable compassion is also part of true steampunk?

Tim Powers: The Anubis Gates

The temporal journeys of Blaylock's St. Ives share a kinship with the time hopping in Tim Powers's *The Anubis Gates*. But there is even less attention to ideology in *The Anubis Gates,* radical, anarchist, or humanitarian. When I explained my research project to Powers at the 2009 Eaton Science Fiction Conference, he bemusedly asked about *The Anubis Gates*: "So do you think it's steampunk?" Powers would ponder the question again at Steamcon later that same year. If steampunk is supposed to be a subgenre of science fiction, then Powers's contribution must be excluded, as it contains even less science than space opera. It involves time travel, so one might argue its relationship to Wells; but the time travel of *The Anubis Gates* is affected through a scientific manipulation of holes created by magic, a hybrid of fantasy with unexplained science. However, as Powers openly stated during a panel at the Eaton conference, his books are more fantasy than they are science fiction, unless one allows for spiritualism as a form of nineteenth-century science. Since *The Anubis Gates* takes place in the early nineteenth century, and because they are friends, Jeter lumped Powers in with his and Blaylock's "Victorian fantasies" in his offhand remark in *Locus* that birthed the term "steampunk." For this reason, regardless of how one defines it today, *The Anubis Gates* is part of how steampunk begins.

At its core, *The Anubis Gates* is an adventure story. Like Jeter and Blaylock, Powers did not write a novel of ideas. And at the risk of spoiling the surprise, it is, once again, not Moorcock's politically charged steampunk. It is simply filled with page-turning cliff-hangers and contrived coincidences that permit the hero to survive his adventures. The protagonist of *The Anubis Gates*, Professor Brendan Doyle, joins the league of pulp characters who can take a severe beating and persevere. Powers is a superior writer of escapist fiction; he simply has no higher agenda, exemplified best by a comment he made at the Eaton conference: he related how people often tell him Bram Stoker's *Dracula* (1897) is about the plight of nineteenth-century women, to which he replies: "Really? I thought it was about a creature that stays immortal by drinking blood!"

The Anubis Gates embraces this literal approach, stubbornly resisting any reading deeper than "the good guy is now trying to escape from the bad guy" or "the heroine is now trapped by the evil, sorcerous clown." The book jacket notes, "Only the dazzling imagination of Tim Powers could have assembled such an insane cast of characters: an ancient Egyptian sorcerer, a modern millionaire, a body-switching werewolf, a hideously deformed clown, a young woman disguised as a boy, a brainwashed Lord Byron, and finally, our hero, Professor Brendan Doyle"— which is no summary whatsoever.[69] Rather, it merely lists the motley cast of characters of *The Anubis Gates*, which might very well be the only way to tantalize a potential reader without giving away the novel's surprises. David C. Kopaska-Merkel summarizes *The Anubis Gates* as follows: "The plot... is similar to those of some of Powers' other novels. The protagonist encounters a problem, struggles against it, and gives himself up to drugs and denial but pulls himself together in the end."[70] Reducing the plot to this barest skeleton is informative for my argument: once again, the Californian steampunk writers fail to produce the weight of content so often attributed to early steampunk writing.

Further, *The Anubis Gates* is entirely unconcerned with industrial technology, supposedly essential to steampunk, focusing instead on thaumaturgic technology: magic. *The Anubis Gates* plays with Egyptian magic particularly, utilizing the nineteenth-century's generation of and their subsequent fascination with the mummy's curse, of Tutankhamen as a seeker of "secret mystical knowledge."[71] Accordingly, it is contemporary magic for the nineteenth century, going so far as to behave within the boundaries of a nineteenth-century worldview; in *The Anubis Gates*, an Egyptian sorcerer speculates that the binding of the ancient Egyptian gods coincided with the rise of Christianity: "They reside now in the Tuaut, the underworld, the gates of which have been held shut for eighteen centuries by some pressure I do not understand but which I am sure is linked with Christianity."[72] There is a verisimilitude gained including Christendom and ritual magic as a part of the fictional universe, if one wishes to write fiction in the British Empire or colonial Europe in the nineteenth century. China Miéville's Bas-Lag can be as godless as its author wishes it to be because it is a secondary world that echoes, not emulates, a Dickensian London. In real-world England, however, magic was a historical precursor to science. It is, if you will, protoscience, or even the science of its day. Accordingly, magic was a sort of technology in the Romantic, Victorian, and Edwardian periods. Serious thinkers such as William Butler Yeats and Evelyn Underhill were joining groups like the Hermetic Order of the Golden Dawn. The working magic of *The Anubis Gates* plays on this real-world analogy, but it is ultimately as fantastic as steam, aether, or clockwork imaginings in steampunk texts. Nevertheless, Powers's magical war between Christian miracle and Egyptian sorcery is a footnote in his tale; it tells the reader why Egyptian magic has lost its power but it does not figure largely in how the protagonist defeats the sorcerers who use it. In this Powers is more like Jeter than Blaylock, using Christianity as a plot device, not an expression of the author's Catholicism.

How, then, can we have steampunk proper and true? These are essentialist—or, to borrow from Nevins, prescriptivist—terms, which imagine steampunk as some fixed entity we can point to and say, "See? There's the truth." One wonders why steampunk adherents, who often espouse the radical individuality inherent in steampunk, feel any need to appeal to the authority of these early texts, as though the writers were penning steampunk scripture: Meister Moorcock and the Holy Californian Trinity. It is a fractious scripture, with Moorcock pontificating his radical, political doctrine on the one hand and the choir of Powers, Jeter, and Blaylock singing whimsical, romantic, and dissonantly polyphonic hymns on the other.

I do not wish to invalidate the political fervor of steampunks like Killjoy. But essentialism, the idea of a true or proper steampunk, seems antithetical to a punk ethos. I am bemused by a contemporary steampunk that appeals to seminal steampunk as authoritative instead of breaking free of any perceived conventions contained therein. Rather than erroneously championing Jeter, Blaylock, and Powers's use of Mayhew as incisive social commentary, shouldn't contemporary steampunk find ways to appropriate Mayhew for a more intentional critical conversation between past and present? Why force these writers' work to be more than it is when one could create the social commentary one must strain to find therein? To be fair, some modern steampunk does indeed do this, or something very like it. Karin Lowachee turns an unromantic steampunk gaze upon the relationship between colonial powers and indigenous people in *The Gaslight Dogs* (2010). The true villain of Jay Kristoff's *Stormdancer* (2012) and *Kinslayer* (2013) is arguably not the corrupt Shogunate but the ecological blight resulting from the recovery and refining of *Chi*, a fictional fuel.

To be fair, if steampunk's romantic vision can address serious issues, then should it not be equally permissible to do the opposite and lose the political subtext of Moorcock on the way to generating a romantic adventure story? This may be objectionable to Killjoy, but it is no less within the tradition of steampunk, if we allow Jeter and company to form the foundations along with Moorcock. Otherwise we will be prescriptivists, essentialists, dictating how steampunk must be. If all steampunk needed to be politically motivated, then we would arguably be without Gail Carriger's Parasol Protectorate series (2009-12), one of steampunk fiction's most successful series. If all steampunk needed to be science fiction and not fantasy, we'd be without Scott Westerfeld's flying whale ships in his Leviathan trilogy (2009-11).

Although I would prefer to see what steampunk could become, unencumbered by concepts of fidelity to steampunk proper and true, there are already steampunk texts that engage in both ends of the spectrum, which seminal steampunk reveals: a combination of countercultural punk ethos and whimsy—Moorcockneyed Mayhew, if you will. Greg Broadmore's Dr. Grordbort's series provides a strong example of this spectrum from contemporary steampunk. At the purely surface level, the Dr. Grordbort's books and the art that inspired them are set in a fictional world that draws on 1930s space opera and serials, the figure of the Great White Hunter, and present-day gun culture in the United States. Those three elements alone could easily end up perpetuating misogynist, patriarchal, and ethnocentric attitudes: the series often implies that owning one of Dr. Grordbort's weapons will make men more virile and therefore more desirable to women. The hero of the series, Lord Cockswain, cavalierly travels to alien worlds and murders the inhabitants to mount their heads as trophies. However, Broadmore's heavy use of ironic tone renders the use of these elements parodies. One advertisement in *Dr. Grordbort's Contrapulatronic Dingus Directory*, a catalog for a line of ray guns and other retrofuturistic weapons, boasts that owning a "Goliathan 83 infinity beam projector" will "settle your woes."

> Is that wife backchatting and a vote-mongering?
> Man servant not fulfilling his "duties"?
> Perhaps your daughter's buck-tooth suitor's giving unwanted grief? Make their posteriors clench with anxiety by flexing your new Goliathon!
> Some say its ambient radiations increase the manhood.*
> *tumefacterous growths not covered under warranty.[73]

It would be difficult to miss Broadmore's lampoon of machismo and gun culture in his consistent references to phallic compensation through possession of a big gun. But this lampoon is achieved in the pages of the catalog and its sequel, *Victory: Scientific Adventure Violence for Young Men and Literate Women* (2009), in meticulously detailed images of ornate ray guns. The gun designs are strangely realistic, combining elements of real-world firearms both current and antique, with space opera ray guns that borrow from the designs of Buck Rogers and Flash Gordon serials and comic strips.

A blending of both the whimsy and wonder of the Californian steampunks with the political subtext of Moorcock achieves some of the best of modern steampunk and indicates a way forward for all steampunk fans. For those like Killjoy and Nevins who feel the need for steampunk to make a statement, to be actively countercultural, steampunk like Broadmore's Dr. Grordbort's series offers postcolonial critique aplenty. However, for those who merely appreciate the series' retrofuturist look and its over-the-top parody of man's dominance over nature, Dr. Grordbort's is a playful lark—text to accompany extremely expensive artworks that look like ray guns.

Ultimately, I reject the notion that one can defend the idea that steampunk is inherently punk, inherently countercultural, or inherently ideological based on the works of Jeter, Blaylock, or Powers. Their texts simply cannot support such an assertion, and academics working in steampunk need to stop making unsupportable claims about these early works that convey the sense that they are serious, subversive works when they are primarily good entertainment. Although Moorcock can obviously support such a claim, his own words, repeated again here for the reader's ease, do not: "There are an infinite number of possible societies. In an infinite universe, all may become real sooner or later. Yet it is always up to mankind to make real what it really wishes to be real. Man is a creature capable of building almost anything he pleases—or destroying anything he pleases."[74] Even if steampunk is inherently political, and because of its genesis in the writing of Moorcock is anarchist by association, is there anything less anarchistic than imposing boundaries for what steampunk must be? Worse yet, what sort of anarchist needs the authorization of books that are decades old to justify the appropriation of the steampunk aesthetic for political ends? Steampunk is not an actual entity. It is not an ontological reality. It is an arbitrary literary category that inspired cinematic expression, which in turn inspired artwork, music, more literary creations, and, yes, a subculture. However, ultimately, we made it, and we are the ones who determine what it will become and who will determine what steampunk is today, regardless of what it was thirty years ago.

NOTES

1. Diana M. Pho, "Beyond Victoriana," *Facebook*, May 6, 2013, https://www.facebook.com/BeyondVictoriana.

2. Jonathan Greyshade, "The Nine Novels That Defined Steampunk," *Steampunk Workshop* (blog), April 29, 2013. http://steampunkworkshop.com/.

3. See Margaret P. Ratt, "Putting the Punk Back into Steampunk," *SteamPunk Magazine* 1 (2006): 2; Margaret Killjoy, "You Can't Stay Neutral on a Moving Train (Even If It's Steam-Powered)," *SteamPunk Magazine* 7 (2010): 5-7.

4. Rebecca Onion, "Reclaiming the Machine: An Introductory Look at Steampunk in Everyday Practice," *Neo-Victorian Studies* 1, no. 1 (2008): 139.

5. K. W. Jeter, "On Steampunk and 'Steampunk,'" in *Infernal Devices and Morlock Night* (Nottingham, U.K.: Angry Robot, 2011), 6.

6. For political activism, see Margaret Killjoy, "Steampunk Will Never Be Afraid of Politics," *Tor.com* (blog), October 3, 2011, http://www.tor.com/; for postcolonialism, see Jaymee Goh, "There Is Totally Punk in Steampunk," *Tor.com* (blog), October 19, 2009, http://www.tor.com/; Christine Ferguson, "Surface Tensions: Steampunk, Subculture, and the Ideology of Style," *Neo-Victorian Studies* 4, no. 2 (2011): 70.

7. Ferguson, "Surface Tensions," 68.

8. Jess Nevins, "Introduction: The 19th-Century Roots of Steampunk," in *Steampunk*, ed. Ann VanderMeer and Jeff VanderMeer (San Francisco: Tachyon, 2008), 10.

9. Brian J. Robb, *Steampunk: An Illustrated History of Fantastical Fiction, Fanciful Film, and Other Victorian Visions* (Minneapolis: Voyageur Press, 2012), 31.

10. Killjoy, "You Can't Stay Neutral," 6.

11. Dru Pagliosotti, "Love and the Machine: Technology and Human Relationships in Steampunk Romance and Erotica," in *Steaming into a Victorian Future: A*

Steampunk Anthology, ed. Julie Anne Taddeo and Cynthia J. Miller (Lanham, Md.: Scarecrow Press, 2012), 65–88.

12. Killjoy, "You Can't Stay Neutral," 6.
13. Jess Nevins, "Prescriptivists vs. Descriptivists: Defining Steampunk," *Science Fiction Studies* 38, no. 3 (2011): 513.
14. Ferguson, "Surface Tensions," 75.
15. Nevins, "Introduction: The 19th-Century Roots of Steampunk," 10.
16. Ferguson, "Surface Tensions," 86.
17. Ibid., 73.
18. Killjoy, "Steampunk Will Never Be Afraid of Politics." Killjoy cites both Michael Moorcock and Alan Moore as pioneers of steampunk. However, Moore's *League of Extraordinary Gentlemen* (1999) was published far too late to be considered a pioneer of steampunk.
19. K. W. Jeter, letter to *Locus,* April 1987.
20. Kelly Link and Gavin J. Grant, introduction to *Steampunk! An Anthology of Fantastically Rich and Strange Stories,* ed. Kelly Link and Gavin J. Grant (Somerville, Mass.: Candlewick, 2011), vii.
21. John Clute, "Steampunk," in *The Encyclopedia of Fantasy,* ed. John Clute and John Grant (New York: St. Martin's Press, 1997), 895.
22. Greg Bear, "Steampunk and Extraordinary Voyages" (panel discussion, Eaton Science Fiction Conference, University of California–Riverside, May 2, 2009).
23. Verne and Wells should not be considered steampunk writers. They might be the grandfathers of science fiction in general, but to reduce them to being primarily or solely the progenitors (or inventors!) of steampunk alone is ridiculous.
24. Clute, "Steampunk," 895.
25. I deal only with Moorcock's *Warlord of the Air* (1971) despite Nick Gevers's contention that Moorcock "pioneered the steampunk form with two major trilogies in the 1970s: *The Dancers at the End of Time* and *A Nomad of the Time Streams*"; introduction to *Extraordinary Engines: The Definitive Anthology,* ed. Nick Gevers (Nottingham, U.K.: Solaris, 2008), 9. One of these trilogies, encompassing *An Alien Heat* (1971), *The Hollow Lands* (1974), and *The End of All Songs* (1976), is collected as *The Dancers at the End of Time* (2000). The other trilogy includes *Warlord of the Air* (1971), *The Land Leviathan* (1974), and *The Steel Tsar* (1981) and is collected as *The Nomad of the Time Streams* (1995). I reference the most recent omnibus editions of these works, released by White Wolf. A complete investigation of these trilogies is beyond my scope here; however, they both deserve greater attention than academia has given them. *Dancers at the End of Time* alone could form an interesting study of seminal steampunk if read as a sort of presciently satirical take on steampunk's view of the past. *Dancers* chronicles the adventures of the decadent Jherek Carnelian, a time traveler from the far future (ostensibly only years away from the end of time) whose obsession with a nineteenth-century married woman results in a series of comical misadventures. Carnelian initially chooses to forego time travel to "his beloved 19th century" because "like most people, he found that the real places were rather disappoint-

ing." Instead he prefers to "indulge in imaginative re-creation of the periods of places." Michael Moorcock, *The Dancers at the End of Time* (Clarkston, Ga.: White Wolf, 2000), 12-13. This preference for a fanciful recreation of the past results in one of Carnelian's servant-robots donning a period costume that combines "a derby, an ulster, chaps and stout brogues" and carrying "several meerschaum pipes in its steel teeth" (13). While the series contains several moments of clever satire of both the late nineteenth century as well as, arguably, the late 1960s and early 1970s in the United Kingdom, here it only reinforces what a study of *Warlord of the Air* reveals: Moorcock's seminal steampunk overtly reflects his political views.

26. Joseph Weakland and Shaun Duke, "Out of Control: Disrupting Technological Mastery in Michael Moorcock's *The Warlord of the Air* and K. W. Jeter's *Infernal Devices*," this volume.

27. Michael Moorcock, *A Nomad of the Time Streams: A Scientific Romance* (Clarkston, Ga.: White Wolf, 1995), 80.

28. Ibid., 94, 105, 122.

29. Wells was Moorcock's inspiration for *Dancers at the End of Time*, which he wrote contemporaneously with *Nomad of the Time Streams*.

30. Moorcock, *Nomad*, 83.

31. Ibid., 132.

32. Ibid., 139-40.

33. Ibid., 135.

34. Ibid., 122; see also 156, 161, 164.

35. Killjoy, "Steampunk Will Never Be Afraid of Politics."

36. Rob Latham, "New Worlds and the New Wave in Fandom: Fan Culture and the Reshaping of Science Fiction in the Sixties," *Extrapolation* 47, no. 2 (Summer 2006): 306; see Michael Moorcock, interview by Margaret Killjoy, in *Mythmakers and Lawbreakers: Anarchist Writers on Fiction*, ed. Margaret Killjoy (Oakland, Calif.: AK Press, 2009), 117-23.

37. Nevins, "Introduction: The 19th-Century Roots of Steampunk," 8.

38. K. W. Jeter, *Morlock Night* (New York: DAW Books, 1979).

39. Ibid., 9.

40. James P. Blaylock, *The Adventures of Langdon St. Ives* (Burton, Mich.: Subterranean Press, 2008), 469.

41. Jeter, *Morlock Night*, 54.

42. Ibid., 55.

43. Robert Charles Wilson, "The Night Wind and the Morning Star," in *"The War of the Worlds": Fresh Perspectives on the H. G. Wells Classic*, ed. Glenn Yeffeth (Dallas, Tex.: BenBella Books, 2005), 153-64; Mercedes Lackey, "In Woking's Image," in Yeffeth, *"The War of the Worlds,"* 215-24.

44. Jeter, *Morlock Night*, 34.

45. Ibid., 41.

46. Greyshade, "Nine Novels."

47. Jeter, *Moorlock Night*, 70-72.

48. Henry Mayhew, *London Labour and the London Poor: A Cyclopaedia of the*

Condition and Earnings of Those That Will Work, Those That Cannot Work, and Those That Will Not Work, 2 vols. (1851; repr., London: Frank Cass, 1967), 2:152.

49. Ibid., 2:153.
50. Jeter, *Morlock Night*, 71.
51. Mayhew, *London Labour*, 2:154.
52. Jeter, *Morlock Night*, 76–77.
53. Mayhew, *London Labour*, 2:151.
54. Julia Anne Taddeo and Cynthia J. Miller, introduction to Taddeo and Miller, *Steaming into a Victorian Future*, xv.
55. Mayhew, *London Labour*, 1:3, 159, 180–81.
56. Blaylock, *Adventures of Langdon St. Ives*, 67; Mayhew, *London Labour*, 1:3, 2:145–46.
57. Blaylock, *Adventures of Langdon St. Ives*, 107; Mayhew, *London Labour*, 1:67–68; Blaylock, *Adventures of Langdon St. Ives*, 70–71.
58. Blaylock, *Adventures of Langdon St. Ives*, 15.
59. Ibid.
60. C. S. Lewis, *On Stories: And Other Essays on Literature* (Orlando, Fla.: Harcourt Books, 1982), 64.
61. Blaylock, *Adventures of Langdon St. Ives*, 469.
62. Ibid., 40.
63. Again, it should be noted that although "The Hole in Space" has a 2002 copyright, it was originally written in 1977, shortly after "The Ape Box Affair," which is why it appears second in *The Adventures of Langdon St. Ives*. This delay in publication was due to simple rejection, not Blaylock's awareness that it did not fit the mold of nascent steampunk.
64. James Blaylock, "Meet James Blaylock" (public interview, Steamcon [steampunk convention], Seattle, Wash., November 20, 2010).
65. C. S. Lewis, *Perelandra* (1943; repr., Toronto: Simon & Schuster, 2005), 152.
66. Roz Kaveney, "James P. Blaylock," in Clute and Grant, *Encyclopedia of Fantasy*, 121.
67. Blaylock, *Adventures of Langdon St. Ives*, 458.
68. Ibid., 448.
69. Tim Powers, *The Anubis Gates* (New York: Ace Science Fiction Books, 1983).
70. David C. Kopaska-Merkel, "*The Anubis Gates*," in *Magill's Guide to Science Fiction and Fantasy Literature* (Pasadena, Calif.: Salem Press, 1996), 28.
71. Roger Luckhurst, *The Mummy's Curse: The True History of a Dark Fantasy* (Oxford: Oxford University Press, 2012), 89.
72. Powers, *Anubis Gates*, 11.
73. Greg Broadmore, *Dr. Grordbort's Contrapulatronic Dingus Directory* (Milwaukie, Ore.: Dark Horse, 2008), 4.
74. Moorcock, *Nomad*, 135.

The Alchemy of Aether
Steampunk as Reading Practice in Karina Cooper's Tarnished *and* Gilded

LISA HAGER

In the early twenty-first century, steampunk, a literary genre and a maker subculture once primarily known by its community and fandoms, has become increasingly visible and popular in mainstream culture.[1] Steampunk's leap into popular culture, which is part of the broader movement of geek subcultures into U.S. mainstream media,[2] means that not only do more and more people actually know what steampunk is, but also, perhaps more interestingly, steampunk has carved out its own long-term niche in U.S. popular culture. For if steampunk has gotten so popular that people within the subculture can wonder if we have reached "peak steampunk,"[3] this once marginal literary genre and fan subculture has achieved a level of cultural saturation that lends itself to long-term social and cultural influence.

As a literary genre, steampunk's popularity is also part of a growing body of neo-Victorian literature, which has garnered much scholarly attention of late. Specifically, steampunk has become increasingly central in these conversations as a result of its extensive usage of nineteenth-century fashion, literature, and design as Victorian studies continues to interrogate its own role creating the Victorian. Steampunk's growing presence in this discourse is evidenced by publications like Rachel A. Bowser and Brian Croxall's 2010 special issue of *Neo-Victorian Studies* and Julie Anne Taddeo and Cynthia J. Miller's *Steaming into a Victorian Future: A Steampunk Anthology* (2013), as well as its strong presence in panels at academic conferences like Neo-Victorian Cultures: The Victorians of Today, hosted by Liverpool John Moores University in the summer of 2013, and more general Victorian studies conferences like the annual conference of the North American Victorian Studies Association. In looking at steampunk, scholars continue to demonstrate the necessity of exploring the influence of the genre's reimagined nineteenth century on literary texts and made objects that revise its history and technology. This innovative and provocative work coming out of Victorian studies' engagement with steampunk, as exemplified by many of the chapters in this volume, suggests that steampunk studies has become one of the central ways in which Victorian studies situates itself within twenty-first-century culture.

Building on these existing conversations regarding steampunk as a reimagining of nineteenth-century culture, I argue that steampunk literature offers the field of Victorian studies a method of contextualizing its own reading practices within the influence of nineteenth-century culture and identifying methodological difficulties intrinsic in studying a period that continues to haunt our present so insistently, specifically in regards to cultural discourses of science, aestheticism, and women's sexuality and agency.[4] At its core, steampunk is both a creative and critical practice in which aesthetics functions as the central mode of creative and critical response. Steampunk's self-reflective consumption and critique of nineteenth-century culture positions the interpretative act as always already bound up in a nexus of competing political, social, and economic forces. As such, steampunk offers Victorian studies productive intersections with the work of nonacademic experts, like fashion designers and other makers. By putting the academic textual work of interpreting Victorian literary culture in conversation with nonacademic material work of reimaging that same literary culture, we have the opportunity to envision critical work as taking place in multiple overlapping arenas and media, fostering the exchange of ideas across them. Furthermore, it is essential that Victorian scholars seek out these experts from outside of the academy as we continue to reflect on our critical practice and, in this time of dwindling state support of higher education, articulate the value of Victorian studies and public humanities.

As a literary genre and a maker movement, steampunk fashions new art by mixing historical fact and alternate historical imaginings to present a fiction whose aestheticized science of beautiful technology creates space for questioning conventional narratives of gender and sexuality. This dynamic between aesthetics and function is central to Karina Cooper's *Tarnished* (2012) and *Gilded* (2012), the first two novels of her St. Croix Chronicles,[5] and its heroine's struggles with the conflicts between the requirements that society places on her as an heiress of marriageable age and her obsession with solving mysteries—mysteries that increasingly center around the dangerous science of alchemy and its key element, aether. By looking at this popular romance novel series,

I trace how Cooper's use of aether and alchemy "punks" the intersecting Victorian ideologies of gender and class while simultaneously revealing the continuing hegemonic power of these ideologies in our conceptions of gender and sexuality. In so doing, Cooper's reading and reimagining of Victorian London demonstrates how steampunk literature works as popular form of enacted literary criticism, connecting both academic and fan cultures. In its potential to enact this criticism, popular steampunk like Cooper's offers a chance for both scholars and members of steampunk communities to reconsider the past and what we continue to inherit from the nineteenth century and how we conceptualize that inheritance.

Conceptualizing steampunk literature as a mode of reading offers Victorian studies an entry point into the genre through which we can more fully understand the implications of steampunk's mobilization of Victorian tropes, ideas, history, and technology. Scholars of Victorian literature and culture have long noted the influence of nineteenth-century British literature and culture on twentieth-century and twenty-first-century literature, especially the ways in which such works draw parallels between our own time and Victorian England. Exemplifying this common theme, Jess Nevins notes, "The social, economic, and political structures of the Victorian era are essentially the same as our own, and their cultural dynamics—the way in which the culture reacts to various phenomena and stimuli—are quite similar to ours."[6] As Steffen Hantke suggests, it is this timely quality of steampunk that gives it the explanatory power to reveal the workings of our own culture: "What makes the Victorian past so fascinating is its unique historical ability to reflect the present moment."[7] Extending this argument by considering what steampunk specifically adds to the conversation about the use of the Victorian past, Karen Hellekson describes the genre's willingness to play with the supposedly firm facts of history: "[Steampunk texts] make readers rethink their world and how it has become what it has. . . . And they foreground the 'constructedness' of history and the role narrative plays in this construction."[8] In other words, these critics position steampunk's neo-Victorian world as a mirror that both reflects our twenty-first century literary and cultural discourses and brings into relief the essential malleability of history.

Steampunk literary work, as part of alternate history literature, builds its world by answering the "what if?" question of science fiction and fantasy with tweaking nineteenth-century history and literature. In taking these liberties with historical narratives, steampunk, according to Bowser and Croxall, insists that "anachronism is not anomalous but becomes the norm."[9] Once we start to see how possible the seemingly wildly anachronistic narratives might be, even the most stable and foundational cultural narratives begin to bear traces of anachronism and subjective accuracy, particularly within this critical narrative of the nineteenth century mirroring the twentieth and twenty-first centuries. In order to avoid these critical fallacies, the key concept here is one of balance: understanding both the uniqueness of Victorian literary culture as well as the extent to which we create that literary culture by reading its material texts from a twenty-first-century point of view. As Simon Joyce indicates, layers of mediation create an ever-shifting temporality: "We never really encounter 'the Victorians' themselves but instead a mediated image like the one we get when we glance into our rearview mirrors while driving. The image usefully condenses the paradoxical sense of looking forward to see what is behind us, which is the opposite of what we do when we read history in order to figure out the future."[10] Joyce's comments suggest that the past, present, and future come into existence in the moment of reading and that these readings change depending on one's viewpoint. In its playful and often snarky self-awareness, steampunk literature is particularly well suited to this sort of reading practice in that as an alternate history genre, it begins with the deep awareness of the impossibility of knowing the truth of the original historical material. Moreover, it also means that texts' interpretations and reworkings of Victorian culture ultimately make visible the notion that any encounter with the past is a reading that takes place within the context of the present but still remains distinct from that present.

One of the primary and perhaps most obvious methods by which steampunk reads Victorian literature is through its deployment of Victorian aesthetics and its insistence on the relationship between aesthetics and technology. Mike Perschon argues that this quality defines steampunk in the popular imagination: "Steampunk [is] an array of visual markers which, when combined, constitute the look popularly understood as steampunk."[11] In commenting on recent steampunk literary work, Ann VanderMeer and Jeff VanderMeer argue that "steampunk has indeed become an aesthetic toolbox for a range of approaches."[12] Aesthetics are perhaps the most recognizable feature of steampunk as literary genre and subculture, and much of the genre's ethos is embedded in those aesthetics.[13] In objects like Jake von Slatt's mods, such as the "Victorian All-in-One PC" and the "Steampunk Stratocaster," which reenvision the computer and other technological devices as being powered by gears and steam, steampunk eschews smooth uniform modernity in favor of an approach that celebrates the bespoke, the gritty, and the unfinished. In much the same way as the outer surface of a Möbius strip becomes the inner surface, so too do the inner workings of steampunk inventions become the visible aesthetics of the object and the aesthetics, in turn, become the inner workings. In making such visible workings simultaneously aesthetic and functional, steampunk aesthetics dramatizes our understanding and analysis of the nineteenth century; it reads our readings of the Victorian period as well as offering its own interpretations.

Aether: Steampunk's Uncertainty Principle

Steampunk consequently both enables us to know the Victorian period and stages the incomplete nature of that knowing. This vexing relationship to knowledge is reflected in the often visible workings of steampunk objects and technology that seem to reveal function even as that function is frequently predicated on fictional technologies and materials, like aether. Aether was believed by the Victorians, including such scientific luminaries as James Clerk Maxwell and Sir William Thomson, Lord Kelvin, to be the element through which light traveled, and as such surrounded and connected all living and nonliving objects.[14] By theorizing that aether connected the universe and conducted electromagnetic energy, these nineteenth-century scientists were able to understand light's wave and particle functions. As a conceptual element, aether works as conductor and connector, allowing energy to cross vast distances and creating the links between the most unlikely objects and people.

In this framework, aether acts as the basic building block of life and structure; as such, science and technology based on aether can play with our notions of reality. In steampunk literature, this fictional element is often associated with anachronistic or fantastic technologies like the aethographor, a long-distance wireless communication device in Gail Carriger's Parasol Protectorate series (2009–12), or the alethiometer, which gives true answers to any question in Philip Pullman's His Dark Materials series (1995–2000). Much like the Victorians used the concept of luminiferous aether to grasp the contradictory behavior of light as both wave and particle, writers and makers of today often use aether to explain what cannot be explained within fantastic fictional steampunk worlds.

This quality of aether becomes even more powerful when it is connected with the science of alchemy. Alchemy, a science best known for its goal of turning any metal into gold, is primarily concerned with transformation of elements based on equations that seek to symbolically represent their essence. In the St. Croix Chronicles, Cooper connects aether with alchemy in order to create a science that exceeds the nineteenth century's actual scientific knowledge. Moreover, given alchemy's focus on symbolically representing the intrinsic properties of elements and concepts, this science operates as a sort of scientific aestheticism in that invoking alchemical symbols with aether as a catalyst enables one to transform physical reality itself by manipulating representations.[15] Thus, in alchemy, the symbolic representation of a substance more fully captures its properties than the seeming "real" properties of the substance. For example, alchemy, as we discover in *Tempered* (2014), the series' fourth book, enables the protagonist's mysterious guardian, Oliver Ashmore, to defy mortality by stealing the life force of his descendants once he has painted their portraits. Here and throughout the novels, alchemy transfigures aesthetic signification into a truth that exceeds the supposed truth of the real, paralleling steampunk literature's production of literature from literature as an interpretive practice. Cooper's aether-based alchemy is thus transformative (by reworking Victorian reality and the conventions of Victorian fiction into an alternate history) and revelatory (by pointing to our desire as readers of Victorian culture to know the essence of the period and to see ourselves in it).

Cooper's *Tarnished* and *Gilded* follow Cherry St. Croix, who moves between the highest echelons of London society and the demimonde of London below the polluted fog, which high society has literally risen above, to satisfy her addiction to opium and need to escape the restrictions of being a respectable young lady. When we meet Cherry for the first time in *Tarnished*, she seems to have mastered the difficulties and pleasures of the liminal life, moving between her two identities in both parts of London. Cherry is an orphan, the daughter of a society belle who married down when she became the wife of St. Croix, a mad scientist who is presumed dead. Before Cherry is found by her guardian and safely ensconced in a London townhouse with a chaperone, she was a child slave, forced to perform as a trapeze artist and thieve in Monsieur Marceaux's Traveling Circus. In the circus, she was also forcibly addicted to the opium that she still requires to sleep. As an adult, Cherry has turned her circus skills to her advantage as a bounty hunter hired by clients in both Londons, but she must choose between her double life and the powerful security of marriage to Earl Compton as her opium addiction and obsession with solving the intertwined mysteries of her parents' work and Jack the Ripper's murders threaten to take over her life completely.

In this world, aether functions as a sort of quantum field that has transformative properties and that disturbs social and spiritual order.[16] Aether powers airships and makes possible alchemical science in which matter and spirit can be dramatically transformed. As the novel's plot deeply enmeshes Cherry in the element's uncertain properties, she becomes increasingly conscious of her departures from conventional femininity even as society attempts to reassert its order and control. She offers us a reading of twenty-first century gender in relation to our own readings of Victorian gender, standing in for us as readers of Victorian culture and steampunk's fictional reworkings of that literary culture. Furthermore, this critical practice is intimately connected with scientific knowledge as a means of power and agency, as Cherry consistently connects the freedom to study alchemy with true independence. Within this reading, aether's simultaneously mystical and technological properties make it the exemplar of steampunk's aesthetic science, functioning according to certain conventional scientific principles and yet revealing its full power only in the symbolic logic of alchemy.

In Cooper's London, aether-based technology serves to render this nineteenth century markedly different from the historical past while using that difference to reframe nineteenth-century concerns about women's mobility. Here, the divide between the working classes and the upper classes has become even more pronounced than in the real nineteenth century, as the wealthy have had their buildings and districts elevated above the pollution-filled fog on a complex system of stilts: "Her Majesty retained . . . a decided view on etiquette and propriety. The end came with a simple declaration: *Rise above it.* . . . The end result was the cleaving of London's well-to-do from its poor, its immigrants and those who couldn't maintain appearances."[17] One's social standing is now physically represented in terms of one's vertical standing above the fog.

Transportation between London above and London below depends on aether-powered airships and gondolas, both of which Cherry makes extensive use in her frequent clandestine travels between the two Londons. In giving such consistent attention to Cherry's mode of travel, Cooper refigures Victorian concerns over urban young women's use of trams, bicycles, and the Underground. For the Victorians, urban mobility suggested not only women's increasing personal independence but also their modernity. The fraught nature of this access to transportation is perhaps most notably exemplified in the freedom and tragedy that such travel brings to Monica Madden in George Gissing's *The Odd Women* (1893). A shopgirl by profession, Monica's use of various forms of London public transportation enables her to move freely around the city and meet Widdowson, whom she marries to escape the drudgery of her life but whose paranoid possessiveness ultimately leads to her death.[18] Like Monica before her, Cherry's skillful movement between London's two levels enables her independence in her double life as a "collector," an all-purpose bounty hunter, by night and a society heiress by day as she hunts both Jack the Ripper and the other mysterious killer of lower London's prostitutes.

In her day hours, Cherry travels exclusively by means of the gondolas that have taken the place of horse-drawn carriages and hansom cabs. Well aware of transportation's class implications, Cherry herself notes that "you could tell a great deal about a family by their gondola." Given her family's problematic class position, "The St. Croix gondola is not the finest of them upon the drift."[19] Yet the display of wealth involved in the gondola itself is not the most important part of its function as a class marker; the real tell of one's position is the skill of its operator: "Fortunately for my already fragile reputation, Booth was an excellent gondolier."[20] Here, the importance that Cherry places on the piloting of her butler and gondolier, Mr. Booth, demonstrates a keen awareness of the necessity of conforming to class and gender expectations in her mode of transportation. As Cherry's comments regarding Booth's deft piloting throughout the series make clear, she is well aware that his work maintains her respectability in the eyes of society. In addition, she also implies the extent to which the manipulation of aether is an art that requires a person to occupy the space between foggy London below and the clean air of London above: "He'd mastered the levers lining the driver's seat to such an extent that the bottom of the gondola only just skimmed the fog."[21] By locating Booth's ability to support Cherry's class status in his liminal movement in the aether between the boundaries of the two Londons, Cooper highlights how aether connects these two supposedly separate class-stratified worlds. As the element existing between all things, aether serves as the connective tissue between both Londons even as it also powers movement between them. Foreshadowing its more subversive uses in alchemy, aether-fueled technology and the expert operation of such devices highlights class distinctions even as it also connects both Londons, serving as a constant reminder of dependence of London above on London below.

Further pointing toward the centrality of aether and its unstable social and physical properties, Cherry's all-consuming obsession with solving murder mysteries in both *Tarnished* and *Gilded* continually circles back to her parents' experiments with aether-fueled alchemy. In *Tarnished,* her presumed-dead father drugs her with an opium-based substance, móchù, that loosens the bonds between a body and its consciousness as he attempts to put her dead mother's consciousness into Cherry's body. Cherry falls victim to his plot while tracking his partner, whose collecting and killing of prostitutes, or "sweets," has earned him the nickname "sweet tooth" among the women of the Midnight Menagerie, a pleasure garden in the style of Vauxhall Gardens controlled by the Chinese mafia. In *Gilded,* Cherry is tasked with solving the murder of several professors. Cherry discovers that the crimes were committed by a bluestocking using alchemy to make herself invisible so that she could get revenge on those who refused to admit women into institutions of higher education. As she attempts to solve these mysteries, Cherry is courted by Earl Compton, whose proposal of marriage would give her a life of luxury and learning in exchange for conforming to society's conventions. Cherry eventually accepts his proposal to escape her debt to the Midnight Menagerie, but she becomes a widow on her wedding day when the sweet tooth murders her new husband. In each of these plots, Cooper locates Cherry's vulnerabilities to villainous machinations and a powerful social order in her parents' connection with aether and the effects of her encounters with aether through alchemy.

Cooper emphasizes aether's centrality and instability in these plots as they continually circle the power of alchemy to rearrange the order of society and the universe. In addition to the class transgressions of their marriage, both Cherry's father, Abraham St. Croix, and her mother, Josephine, were deeply involved in alchemy. The occult nature of her father's research is well known from the series' beginning to the point that everyone, including Cherry herself, calls her father "Mad St. Croix."[22] Cherry herself comes to understand the depth of that madness when her father uses the alchemical drug móchù to facilitate the exchange of her mother's consciousness for her own, and she nearly loses control of her own body: "I felt it; I lived it, I struggled against it as the pressure built and built. As it thrashed against the boundary of *me.* As it fought for purchase . . . It was trying to overtake me. It was trying to *devour* me!"²³ Here, Cherry's father is presumably destroying Cherry's consciousness in order to replace it with her mother's; despite the failure of the procedure, the process has the unintended effect of allowing Cherry's mother to periodically take over Cherry's body.²⁴ The aether in the drug alters that most basic of bonds, the connection between body and mind, dramatizing Victorian culture's anxieties regarding the boundary between them as it sought to elevate the masculine mind over the feminine body and position the body as a readable text revealing moral character.²⁵ As a key component in steampunk technology in this series and throughout the genre, aether, when distilled in alchemical formulas, then throws into question the basic rules of life and death, asking readers to reevaluate their own understandings of the line between the living and nonliving.²⁶

Aether reconfigures these most fundamental alchemical structures; likewise, it infects Cherry's body and irrevocably alters her lives in the two Londons, pushing her increasingly outside the conventional narratives for women in either London as she becomes further enmeshed in her family's alchemical heritage. Critically, Cooper ties this dramatic upheaval to Cherry's experience of sexual pleasure, which revises Victorian notions of women's sexuality, be they wives or prostitutes, as dependent on male sexuality.²⁷ Cherry's first kiss with Compton happens when they go to view an exhibit on galvanism, the effects of electricity on flesh, put on by a professor whom we later learn is her presumed-dead father: "The exhibit around us had been put together for one reason: to study the effects of electricity on dead tissue. But had the odd professor asked me, I could have written a proposal on the effects of electricity through live flesh on the spot." Though he initiates the kiss, she "lean[s] closer" to prolong the moment and elicits "a low note—surprise, maybe."²⁸ Cherry is a full and equal participant in this moment of sexual pleasure, and her suitor is surprised to feel a woman's desire equal to his own. In describing the pleasure of her first kiss, Cherry borrows from the language of her father's scientific work to explain the intense physical reaction she experiences with this intimate touch. Like the aether that her father is experimenting with, this moment of desire connects her with the earl because it establishes an unexpected bond and rearranges the conventional social order, as it marks Compton's clear pursuit of her as partner in marriage.

Cooper further explores this dynamic in Cherry's experiences with Michajah Hawke, the ringmaster of the Midnight Menagerie, which serve to more fully establish the link between Cherry's sexuality and her complicated relationship with aether that results from her family's dealings with alchemy. When she accidently comes into contact with móchù, Cherry survives because Michajah keeps her tethered to her body through oral sex: "High, keening pants filled the room and I realized somewhere that it was me. That I struggled to breathe and had no ability to censor myself. That I was shamelessly encouraging him with every dip of his tongue, every rasp of his lips and soul-shocking skim of his teeth."[29] This intense physical pleasure serves to connect her body in the moment of orgasm, when her mind is filled entirely with the sensations of her body, thus enabling her to prevent her mother from completely invading her body. Hawke fights the drug's disassociating effects by giving Cherry a sexual experience that is all about her pleasure and, as such, frustrates patriarchal society's focus on penetrative sex and the disavowal of feminine pleasure reproduction. The energy intended to destroy the connection between Cherry and her body is instead turned into waves of pleasure in which she is most intensely present as a physical being. This power of aether within the mystical science of alchemy is rendered visible through the golden glow of Cherry's body throughout their encounter, literally embodying the fundamentally aesthetic nature of this science. This golden color alludes to alchemy's popularly known goal of turning base metals into gold, and the extent to which this sex act's subversiveness enables Cherry's body to transmute the mystical experience of the aether-laced drug from that of another's will being imposed upon her into a moment of self-awareness as she claims her sexuality.

Having established Hawke as the attractive bad-boy alpha male from the beginning of the series, Cooper pushes her readers to reconsider how we envision male sexuality in the nineteenth century and in our time. Hawke, as we discover later in the series, is himself an alchemist whose connection to aether is embodied in the blue flecks of his brown eyes that expand when he taps into that power. It is this power that enables him to save Cherry. When Cherry wakes after this experience and thinks that Hawke has taken advantage of her "drug-addled memory" to violate her, this response acts as the voice of conventional narrative.[30] Cherry reads her sexual experience through a narrative of women's sexuality that centers on the victimization of women by physically stronger men, a common trope in many Victorian novels as well as today's popular culture. However, Cherry is surprised to find out from her trusted friend, Zylphia, that "all he [Hawke] did was keep you from giving in," which is later confirmed by Hawke himself, suggesting a more complex sexual character for even this most clichéd of romance fiction's masculine characters and requiring us to reevaluate our narratives of men's sexual desire.[31] Hence, as Hawke's sexual healing of Cherry through his own connection to aether as an alchemist punks the genre's expectations of masculine sexuality, it also calls into question our understanding of Victorian sexuality and how we, as twenty-first-century readers, envision ourselves as liberated from the repressive mores of the nineteenth century.

Alchemy as Fictional and Academic Reading Practice

Cooper continues to develop this doubled reading practice—one in which both the nineteenth and twenty-first centuries must be reread—in *Gilded*, the series' second book, as Cherry's investigations into the murders of several professors suggests an affiliation between the intellectual ability to understand hidden symbolic meanings required by both alchemy and detective work. Lady Rutledge, one of her dead mother's friends, assigns Cherry a mystery as an assessment. She wants to know if Cherry has her mother's mind as well as her looks: "Your mother was a brilliant woman. You've inherited her looks, what of her senses?"[32] In particular, Lady Rutledge wants to know whether Cherry shares her mother's ability to make connections among the seemingly disparate elements required by detective work and alchemy. Tied by these associations to her mother from the beginning of the series, this parlor game mystery leads Cherry to discover that Miss Hortense Hensworth is using alchemy to make herself invisible so she can murder the professors who prevent women from taking degrees at London's King's College. Cherry may not agree with Hensworth's methods, but she thinks, "Give them the very devil" in response to Hensworth's letter to the *London Times*, in which she argues the following: "A woman's mind is by definition a mind suited to searching for the unknown. Centuries of subjection by the male of the species has left us with only one task—to raise the young of the men who choose us. But by that very definition, do we not exercise an aptitude for creative and logical endeavors?"[33] In this manifesto, Hensworth positions women as experts on the marriage market and in child rearing, both of which require no small amount of creative problem solving, as demonstrating their capacity for intense research and scholarship. Given Hensworth's alchemical experiments with aether to render herself invisible, this "unknown" that she highlights is more than scientific study in a general sense; it is also the commitment and ability to explore the science of aether, an element that scientists struggle to measure, see, and know.

In this context, then, Hensworth's tragic fate and Cherry's attempted retreat into marriage in accepting Compton's proposal illustrate the costs of making such leaps into the unknown for women within this steampunk Victorian England. Through her investigations, Cherry discovers that, as with any experiment involving aether, there is a price to pay: "Like most scientific endeavors, there were drawbacks to be had. Drawbacks that could build, like a slow poison or a quiet, subtle killer."[34] Though Cherry's assessment refers to the effects of Hensworth's invisibility formula on the body, it also applies to Hensworth's quest to go beyond the limits that society has placed on her as a woman, something that she shares with Cherry and Cherry's mother, who was ostracized after her déclassé marriage and scandalous scientific experiments. Cherry becomes aware of that price after Hensworth falls to her death during a ball at King's College, unnoticed and unmourned as an invisible corpse in the courtyard. Hensworth turns herself invisible in order to fight against the absence—the invisibility—of women in higher education. In the process, we see alchemy's powerful ability to render ideas invoked symbolically into physical, visible reality even as it ultimately makes her physically and socially invisible in death. Thematically, this excessive effect highlights the visibility of nineteenth-century women's invisibility to twenty-first-century readers.

Ultimately Cherry chooses the security of marriage and position in an attempt to avoid the fatal effects of this steampunked Victorian society's inability to accommodate women's scientific intelligence and agency. Initially Cherry insisted that she would not marry despite the intense social pressure to do so: "I'd rather drill holes through my fingernails than marry. In less than a year, I would inherit everything of my father's. If I married, common law dictated that everything that was mine belong solely to my groom. . . . Bugger that for a lark."[35] Alluding to legal principle of coverture, which subsumes a wife's legal identity and property under that of her husband upon marriage, Cherry explicitly links ownership of her property with ownership of herself. The earl's offer is one of safe harbor and social propriety: "I offer you shelter, kindness, and support. All I ask is that you fit the demands of a future marchioness." However, for Cherry, "the price [appears] far too high."[36] Though marriage would be easier, providing a permanent place for her and the staff who have become her family, Cherry initially chooses to the keep her individuality and her ability to move between the two Londons.

Yet once Cherry comes to understand all too well the price of her individuality, the drawbacks that inevitably follow a woman's encounters with breaking the rules and aether, she accepts the earl's offer. Cherry is attracted to Compton, but she only consents to be his wife once she understands that he is "a kindred spirit in the fight against the world that would take from us our freedoms. Our happiness."[37] Still, he and the position he offers Cherry as his wife would force her to change her life dramatically: "I would have no choice. To earn the right to be a woman of intellect and stature . . . I would have to play by the rules. Freedom would mean nothing if I lacked the status to use it."[38] Cherry does not make her choice lightly; instead, she mercilessly assesses the social power she must gain as a woman in society in order to have the freedom to pursue her own scientific studies. Her new position gives her undeniable social power while shielding her from society's reach as long as she fulfills the conventional forms and functions of being a countess. In being visibly conventional, she can study alchemy's aether-fueled transmutation of the symbolic into the real.

For readers of Victorian fiction, the sort of bargain that Cherry has made will seem familiar; middle- and upper-class women often had few options beyond marriage for having any kind of secure social position, as seen in novels like Mary Elizabeth Braddon's *Lady Audley's Secret* (1862) and Grant Allen's *The Woman Who Did* (1895). However, it is here that Cooper troubles this Victorian narrative. Cherry and her new husband do not live happily ever after, or even unhappily ever after. When the newly married couple pauses as they wait for a cab in London below on their way to the docks to depart on their honeymoon, the sweet tooth, the collector and murderer who had been working with Cherry's father, tricks Cherry into leaving her husband alone in the fog and murders him.[39] In one instant, Cherry's new life is destroyed, taking her old one along with it now that her new mother-in-law controls her entire fortune. In the moment when Cherry decides to pursue the murderer, the true effects of her father's drug fully reveal themselves. The móchù has exacerbated her addiction to opium and precipitates her obsession with catching the sweet tooth. At the beginning of the series, Cherry painstakingly stalks and plans in pursuit of her marks, yet here she pursues her most dangerous quarry with no weapons and in the constricting dress and corset of a proper society wife. She does so because she cannot resist the "challenge" of the sweet tooth's whistle.[40] Much like her parents and even Hensworth, Cherry has been infected by aether's ability to turn focus into obsession. Aether's far-reaching effects through alchemy amplify the troubled qualities of Victorian courtship narratives that structure so many nineteenth-century novels. Moreover, it also prevents this romance novel from having its clichéd ending, exposing the extent to which twenty-first century visions of Victorian life and literary culture depend on an imagined past.

By reconfiguring such familiar novel plots, Cooper's *Tarnished* and *Gilded* give readers a different approach to cultural inquiry of the Victorian period, making it accessible without falling into simulacrum. Cooper's deployment of alchemy as a science grounded in aesthetics blurs the lines between the symbolic and the real and in doing so suggests a methodology for thinking through what we cannot know about the historically distant and yet ever-present nineteenth century. Further, her mobilization of aether in this alternate history reminds us of our own desire to fill in gaps, which makes visible the ultimate elusiveness of historical and cultural certainty. In this series and in steampunk literature more broadly, aether and the alchemy it makes possible stage many of the more progressive themes and ideas, but full understanding of this fictional element remains just beyond our grasp, reminding us of intrinsic otherness of the nineteenth century. Consequently, when we read steampunk fiction looking only for the relationship between the twenty-first and nineteenth centuries, these readings risk a flattening of Victorian culture. In overemphasizing the similarity between our present and this past, we lose the depth and specificity of Victorian literary culture, and the nineteenth century becomes an empty, mirrored shell; in other words, there's no "there" there if steampunk's only function is to show us ourselves. Moreover, this insistence on the continuity of the past with our present causes us to lose the particularity of our current cultural debates as they are transformed into inevitable and timeless problems, foreclosing the possibility of change or progress.

We might, then, look at steampunk artists as interpretive critics in the vein of Oscar Wilde's "Critic as Artist" (1891), where the true artist is a critic who makes art from art. Any critical study of steampunk literature must recognize this interpretive turn in the genre. Indeed, we ought to envision steampunk and neo-Victorian authors and Victorian studies scholars as offering different but essential kinds of critical understanding of Victorian literature and culture. This recognition of expertise within and outside of academia also reflects the permeable boundaries of nineteenth-century definitions of expertise and academic knowledge. Such an understanding of criticism opens connections between academia and fan cultures, mapping additional conceptual and social paths through which Victorian studies as a discipline is uniquely positioned, through steampunk, to take an active role in making the humanities a vital part of public life.

NOTES

1. Steampunk has become so ubiquitous that one can even purchase readymade steampunk Halloween costumes in a bag at most U.S. party stores and online retailers. Such products indicate that there is a readily available vision of what constitutes steampunk in the popular imagination.

2. Spurred by sharing of geek fan culture content over social media as well as the popularity of such content in television and films, what was once a set of intersecting niche subcultures has become fairly legible throughout the United States. TV shows like *The Big Bang Theory* (2007-present) and films like those that comprise the Marvel Cinematic Universe have introduced billions of people worldwide to both the interests of these fan subcultures and the social norms of how these subcultures function. Consequently, while the intense focus of fan subcultures on particular styles, characters, comic books, films, and television series remains a unique quality, there has been a perceptible shift in which the broader culture has become fully aware of these subcultures and embraced their enthusiasm, largely in the form of advertising and merchandising.

3. Austin Sirkin, "Has Steampunk Peaked in the U.S.?," *An Educated Guess* (blog), August 25, 2013, http://austinsirkin.tumblr.com.

4. The nineteenth century is present in the twenty-first century because its historical distance is near enough to enable us to see the emergence of a variety of cultural and economic institutions while simultaneously far enough to allow us to tell ourselves the story of our own advancement and progress. As John Kucich and Dianne F. Sadoff note, "Rewritings of Victorian culture have flourished, we believe, because the postmodern fetishizes notions of cultural emergence, and because the nineteenth century provides multiple eligible sites for theorizing such emergence." "Introduction: Histories of the Present," in *Victorian Afterlife: Postmodern Culture Rewrites the Nineteenth Century*, ed. John Kucich and Dianne F. Sadoff (Minneapolis: University of Minnesota Press, 2000), xv.

5. At the time of this essay's composition, only the first two books of the series were available. The series currently comprises the following novels: *Tarnished* (2012), *Gilded* (2012), *Corroded* (2013), *Tempered* (2014), *Engraved* (2014), and *Transmuted* (2015). In addition, there is also one electronically published St. Croix Chronicles novella, *The Mysterious Case of Mr. Strangeway* (2013).

6. Jess Nevins, "The Nineteenth Century Roots of Steampunk," *New York Review of Science Fiction* 21, no. 5 (2009): 5.

7. Steffen Hantke, "Difference Engines and Other Infernal Devices: History According to Steampunk," *Extrapolation* 40, no. 3 (Fall 1999): 245.

8. Karen Hellekson, "Toward a Taxonomy of the Alternate History Genre," *Extrapolation* 41, no. 3 (Fall 2000): 255.

9. Rachel A. Bowser and Brian Croxall, "Introduction: Industrial Evolution," *Neo-Victorian Studies* 3, no. 1 (2010): 3.

10. Simon Joyce, *The Victorians in the Rearview Mirror* (Athens: Ohio University Press, 2007), 4.

11. Mike Perschon, "Steam Wars," *Neo-Victorian Studies* 3, no. 1 (2010): 128.

12. Ann VanderMeer and Jeff VanderMeer, "What Is Steampunk?," in *Steampunk II: Steampunk Reloaded*, ed. Ann VanderMeer and Jeff VanderMeer (San Francisco: Tachyon, 2010), 11.

13. Perhaps the most recognizable symbol of steampunk's aesthetics is the cog. While steampunk cogs and gears have gotten so ubiquitous as to give rise to parodies, as exemplified by the popular YouTube video and song "Just Glue Some Gears On It (And Call It Steampunk)" by Reginald Pikedevant, their very pervasiveness within steampunk literary and material culture points toward their importance; "Just Glue Some Gears On It (And Call It Steampunk)," *YouTube*, 2:52, November 29, 2011, https://www.youtube.com/watch?v=TFCuE5rHbPA. Cogs are closely associated with the Industrial Revolution, gentlemen inventors, and, to borrow Thomas Carlyle's term, captains of industry. Though not present in all steampunk texts or objects, they do metonymically represent both steampunk's central concern with the interplay between aesthetics and technology as these previously utilitarian machine parts also become aesthetic signifiers of the genre, blurring the boundaries between what is beautiful and what is useful.

14. For further discussion of the history of these theories, see P. M. Harman, *Energy, Force, and Matter: The Conceptual Development of Nineteenth-Century Physics* (Cambridge: Cambridge University Press, 1982).

15. Cooper explores this part of alchemy in greater detail in chapter 14 of *Tempered* as Oliver Ashmore teaches Cherry the twenty-two trumps of alchemy's tarot deck, which encapsulates its central concepts.

16. This sort of unknown element seems to be a common means for upending conventional power dynamics. As I have discussed elsewhere, chemical X in the animated television series *The Powerpuff Girls* (1998–2007) functions similarly. See Lisa Hager, "'Saving the World before Bedtime': *The Powerpuff Girls*, Citizenship, and the Little Girl Superhero," *Children's Literature Association Quarterly* 33, no. 1 (Spring 2008): 62–78.

17. Karina Cooper, *Gilded* (New York: Avon Books, 2013), 29.

18. For further discussion of Monica Madden and transportation, see Arlene Young, "Character and the Modern City: George Gissing's Urban Negotiations," *English Literature in Transition, 1880–1920* 49, no. 1 (2006): 49–62; Maria Teresa Chialant, "The Feminization of the City in Gissing's Fiction: The Streetwalker, the Flâneuse, the Shopgirl," in *A Garland for Gissing*, ed. Bouwe Postmus (Amsterdam: Rodopi, 2001), 51–65; Josephine A. McQuail, "'Woman as an Invader': Travel and Travail in George Gissing's *The Odd Women*," in *Gissing and the City:*

Cultural Crisis and the Making of Books in Late Victorian England, ed. John Spiers (New York: Palgrave, 2006), 139-51.

19. Karina Cooper, *Tarnished* (New York: Avon Books, 2012), 42; Cooper, *Gilded,* 65.

20. Cooper, *Tarnished,* 42.

21. Cooper, *Gilded,* 66.

22. It is worth noting here that this research is later revealed in *Tempered* to be the work of Cherry's mother and to be almost entirely aimed at destroying the alchemical bond that enables Oliver Ashmore (Nicholin Folsham), Cherry's mysterious guardian, to prolong his life by stealing the life force of his descendants after he has painted (i.e., aestheticized) them.

23. Cooper, *Tarnished,* 237.

24. Cherry realizes the extent of her mother's influence in the final chapters of *Tempered* when she discovers that her mother was the guiding force behind all of her father's schemes.

25. Pamela K. Gilbert's work on sensation fiction and disease in the nineteenth century explores these ideas in more detail; see *Disease, Desire, and the Body in Victorian Women's Popular Novels* (Cambridge: Cambridge University Press, 1997), and *Mapping the Victorian Social Body* (Albany: State University of New York Press, 2004).

26. This interrogation of the boundary between the living and nonliving is a central theme of steampunk, as I discuss elsewhere in my study of Joss Whedon's TV show *Firefly* (2002-3) and its film sequel, *Serenity* (2005); see Lisa Hager, "Aiming to Misbehave at the Boundary between the Human and the Machine: The Queer Steampunk Ecology of Joss Whedon's *Firefly* and *Serenity,*" in *The Philosophy of Joss Whedon,* ed. Dean Kowalski and Evan Kreider (Lexington: University Press of Kentucky, 2011), 182-93.

27. Cooper is definitely not alone in connecting steampunk and sex. For variety of viewpoints on the subject, see Professor Calamity et al., *A Steampunk's Guide to Sex* (New York: Combustion Books, 2012).

28. Cooper, *Tarnished,* 177.

29. Ibid., 238.

30. Ibid., 246.

31. Ibid., 250.

32. Cooper, *Gilded,* 58.

33. Ibid., 200.

34. Ibid., 299.

35. Cooper, *Tarnished,* 46.

36. Cooper, *Gilded,* 218-19, 349.

37. Ibid., 328.

38. Ibid., 329.

39. In Cooper's fictional universe, there are two murderers killing prostitutes in London during the action of the book. The first is Jack the Ripper, whose victims are streetwalkers, called doxies in the nineteenth century, and whose nearly illiterate letters to the papers suggest that he himself is also working class.

The second is known as the sweet tooth, a dandy and a collector who has been murdering the Midnight Menagerie's kept women in order to provide Cherry's father with organs for his alchemical experiments. In *Corroded*, Cherry discovers that the sweet tooth is actually her good friend and fellow science enthusiast Theodore "Teddy" Helmsley.

40. Cooper, *Gilded*, 349.

9

Out of Control
Disrupting Technological Mastery in Michael Moorcock's The Warlord of the Air and K. W. Jeter's Infernal Devices

JOSEPH WEAKLAND AND SHAUN DUKE

Several critics have tried to make sense of how and why steampunk represents technology. Rebecca Onion, for example, writes that "many people who participate in this subculture see reading, constructing, and writing about steam technology as a highly [liberatory], countercultural practice (hence, the word 'punk')."[1] Despite their differences, then, steampunk shares with cyberpunk (and other technopunk offshoots) a commitment to imagining how the "self-taught tinkerer [might] master important pieces of machinery that, in the current technological landscape, would be the exclusive province of specialists." In Onion's formulation, steampunk often imparts an "expanded capacity for mastery" to "unlikely subjects," namely, "women, children, and members of the working class."[2] Rachel A. Bowser and Brian Croxall echo this thesis in the introduction to their coedited special issue of *Neo-Victorian Studies* on steampunk, once more underscoring mastery over technology. They present steampunk as a "world in which individuals are masters of their tools, rather than being restrained by warranties, EULAs, and DRM."[3] The editors also emphasize control over the machine: steampunk offers "an opportunity to consider what it would be like to be in control of technology," and, finally, "steampunk's rise in the last few decades ... has everything to do with this punk sensibility regarding technology: a politics of taking back control."[4]

We do not disagree with Onion, Bowser, or Croxall in their analyses of steampunk's technological politics. However, we believe the emphasis on technological mastery and control identified in first-wave steampunk criticism invites further investigation. Stefania Forlini helps us understand some of the limitations of this ideology when she writes, "Although the 'democratization of mastery' emphasised by the DIY component of steampunk effectively critiques the fundamental opacity of contemporary technology, it is premised on an unrealistic understanding of the human and its relation to technology."[5] Indeed, we increasingly find ourselves in a world of "ambient intelligence" that displaces the human as the central autonomous agent within the system.[6] From this perspective, emergent technologies like ubiquitous computing and augmented reality are saturating our environment to such an extent that "boundaries between subject and object, human and nonhuman, and information and matter dissolve."[7] Consequently, critiques of technological culture predicated on regaining mastery and control might better give way to more systemic ways of thinking in which the human is only one player within a larger network composed of multiple human and nonhuman actors.[8] As R. L. Rutsky notes,

> This acceptance of the autonomy of techno-cultural processes implies a shift in the relation of human beings not only to technology, but to others. It implies a politics that is no longer based solely on the knowledge and actions of a "human subject." From this perspective, humanity can no longer be defined in opposition to its others, whether that otherness is technological, irrational, primitive, or simply monstrous. . . . Neither masters nor slaves, subjects nor objects, [we] nevertheless have an agency, even if that agency—no longer simply human—cannot be divorced from the complex web of forces around [us].[9]

Accordingly, our chapter explores how two early works of steampunk fiction disrupt the ideology of technological mastery: Michael Moorcock's *The Warlord of the Air* (1971) and K. W. Jeter's *Infernal Devices* (1987). Bowser and Croxall recognize the importance of asking whether "the contemporary fascination with steampunk technology, style and surfaces is not merely a re-inscription of the values of the Edisonade."[10] These two early works subvert many elements of the Edisonade, and they can help us understand how contemporary steampunk relates to what came before it.

Steampunk, like other science fictions, extrapolates nascent, unevenly distributed technological developments into imaginary worlds. In doing so, such fictions allow us to formulate hypotheses regarding how disruptive technologies—once they become more widely distributed—might perturb and even transform the various systems with which they come into contact. Unlike most science fiction, however, steampunk performs this investigation by moving into alternative pasts or in multiple temporal directions simultaneously. For this reason, steampunk is a valuable source of cultural production for exploring our contemporary technological environment. In drawing on reimagined pasts in order to estrange us from the present and future, steampunk offers another set of game rules through which to imagine, model, and attribute meaning and value to an array of disruptive technologies.

We begin by examining how early steampunk fiction challenges the representations of technology it inherits from its sources. *The Warlord of the Air* is the first novel in Michael Moorcock's Nomad of the Time Streams series, which presents multiple alternative histories in which non-Western peoples develop or acquire technologies more advanced than their European or American counterparts. In *The Warlord of the Air*, utopian steampunks use state-of-the-art machines to defend their cosmopolitan society against the world's empires. Moorcock draws on the familiar narrative of technical mastery and pushes it in the direction of countermastery, but he remains ambivalent about its prospects. On the other hand, K. W. Jeter's *Infernal Devices* questions the imperative of technological mastery itself, satirizing an aristocrat who would destroy Earth simply to demonstrate his scientific and technical knowledge to aliens. We conclude by surveying several contemporary steampunk texts that exemplify the genre's conflicting tendencies. Contemporary steampunk remains largely committed to the politics of technological mastery. However, it reassigns mastery to imagine how technological spaces might be opened to those historically "repressed by patriarchal, Western scientific-technological thought and culture."[11] Steampunk fictions allow us to imagine decolonizing technology, but it remains to be seen how helpful they will be in making sense of the movement toward ambient intelligence.

The Warlord of the Air *and Utopian Binaries*

Much of Moorcock's novel takes place in colonial India. The British Empire and its subsidiaries understood that the industrial technologies and related knowledges that formed the foundations of late Victorian science were crucial tools for colonial expansion.[12] The invention of ships capable of global sea travel, the use of steamboats to support the colonization of Africa, the advances in medicine in the colonies—in all these, technology has been central to the growth and expansion of colonial empires.[13] At the same time that it enabled conquest, technology also played a role in the social makeup of Britain's colonies. Some British authorities, for example, saw India as a "social laboratory [for the policies] that could be transferred to Britain and other parts of the empire." As such, state-sponsored institutions like the East India Company became "channels for the diffusion of Western science and technology in Colonial India."[14] While the motivation for this project was multivalent, one pressing concern for British colonizers was the need for docile and useful colonial subjects. Lord George Curzon, viceroy of India after the 1897–98 famines, famously said that "[in] the proportion as we teach the masses, so we shall make their lot happier, and in proportion as they are happier so they will become more useful members of the body politic."[15] Technology was thus integral to the success of the colonial project in India, not just in terms of its use to build and maintain the colonies but also in terms of the ability of the colonial system to produce new subjects. As Aihwa Ong contends, "education is a social technology" and a "technology of power involved in the construction of modern ethics and knowledges [and] skills that shape new kinds of knowledgeable subjects."[16] For the purposes of our discussion, then, colonial technology has at least two general and interrelated functions: first, it produces the asymmetries of material power that allow the colonial apparatus to take hold, and second, as Ong argues, it aids in the creation of colonial subjectivities.

These historical details and theoretical conceptions of colonial technology—specifically those related to the British Empire—help us understand the world that Moorcock reimagines in *The Warlord of the Air*. In the opening chapter of the novel, Moorcock's fictional grandfather, sent in 1903 to the fictional Rowe Island in colonial India at the request of his physician, meets Oswald Bastable, an opium addict whom the elder Moorcock describes as "some wretch whom the East had ruined, who had discovered a weakness within himself which he might never have found if he had stayed safely at home in England."[17] Curious about Bastable's condition, the senior Moorcock takes Bastable under his care and convinces the man to relate his story. During a military mission for the British Empire to confront a radical religious leader in a sacred city in the Indian mountains, the city's temple is destroyed by an earthquake; as the only survivor, Bastable awakens in 1973, where immense dirigible-style ships rule the air and the still-existent empires have directed vast social changes. These advances, however, are eventually (and deliberately) undermined by the novel's villain, General O. T. Shaw. A utopian binary structures the novel, with the utopian dream of Empire on the one side and the equally utopian dream of anticolonial revolution on the other. The novel uses this binary to explore what changes might be possible once advanced technologies pass from imperial control into the hands of those excluded or exploited by the system. Bastable, at first a loyal subject of Empire, has access to its bounties by dint of having been inculcated into this system. Later he comes to question Empire when he meets the revolutionary, cosmopolitan character Shaw, who rejects Britain's program of colonial violence. Through Shaw and his rebel stronghold, Dawn City, Moorcock imagines a form of technological countermastery in which the "unlikely subjects" whom Rebecca Onion identifies gain access to the tools of Empire for the purpose of dismantling it.

Bastable first experiences the utopian dream of Empire when he arrives in 1973. He discovers that Nepal has become a major component of the British Empire and that the city of Katmandu—and thus the Empire at large—is filled with motorized vehicles, great towering structures for docking flying ships, and other medical and technological advances. The Empire has also managed to establish a relatively stable peace; violent confrontations, we are told, are few and far between. Understandably impressed, Bastable declares that "[the] carping critics of Imperialism in my own day would have been silenced pretty sharply" if they could see this new world. All of these advances have been doubled in London and nearby Croydon, where "poverty had been banished! Disease had been exiled! Misery must surely be unknown!"[18] The only sore point, as far as Bastable is initially aware, is the anarchists and nihilists (terms the Empire uses to describe its remaining enemies), who sabotage the Empire's remaining efforts to create utopia. These utopian sentiments were not uncommon in the British Empire, particularly with regard to India and its nearby territories. For example, in a November 1905 speech in our own world, Lord George Nathaniel Curzon described Britain's desire not simply to maintain power but to eliminate the role of misery in everyday life, pushing India and Britain, its master, closer to a better world.[19] Thus, Curzon's argument for the creation of a stronger colonial India through closer integration to Britain is at the very least utopian in thought, but not necessarily in form.[20] Moorcock's future on its face appears to offer a vision of what Curzon's idea of Empire might have looked like, provided that technological innovations could actually make such a vision possible.

However, General O. T. Shaw and Count Rudolfo Guevara—a nationalist revolutionary—soon bring this world into question. After they imprison Bastable, Guevara and Shaw each explain his own perspective on the Empire and suggest that its utopia is false. They point out how the imperial center is only accessible to a select few (as it was when empires dominated the globe): "You have seen only the cities. Do you know that Indians are only allowed to come to the cities if they have permission from the government?" Guevara also argues that the hospitals and welfare programs only exist to prevent the "pool of available labour [from dying] altogether," and that the British Empire artificially influences the prices to increase its own wealth ("the Indian starves so that the Briton may feast").[21] Thus, while Bastable has enjoyed the fruits of the Empire's scientific and technological innovations, indigenous subjects are kept on the outside by economic stagnation and apartheid-style spatial politics.

The novel continues to draw out the inherent contradictions in this perceived utopia when the action moves to Dawn City, General Shaw's counterutopia. Dawn City represents the desire for an equitable, anticolonial, antinationalist, and antiracial utopia and forms the basis of Shaw's politics. When Bastable arrives in the city, which is all white buildings, fountains, and greenery, he internally remarks, "It seemed so peaceful, so civilized!" He quickly discovers that not only is this city more advanced than London herself—"It has every amenity—and some which even London cannot boast"—but it also houses exiles from India, Europe, Russia, America, and France, all working toward a common goal.[22] Whereas the Empire that Bastable witnesses when he first arrives in 1973 provides the illusion of advancement in the form of cities populated by proper imperial subjects, Dawn City actualizes the utopian vision by putting the amenities of the state, and the knowledge therein, within the hands of a miniaturized world. Unlike the protagonists of the Edisonades, or for that matter much of early science fiction and fantasy writing, Shaw is not the white male master and inventor. Rather, it is Shaw's identity as a biological and ideological cosmopolitan that makes his character so interesting. This is not to suggest that Moorcock's novel does not immediately attempt, through Bastable's perspective, to present Shaw as some version of the yellow peril. In fact, Bastable's constant references to Shaw's Eurasian features, terrorism, and piracy—from which the title "The Warlord of the Air" is derived—establish the orientalist narrative that the novel challenges.

Shaw openly discusses his desire to rid the world of empires, for doing so would be to remap the globe with the template of Dawn City, wiping out national and social boundaries. Dawn City provides Bastable with a physical template of a possible and presumably better future, and it represents Shaw's desire for "a utopia that would exist for all."[23]

Through the technical advancements of Dawn City, and with the guidance of Shaw, Bastable is able to see with his own eyes the terrifying underbelly of imperialism: all of Guevara's critiques are viewable on film (Moorcock uses the word "kinema"), which Shaw gladly screens for his imperial guest, remarking that "[this] is how your kind of power is used when others threaten it."[24] Though obviously a form of propaganda, these films stand in for the educational technologies through which Dawn City creates subjectivities that oppose Empire. Shaw's vision is to free people from the impositions of Empire; he argues that Africa and the East would have arrived at Dawn City on their own if Europe had let them be. Though expanding this vision across the globe would require conquest, Shaw believes his actions to be just insofar as he fights on behalf of oppressed peoples and against an authority that abuses its power. Though Shaw recognizes that he too will have to use force to achieve his goals, he differentiates that force by arguing for its moral necessity.

Bastable, however, charges Shaw with courting death and destruction for a fantasy that, he believes, is impossible without a means for actualizing the necessary change: war machines capable of standing against the Empire. The death knell to Bastable's imperialism comes when Shaw reveals his trump card: flying machines much faster and more agile than anything the empires of the world have yet produced. Bastable responds, "I had to face the fact that the people of Dawn City were my comrades now." This moment also highlights the sudden truth of an early statement made by Guevara: "Europe has used up its dream. It has no future. The future lies here, in China, which has a new dream, a new future.... Europe is dying.... But before she dies, she offers certain notions of what is possible to the countries she has dishonoured."[25] Shaw's—and to a lesser extent Guevara's—anticolonial arguments reflect those of Aimé Césaire's, namely the suggestion that the conditions under which the Empire operates, while seemingly benevolent, are in fact markers of a dying civilization. Césaire argues that "Europe is unable to justify itself either before the bar of 'reason' or before the bar of 'conscience'"; in other words, *"Europe is indefensible."*[26] Bastable ponders the very same idea with Guevara, and Shaw later implies that the crimes of the Empire have made its ideological defense impossible. It is not insignificant, then, that Bastable initially refuses to accept the premise set before him. For him, the Empire of the 1970s is a better world, but it is also a world that hides its failures, obscures reality with glittery cityscapes, and smashes dissent. Shaw's vision, it becomes clear, is an immeasurably better one than anything the British Empire has thus far provided, but it is still, Bastable fears, governed by the logic of conquest inherited from the very thing Dawn City hopes to subvert.

While Moorcock critiques the world as it is through the variant worlds that might have been, the conclusion of *The Warlord of the Air* supports Jess Nevins's suggestion that steampunk "rarely offers a solution to the problems it decries."[27] The genre may criticize or tear down the foundations, but it never completes the utopian dream of an answer. In the case of Moorcock's novel, the duality of utopianism, split between two technologically oriented visions, never permits one to cancel out or override the other. One vision (nationalistic, imperial) is in conflict with another (hybrid, cosmopolitan). Each remains locked within what Donna Haraway terms the "dialectic of apocalypse with the other."[28] On both sides of this dialectic, technics functions as an instrument to achieve power, which quickly leads to an instrumental ethical stance toward human (and nonhuman) life. *The Warlord of the Air* makes this evident when Shaw, despite the obvious collateral damage, drops an atomic bomb on Hiroshima in order to strike a blow against the Empire. The solution for which the novel appears to search is deferred, leaving the reader with two terrifying possibilities: the continuation of the world system of "benevolent" empires or a world made anew by freedom fighters with nuclear weapons. Those who look to early steampunk fictions like *The Warlord of the Air* for evidence of the genre's countercultural roots would do well to note Moorcock's fundamental ambivalence regarding DIY technology. In his vision, simply appropriating advanced technology does not guarantee a better world.

Infernal Devices *and the Natural-Born Cyborg*

The Warlord of the Air stages an alternate history of countermastery to explore technology's role in patterns of colonial domination. While less overtly political than Moorcock's novel, K. W. Jeter's *Infernal Devices* represents a subtle development in steampunk's imaginative engagement with technics. Specifically, his novel takes aim at the very coherence of technomastery, revealing its thorough penetration by and reliance on external technology. Once disrupted in this way, as Forlini writes, "the possibility of human mastery over technology is replaced by what we might call mutual constitutivity in which humans make and are made by technological things." According to Forlini, such a perspective allows us to "glimpse a slippage between our treatment of things and our treatment of people" and "might lead us beyond relationships of domination."[29] *Infernal Devices*, published nearly sixteen years after *The Warlord of the Air*, hints at a way beyond the dialectic of apocalypse and anticipates the steampunk of authors such as Neal Stephenson (*The Diamond Age*, 1995) and China Miéville (*Perdido Street Station*, 2000).

Following Mike Perschon's argument in this volume,[30] we acknowledge that there is no easy or necessary connection between the work of Moorcock and Jeter, as Perschon persuasively argues that Moorcock cannot be neatly grouped with the later work of American writers Jeter, Blaylock, and Powers. However, *Infernal Devices* is arguably among the more interesting early steampunk works to address technology. We also believe that Jeter's later novel, *Noir* (1998), ranks among the most literary examples of cyberpunk and establishes him as a significant science fiction author.[31] Even so, we want to anticipate the possible objection that our attempt to locate posthuman potentiality within *Infernal Devices* imposes a theoretical understanding on what might be better understood as a relatively conventional work of genre fiction. If our reading of Jeter's novel is willful, it is for the purpose of magnifying those elements of the novel—and by extension other steampunk fictions—that challenge human mastery and control over technology.[32]

Accordingly, we contend that *Infernal Devices* allows us to glimpse what Andy Clark calls the natural-born cyborg, an image of humans as "products of a complex and heterogenous developmental matrix in which culture, technology, and biology are . . . inextricably intermingled."[33] The natural-born cyborg is not primarily a product of contemporary digital technology and information networks but rather a conception of humans as always already cyborgic, hybrid entities that extend their mental processes into the external world through technical capacities such as language and tool making. Clark writes,

> It is only our metabolically based obsession with our own skin-bags that has warped the popular image of the cyborg into that of a heavily electronically penetrated human body; a body dramatically transformed by prostheses, by neural implants, enhanced perceptual systems, and the full line of Terminator fashion accessories. The mistake—and it is a familiar one—was to assume that the most profound mergers and intimacies always involved literal penetrations of the skin-bag.[34]

In other words, the natural-born cyborg reminds us that we are not cyborgs because of current technologies in the twenty-first century that penetrate our bodies. Instead, we are (always already) cyborgs because of the way our agency is distributed among nonhuman objects and the way our interactions with any technology fundamentally affects our embodiment, even at invisible neurological levels. According to the idea of technogenesis, for example, humans coevolved (and continue to coevolve) with their tools. As N. Katherine Hayles observes, "The view that bipedalism coevolved with tool manufacture and transport is widely accepted" among paleoanthropologists.[35] This makes the natural-born cyborg useful for thinking through human–technology relations in the nineteenth century as it is in the twenty-first, and it may allow us to sidestep a possible charge against steampunk—namely that the movement returns to the nineteenth century to imagine how humans might be insulated from (or reacquire mastery over) technology. The concept of the natural-born cyborg collapses the subject–object distinction between user and tool. In doing so, it helps us test whether steampunk fictions are capable of representing technology as something other than a tool to be mastered.

Before we begin to discuss *Infernal Devices* through this lens, we will first provide a brief description of the plot. Englishman George Dower is the novel's protagonist and first-person narrator. George's father was a brilliant inventor and repairman who built many gadgets for noblemen in London. When his father passes away, George takes over the family business: a repair shop for clocks and other mechanical devices. Much to George's continuing dismay, he is much less skilled a repairman than his father. *Infernal Devices* takes the form of George's written statement concerning the misfortunes that befall him after encountering Lord Bendray, a member of the parodic Royal Anti-Society. George's father built a device for Bendray known as the Cataclysm Harmonics, which uses vibrations "to split the earth to its core."[36] Bendray is missing a key component for his machine, however, and the plot centers around his attempts to reacquire it from George's possession. Of course, George isn't aware of most of his father's activities, nor does he know of the device's existence or whereabouts. Bendray's scheme embroils George in several misadventures in Jeter's version of nineteenth-century London, where the enigmatic character known as the Brown Leather Man helps George foil Lord Bendray's plot.

Even in the novel's opening pages, it is clear how nondigital technologies can have significant consequences for human identity. The story's events cause quite a scandal around George's public image. George begins his written testimony by imploring his reader to "read no further" should he or she be unfamiliar with the Dower name: "Small chance of that, I know, as the infamy has been given the widest circulation possible. The engines of ink-stained paper and press spew forth unceasingly, while the even more persuasive swell of human voice whispers in the drawing room and tenement the details that cannot be transcribed."[37] With this observation, *Infernal Devices* begins a subtle investigation into technology, language, and subjectivity. George recognizes his person as dispersed and mediated through writing technologies ("the engines of ink-stained paper and press"). His sense of self is inextricably bound to the technological reproduction of his story and its "circulation" among the paper's readers. Later, the character Scape reveals to George that he has seen the future through a viewing device George's father built. Scape reflects that the many hours spent watching the twentieth century has transformed his speech, imbuing it with contemporary American colloquialisms and providing him with a "future personality" and a "new improved brain."[38] This is consistent with the "cognitive and morphological changes in the brain" brought on by emergent media, such as reading on the Web.[39] Thus, while the novel's characters, and perhaps even the author himself, lack a clear language to describe the process, *Infernal Devices* depicts the "co-evolutionary spiral in which humans and tools [speech, writing, old/new media] are continually modifying each other."[40] Likewise, Dower's written narrative is a technology of the self whereby George hopes to restore his name. It is unlikely that this protocybernetic conception of human language and subjectivity would have been available to George before he experienced the events he recounts. He reflects, "Restoring my name, my father's name, seems a shallow vanity now. What matter glory or ignominy, when such visions have altered the world in my sight?"[41] These world-altering visions are those of the natural-born cyborg. Through them, the narrative questions the Royal Anti-Society's drive toward technomastery.

The novel's central conflict concerns "Lord Bendray's investigations into the so-called Cataclysm Harmonics by which he meant to split the Earth to its core."[42] By sealing himself within a hermetic carriage (an airtight Victorian-era space capsule), Bendray hopes to survive Earth's destruction and make contact with an alien race that he believes will accept him as an equal after he has demonstrated the scientific and technological know-how necessary to destroy the planet. According to his logic, "Surely, creatures that are capable of shattering the world on which they live would be perceived by those intelligences as beings worthy of respect and attention. It stands to reason." As its name suggests, the hermetic carriage will insulate Bendray and his house servants even while Earth turns to dust. The vessel's "signal flags and lights" and Union Jack will then allow for communication with the aliens.[43] In desiring to become quite literally a "man in space," or "an ultimate self untied at last from all dependency," Bendray represents the apocalyptic drive of technological mastery that would culminate in the twentieth-century nightmare of nuclear proliferation and mutually assured self-destruction.[44] Bendray reveals his distorted view of science when he declares, "We can't let mere sentiment intrude. This is *Science*."[45] In this way, Bendray's ideology erases embodiment; he is seduced by "fantasies of unlimited power and disembodied immortality."[46]

Infernal Devices offers another glimpse of the natural-born cyborg by challenging the ontological division between human and machine. This occurs when George encounters the Paganinicon, a clockwork replica of George built by his father. When George questions the Paganinicon as to its functioning, George's mechanical double lifts its shirt, revealing, to George's "utter amazement," no "heart, no bone, no human ligament or vein. Inside a metal cage, gears whirred and meshed. Wound springs inter-twined with each other, and ticked off the slow measuring of his artificial life." The Paganinicon then puts his own question to George, asking, "If I were to open you up—would you see anything less remarkable? Less intricately dazzling, in its squelching, spongy way? Lungs and heart and spleen, all the rest—ticking away, as it were."[47] George, however, insists on maintaining a clear distinction in kind between the organic and the machinic, arguing that "human beings [are] not made; except, perhaps, by God," and that "the operations of an invisible creator are meant to be beyond our comprehension; such are mysteries. But clockwork—gears and wheels and springs—that is another matter." The Paganinicon seizes on this, reminding George of his own powerlessness to comprehend, much less repair, many of the devices in his father's shop: "I know as well as you do that the simplest watch is as much a befuddlement to you as the workings of the heart that beats inside your chest."[48] With his argument, the Paganinicon claims for technology autonomy and even agency that exceeds human understanding and control. In destabilizing George's ontological frame of reference, his clockwork twin forces him to confront how the machine "unsettles or disorganizes the conventional boundaries between subject and object, self and other, the human and the technological."⁴⁹ If machines take on the characteristics of living organisms, how can we distinguish the two? Dower learns from the Paganinicon that their brains are linked to a cybernetic "governing mechanism," one that not only "[regulates] two creatures, one of flesh and blood, the other made of clockwork," but that also functions as the trigger for Bendray's Cataclysm Harmonics.⁵⁰ George is not reclaiming the machine; machines are reclaiming him as a component within their systems.

Finally, through the character of the Brown Leather Man, *Infernal Devices* gestures, albeit incompletely, toward the human and nonhuman toll of technological development, or "to those supposedly nontechnological 'other' cultures and discourses that modernity has always devalued, excluded, or repressed."⁵¹ We first encounter the Brown Leather Man in the novel's opening pages when Creff, Dower's assistant, announces that "a crazed Ethiope" is at the door of Dower's shop. The reader later learns that the Brown Leather Man is actually one of a fantastic variety of mermaidlike humanoids who live off the coast of Northern England. The Brown Leather Man is variously coded by Creff and Dower as an "Ethiope," "a murderous savage," and an "anthropophagi" because of a dark leather suit he wears to retain moisture while traveling on land.⁵² The Brown Leather Man's race of selkies, as the humans call them, lay their eggs in seaweed; they are driven almost to extinction when Bendray solicits George's father to develop a commercial seaweed extractor that destroys the selkie breeding grounds. The remaining scattered selkies interbreed with humans in the rural areas around London, and Lord Bendray creates a shadow economy based on the prostitution of selkie women. Even as they are exploited, the Brown Leather Man and selkie-human offspring represent an irruption of hybridity within England itself. They function as a reminder of the repressed human, nonhuman, and environmental toll of Western scientific and technological development.

In seeing "the gears and furious machinery of the world that lie unreckoned beneath our feet," George has glimpsed the natural-born cyborg, as well as the impossibility of complete technomastery.⁵³ If *Infernal Devices* comes close to offering a solution to the relationships of domination Forlini describes, then it is in George's somber closing address to the reader: "No longer can I note, as other men do, the passing hours upon the heaven's gilded face, without a vision of a hidden master-spring uncoiling to its final silence. I await the day when all clocks shall stop, including the one that ticks within my breast. Do thou the same, Reader, and profit from my example."[54] Even as he has been alienated from the community, sealed within his shop, George can no longer maintain firm boundaries between clockwork devices and the clockwork of life itself. Both human and machine are finite, and, as George's metaphoric language suggests, just as the human constructs the machine, so does the machine construct the human.

Rebuilding the Past to Construct a Different Future

Steampunk's contemporary moment is filled with debate, in no small part because, as Mike Perschon suggests in his essay in this collection, some critics long for a steampunk which inherits the political fervor of its suffix: punk. In some respects this critique is a fair one, as many steampunk texts have tended toward, as Paul Jessup argues, "Empire worship and a hidden undercurrent of racism,"[55] while others have capitalized on the genre's commercial viability. Likewise, science fiction author Charles Stross contends that a great deal of contemporary steampunk texts simply ignore the social conditions of the Victorian era,[56] while Amal El-Mohtar has called for "retrofuturism [or steampunk as it might be imagined in non-European settings] that plays with our assumptions and subverts our expectations."[57] Though we are not concerned here with the quality or accuracy of these arguments, we are concerned with the methods by which steampunk imagines technology differently. Moorcock certainly provides the sort of anticolonial vision of the future that Stross and Jessup desire, and Jeter engages in the playful questioning of the human subject familiar even to readers of cyberpunk. Nonetheless, the genre's contemporary moment is one of conflicting tendencies, at once an unchallenging pulp reimagining of Victoriana, a political decentering of Europe as the focal point, and a rejection or examination of Victorian social mores, sometimes from the perspective of the marginalized. These various camps are arguably united, however, by their concern with reclaiming technology as a tool to be (re)mastered, and the wealth of posthuman speculation in other recent science fiction is rare in steampunk. Thus, we are not certain that steampunk is as useful as other science fiction for thinking about contemporary technoculture, especially in light of the rise of ambient intelligence. Indeed, we would suggest that the long-term viability of steampunk will largely depend on its ability to leverage speculation concerning alternative pasts to confront a range of disruptive developments within our contemporary technological environment: anthropogenic climate change, geoengineering, bioengineering, 3-D printing, and drone technologies, among others. As we conclude, however, we will leave this question to the side in favor of charting how the paradigm of technological countermastery operates—or fails to operate—in some of the contemporary fiction.

The Buntline Special (2010), by Mike Resnick, the first in his Weird West series, is a prime example of the steampunk text that fails or refuses to engage in a countercolonial, countercultural, or counterhumanist project.[58] Set in an alternate nineteenth-century America where Thomas Edison and Ned Buntline have turned Tombstone, Arizona, into a steam-powered city with streetlights and horseless carriages, the novel also addresses the politics of westward expansion of human settlements by a fledgling United States, which has thus far been thwarted by a magic-wielding Geronimo. Tombstone, as such, is in an unspoken half-truce with Geronimo and remains largely exterior from the United States proper, operating as a free state. Resnick's novel is unabashedly a pulp affair, drawing from historical embellishments of popular American West figures and the western genre more generally. It is likewise a novel embedded within the discourses of early American imperialism. The narrative's central concern lies in the technological conflict between Edison/Buntline, Geronimo, and the United States. Doc Holliday, hired to protect Edison and Buntline by the U.S. government, soon discovers that the two geniuses have been hard at work on a technological solution to Geronimo's magic, thus opening Tombstone and its residents to the colonial agenda that lies at the heart of manifest destiny. The novel's pulp leanings are a deliberate throwback to Old West adventure novels. They are also a return to America's conquest narratives and their violent implications, particularly as they relate to the imagined and real technological divisions between the growing nineteenth-century U.S. population and the Native Americans who opposed them; this includes the notion that Euro-American culture was superior partly as a result of its technological advancements. Like Moorcock's *The Warlord of the Air*, though, Resnick's novel shifts the power dynamics slightly, such that Geronimo's threat is more acute, but notably without the revolutionary and anticolonial focus. In *The Buntline Special* and sequels such as *The Doctor and the Kid* (2011), Geronimo and other Native Americans wield only magic, never advanced technology, while Edison and other characters deploy the usual array of steampunk gadgets and weapons. The only android or cyborg characters to be found are the robotic female sex workers Edison designs for Tombstone's brothels.

Another, and quite different, example of contemporary steampunk's engagement with the technological can be found in N. K. Jemisin's "The Effluent Engine," originally published in *Steam-Powered: Lesbian Steampunk Stories* (2011). Editor JoSelle Vanderhooft argues that the undercurrents of hostility in steampunk "have lead [sic] plenty of writers at all levels in their career to dismiss the genre as nothing more than fuel for white, straight, male imperialist fantasies."[59] The anthology works to challenge these assumptions by exploring traditionally marginalized groups in alternative pasts. Jemisin's story certainly fits the bill. It features a Haitian spy who seeks the help of a black American, Rillieux, and his amateur scientist sister, Eugenie, to develop a method for converting rum effluent into airship fuel. The story, however, avoids the simple utopianism of a postracial, postimperial past and instead pits its protagonist, Jessaline, against the politically charged social climate of a slave-owning southern America. Though Haiti has become a trading partner with the United States, this is largely out of necessity: the United States needs sugar and Haiti needs guns, so naturally the two have come to an agreement. But the relationship is a limited one. Jessaline reminds the reader that even if the United States "alone was willing to treat with Haiti," the real-world politics of the antebellum period could not be ignored: "Haiti was the stuff of American nightmare: a nation of black slaves who had killed off their white masters."[60] Likewise, the narrative openly discusses the limitations of gender and race in nineteenth-century America, while Jessaline's Haiti appears to have few such limitations. Most importantly, the story positions a burgeoning superpower with all the trappings of patriarchy and racism (the United States) against a small sovereign state controlled by freed slaves with the technological might to stand on its own before giants (Haiti). Thus, while *The Buntline Special* engages the pulp in the service of a traditional and unchallenged Victorian setting, Jemisin's "The Effluent Engine" decenters the traditional subject of the Victorian era in favor of technocultural critique.

Though steampunk has rightly received criticism for its nostalgic and revisionist reimagining of history—particularly in its use of imperial symbols and social structures without the trappings of their historical origins—an undercurrent of culturally aware narratives have found a home within the genre. Cherie Priest's *Boneshaker* (2009) and Shelley Adina's *Lady of Devices* (2011), for example, feature female heroines who use technology to break out of the roles imposed on them by patriarchal culture. Further, efforts such as the *Beyond Victoriana* blog, Rosemary Lim and Maisarah Bte Abu Samah's Asian steampunk anthology *The Steampowered Globe* (2012), and Sarah Hans's anthology *Steampunk World* (2014) and its proposed follow-up, *Steampunk Universe*, give voice to steampunk writers and artificers working outside of a "Western-dominant, Eurocentric, [and heteronormative] framework."[61] The genre will likely always demonstrate its conflict between the anachronistic nostalgia for a magically "better" Victorian milieu and the equally anachronistic remapping of contemporary racial, political, and social awareness over the past. However, as is apparent in the influx of diverse authors and characters in contemporary steampunk, the potential for a challenge to these anachronisms will also be present, giving weight to an undercurrent of critical steampunk that has existed in the genre from the beginning.

NOTES

1. Rebecca Onion, "Reclaiming the Machine: An Introductory Look at Steampunk in Everyday Practice," *Neo-Victorian Studies* 1, no. 1 (2008): 139.

2. Ibid., 151, 152.

3. Rachel A. Bowser and Brian Croxall, "Introduction: Industrial Evolution," *Neo-Victorian Studies* 3, no. 1 (2010): 20.

4. Ibid., 23, 21.

5. Stefania Forlini, "Technology and Morality: The Stuff of Steampunk," *Neo-Victorian Studies* 3, no. 1 (2010): 81.

6. For in-depth discussions concerning ambient technology, see Adam Greenfield, *Everyware: The Dawning Age of Ubiquitous Computing* (Indianapolis, Ind.: New Riders Publishing, 2006), Malcolm McCullough, *Ambient Commons: Attention in the Age of Embodied Information* (Cambridge, Mass.: MIT Press, 2013), and Thomas Rickert, *Ambient Rhetoric: The Attunements of Rhetorical Being* (Pittsburgh, Pa.: University of Pittsburgh Press, 2013). For these theorists, the term "ambient" has at least two general meanings. First, it refers to a lived technological reality—that is, the moment in which computation becomes coextensive with the environment itself. In the second sense, ambience functions as a metaphor for thinking through the ontological disruption the first implies.

7. Rickert, *Ambient Rhetoric*, 1.

8. Forlini, "Technology and Morality," 81. She draws on Bruno Latour's theory of networks to make this point.

9. R. L. Rutsky, *High Technē: Art and Technology from the Machine Aesthetic to the Posthuman* (Minneapolis: University of Minnesota Press, 1999), 157.

10. Bowser and Croxall, "Introduction: Industrial Evolution," 22. John Clute describes the Edisonade as "a kind of science fiction in which a brave young

inventor creates a tool or a weapon (or both) that enables him to save the girl and his nation (America) and the world from some menace, whether it be foreigners or evil scientists or aliens; and gets the girl; and gets rich"; John Clute, "Yore is Us," *The Infinite Matrix*, November 29, 2001, http://www.infinitematrix.net/.

11. Rutsky, *High Technē*, 123.

12. What constitutes science is important, although we do not have the space to explore that issue here. For an entrée into the subject, see Colin Scott, "Science for the West, Myth for the Rest? The Case of James Bay Cree Knowledge Construction," in *The Postcolonial Science and Technology Studies Reader*, ed. Sandra Harding (Durham, N.C.: Duke University Press, 2011), 175–97.

13. For an in-depth look into the relationships between Western empires and science, see Daniel R. Headrick, *Power Over Peoples: Technology, Environments, and Western Imperialism, 1400 to the Present* (Princeton, N.J.: Princeton University Press, 2010). Another invaluable resource is Headrick's *The Tentacles of Progress: Technology Transfer in the Age of Imperialism, 1850–1940* (Oxford: Oxford University Press, 1988).

14. Zaheer Baber, *The Science of Empire: Scientific Knowledge, Civilization, and Colonial Rule in India* (Albany: State University of New York Press, 1996), 186. For a more nuanced account of the colonial relationship to technology and education, see Zaheer Baber, "Science, Technology, and Colonial Power," in *Social History of Science in Colonial India*, ed. S. Irfan Habib and Dhruv Raina (Oxford: Oxford University Press, 2007), 102–58.

15. Baber, *Science of Empire*, 185.

16. Aihwa Ong, *Neoliberalism as Exception: Mutations in Citizenship and Sovereignty* (Durham, N.C.: Duke University Press, 2006), 139.

17. Michael Moorcock, *The Warlord of the Air* (1971), in *The Nomad of the Time Streams* (London: Grafton, 1988), 12.

18. Ibid., 49, 55.

19. George Nathaniel Curzon, *Lord Curzon's Farewell to India, Being Speeches Delivered as Viceroy and Governor-General of India during Sept.-Nov. 1905*, ed. Rustomji Pestonji Karkaria (Bombay: Thacker & Company, 1907), 13–14.

20. Curzon was not beyond criticism even in his day. Charles James O'Donnell, amusingly enough, disliked Curzon (either as a person or a politician) so much that in 1903 he wrote an entire book in which he declared that Curzon had "trodden under foot every principle of sober statesmanship and very often justice, tact, and foresight in dealing with a vast population, which our taxation has brought to the verge of ruin." *The Failure of Lord Curzon: A Study in "Imperialism"—An Open Letter to the Earl of Rosebery* (London: T. Fisher Unwin, 1903), 9.

21. Moorcock, *Warlord of the Air*, 106, 105.

22. Ibid., 114.

23. Ibid., 127.

24. Ibid., 129.

25. Ibid., 135, 122.

26. Ibid., 31, 32.

27. Jess Nevins, "Introduction: The 19th-Century Roots of Steampunk," in *Steampunk*, ed. Ann VanderMeer and Jeff VanderMeer (San Francisco: Tachyon, 2008), 10.
28. Donna J. Haraway, *Simians, Cyborgs, and Women: The Reinvention of Nature* (New York: Routledge, 1991), 177.
29. Forlini, "Technology and Morality," 81, 91.
30. Mike Perschon, "Seminal Steampunk: Proper and True," this volume.
31. Steven Shaviro's examination of network culture, *Connected* (2003), discusses *Noir* at length.
32. Our reading of *Infernal Devices* is certainly at odds with the antitechnological rhetoric of Jeter's introduction to its 2011 reprinting.
33. Andy Clark, *Natural-Born Cyborgs: Minds, Technologies, and the Future of Human Intelligence* (Oxford: Oxford University Press, 2003), 86.
34. Ibid., 28.
35. N. Katherine Hayles, *How We Think: Digital Media and Contemporary Technogenesis* (Chicago: University of Chicago Press, 2012), 10.
36. K. W. Jeter, *Infernal Devices* (New York: Angry Robot, 2011), 16.
37. Ibid., 15, 16.
38. Ibid., 294-95.
39. Hayles, *How We Think*, 26.
40. Ibid., 45-46.
41. Jeter, *Infernal Devices*, 19.
42. Ibid., 16.
43. Ibid., 199, 200.
44. Haraway, *Simians, Cyborgs, and Women*, 150-51.
45. Jeter, *Infernal Devices*, 201.
46. N. Katherine Hayles, *How We Became Posthuman: Virtual Bodies in Cybernetics, Literature, and Informatics* (Chicago: University of Chicago Press, 1999), 5.
47. Jeter, *Infernal Devices*, 256.
48. Ibid., 257.
49. Rutsky, *High Technē*, 153.
50. Jeter, *Infernal Devices*, 262.
51. Rutsky, *High Technē*, 3.
52. Jeter, *Infernal Devices*, 20, 21.
53. Ibid., 368-69.
54. Ibid., 369.
55. Paul Jessup, "The Future of Steampunk" *Mad Hatter's Bookshelf and Book Review* (blog), October 15, 2010, http://booktionary.blogspot.com/.
56. Charles Stross, "The Hard Edge of Empire," *Charlie's Diary* (blog), October 27, 2010, http://www.antipope.org/charlie/.
57. Amal El-Mohtar, "Towards a Steampunk without Steam," *Tor.com* (blog), October 29, 2010, http://www.tor.com.
58. Michael D. Resnick, *The Buntline Special: A Weird West Tale* (Amherst, Mass.: Pyr, 2010).

59. JoSelle Vanderhooft, "Introduction: Build a Better Engine," in *Steam-Powered: Lesbian Steampunk Stories,* ed. JoSelle Vanderhooft (Round Rock, Tex.: Torquere Press, 2011), n.p.

60. N. K. Jemisin, "The Effluent Engine," in Vanderhooft, *Steam Powered,* n.p.

61. Diana M. Pho, "About *Beyond Victoriana,*" *Beyond Victoriana* (blog), http://beyondvictoriana.com/about/. For the call for submissions to the proposed *Steampunk Universe,* see Sarah Hans, "Special Call for Submissions: *Steampunk Universe,*" *Sarah Hans* (blog), July 6, 2015, http://sarahhans.com.

CONTRIBUTORS

RACHEL A. BOWSER is associate professor of English at Georgia Gwinnett College. Her previous work on steampunk and Victorian fiction has been published in *Studies in the Novel*, *Neo-Victorian Studies*, and *Genre*.

KATHRYN CROWTHER is assistant professor of English at Georgia State University Perimeter College. She has published on Victorian literature and nineteenth-century print culture and has articles forthcoming on digital pedagogy in the literature and composition classroom.

BRIAN CROXALL is digital humanities librarian at Brown University. His research on steampunk, nineteenth-century technologies, and digital culture has been published in *American Imago*, *Journal of Digital Humanities*, *Neo-Victorian Studies*, *Johns Hopkins Guidebook to Digital Media*, and *Writing and Pedagogy*.

SHAUN DUKE is a PhD candidate at the University of Florida studying Caribbean literature, science fiction, and postcolonialism. He has published in *Science Fiction Studies*, *Science Fiction Film and Television*, *Extrapolation*, *Journal of the Fantastic in the Arts*, *Strange Horizons*, and *Crimethink*.

STEFANIA FORLINI is associate professor of English at the University of Calgary. Her recent publications can be found in *Digital Humanities Quarterly*, *IEEE, Transactions on Visualization and Computer Graphics*, *Neo-Victorian Studies*, *English Literature in Transition, 1880–1920*, and in the edited collection *Bodies and Things in Nineteenth-Century Literature and Culture*.

LISA HAGER is associate professor in the departments of English and gender, sexuality, and women's studies at the University of Wisconsin-Waukesha, where she codirects the LGBTQIA Resource Center. She has published articles on Victorian sexology, the New Woman, aesthetics, steampunk, queer studies, and digital humanities. Her current book project looks at the relationship between the New Woman and the Victorian family.

MIKE PERSCHON is assistant professor of English at MacEwan University in Edmonton, Alberta. His writing on steampunk had appeared in the anthology *Steaming into a Victorian Future*, as well as magazines and journals such as *Locus*, *Neo-Victorian Studies*, *Verniana*, and *On Spec*.

DIANA M. PHO is an independent scholar, science fiction and fantasy editor, activist, and performer. She runs *Beyond Victoriana*, an award-winning blog on multicultural steampunk and retrofuturism, and has published academically in *Fashion Talks: Undressing the Power of Style*, *Steaming into a Victorian Future*, and the *Journal of Victorian Culture Online*.

DAVID PIKE teaches literature and film at American University. His books include *Canadian Cinema since the 1980s: At the Heart of the World*; *Metropolis on the Styx: The Underworlds of Modern Urban Culture, 1800–2001*; *Subterranean Cities: The World beneath Paris and London, 1800–1945*; and *Passage through Hell: Modernist Descents, Medieval Underworlds*. He has published widely on nineteenth- and twentieth-century urban literature, culture, and film.

CATHERINE SIEMANN directs the writing center at the New Jersey Institute of Technology. She has published on Victorian literature and on popular culture in *Law and Literature*, *Nineteenth-Century Gender Studies*, and *Neo-Victorian Studies*, and in the edited collections *Steaming into a Victorian Future*, *Ada's Legacy*, and *Fighting the Forces: What's at Stake in "Buffy the Vampire Slayer."*

JOSEPH WEAKLAND is a Marion L. Brittain Postdoctoral Fellow at the Georgia Institute of Technology and editorial associate at the Center for Environmental and Sustainability Education at Florida Gulf Coast University. He recently collaborated with University of Florida's Nanoscale Research Facility to chart the rhetorical processes by which nanoscale materiality acquires meaning and value in digital culture.

ROGER WHITSON is assistant professor of English at Washington State University, author of the forthcoming *Steampunk and Nineteenth-Century Digital Humanities: Literary Retrofuturisms, Alternate Histories, Media Archaeologies* and (with Jason Whittaker) of *William Blake and the Digital Humanities: Collaboration, Participation, and Social Media,* along with articles on Blake, digital humanities, steampunk, and digital pedagogy.

INDEX

A Count Named Slick-Brass, 141-45
Adventures of Langdon St. Ives, The (Blaylock), 166-70
Adventures of Luther Arkwright, The (Talbot), 18-24
aestheticism, 97-117
aether, 183-90
Against the Day (Pynchon), xv, 15-18
alchemy, 183-94
Alice in Sunderland (Talbot), 25-28
alternative history: American Civil War, 58-62; British empire, 201-6; computing, 52-58; the Great Stink, 52-58; Industrial Revolution, xxv-xxvi, xxxix, 52-58; Jack the Ripper, 196-97n39; Napoleonic War, 22; nineteenth-century America, 213-14; September 11, 2001, attacks of, 25; World War I, xxiv-xxx
amputees, 74-91
anglophilia, 127-46
anthologies, steampunk, xiv-xv
Anubis Gates, The (Powers), 170-72
"Arbeitskraft" (Mamatas), 78-79
Arnold, Matthew, 107
ArtificerMade, 89
Arts and Crafts movement, 114. *See also* Morris, William
Ay-leen the Peacemaker, xiv, 68n4. *See also* Pho, Diana M.
Aylesford Skull, The (Blaylock), 169

Babbage, Charles, 53, 79, 85
Behemoth (Westerfeld), xxviii-xxix
Benjamin, Walter, 65
Beyond Victoriana (blog), xiv, 68n4, 215
BioShock (video game), xvi-xviii
Blair, Kirstie, 73-74
Blaylock, James: *The Adventures of Langdon St. Ives*, 166-70, 172-75; *The Aylesford Skull*, 169; *Homunculus*, 166-70; *Lord Kelvin's Machine*, 169
Bogost, Ian, 49n44
Boneshaker (Priest), 4, 58-62, 93n17
Boondocks, The (McGruder), 144-45
Bowser, Rachel A., xi-xlvi, 13, 58, 65-66, 86, 181-82, 199
Broadmore, Greg, 173-75
Bryant, Levi, 34
Bulloff, Libby, 97-100
Buntline Special, The (Resnick), 213-14

Carroll, Lewis, 28
Casshern (Kiriya), 80-81
catastrophism. *See Principles of Geology*
Catastrophone Orchestra and Arts Collective, 87, 100
Catholicism, 168, 172
chap-hop, 129-34
Chen, Anna, 137
Civil War (United States), 83
Clark, Andy, 207

223

Clayton, Jay, 7, 56
commodity fetishism, 97–117
conferences/conventions, steampunk, xiii–xiv
cookbooks, 40–43
Cooper, Karina, 179–94; *Gilded*, 184–94; *Tarnished*, 184–94; *Tempered*, 184
cosplay: conventions, xi–xiv; disability, 91, 96n58; race, 141–45
"Critic as Artist, The" (Wilde), 107, 193
critical making, 33–47
Crowther, Kathryn, 73–96
Croxall, Brian, xi–xlvi, 13, 58, 65–66, 86, 181–82, 199
Crystal Palace, 19, 20
cyberpunk, 53, 58, 161–63, 199, 207, 212
"Cyborg Manifesto, The" (Haraway), 95n44
cyborgs, 95n44, 207–12

Dancers at the End of Time, The (Moorcock), 176–77n25
dandyism, 97–117
DARKsteam. *See* Grunbaum, Maurice
Darwin, Charles, xxii–xxvii, xxxi–xxxiii, xxxix
David, Milton, 137–41
Degeneration (Nordau), 103
descriptivism, xlivn23
Dickens, Charles, 84
Difference Engine, The (Gibson and Sterling), 52–58
Di Filippo, Paul, xxx, 78
digital humanities, 44–47
disability, 73–92
"'Discreet Companion' Ladies' Raygun, The" (Friedrich), 36–37
Dishonored (video game), xvi–xviii
Disraeli, Benjamin, 68n7
Dr. Adder (Jeter), 161
Dracula (Stoker), 171
Dragon*Con, xi–xii, xiii

DSM (*Diagnostic and Statistical Manual of Mental Disorders*), xxxv–xxxvi
Duke, Shawn, 45–46, 199–218

Eagan, Aaron, 42–43
East India Company, 131, 202
ecocriticism, 51–67
Economy of Machinery and Manufacture, The (Babbage), 85
"Effluent Engine, The" (Jemisin), 214
Engels, Friedrich, 79
erotica, steampunk, xv
Esmail, Jennifer, 82
evolution, xxii–xxvii, xxxi–xxxiii, 108

Falksen, G. D., 75
fan culture, xiii–xiv, 33–47
fashion, xv–xvi, xviii, xliiin13
feminism. *See* gender studies; sexuality
Ferguson, Sarah, 155–56
festivals, steampunk, xiii–xiv
Fiddlehead (Priest), 61
Foran, Colin, 97–100
Ford, Ford Madox, 3–4
Ford, Henry, 84
Forlini, Stefania, 33, 37, 97–125, 199–200, 206–7
Foucault, Michel, 63
Freedgood, Elaine, 101–2, 106
Freud, Sigmund, xxxvii–xl
Friedrich, Molly, 36–37

Garland-Thomson, Rosemarie, 81–82, 87
Gavin, Adrienne E., 84
gender studies, 179–94
geology. *See* Lyell, Charles
Gibson, William, 52–58
Gilded (Cooper), 184–94
Gissing, George, 186
"Giving Mouth, The" (MacLeod), 78
Goh, Jaymee, 91, 129, 135, 136
Goliath (Westerfeld), xxix–xxx
Grandville (Talbot), 22–25

Index

Great Exhibition, 78, 101-3. *See also* Crystal Palace
Great Stink, 52-58
Greyshade, Jonathan, 153, 164
Grossman, Lev, 79-80
Grunbaum, Maurice, 141-45
Guetta, David, 140-41
Gupta, Savan, 141-45

Hager, Lisa, 179-97
Haiti, 214
Hans, Sarah, 215
Haraway, Donna, 95n44
Hayles, N. Katherine, 116-17, 208
"Heart Is the Matter, The" (Kent), 78
Heart of Empire (Talbot), 21, 22
Hebdige, Dick, 127-28
Hellekson, Karen, 181
historicism, 45-46
homologies, xxiii-xxxi, xxxii-xxxiv. *See also* On the Origin of Species
Homunculus (Blaylock), 166-70
How We Think (Hayles), 116-17
hybridity, xxiii-xxxi, xxxii-xxxiv

IBM, xviii-xix, xxxviii
imperialism, 127-46, 199-215
India, 201-6
Inexplicables, The (Priest), 59, 61
Infernal Devices (Jeter), 165, 206-12

Jacaranda (Priest), 59, 61
Jacob, François, xxxi-xxxii, 108
Jacques, Jeff, xx, xxi
Jagoda, Patrick, 54
"Jekyll and Hyde" (YouTube video), 138-39
Jemisin, N. K., 214
Jessup, Paul, 212
Jeter, K. W.: *Dr. Adder*, 161; *Infernal Devices*, 165, 206-12; *Morlock Night*, 14-15, 18, 161-66; *Noir*, 207
Jha, 135. *See also* Goh, Jaymee
Joseph, Gerhard, 85
Joyce, Simon, 182

Keep, Christopher, 82
Kent, Melissa, 78
Kiernan, Catherine, 90-91
Killjoy, Margaret P., 113, 155-71
Kiriya, Kazuaki, 80-81
Kotite, Erika, 42
Kucich, John, 194n4

Land Leviathan, The (Moorcock), 160-61
Lansdale, Joe, 15
Latour, Bruno, 34, 45
League of Extraordinary Gentleman, The (Moore and O'Neill), 16-18, 30-31n20
Lee, Vernon, 107-10, 116, 121-22n42, 122n45
Leviathan (Westerfeld), xxiv-xxx
Lim, Rosemary, 215
Lohman, Sarah, 49n34
London, 3-31; *The Difference Engine*, 52-58; *Infernal Devices*, 206-12; *Tarnished*, 184-87; *The Time Machine*, 3-28; *The Warlord of the Air*, 201-6
London Labour and the London Poor (Mayhew), 14-15, 164-65, 166, 172-73
Lord Kelvin's Machine (Blaylock), 169
Lyell, Charles, xxii-xxiv, xxxiii

MacLeod, Ian, 78
Make Magazine, 36-40, 47n12
Mamatas, Nick, 78-79
Mao, Douglas, 107
Marius, the Epicurean (Pater), 107
Marx, Karl, 102-6
masculinity, 74, 130-34
materialism, 96-117
Mayhew, Henry, 14-15, 164-65, 166, 172-73
McGruder, Aaron, 144-45
Miéville, China, 50n55, 62-65
Minaj, Nicki, 140-41
Moorcock, Michael, 172-75;

The Dancers at the End of Time,
176–77n25; *The Land Leviathan*,
160–61; *The Nomad of Time Streams*,
158; *The Warlord of the Air*, 157–61,
201–6
Moore, Alan, 16–18, 30–31n20
Morlock Night (Jeter), 14–15, 161–66
Morris, William, 102, 114
Mr. B the Gentleman Rhymer, 129–34
Mullins, Aimee, 88
multiculturalism, 127–46
music, 129–41. *See also* chap-hop;
steamfunk

Native Americans, 213–14
Neo-Victorian Studies (journal), 179
Nevins, Jess, xlivn23, 154–56, 172–75, 181
New York City, xxxiv–xxxv
Noir (Jeter), 207
Nomad of the Time Streams, A (Moorcock), 158
Nordau, Max, 103

object relations, 33–47, 97–117
O'Connor, Erin, 83
Odd Women, The (Gissing), 186
Ojetade, Balogun, 137–41
O'Neil, Kevin, 16–18, 30–31n20
Onion, Rebecca, 86–87, 110, 154, 199
On the Origin of Species (Darwin), xxii–xxvii, xxxi–xxxiii
Otomo, Katsuhiro, *Steamboy*, xlvn54, xlvin72, 80, 88
Our Mutual Friend (Dickens), 84

Pal, George, 8–13
Paris, 22–25
Pater, Walter, 106–8
Perdido Street Station (Miéville), 50n55, 62–65
Perschon, Mike, xl, 4, 129, 153–78, 182, 207, 212
Pho, Diana M., 12–13, 45–46, 127–49, 153. *See also* Ay-leen the Peacemaker
phossy jaw, 60, 79

Picture of Dorian Gray, The (Wilde), 107
Pike, David, 3–31, 60, 63
Pistorius, Oscar, 88
Poirier, Monique, 135–37
postcolonialism, 127–46, 199–215
Powers, Tim, 170–75
prescriptivism, xlivn23
Priest, Cherie: *Boneshaker*, 4, 58–62, 93n17; *Fiddlehead*, 61; *Jacaranda*, 59, 61
Principles of Geology, The (Lyell), xxii–xxiv
Professor Elemental, 129–34
Professor Layton (video game series), xvii–xviii
prosthetics: athletes, 88; capitalism, 85–86; fetishization of, 89–91; material culture / materialism, 86–92; in nineteenth century, 81–86; in steampunk literature and film, 74–81; technology of, 83–85
psychoanalysis. *See* Freud, Sigmund; PTSD; trauma
PTSD (post-traumatic stress disorder), xxxv–xxxvii
Punch (magazine), 103, 104, 105
Pynchon, Thomas, 115; *Against the Day*, xv, 15–18

Questionable Content (web comic), xx, xxi

race, 127–46
Rancière, Jacques, 114–17
Ratt, Margaret P., 111
recipes, 40–43
religion. *See* Catholicism
Renaissance, The (Pater), 106–7
Resnick, Mike, 213–14
Ruskin, John, 107
Rutsky, R. L., 200

Sadoff, Dianne, 194n4
Samah, Maisarah Bte Abu, 215
San Francisco, 60
science. *See* aether; alchemy; Darwin,

Charles; evolution; geology; Jacob, Francois; Lyell, Charles; technology
Science (journal), xxxi
Seattle, 4, 58-62
Sennett, Richard, 34-35
September 11, 2001, attacks of, xxxiv-xl
sexuality, 179-94
Shealy, Jim, 37-40
Siemann, Catherine, 51-70, 76
"Sir Ranulph Wykeham-Rackham, GBE, a.k.a Roboticus the All-Knowing" (Grossman), 79-80
Smythe, Kimric, 37
Sonnenfeld, Barry, xix, 76, 80
"Steam Arm, The," 73-74
Steamboy (film), xlvn54, xlvin72, 80, 88
"Steam Dancer, The" (Kiernan), 90-91
steamfunk, 137-41
Steam Man of the Prairie and the Dark Rider Get Down, The (Lansdale), 15
Steampowered Globe, The (Lim and Samah), 215
Steampunk Cookbook, The (Stockton), 42
SteamPunk Magazine, xxxi, 97-100, 110-13
Steampunk World, The (Hans), 215
Sterling, Bruce, 34, 46, 52-58, 100
stirling engine, 37-40
Stockton, Elizabeth, 42
Stoker, Bram, 171
Stones of Venice, The (Ruskin), 107
Stross, Charles, 127, 212
Supersizers Go, The (TV show), 40-43
Sussman, Herbert, 85
Sybil (Disraeli), 68n7

Talbot, Bryan: *The Adventures of Luther Arkwright*, 18-24; *Alice in Sunderland*, 25-28; *Grandville*, 22-25; *Heart of Empire*, 21, 22
Tarnished (Cooper), 184-94
technology: aesthetics of, 13-14; cooking, 40-43; disability, 81-92; environmental crisis, 51-67; imperialism, 199-215; prostheses, 81-92; transportation, 22, 184-87. *See also* stirling engine
television series, steampunk, xvi
temperance movement, 49n34
Tempered (Cooper), 184
Tesla, Nikola, xxix
Theoretics, 138-39
Thomson, Rosemarie Garland. *See* Garland-Thomson, Rosemarie
time: geologic formulations of, xxii-xxiv; steampunk paradigms of, xxxviii-xl; trauma, xxxvii-xl
Time Machine, The (1960 film), 8-13
Time Machine, The (2002 film), 8-13
Time Machine, The (Wells), 5-6, 8-13, 161-63
tinkering, xxx-xxxiv, 98, 108, 113
trauma, xxxiv-xl. *See also* Freud, Sigmund; PTSD
"Turn Me On" (Guetta), 140-41

uniformitarianism, xxii-xxiv, xxxiii, xxxix. *See also Principles of Geology*
urban studies, 51-67. *See also specific cities*

VanderMeer, Ann, xiv, 156, 182
VanderMeer, Jeff, xiv, 66, 156, 182
Victoria (Di Filippo), 78
Victorian era: aestheticism, 96-117; alternative history, xxv-xxvi, 52-58, 184-87; cities, 3-28, 52-58; cuisine, 40-43; disability, 81-86; imperialism, 199-215; industrialism, 81-86; materiality, 96-117; science, xxii-xxiv
Victorian studies, 179-94
video games, steampunk, xvi-xviii
Vintage Tomorrows (Smythe), 37

Warhol, Andy, 80
Warlord of the Air, The (Moorcock), 157-61, 201-6
War of the Worlds, The (Wells), 163, 167
Weakland, Joseph, 45-46, 199-218

web series, xvi
Wells, H. G., 159; *The Time Machine*, 5-6, 161-63; *The War of the Worlds*, 163, 167
Wells, Simon, 8-13
Westerfeld, Scott, 173; *Behemoth*, xxviii-xxix; *Goliath*, xxix-xxx; *Leviathan*, xxiv-xxxi
Whitson, Roger, 33-50, 88, 111

Wilberforce, Samuel, xxiii-xxiv, xxxix
Wild Wild West (film), xix, 76, 80
Wilde, Oscar, 97-117, 193; "The Critic as Artist," 107, 193; *The Picture of Dorian Gray*, 107
Willeford, Thomas, 75
World War I, xxiv-xxx

zombies, 59-60